The Magnetized Corpse

Jules Janin

The Magnetized Corpse
and Other Paradoxical Tales

translated, annotated and introduced by
Brian Stableford

A Black Coat Press Book

ISBN 978-1-61227-248-1. First Printing. January 2014. Published by Black Coat Press, an imprint of Hollywood Comics.com, LLC, P.O. Box 17270, Encino, CA 91416. All rights reserved. Except for review purposes, no part of this book may be reproduced or transmitted in any form or by any means, electronic or mechanical, including photocopying, recording, or by any information storage and retrieval system, without permission in writing from the publisher. The stories and characters depicted in this novel are entirely fictional. Printed in the United States of America.

TABLE OF CONTENTS

Introduction

Jules Janin was born in Saint-Étienne, in the département of the Loire, in 1804, the son of an advocate. He came to Paris to attend the prestigious Lycée Louis-le-Grand, and then to prepare for a career in law, but he gave scant attention to his studies. Having twice been a schoolfellow of Edgar Quinet, his law studies briefly overlapped with those of Honoré de Balzac, and like them, Janin became avidly involved in the capital's literary life, launching himself into journalism at the earliest opportunity.

Janin wrote articles and stories for several periodicals during the 1820s, including *Le Figaro* and the two key periodicals of the burgeoning Romantic Movement, the *Revue des Deux Mondes* and the *Revue de Paris*. According to Albert de La Fizelière, who assembled two posthumous series collecting his works after his death in 1874—comprising a dozen volumes in all, issued between 1875 and 1878—Janin published numerous unsigned items that he never acknowledged, but even if that claim is slightly exaggerated, he was unusually prolific. He admitted, however, that most of his work was produced in haste. La Fizelière's introduction to the collection of early stories entitled *Petit Contes* begins by quoting Janin's contention that "long works scare me" and that "the idea of composing a book, an entire volume, frightens me and discourages me in advance," and he does, indeed, seem to have been a natural sprinter rather than a marathon runner, irrepressibly enthusiastic in producing short pieces, but far less so in the matter of long ones.

Even so, it was a novel, albeit not a very long one—it was probably intended as a short story, but took the bit between its teeth and carried its author away—that first shot Janin to fame, when he published *L'Âne mort et la femme guillotinée* (tr. as *The Dead Donkey and the Guillotined Wom-*

an) in 1829, causing something of a sensation. The work was subsequently hailed by critics as the culminating specimen of *roman frénétique* [frenzied fiction], that being one of the labels invented in parallel with the English notion of "Gothic novels" for application to French products associated with the fad. The story tracks the career of an unfortunate young woman spoiled and corrupted by the struggle for existence in French society, who follows an inexorable path of misfortune and moral degradation all the way to the guillotine.

Balzac loved *L'Âne mort et la femme guillotinée*, and wrote a brief sequel to it. Pétrus Borel also admired it, and followed it up with his own archetypal collection of similarly cynical tales, *Champavert: contes immoraux* (1832; tr. as *Champavert: Immoral Tales*), which now seems the archetypal, although it was not the first-published, collection of what were subsequently to become better known, thanks to the Comte de Villiers de l'Isle-Adam, as *Contes cruels* [cruel tales][1]. The first such collection to be published was actually S. Henry Berthoud's *Contes misanthropiques* [Misanthropic Tales] (1831)[2], although it seems probable that Janin, Borel and Berthoud—and Balzac too—were all writing stories of the relevant kind in parallel, between 1828 and 1831.

None of the labels invented to describe the new kind of fiction in which Janin was dabbling was truly convincing in its accuracy, and people kept trying to find better ones, without much success. Villiers tried again, weakly, in *Histoires insolites* [unusual stories] (1888), Léon Bloy hazarded *Histoires désobligeantes* (1894; tr. as *The Tarantulas Parlor and Other Unkind Tales*) and Jules Richepin *Contes sans mo-*

---

[1] A number of which were published by Black Coat Press in *The Scaffold* (ISBN 978-1-932983-01-2) and *The Vampire Soul* (ISBN 978-1-932983-02-9).
[2] A number of which were published by Black Coat Press in *Martyrs of Science* (ISBN 978-1-61227-229-0).

rale [Tales without Morals] (1923)[3], but the essence of such work remained, in spite of its occasional fashionability—it enjoyed a second heyday in the *fin-de-siècle* era—frustratingly beyond clear-cut descriptive grasp. Janin's work reflects that elusiveness, perhaps more clearly than any of his contemporaries, partly because the phases of his experimentation were more obvious and more adventurous, and partly because his struggle to find an appropriate label for it was so perversely confused.

The struggle in question is also reflected in the fact that the relevant genre has evaded explanation as well as precise description; critics still do not know exactly what to make of *L'Âne mort et la femme guillotinée*, and various accounts of its nature and significance can be found in commentaries, ranging from its representation as a straightforward horror story or a plaintive complaint against the iniquities of social injustice to the allegation that it was a parody of the *roman frénétique* intended as a joke. It certainly lacks the ferocity of Borel's work in a similar vein, or the slick formularization of Berthoud's, and it does seem curiously light-hearted for a work with such a grim theme and cynical tone, but it is definitely not a parody, and the probability is that its cynicism is curiously light-hearted simply because Jules Janin's cynicism was, in fact, curiously light-hearted.

In the introduction to *Petits contes*, La Fizelière relates another anecdote told to him by Janin, in which, after having read Victor Hugo's grimly dramatic *Dernier jour d'un condamné* (1829; tr. as "The Last Day of a Condemned Man"), which tracks the stream of consciousness of a man on the eve of his execution, Janin immediately began to improvise a "*conte fantastique*" [fantastic tale] entitled "Histoire édifiante d'un homme dévoré par un serpent," tracking the stream of consciousness of a man in the process of being slowly swallowed and digested by a giant python. Unfortunately,

---

[3] A number of which were published by Black Coat Press in *The Crazy Corner* (ISBN 978-1-61227-142-2).

he showed it, while still incomplete, to Charles Nodier, and the two of them were reduced to such side-splitting hilarity by discussion of its contents and possibilities that the tale evaporated in the laughter and was never finished. This is a revealing anecdote in several ways, not least because the term "*conte fantastique*" was one with which Janin was to toy throughout his career, in a rather eccentric fashion, and the one that he settled upon, although he was keenly aware of its impropriety, to describe the kind of story he was writing.

In fact, Janin entitled his first collection of short stories, published in 1832, *Contes fantastiques*, but he began his preface to the collection in question by begging the reader's forgiveness for employing the title deceptively, merely as a lure, and claiming that there was actually very little of the fantastic in the collection. The publisher obviously thought that this prevarication was a trifle too paradoxical, because he amended to the title of the collection, belatedly, to *Contes fantastiques et contes littéraires*, blithely ignoring the fact that equally few of the items in the collection fit the second description, and that the principal literary figure to whom reference is made, the German writer E. T. A. Hoffmann (whose given names were Ernst Theodor Wilhelm, but who substituted A—for Amadeus—for the W in honor of Mozart) is, in fact, the person credited by Janin with pioneering a new kind of *conte fantastique*, and who becomes a fantastic figure himself in the stories in which he features as a character.

The preface to the collection in question—which I have included in this sequence of translations, partly because its flamboyantly tangled argument and method of presentation offer a uniquely precious insight into Janin's attitudes and methods, and partly because it is in itself an item of fantastic fiction comparable to some of Edgar Allan Poe's satirical essays, as well as containing an exemplary short story—pretends to analyze the new genre of *contes fantastiques* popularized by Hoffmann as an art-form typical of an era in which it is no longer possible to produce great literary art, because the world no longer contains subjects suitable for great art, the Revolution having swept all that away irredeemably. As to whether Janin actually believed what he was saying, even he was evidently uncertain, as he adopted two contrasting personas within the piece in order to argue for and against himself.

Within the French Romantic Movement that gathered momentum in the 1820s and enjoyed its first heyday in the early 1830s, Hoffmann was a very popular and influential writer—a fourteen-volume showcase of his works was issued by Eugène Renduel, the Movement's principal publisher, in 1830-32—and Janin was by no means the only French writer to take considerable inspiration from him. No one else, however, took the same strange kind of inspiration from Hoffmann that Janin did, just as no one else was inspired by Victor Hugo's classic novella protesting against capital punishment to write what would nowadays be thought of as a surreal existentialist comedy about a man being swallowed by a python. That was, in a way, the whole point; the one thing Janin wanted more than anything else was not to do things, in his literary work, the way that other people did them. He wanted to be different—in flagrant opposition to the norm, if possible—and was very acutely aware of the awkwardness of trying to do that while working in a profession whose principal *raison d'être* was to court popularity and flatter public opinion. He wanted, in fact, in a particular and perhaps unique sense of the word, to be *fantastique*.

It was, therefore, entirely typical of Janin to begin a collection entitled *Contes fantastiques* by denying that the collection actually contained *contes fantastiques* in the generally-understood sense of the term. In the course of his career he was subsequently to use "*conte fantastique*" several times as a descriptive subtitle, but never on a story that would usually be considered to fit into that category—which is to say, a story including a manifestly supernatural incident. On the other hand, he did write several stories that do contain manifestly supernatural incidents, but never attached the description "*conte fantastique*" to any of them, reserving his own personal significance for the phrase. That strategy might well seem

11

perverse—and it is, that being the reason for adopting it. Even the contention that there is very little of the fantastic, in the commonly-understood sense of the term, in *Contes fantastiques*, is immediately belied by the first two stories in the collection, "Kreyssler" (here translated as "Kreisler") and "Honestus," which are sincerely, albeit rather eccentrically, fantastic.

It is certainly the case that Janin thought there was something very dubious about fantastic fiction, and was never sure that he, as an aspiring great artist, even in an era when great art had supposedly become impossible, ought to be writing it. His one masterpiece of the fantastic, "La Soeur rose et la soeur grise" (1937 in the *Revue de Paris*; here translated as "The Good Sister and the Bad Sister") was so obviously a masterpiece that he reprinted it more than once in the collections of his work that he assembled himself, but the fantastic element of the story is confined to the frame narrative, which consists of a dialogue not dissimilar to, but far more effective than, the one in the Preface to *Contes fantastiques*, in which Janin awards the role of his alter ego to the Devil. Although most of the stories in *Contes Fantastiques et littéraires* were reprinted in his later story collections, occasionally rewritten and retitled, he never reprinted "Kreyssler" or "Honestus"—or, for that matter, "Hoffman et Paganini," here translated as "Hoffmann and Paganini."

Janin also refrained from including "Le Mort magnétisé" (1845 in the *Revue Pittoresque*; here translated as "The Magnetized Corpse") in any of his collections, although he did reprint it in the *Journal des Débats*, in which he had a regular column, primarily employed for his dramatic criticism (the latter version was dismissively reviewed in the *Journal du Magnétisme*, which dutifully reported that the experiment described had been tried, and had not produced the indicated result). Neither of the editors who assembled collections of Janin's works posthumously saw fit to reprint the story either, even though they ought to have realized by then that it is of some historical significance, because it was published several months before Edgar Allan Poe's "The Facts in the Case of M. Valdemar," which has an identical theme, appeared in the December 1845 issue of the *American Review*.

The possibility of any direct influence of Janin's story on Poe's seems remote, and the idea is one that might have occurred to anyone at the time, but the coincidence is all the more striking because Poe, assisted by Charles Baudelaire's translations, was the writer who supplemented and displaced Hoffmann in the affections of the French Romantics and their Decadent and Symbolist successors. It is arguable that Joseph Méry was the French writer most closely analogous to Poe in the range of his short fiction, but in terms of the defiant celebration of "the imp of the perverse," Janin was probably closer to Poe in spirit, although his ambition took him in a different direction; his key position at the *Journal des Débats* from 1830 onwards established him as the most influential dramatic critic of his era, and it is on that kind of work that his reputation now largely rests.

The flagrantly fantastic stories that open and close the present sampler, "Une Histoire de revenant" (tr. as "A Ghost Story") and "Tout de bon coeur" (tr. as "Sincerity") also went unreprinted by the author, although the former was rescued from oblivion by La Fizelière and the latter was included in a later collection of Janin's *Contes, nouvelles et récits* (1884) published be Charles Delagrave. The former was one of Janin's earliest stories, written in 1826; the latter was one of his last, first appearing in the *Musée des Familles* in 1868, two years before his death. Both of them provide typical examples of his determination to work against the established grain. The former sets out straightforwardly to violate the kind of expectation that had already been standardized by popular ghost stories in both anecdotal and literary form. The second pretends—with tongue firmly in cheek—to be abstracted from a book of homiletic fake legends compiled by a Dominican friar, precisely in order to subvert the morality and world-view typically embodied by such "fakelore." Janin was undoubtedly familiar with Henry Berthoud's collection of the legends of

Flanders, into which Berthoud had inserted several of his own imitations, and was probably aware of the latter's further uses of such fakelore in the service of the popularization of science. (Berthoud had been the original editor of the *Musée des Familles*, obtaining that job at the same time that Janin obtained his first editorial appointment, at the *Journal des Enfants*; both writers had probably been in competition for both jobs.)

These parenthetical stories give the lie of another of the disingenuous statements made in the Preface to *Contes fantastiques*, when Janin claims that the fantastic only intruded into his work when he got carried away by a stray whim—although the suggestion that he always made up his stories as they went along, without any pre-planning, rings truer. It is entirely plausible that "Honestus," the longest and most fantastic story in that first collection, really did start out without any clear intention of being fantastic, but simply took off at a tangent. In the same way, "Kreyssler" might plausibly have started out as a kind of aimless doodle, as the author reflected on his sympathy for Hoffmann and attempted to analyze by means of a kind of "free association" what it was about that author's work that so intrigued him.

It is probably significant that two of the subsequent stories to which Janin elected to add the subtitle "conte fantastique," "Le Dîner de Beethoven" (1834 in the *Gazette Musicale*; here translated as "Beethoven's Dinner" and "L'Homme vert" (also 1834, in the *Gazette Musicale*; here translated as "The Green Man") have an obvious kinship with "Kreyssler," each trying in its own way to capture something of the essentially fantastic, or ecstatic, nature of great music. Although Janin did not reprint "L'Homme vert" either—perhaps feeling that it lacked an element of respectability that Beethoven's presence had given the earlier story—it too is a remarkably original and ambitious narrative. It really is fantastic, in a stronger sense than "Le Dîner de Beethoven," although its supernatural element is covert.

Four of the stories that I have included in this sampler, in between the first story and the Preface to the *Contes Fantastiques*, are very early stories, included primarily to illustrate the range of Janin's early attempts to break new literary ground. "Le Rendez-vous" (1826; tr. as "The Rendezvous" is an interesting anticipation of what was to become a standard tactic of his, hybridizing "fiction" and "non-fiction" in a curious kind of alloy, reflected further in "Le Sorcier" (1831; tr. as "The Sorcerer"), and, more elaborately, in "Hoffmann et Paganini." "L'Éclipse" (1828; tr. as "The Eclipse") is interesting as an early example of the "case-study story" that was subsequently to become an important subgenre of the *conte cruel*; Janin evidently thought it more worthy than most of his early stories, because he reprinted it himself, in a slightly revised version, as "La Folle" [The Madwoman]. "Le Voyage imaginaire" (1830; tr. as "The Imaginary Voyage") is a more experimental piece, which provides further endorsement for the assertion that some of the time, at least, Janin really did go wherever the whim of the moment took him while attempting to extrapolate a theme.

It is not impossible that the longest story in the present sampler, "Le Revenant"—translated as "The Revenant"—was also improvised as it went along, with no destination in mind, but that seems unlikely, on close inspection; indeed, the likelier possibility is that it did have a destination in mind but simply failed to reach it, because the author—not atypically—ran out of steam, and hastily adapted what had been planned as a novel into a deeply enigmatic and perhaps unsatisfactory novella. It is difficult to expand that argument, or to discuss the question of exactly how the story is related to the genre of the *conte fantastique*, without going into detail about the twists and turns of its strange plot, so I shall add a brief afterword to the story rather than saying anything further about it here.

It is, I hope, possible that if the stories in this sampler are read as a set—and this is the first time that anyone has ever had the opportunity to do that—then a certain consistency of narrative themes and narrative strategies will become apparent, which is not apparent when the stories are read in isolation, and which reveals something significant about Janin's attitude to the literary fantastic and his contributions thereto. He was by no means the only writer of his day to feel that there as something slightly *infra dig* about writing *contes fantastiques* in the accepted sense of the term, and that it was not what a modern writer with artistic ambitions ought to be doing, except perhaps as a wry joke—but nor was he the only writer of his era who had such a fascination with the possible literary uses of the fantastic that he simply could not let it alone, and could not maintain the false smile by means of which he tried to pretend that he was, in fact, only joking. It is true that his *contes cruels* lack the naked ferocity that Borel and Balzac were able to contrive, and that the only way he could bring himself to compete with Borel's sheer narrative brutality—as he does in the tale enclosed by "Le Soeur rose et la soeur grise"—was to wrap it up very carefully in some kind of gaudy narrative contrivance, but the cruel element is still there, and calling attention to its cruelty in a reproachful fashion, as the narrative voice of "Le Mort magnétisé" does so very conscientiously, does not alter that fact.

Janin was always well aware of the fact that, within the Romantic Movement, he was something of an anomaly. The titanic figures who became the effective leaders of the Movement when it finally took flight, after a long prelude, in 1830, were mostly Republicans—Victor Hugo, Alphonse Lamartine and Edgar Quinet all eventually accepted political office in the Second Republic established after the 1848 Revolution, and the whole movement was hurled into disarray when Hugo and Quinet, along with Alexandre Dumas and several others, were exiled following Louis Napoléon's 1851 coup. Janin, by contrast, not only posed as a nostalgic Royalist who frequently contended that the Revolution had been a colossal tragedy, but as a Bourbonist who disapproved equally strongly of the July Revolution of 1830 and the constitutional monarchy of Louis-

Philippe.[4] He was not the only Royalist member of the Movement, of course, but the others—including Henry Berthoud and Paul Féval—were conventionally right-wing, in combining their support for the crown with religious conservatism, while Janin was a frank and straightforward atheist. Janin was, furthermore, aware of a certain paradoxicality in his own outlook, because, no matter how much he disapproved of revolutions, he was certainly no fan of tyranny and exploitation, and he knew full well that the *ancien régime* had got exactly what it deserved, in recompense for its crimes.

That paradoxicality, which comes across very clearly in the twisted allegory of "Tout de bon Coeur," is supplemented by a more personal one, in that Janin, although by no means short of arrogance and exceedingly touchy in matters of self-respect—he launched more than one libel suit and would probably have fought a lot more duels had he been capable of wielding a weapon with any degree of skill or effect—never really found it possible to approve of himself. Something of a dandy and a rake in his youth, and ever a *bon viveur*, he became morbidly obese long before he wanted to abandon his vices, and was always well aware of what they were costing him, even while he found it impossible to give them up.

Janin was, in fact, too honest a man not to be continually arguing with himself and reproaching himself, about matters of morality as well as issues of literary taste. It is no coincidence that two of his most striking stories, "La Soeur rose et la soeur grise" and "Le Mort magnétisé," are dominated by bitingly critical dialogues with himself—nor is it in the least surprising that, in order to contrive those dialogues, he employed

---

[4] The website of the Académic Française suggests that the failure of Janin's three earlier attempts to get into the Academy before he was finally allowed to take over Charles-Augustin Sainte-Beuve's seat in 1870 occurred because the members thought him "trop Voltairean and "trop Orléaniste." If so, they had obviously not read his works with sufficient attention.

flamboyantly fantastic devices. How could he possibly have done otherwise? There is a similar element of perverse conflict in "Honestus," and when it is missing, in stories in which the key characters are overflowing with sympathy for one another, it is arguably conspicuous by its absence, as the fervent agreements in question are formulated defensively, in opposition to cruel neglect, if not to manifest scorn.

When the fantastic element in Janin's work does not emerge as a dramatization of conflict, it is usually concerned with the quasi-supernatural effects of music, which is, in Janin's view—by no means an uncommon one—the purest of the arts, more refined than the drama that provided the substance of his bread-and-butter criticism, let alone fiction and journalism. That too, however, is not unconnected with self-dissatisfaction, as is obvious with his persistent fascination with "imaginary" music confined to the minds of its makers, which, if externalized, is apt to go wrong, or at least to go unappreciated—because, in his view, music becomes the ultimate form of escapism, of getting away from one's direly unsatisfactory materiality and catching at least a fugitive glimpse of celestial ecstasy.

In that particular opinion, Janin was not at all exceptional or anomalous within the Romantic Movement; indeed, in purely artistic terms, he was one of the most Romantic of all its members, and perhaps more aware than any of his dubious colleagues of the embarrassments corollary to the intrinsic impossibility of isolating the artistic from the political, the personal and the vulgar. He was, and remains, a writer apart, who succeeded more than was entirely good for him in being different, and setting himself up in opposition to what other people thought appropriate. That, of course, makes him all the more valuable as a thinker and as a writer, at least from the viewpoint of readers similarly inclined to self-differentiation, if not to self-reproach.

The following translation of "Une Histoire de revenant" was made from the version reproduced on the website of La

Bibliothèque électronique de Lisieux at *bmlisieux.com*. The translations of the next four stories were made from the London Library's copy of the 1882 edition of *Petits Contes* (volume 3 of *Oeuvres de Jeunesse*) published by the Librairie des Bibliophiles. The translations of the following four items were made from the London Library's copy of the 1863 reprint of *Contes fantastiques et contes littéraires* published by Michel Lévy. The translation of "Le Dîner de Beethoven" was made from the version of volume five of *Catacombes*, published in Paris by Werdet in 1839, reproduced on the Bibliothèque Nationale's *gallica* website. The translation of "L'Homme vert" was made from the Google Books version of the 1841 edition of the *Revue des Feuilletons* (the story is missing from the *gallica* version). The translation of "La Soeur rose et la soeur grise" was made from the London Library's copy of *Contes et nouvelles* (Tome premier) published by the Librairie des Bibliophiles in 1876. The translation of "Le Mort magnétisé" was made from the 1845 volume of the *Revue Pittoresque* contained on *gallica*. The translation of "Le Revenant" was made from the London Library's copy of *Petit romans d'hier et d'aujourdhui*, published in 1869 by A. Sauton. The translation of "Tout de bon Coeur" was made from the version reproduced on the Bibliosem website at *bibliosem.com*.

Brian Stableford

A GHOST STORY

A few friends met up the other day—Frenchmen and foreigners that we had never seen, but whom we had known for a long time: poets, writers, rich men, all people who approved of one another at first glance and understood one another at the first handshake. As no one had come to stand around, we talked about nothing—which is to say that we talked about everything: poetry, politics, even love; to such an extent that, by dint of getting carried away, our imaginations being gradually warmed up as the champagne hit the ice, we ended up talking about ghosts.

One of us, an Englishman, a very cold man externally, one of those fortunate men of the world who can drink without ever getting drunk and eat without ever getting fat, and who was an implacable mocker to boot—in a brief, as dangerous as any Englishman who has read Voltaire—on listening to us talking about ghosts, declared with perfect composure that he had known a man who was the friend of another man who had seen a ghost.

"The whole city of London still remembers it," our Englishman added, "and as true as we're honest men, I believe the story, whose hero is well-known."

As you can imagine, everyone cried: "The story—tell us the story!"

He wanted nothing more than to tell us the story, which he did.

"We all knew Lord Littleton. He was an honest and noble gentleman, rich, happy, capable of controlling his passions. He had passed through his first youth and had arrived in that fine thirtieth year, in which passion reasons, love hesitates and the heart only beats at certain times of the day. In brief, Lord Littleton had a strong mind. Unfortunately, he wanted to be too strong, and that made him do something bad.

21

"Since turning twenty-five he had kept a young, beautiful and passionate mistress, whom he loved as if he wasn't thirty. Poor woman! She hadn't given any thought to the revolution that takes place in a man when his first twenty years are surcharged and overburdened by ten more. She still trusted in her lover's initial declaration: fiery words, ardent embraces, admirable oaths, blazing kisses! She was still there, poor woman; she hadn't changed a single heartbeat, not a single throb of her pulse. You can imagine her fear and pain, therefore, when the lord told her one morning that he no longer wanted to love her, and that, in consequence, he no longer loved her, and that she had to make provision for herself elsewhere—and a thousand other admirable reasons extracted from social convention.

"On hearing him talk like that, she understood quite clearly that he was right, that he was saying what he had to say, that he no longer loved her at all, and that there was only one response she could make. She went out without shedding a tear. She closed the door, and the lord, who was reading a French novel, picked up his book and resumed reading at the page where he had left it, at the moving moment when the hero was embracing the cadaver of his mistress.

"But what do you expect? We're all mortal! It was a four-volume novel that Lord Littleton was reading—which takes you back a few years, for France didn't yet have the octavo novel, that great conquest of modern literature.

"When he'd finished his third volume, therefore, he got dressed, went out and went to dine at his club. That evening, he played a few hands of whist, won, went home, got undressed and went to bed; then as he still had his fourth volume to read, he didn't want to go to sleep before having finished the exceedingly lamentable story. His reading took him to midnight, the time when he usually went to sleep.

"He was about to snuff out the candles and go to sleep when all of a sudden, in the big red leather armchair, in the same place and in the same place that Fanny—the discarded mistress—had always sat, he saw Fanny, or rather her shade.

White and pale, disheveled and sad, she was supporting her head with her hands; her gaze was solemn.

"Evidently, she was waiting until Lord Littleton had finished reading before speaking to him.

"Lord Littleton, seeing Fanny again like that, suddenly realized that she was dead. In fact, she had thrown herself into the Thames earlier that evening, between seven and nine o'clock, during a thick fog; her body hadn't yet been found.

"'Good night, Milord,' Fanny said. 'Here I am, dead, killed by you. You're free—take advantage of it, Milord! In a week's time, at the same hour, midnight next Friday, you'll be one of us!'

"Having said that, she stood up—it really was her elegant figure, as supple as a cane but even slimmer, by God!—and she went out. She didn't even glance at the mirror over the fireplace. As I say, she was dead.

"Lord Littleton had no trouble at first in mustering a little heroism. That's such a fine thing to do, mustering heroism, that one wants to do it for oneself, when one can't do it for others. So the lord did his best to settle down and go to sleep, and even though he didn't get a wink all night, he persuaded himself that he had.

"So, he reached daylight, still repeating the phantom's words to himself: *Goodnight, Milord!*

"That same day, Milord was eating lunch when they brought him Fanny's corpse—so disfigured, alas, so violet and contracted by death, and so horribly small, narrow, dead and deformed, that her lover wouldn't even have recognized her if Fanny hadn't taken the precaution of coming to tell him, the night before, that she was dead: *Killed by you, Milord!*

"Lord Littleton had Fanny buried; he followed her to the graveside. On the way, people said of him: *There's the man for whom she killed herself.*

"As for her, who had killed herself, she had not a word of remembrance. She was, therefore, thrown into her earthly refuge and covered with earth. The gravedigger trampled the earth in question down, stuck a cypress into it, and Fanny's tomb was lacking nothing.

"That funeral took up the whole Lord Littleton's day—a day and a night, in fact, for he couldn't sleep again that night, and he said to himself that, in fact, he was saddened by her death, and that it was the least he could do for Fanny's spirit was spend a sleepless night.

"On the second day, Lord Littleton got up early. He ate well, went riding, tried himself out as best he could, and that evening, was very astonished to be still so wide awake and felling so well that, if he had dared, he would have invited one of his friends to play cards with him all night. But was he not in mourning for Fanny?

"On the third day, Littleton couldn't help remembering what else the dead woman had said: *In a week's time, at the same hour, midnight next Friday.*

"He ordered the removal of the red armchair—the armchair that reminded him too much of poor Fanny.

"And thus, from day to day, the terror made such frightful progress that by the sixth day, the fear was legible in his pale face. On that sixth day Lord Littleton's eyes were haggard, his voice hollow; he could hardly breathe. He was so frightened that he confessed his fear.

"His mother and his friends interrogated him in vain; he only replied in monosyllables. In the end, however, when the evening of the penultimate day came, he confessed his terrors. 'Tomorrow,' he said, 'at midnight. It'll be the end of me; she said so.'

"His mother and his friends had recourse in vain to the encouraging and consolatory words that all those who love you have in their hearts. Nothing made any difference; he was like a condemned man awaiting execution.

"He was somber, anxious, motionless; he shivered every time he heard the clock chime the hour. He cocked his ear as if he could hear someone coming. His friends, seeing him in that sad depression, wanted at least to abridge and deceive his suffering. They took the precaution of putting all the clocks and watches forward by half an hour; they even instructed the watchman to cry the hours falsely.

"The night wore on. Lord Littleton, in bed, asked his manservant: 'What time is it?'

"'Midnight, Your Lordship,' said the manservant.

"'You're mistaken, John,' said the Lord. 'Show me the clock.'

"The clock said midnight.

"'And my watch?'

"The Lord's watch said midnight. In the street, the cry was heard: 'Midnight!'

"Then he got up; he felt himself walking; he felt himself alive; he came and went, light-hearted. He was brave, he was the young and handsome Lord Littleton of old. He was hungry; he was thirsty; he was sleepy."

At this point our narrator paused to draw breath. When he had drawn breath, he drank a glass of champagne.

When he had drunk, he picked up a fruit from a dish, and he was about to eat the fruit, when we all cried: "What about Lord Littleton? Lord Littleton?"

"Lord Littleton?" said the Englishman. "He's as well as you and me, Messieurs. "The hour had gone by without carrying his lordship off; at present, he eats, he drinks, he sleeps, he goes riding, he's always lucky at cards, and he doesn't have a single mistress. I advise you to do likewise."

People generally think that the story of Lord Littleton makes no sense, and I agree with the general opinion.

THE RENDEZVOUS

She hesitated at first, but there was so much resignation and love in my gaze that she finally consented. "This evening," she said, "in front of Notre-Dame." And as swift as lightning, she disappeared, in order to hide her blush, leaving me in one of those moments of intoxication that one only experiences once.

This evening, she had said! All day I thought I could hear that sweet promise murmured in my ear, and the sun had scarcely begun to decline when I found myself under the parvis of the temple, breathless with anxiety and hope. At first I saw nothing, did not think about anything; I was too intent on the impending moment. It required nothing less than the admirable spectacle before which I found myself to draw me out of the obsession that was my everyday life.

That moment of youth, that fugitive and fragile hour which man, in a fit of irony, has called his finest years, is, incontrovertibly, the most inexplicable aspect of the human creature. There is in your depths a malaise, a kind of dolorous joy, that causes you to suffer the torment of Prometheus. Once attained by that fatal malady, everything charming that there is in the actions of the imagination and thought is annihilated, disappearing and giving way to the fantastic images of a sick heart.

That is why, at first, I was cold and insensible at the sight of that beautiful monument of Medieval civilization, that vast and poetic cathedral, the imposing sight of which was still a novelty to me.

It was, however, the exact time at which a beautiful evening magnifies all the prestige of the Gothic temple, whose silvery steeple loses itself in the still-silvery clouds. That mass of stone looming up in the midst of the general silence, an eloquent witness to the perseverance and the piety of our forefathers, was then surrounded by all the harmonies with which Heaven embellishes the work of the creature; the bell renders a Gothic sound; the crow, as old as time, spreads its black wings over the ogives; and through the holes in the belfry, the chattering sparrow seems to defy the reach of humans. To complete the joy, the temple was deserted; there was no cantor in a soutane, no choirboy with a red face; no dispenser of holy water with a shrill voice; no missionary with haggard eyes; the temple was there in all its majesty, without any human creature to mar that sublime ensemble.

We are in a century so incredulous that the idea of atheism and hypocrisy slips in everywhere that one encounters a human being!

For me, without thinking about it, I started studying the edifice with which I was still unfamiliar. Imagine that temple, embroidered with as much grace and delicacy as the veil of a young bride. It is a mass of detail that frightens our imagination. Everywhere, the human chisel has represented, sometimes a Christ on the cross, sometimes the evangelists writing the moral code that was to submit the world to reason, sometimes the apostle St. John with his lamb and that child-like grace that one might have thought escaped from the brush of Rubens. It is a sequence of fantastic images, of holy creations, of naïve miracles, such as one reads in old legends.

All the beliefs of the Middle Ages, with their frank, definite, martial allure are found on those Gothic stones. You find Roman armor there, the barbarian javelin, and, often, the Italian toga on the shoulders of a Vandal. As high as your sight can reach, you perceive a thousand dramatic, lively, passionate scenes like those Shakespeare wrote, sometimes in a poor cabin, sometimes in a magnificent palace: old men, young women, martyrs, murderers—an entire poem.

That is what I would not have seen without you, young woman—without you, whom I had almost forgotten in that mute contemplation.

And as the night, descending from the height of the belfry, gradually veiled those various scenes, like the curtain at the Opéra that separates you from the enchantments of the theater, I came to consider the immense door with the double batten that the Swiss with the worried expression had just closed noisily. I considered, attentively, the beautiful face of the Virgin sculpted on the door: a celestial woman that some poor artist had found buried in obscure wood.

That door has suffered the dire effects of time! All color is lost; numerous cracks furrow that beautiful body. However, it has a real beauty, an ineffable grace, like everything that is spontaneous in the arts.

I was standing there, contemplating those beautiful hands and that angelic smile, when a light and soft footstep, and the harmonious breath that announces the beating of a heart, caused me to turn my head abruptly.

It wasn't her.

It was an old woman wearing the habit of the Sisters of Charity, and that white head-dress that adorns them, and that gross ebony rosary that they carry with as much assurance as a young colonel carries his sword. The woman had seen long days; she was doubtless coming from visiting the loft of a poet or an orphan, returning in the evening to a vast edifice that she had chosen for a dwelling because it is consecrated to suffering humanity. I saw then that I was beside the Hôtel-Dieu.

Oh, whoever you are, if you think you know all that is beautiful in the arts, go study them under the empire of a great passion; let the whim of your mistress fix you for entire hours before those monuments that disdain your young inexperience. Only then will you sense that there is something that floats above the work of centuries, how perseverance is no less useful in comprehending the work of genius than in creating them, how the human soul is magnified in the contemplation of masterpieces that our century no longer understands.

She didn't come that evening, but I went home half-consoled.

THE ECLIPSE

Three years ago, in Montmartre, in the house of Doctor Blanche, the indefatigable healer of all kinds of madness, who treats his patients with tender care with well-being and with liberty, as others do with isolation, cold showers and misery, there was a woman whose madness was singular and touching.

The woman in question, still young, whose face was tender and whose smile was full of charm, had no other madness than this: she imagined that she was the fiancée of the sun. They had been promised to one another in marriage, she and the sun, one fine autumn day, and that day, the sun had covered his resplendent face with his most beautiful veil of clouds, in order not to dazzle his beloved suddenly. Since then, she had been his as he was hers; she had felt her husband's burning kiss on her hand, and now she no longer lived for anyone but him.

The sun was her joy, her glory and her triumph, poor woman; she got up at the very moment when her flamboyant beloved threw his first rays into the sky; she had her eyes fixed on her spouse's rise, and she greeted him with her gaze, as the birds greet him with their songs, as the river greets him with its murmur as the rose greets him with its perfume.

The more beautiful nature was at sunrise, the more serene the sky, the more joyful was creation entire, the happier the poor madwoman was; was it not her divine spouse who was casting light and heat everywhere? Was he not the king of the world? Had she not spent an entire night of transports in his arms, the arms of the master of creation? The soul of the world was his, and hers!

Thus, in a perpetual and divine ecstasy, she followed every step of the sun; she collected his least rays. The higher the sun rose in the sky, the greater that poetic enthusiasm became. It was scarcely possible to persuade the madwoman to take her meals every day, so obsessed was she with her celestial passion; and even then, to make her eat, it was necessary to tell her that her divine spouse had gilded the fruits, had yellowed the wheat, had ripened the grapes; thus, she had the right to sit down at the immense table that the sun charged with foodstuffs in his course.

When she took her meals, therefore, the madwoman offered libations to the sun; in his honor she poured a drop of milk in the morning, and emptied her glass to his health. Then, when the day began to decrease and the luminous radiance went to fade away in the distance in the Seine, the tender bride of the sun became as anxious as the wife of a poor herring-fisherman might be, whose husband has been away for two months and who hears the sea roaring.

"What will become of my husband?" the madwoman said. "As long as he is not wounded on the road, please God!"

Gradually, the sun went away, giving way to the night. Then the madwoman put her hands together and, in a mysterious tone and in her softest voice, she said to her spouse: "Wait for me! Wait for me!"

Then she went back into her room in all haste, because she did not want to make the sun wait.

Singular and fortunate madwoman! A pleasant delusion! To see her soul attached to the heavens by a ray of sunlight! To have no other passion than that, a serene sky! To have nothing to fear but the clouds that veil the day star! To be happy every time that nature is happy! To open her soul to the gentle heat, as the earth does, and receive its benevolent influence! To sing a canticle of love in a low voice, and only to be jealous of the grass of the fields!

Such was the life of the poor madwoman for two years. Not that she did not have her chagrins, just as she would have done had she had her reason; for, as soon as winter came and she saw the face of the sun, her spouse, grow pale and tremble beneath the snow as a mortally wounded handsome young man might; as soon as she saw that immense glory obscured by thick clouds, as happens to the greatest man of this world, whose glory is obscured by envy; then the unfortunate creature became the saddest of human creatures. No more repose; no more smiles; no more songs; no more celebrations in her heart! Can you not see her spouse, freezing and trembling up there, resting his weary head on the ice-capped mountains?

How long and sad the days of winter seemed to the madwoman! It was a real, incredible suffering; it was a love-sickness such as the privileged companions of a few great unfortunate men have experienced over the centuries. The greater and more elevated in the world is the man a woman loves, the more impatiently she supports the great misfortune of seeing him humiliated, obscured, trembling, scorned, vanquished or captive. Hers was almost the dolor of the mother of the Emperor when she saw her son in chains on his rick in the middle of the sea!

But the dolor of that noble mother, an immense queen still standing in the ruins of Rome, is an eternal dolor. Her fallen star will never rise again. The sun is more fortunate; his defeat is temporary; he has soon pierced the thickest cloud; he is victorious, he returns; there he is; the sun has his Hundred Days twice over, every year. I'm only talking about the sun of France.

So, when, in spring, Dr. Blanche's poor madwoman recovered her spouse as she had left him, in the month of May, when she saw him once again as resplendent as ever, and all the leaves of the trees sprang forth at his coming as the sparks do beneath the blacksmith's hammer, then the sweet joy returned to the poor woman's heart; then she quit her mourning, put on her brightest dress, and sang her sweetest hymn.

"Rejoice in Heavens and on earth; rejoice, stars of the firmament and waves of the river, angels up above and humans down below, rejoice! My husband the sun was ill, and had returned to health; he was absent, and has returned!"

And indeed, nature entire obeyed the poor madwoman; nature entire rejoiced; the madwoman's husband had returned.

That joyful madness lasted ten more years without it be-ing possible to cure it—but the woman was so happy! Why, then, cure her happiness?

It is now three years since the wife of the sun died, and her death was as touching as her life.

It was a beautiful autumn day; it was noon; the gentle and calm sun was launching his purest rays upon the earth and his wife.

The sun's wife, sitting on the lawn next to the large ap-ple-tree, was following the steps of her august spouse in the sky. Her heart had never been more full of love, her gaze had never been more tender; her dream had never been closer to being a reality.

They understood one another so well, she and her spouse the sun! She had such a piercing gaze for him, and he for her. He was marching so slowly in that enclosed field of azure, doubtless in order to have time to see her kneeling before him.

But, O Heaven! Suddenly, that powerful radiance of na-ture pauses and is troubled; suddenly, the sun disappears, no longer as before, by degrees, on the edge of the river, after having shaken the brilliant dust off his robe and his feet; he pauses abruptly, entirely; he hides; one can no longer see him!

Where is he?

"Yes!" she cries. "Yes, my spouse is with my rival! Yes, he's unfaithful! Yes, he's gone during the day, and won't come back this evening."

And as she only lived in order to see him during the day, to wait for him during the night, to greet him at dawn, to sing to him in spring, to admire him in summer, to bless him in autumn, to weep for him in winter, to love him at all times, the poor woman, on seeing him disappear suddenly like that, ab-ruptly, without knowing where he was going, without know-ing whether he would come back, the poor woman died during the eclipse: died of jealousy, despair and love.

She had scarcely been dead for a second when the sun, disengaged from his innocent encounter with the moon, tran-quilly resumed his course—but it was too late; the drama was concluded, and the immortal spouse, still the object of such a violent love a little while before, now only struck extinct, closed eyes with his radiance.

Yes, it was obvious that the poor woman was really dead, for the sad and calm ray of sunlight that posed itself upon her, as if to ask her forgiveness for that involuntary absence, did not wake her up.

THE IMAGINARY VOYAGE

Angling[5]

Truly, it's a shame to be here all alone. Walls the color of a fireplace, extremely ugly men, and what women! I'm weary of the noise of the city, the mud, the Opéra, the rumors. If the word nature—a beautiful word—hadn't been abused to such an extent, I'd say that I want more nature. I've seen it somewhere.

On a dazzling summer's day, toward the silence of noon, when the light is everywhere, enjoying itself in the blue sky, in the flowering wheat, in the green water, slipping through the clouds as if through swans' wings; when everything falls silent—birds, insects, demoiselles with broad necklines—when life, humans, plants and animals, have paused everywhere, during that waking sleep, more beautiful than a beautiful dream, I saw a pretty scene full of grace; you'll recognize it, for I'm leaving—and what man knows, when he leaves, whether he'll come back?

On the edge of the water, a wave hidden by the grass that snakes smoothly over the clay, and which glides like a snake through the meadow laden with trees and fruits, joyous reflections of a rural abundance; I can say it; I've seen it.

I've seen three anglers who weren't asleep: three passionate, active anglers, interested as one might be in a drama or a ghost story; not anglers like the ones you've often seen, vulgar anglers, some tall, stiff, thin, suntanned fellow with a stupid gaze and an idiotic smile, his arm extended and at the

---

[5] I have translated *La Pêche* in the literal sense given by context, but it is perhaps not irrelevant that it could also be translated as "The Peach."

end of that arm an old line, and at the end of that line a hook, and at the end of that hook a worm, and at the end of that worm, nothing.

My anglers were laughing, singing, admiring, as ready to deliver their fish to the frying-pan as to return it to the warm waves. Mute inhabitant of the reeds, poor animal with cold sensations, modest tastes, still shining with a thousand colors, gilded carp; pike, open your wide jaws like a shark at sea; slither, eel; live and grow long; that was what my anglers would have done with their captives, if the fish had had a voice. If it had only uttered the plaintive call of the skylark; if its eye had expressed the frank fear of the sparrow caught in a barn!

But for mute dolors one has no compassion; a plaint is a confession of weakness that often touches human pride; humans want to appear the stronger.

But I'll get back to my three anglers.

The first was a child already grown, a man by comparison with his brothers, skillful at casting the hook, more skillful at bringing the captive fish back with the net. The other anglers—oh, as for them, you've never seen prettier.

A small pale child, plump, fresh, blue-eyed, a good boy, devoid of malice, devoid of envy, almost naked, as curious as a puppy putting his nose to a carriage door for the first time. The little boy plunged his nose into the net, and at every movement of the fish he closed his eyes as if he were afraid, and more than one drop of water splashed his pretty face, an innocent punishment for an innocent curiosity.

My third angler was a little girl, gross, chubby, already mischievous, with little rounded arms and a good hand, which she plunged into the net; one might have thought that there was one eel more in the net, the little hand agitating without seizing anything, the fish slipping between her fingers, so frail.

Grow up quickly, little one, grow, be as beautiful as Charlotte; grown up like her, you won't need either to cast the hook or extend the net, or to lean over toward the bank; young men, noble prey, will be your captives, if you wish, at a glance; and the old one will regret no longer being, in your eyes, anything more than that paltry small fry that your brother will throw back into the water.

Charlotte

Have I not named Charlotte? Alas, that's a name whose echo is prolonged for me, which resounds, here in the heart, here in the head; it's a permanent vision; I can see her, I can touch her. I say to her: "I love you, Charlotte, capricious creation made for the torment of my life; since you're here, evoked, stay with me, that I might still see you."

Charlotte is grown up and beautiful; her complexion is bronzed as she has black hair; she's a young woman with a haughty expression, but who smiles at intervals, which corrects her pride. There's no woman like Charlotte in France or in England; she isn't a daughter of Europe; she's a plant that needs too much sun and cold earth would stifle her, and also dainty and frail at her extremities—but what a noble breast! And within that breast, what a noble heart!

When one is a young man, a new, true man, and when the moment comes that shows you the predestined woman, the one that one recognizes without ever having seen her and about whom one says to oneself in a whisper; "That's her," it happens that, memory bearing her to the heart, you remember everything about that woman you have judged with a glance; you know the color of her garments and her figure, all the way to the slightest crease in her sleeve; you know the arrangement of her hair, the little hat that ornaments her head and the white feather that falls back gracefully over her neck; you could say how her beautiful neck was uncovered, how her beautiful hands were bare, what tune the young woman was humming, which keys she was touching on the harmonium; not only do you have the details, but you also have the ensemble; more than that, neither her dress, nor her attitude, nor her face, nor her gaze, nor her smile, nor her hand makes you recognize her;

that's something you've forgotten: a gaze that escapes you, a sense of which you're ignorant; that sense is the sixth sense.

It is with the sixth sense that I loved Charlotte.

The sixth sense—long live magnetism and glory to Mesmer!—the perfect sense, the divine sense, the unique sense, the sense that awakens the dead man, the sense clad in the material envelope, the soul's sense…give me a name, Charlotte! Whatever its name is, it's with the sixth sense that I loved Charlotte.

Grab you via the eyes, and you'll be infatuated for a day; grab you via the sixth sense, and you'll be in love until you die.

It was via the eyes that Andromeda's lover was captured, via the eyes that Cleopatra was taken. Antonia and Sappho were taken via the sixth sense.

O Saint-Preux![6] O Lovelace! Would you like to escape, one, the philosophy of your mistress, the other, your own virtue? Would you like to become simple bourgeois, very happy and with very little of which to complain? Incline solitary toward some beauty in the audience, attentive to the play, or awaiting a cavalier at a ball.

But what did I do to you, Charlotte? Why welcome me? Why did you interrupt the song you had commenced when I arrived? Why did you suspend that chord, scarcely-born, that your capricious fingers interrupted at the sight of me? Why, in sum, did I place myself, from the very start, so close to you?

Charlotte, without that, I was happy. I had all of the spring, with its roses; without you, I was free and content; I lived untroubled, a futile observer of petty things; the historian impassioned by the infinitely small, the crazy lover of the sun, of the light, of the rain falling as dew, of the cricket singing in the blazing hearth, the glow-worm hiding under a rose-leaf,

---

[6] Saint-Preux is the protagonist of Rousseau's *Nouvelle Héloïse* (1761), who falls in love with his pupil Julie. Lovelace is the leading male character in Richardson's *Clarissa* (1748)

the timid and fugitive radiance that the eye scarcely suspects and that the breath of an insect can tarnish.

Without you, I would still love the thunder that rumbles in the distance; the mill that goes tick-tock, a monotonous music so favorable to slumber; the cockerel that crows, the bell that tolls, the horse at the plough, the lamb at its mother's teat; the artisan at his door in the evening, the prince passing by with his soldiers, the great lady of the opera and her caleche; I would love all of that Charlotte, and I wouldn't love you!

But now, here you are in my sixth sense. There you are, sovereign mistress, placed there, giving my heart all emotions, my head all transports, my arteries their sudden movement; you're there, always there, there forever.

The Valley

I'm already far away from that city of noise and mire, here I am over the most beautiful valley of which Theocritus ever dreamed. My valley is situated under a Greek sky. First you see mountains placed like so many steps rising up to the sky. The sky above is stormy. There stands the first summit of the mountains, the hardened stone, raised up by some giant before the deluge, beneath its crust of ice and snow. In the greatest heat of summer, you find snow up there, glittering like a diamond; you hear the torrents tumbling, you see the eagle disappearing into their inaccessible dwellings, veritable companions of the winter. That's the first terrain overlooking my valley.

Lower down, the ground is laden with a dark forest of tall pines and poplars; majestic branches that the sun sways, a somber horror made for prophecies, sudden noises, unexpected eruptions, flames when lightning strikes; an entire, unknown, mysterious world about whom no one says anything; a world that Byron would have loved but into which Charlotte and I don't go. Charlotte's hands are delicate; they would break on the rocks; then, having arrived up there, Charlotte would be afraid. We'll remain in the valley, sheltered, in the lukewarm wind; at the very most, we might risk ourselves on the lower slopes on feast-days.

In the lush pasture, in the green and bushy meadows, where the streams murmur, where the white heifers hang from the flanks of the rock, where the capricious goats balance on the brink of the abyss, where the mules rejoice in the sunlight, we go in pilgrimage, all alone with our love, all alone outside the world, like Lucretius' sailor who sees the tempest at his feet.

But I'll place my house, my domestic roof, in the depths of the valley, on the other side of the river, under a few large trees and facing a ruined temple: ruins in marble, partly broken columns, capitals devoured by the winter wind; we'll be able to see the temple from our window, lit by the moon, and it will seem to us to be magnified by the shadow cast at our feet. Pious monuments of ancient religion, beautiful remains of antique art, the religion to which you were consecrated is abolished, the art that raised you is lost, but you remain standing, the last witnesses of those vanished forces. Alas, if you were to die, Charlotte, I would not even be like that insensible debris; I would die; I would follow you, you who made me feel that I had a soul, you for whom I would die!

Beautiful dreams! And I'm alone! And yet, I'm leaving. Italy, Spain, America, where, then, shall I go? Where is Charlotte? Charlotte is in my thoughts, she guides me, she rests upon me; it is on her that I built those brilliant châteaux in the land of chimeras, which crumble like palaces of cloud, like the villages one sees in the fire, in winter, with their tall bell-towers, their minarets, their obelisks, their tombs. To leave—but where, then, to find rest? To learn more! What fatigue! I prefer remembrance.

Children

We'll have two children, Charlotte and I: a little boy and a little girl, who will be called after her mother. Our daughter will be the older of our children: a pretty child with a fine profile, long hair, a dreamer at the age of ten; she'll be the one to support her brother, she who teaches him his first steps, his first words, who will receive his first caresses, for we shan't be jealous of our daughter, shall we, Charlotte? Besides which, our son will be so beautiful.

A stout and jovial boy, always laughing, his hair untidy, a broad chest, sturdy arms; a well-built boy, very bold, fearing nothing in the dark, liking the sound of drums and trumpets, playing fearlessly with dogs and horses, sleeping all night, playing all day; intelligent, active, already passionate, preferring his other to his father, loving his sister as much as his mother. A pleasant couple, youthful and cheerful, I can see you in advance in my heart.

Oh, it's when one is a father, most of all, that spring is beautiful, that poetry is true, that death is gentle: one is represented on the earth; someone remains after you to bear your name, your face, who ornaments you with his virtues and his talent, who repairs your domestic roof and continues your benefits; it's then that one can die.

A Halt

With her, my life was complete; every instant was a separate life for me, every corner of the earth a world. With Charlotte, I was a simple man, a happy man. Every season had its pleasures for me. In summer, I roamed the forests and meadows with her, the entire countryside; we often paused on the edge of a stream, on the summit of a mountain, in a forest clearing. Let's call a halt, uncouple our horses, set up a table on the grass; sit down beside me, Charlotte; our guide is leaning on the carriage, and there he is, devouring political newspapers, weighing the destiny of empires, setting Europe in equilibrium, marveling over the destiny of kings who wander the roads, seeking a shelter they cannot find. Thus our great politician waits patiently for dinner to be ready, while the child plays, the ox ruminates, the dog barks and the cricket

40

hidden in the grass sings his noonday song and the spider spins her web, glittering like the rainbow. Do you understand that happiness was there, Charlotte?

Charlotte, happiness is repose; it's the dream without sleep that the shadows give us; it's that half-noisy calm that is nothing like the fearful calm of darkness; it's the movement of the invisible world that one can encounter anywhere, in the calices of flowers, in the treetops, in the grass, on vines that climb everywhere; life with you, with the woman one loves, with the wife who gazes at you, smiles at you, speaks to you: that's how I make my happiness.

And after the meal, after the slumber when the shadows extend over the plain, it's the pleasure of resuming one's route, of reharnessing one's good well-rested horses, of climbing back into the rural vehicle; of feeling oneself jolted beside the woman one loves, of hearing her cries of fright during the descent, of drawing closer to her in order to reassure her, and squeezing her arm at every jolt.

Alas, you're the one who didn't want it, Charlotte. But I'm leaving.

Winter

And the winter would still have made poetry. It's a good time for the poet and for lovers. It's cold outside, the north wind is blowing, the snow is falling, the river has stopped flowing, the trees are all white with frost, the poultry-yard is mute; then you shut yourselves in together to practice egotism *à deux*. What conditions for wellbeing then! You have an entirely closed room, paintings, engravings, a large mirror to reflect your image, Charlotte; a good oak-log fire, and your feet on a carpet with a floral pattern, and thick cushions around the apartment, and for me a large armchair, and perfumes to my right, and antique vases on the mantelpiece and to one side an open piano, and above the piano shelves laden with books, and silk curtains at the windows, and all that lit by an alabaster lamp; and above you the bust of Shakespeare, old

41

William, who dominates the whole petty universe, and then you say to me, Charlotte: "Read me something from one of your homeland's great poets."

"I'll read you some verses by Lamartine, Charlotte."

And the young woman gets ready to listen; she leans her pretty arm on the back of her winged armchair; she's all soul.

"Yes, I'll read you something by our poet. Let's go to Heaven, since there's a God; let's quit the earth; come, no longer having any but angelic passions, let's love as the angels do, let's weep as the angels do; the poem by Lamartine is love; all his thought is love.

"Would you like new verses, Charlotte? You know all the others by heart.

"There's revolution in the world as well; liberty dominates all other needs; poetry itself falls silent before great changes. Let's be just toward genius, we simple mortals.

"Listen to the verses, Charlotte."

> The inspirational breath that makes the human soul
>   A melodious instrument
> Disdains the palace of sovereign pomp.
> What are the purple and the gold that scarcely descend
>   From the radiant palace of the heavens?
>
> It falls at random on the solitary tree,
>   On the pastor's cabin
> Beneath the indigent thatch of the earth's poor
> And covers, smiling, a glorious mystery
>   In a cradle moist with tears.
>
> It's Homer asleep, that a masterless slave
>   Warms with his love alone;
> It's a child, expelled from the shade of his beech
> Weeping for the goats his feet lead to pasture,
>   And one day will be Virgil.

Thus, instinct hides in nature entire
    Ripening for immortality,
The pearl on the sea bed, gold in the bosom of stone
Diamond in the shadow where light languishes
    Its glory in obscurity.

Glory, bird divine, phoenix born of itself,
    Which comes every hundred years, anew,
To pose upon the earth and on a name it loves,
And one sees it die there, like its emblem,
    But whose cradle no one knows.

Don't be astonished that an angel of harmony
    Comes from on high to awaken you,
Remember Jacob! The dreams off genius
Descend upon brows that have, in insomnia,
    Nothing but stone for a pillow.[7]

"Or would you rather have an elegy, Charlotte? A prayer
to the angel of death? Listen, the wind's groaning and lifting
the yellow leaves in swirls; listen to these verses."

My gaze pauses, fixed upon a tomb;
Tomb, dear maintenance of bitter dolor,
Where the sacred grass that covers my mother
    Grows beneath the hamlet's tears.

There, when veiled angel with a woman's features
In God, his light, had exhaled her soul,
As one blows out a lamp as day approaches,
In the altar's shadow, which she loved not long ago,
I have dug myself a narrow dwelling,
    A doorway to the other abode.

---

[7] These are the opening stanzas of Lamartine's "Le Génie dans
l'obscurité" (1828).

There sleeps in hope the one whose smile
Still seeks my eyes at the hour when all expires,
That heart, source of mine, bosom that conceived me,
That breast that nourished me with milk and affection,
Those arms that were nothing but a cradle of caresses,
    Those lips from which I received everything.

There sleep sixty years with one sole thought,
Of a life uniquely spent in doing good,
Of innocence, love, hope and purity,
So many aspirations repeated to her God,
So much faith in death, so much virtue cast
As a pledge to immortality.

So many sleepless nights watching over suffering,
So much pain retrenched to nourish indigence,
So many tears ever ready to unite with others,
So many sighs burning toward another homeland,
And so much patience in supporting a life
    Whose crown was elsewhere.

And all that, Why? For a hole in the sand
To absorb forever that imperishable being.
For the vile furrows to be fattened,
For the grass of the dead that covers her tomb
To grow thicker and greener beneath my feet,
    A little ash was enough.

No, no; to light three footsteps on the grass
God would not have created that immense light,
That soul of the long gaze and heroic effort.
On that cold stone the gaze falls in vain,
O virtue, your aspect is stronger than the grave
    And more evident than death,

And my eyes, convinced of that great testimony,
Are raised from the ground and emerge from the cloud,

And my tenebrous heart recovers its torch.
Happy the man to who God has given a saintly mother;
In vain is life hard and death bitter;
   Who can doubt upon her tomb?[8]

And Charlotte's eyes were bathed with tears, tears steaming gently through her pretty fingers.

"Enough, enough," she said to me. "Leave or Lamartine there, I can't cry anymore." And then she added, smiling: "And then, Arthur, let's wait until I'm a mother, and sixty years old."

Return to the Fields

It's not that I would have refused Heaven a more numerous family. No, I'm too happy being loved not to have held out my arms to each of my children; childhood is a blessing for the cottage. How many times in the evening, in our Grand Duchy, in the middle of a farm situated on the banks of the Avon with the cold green waves—Shakespeare's homeland—have I not been witness to the tender emotions of a father, when he comes home at midday to have his meal. His eldest son, on a shoulder already strong, carries a spade; his eldest daughter, who already serves as a mother to her youngest sister, comes to meet him while the second son, impatiently awaiting his father, rolls toward him like an animate ball, and its him that his father kisses first, while the mistress of the house prepares the frugal meal.

Alas, those scenes of rural pleasure make me feel ill; they remind me cruelly of all the happiness of which I dreamed, and which I have lost; they remind me of my isolation in this world, my sadness in that joyful crowd, my idleness among the people who work. Woe betide you, Charlotte,

---

[8] These stanzas come from Lamartine's "Le Tombeau d'une mère" (1829)

45

I am neither a husband nor a father, and it was you who wanted that!

Alms

And of what benefits you deprived yourself! You'll never know what the domestic hearth is and the royalty of the family, when a woman is everything for those who surround her, everything for her husband, everything for her children: the children to whom she teaches benevolence, love of their fellows; she teaches them prayer and charity; she speaks simultaneously to their hearts, to their minds, to their souls. She is the visible providence of the entire domain; the birds greet her by singing, the cockerel straightens up in her presence; the peacock spreads his tail; the dog comes running and fawns on her; the horse whinnies. The poor man, above all, feels reassured, understanding that in that hospitable house he will finally find generosity and pity for his indigence; he approaches, leaning on his gnarled staff, and asks for a little bread for pity's sake.

And here are the children, looking at him with compassion and astonishment. One cannot conceive that a man might be hungry; the other gives him his snack with a slight sigh of regret, and the mother is glad!

It's just that in an overburdened land, which engenders more people than it can nourish, when the poor, heaped upon the poor, can no longer find alms anywhere, when charity has become a tax imperiously exacted, with all the difficulties that taxation brings, it's rare for the mendicant to find a door that opens by a crack, a hand extended toward him, a consoling smile.

Julie

You've disdained me Charlotte, and I'm leaving. I don't believe, however, that if I'm alone, I'm condemned to the disdain of all women. No, if I had wished, also, to be inconstant,

I could have been; I'll say more; I wanted to be inconstant, but I recognized that my heart could not do it.

Her name was Julie, like Rousseau's Héloïse; she was very genteel, young, naïve, affable, affectionate and brunette; she was a young woman devoid of chagrin, ambition or plans for the future, happy with everything—a flower, a butterfly flying through the air, a rustic song; she saw me one day when I still had eyes moist with tears that you had caused me to shed.

She felt sorry for me; she sat down casually by my side, then looked at me with a soft and tender expression, and said a thousand crazy things to me: that I was a dreamer, a poor builder of chimerical châteaux; a bad fantasist, what do I know? She added that movement was life, that joy was happiness, that it was a grave contradiction to be young and unhappy. Then she talked about her mother, her old father, the work she had begun, her paintings, her verses, her caprices, and the next day's ball, and the white dress she would wear, and ribbons, and the flower that would decorate her corset; and she assured me that I would be her cavalier all evening, that I would dance well and with grace whenever I wanted; that the women at the ball would be beautiful, that there would be a great many of them.

"Never more beautiful than you, Julie," I said, in the end.

The Tavern

I know full well that there are two worlds for travelers: a world of industry and a poetic world; rich England, the land of opium and essence of roses; and you, America, young world, noble cradle of liberty! Into which of those two worlds should I go to be further away from you, Charlotte?

Personally, I like the taverns of joyful England, when the port is full of ships, when the sailors, after a long haul, kiss the adored shore. Then the movement is augmented, life circulates, gold and silver abound, the riches of the two worlds collide on the same soil. Long live industry and commerce!

47

Commerce is the bond between nations, the ambition of the rational man.

Oh, transport me at once, simple shipwright, into the midst of the disorder of the arrival or the sadness of departure; I can already see the landlord's house, his old mother beside the peat fire, his young daughter indifferent to the movement stirring around her; the whole household suspended on the floorboards, the domestic dog, the empty bottles, the fish smoked in Holland, the shore in the distance, the rich merchants in the foreground counting their gold. All these details make up a fine Flemish scene, except for the man turned to the wall, whom you encounter so often in the work of the painters of Flanders.

Yes, to be sure, those are the spectacles that await my voyage, those are the powerful distractions of which I dream; and what do I need, Charlotte, in order to forget you? Movement, and nothing more.

Movement? It's in America or in England; it's everywhere where people hope and work; it's also where I want to go...

The Seraglio

Or rather, am I destined to set forth in a rapid vessel for the Bosphorus of Thrace? Can I not, at the extremity of that green and transparent expanse, perceive in the distance the mountains laden with flax-fields, those cool hills, shelter of hermits, those gilded minarets, those temples consecrated to the crescent, those light feluccas, all the luxury of the Orient, all the repose of that land beloved by Heaven, all those roses, all that slumber. Constantinople is the ultimate city, the ancient rival of ancient Rome; only there do people know how to sleep; only there do people know how to love and be tranquil; everything there is murmurous; everything is prayer; everything is cool; every house is a sanctuary inhabited by young women who belong only to their husbands, and who, along men, know him alone. How you delight me, young sultana, when, in retreat in the depths of the harem and softly lying on a Persian rug, a child suspended from your breast, an infant lying at your feet, an infant before you supported by his nurse, you lend your ear to a reading of the Thousand-and-One Nights, alternately thoughtful and laughing, thinking to yourself that all the enchantments related to you cannot equal all the happiness that you enjoy in reality.

The Shipwreck

And I'm leaving! Adieu. Less happy am I, alas, than the poorest sailor in the port whose wife is waiting for him on the shore, her heart anxious and her eyes tearful: poor woman, who consults the storm, who is troubled by the slightest change in the sky, and who is thinking about her poor family and her imminent widowhood.

And I too am leaving, never to return.

May Heaven ensure that I do not wander for a long time in this world, uninhabited for me. I prefer exile to a favorable tempest that might break me against the rocks if the homeland. And then again, it's beautiful, a tempest in an agitated sea: the wind howls, the sea groans, the vessel floats, sometimes in the abyss, sometimes in the sky. Meanwhile, the passengers throw their wealth into the sea, the inexorable goddess! The sailors curse, the captain is calm, the women pray; I alone, O Sea, have no gold to throw you; I alone have no blasphemy or prayer, no regret or remorse; I'm alone.

Adieu, Charlotte.

THE SORCERER

I once knew a sorcerer who really was deemed to be a good sorcerer. He had the same reputation in his art that Félix or Monsieur Viennet, two famous makers of brioches, might have in their respective trades. He was, as you can imagine, an old man with a white beard and a black cat, whose walls were ornamented with the stuffed crocodiles of Molière's Miser "so favorable to being hung on a wall."

He wore spectacles, and only dyed his hair on the day of the Sabbat; he went astride a broomstick, it was said, "but I didn't see the horse jump"; in a word, he was a very knowledgeable sorcerer in his time; he predicted, almost reliably, storms of March, sleigh-races in January and harvests in Autumn; and when a marriage was made, he never failed to shake his head with a terrible significant and skeptical expression.

When he went out, the beadles covered their faces, the vicar made the sign of the cross, and the little children, bolder, shouted after him: "Hey! The sorcerer! There goes the sorcerer! Dog of a sorcerer!"

Praise God, he was also clever and fêted. His grain-loft was never empty. If a vessel sailed, an uncle was dying, a child fell ill or a young man returned to the regiment:

"Will there be a shipwreck, sorcerer?"

"An inheritance, sorcerer?"

"A recovery, sorcerer?"

"Fidelity, sorcerer?"

To which he responded: calm; testament; health; fidelity.

Merchant, nephew, mother and lover leapt for joy; the sorcerer's satchel was filled.

And when the tempest howls, the old man lives, death arrives, and the soldier comes back with a brunette canteen-stewardess on his arm, what does the sorcerer care? His prediction has been made and paid for. It's a fine profession, that of sorcerer!

Alas, though, what misfortunes he had to suffer in the course of his long life! The day when it was decided that sorcerers would no longer be burned was a disastrous one for his art. The day when it was decided that no one was any longer a sorcerer finished him off. From that day on, he was no more than a vulgar sorcerer, a sorcerer of chambermaids, coachmen and great lords. No more politics for him, no more important deaths to predict, no more invasions, no more eternal wars; he was reduced to family quarrels, the porter's castles in Spain, the ambitions of the antechamber. Except that, for a last resort, he still had love. Love is superstitious everywhere and always: a great sorcerer, which has need of belief in sorcerers; a blind child, which wants to see.

"I'll live in my predictions of love," the sorcerer said. "Love's an old story, hackneyed and monotonous, always moral and interesting; I'll keep telling them the old story. At any rate, there'll be enough to live on for twenty years with that."

Then came clients old and young, albeit less numerous and less curious than before.

"I'm bored, Master," said the young woman. "I'm sixteen; I can't sleep; I dream; I'm hastening toward an unknown goal; Master, look at my hand."

What a hand! Shallow lines; the breath of the wind over the gilded furrow; the wind bending the flowering lilac, laves deeper tracks. The hand is soft and velvety; the tissue is brand new, the fatal M line is scarcely visible in such a pretty hand.

"My child," says the visionary, "Your suffering will come to an end. You'll love a handsome young man who will come from the Orient or the Occident—but he'll come, be sure of it; you'll meet him one day in spring, or autumn, or even winter, in the intoxication of a ball. You'll recognize him by his smile, by the sound of his voice, by his tender gaze, or by his entire person; you'll think you've seen him before, already loved him; you'll think you recognize him, and you'll say: *That's him!*"

Such were the predictions of love for the young—when a woman still has her mere gaze for make-up, a rose in her hair for her only adornment, without a single ring on her fingers, or an antique cameo in her bracelet, not a pearl around her neck nor a ruby on top of her head; rich simplicity, imposing adornment, just compensation for your fifteen years, young woman, forced to adorn yourself as the Idyll of Despréaux was adorned.[9]

Full of hope and faith in the sorcerer's words, the poor child goes away. Where, then, is the one who is due to come? She searches he Orient and the Occident, is expectant in the vintages of autumn, beneath the lilacs of spring, in the perfume of winter balls. She will recognize him, the sorcerer has said, recognize him by his voice, his gesture, his gaze; she searches everywhere, but she does not recognize him; she cannot say: "That's him!"

She's so impatient, she's so anxious. And the insomnia comes back worse than before, and in the evening she look at herself, trembling: her pretty foot, her shapely leg, that same corsage, her entire person—all of it futile, widowed, although so beautiful, so fresh!

The she goes up to the sorcerer's attic again.

"You were mistaken, Father. I've seen nothing in the Orient, nothing in the Occident, nothing in summer or winter; I haven't recognized anyone; I'm still alone and weighed down by ennui. Look at my hand again, if you please."

And the sorcerer looks at it again, that hand, and on that hand, a few shallow wrinkles, like the tracks that the bitch in *Zadig* imprinted in the sand with her ears; and the sorcerer doesn't know what to say; his art has reached its limit. What! No one to caress that pretty face! No one to throw himself at

---

[9] The reference is to the poetry of Nicolas Boileau-Despréaux (1636-1711), more usually known simply as Boileau, and more influential as a critic than a poet.

those young knees! To kiss that hand, no one! To make that heart beat faster, no one! My God, what century are we living in? What world? The sorcerer cannot understand it.

O sorcerer! The world of love is entirely disrupted; men have separated from women; there are no more young men; they're arrogant, politicians, warriors, scientists; they wear beards! They're everything, our young men, except amorous: artists, drunkards, bold swashbucklers for amorous quarrels, hoarse singers beneath windows left ajar. What can you predict, then, for young women? Why do you talk to them about seductions and soft words? There are no more seductions today, no more soft words; no more savant assaults *à la* Lovelace, of which Bisson was the Polybe and the Folard.[10]

If you want to be a sorcerer, a long-term sorcerer, when a young woman comes to you and reaches to you with her hand in order to receive the obol of the future, do violence to her heart, in order that her heart shall fall silent; take no notice of your fine passion for women; predict, instead of the joys of love, a complete neglect, a shameful celibacy, a faded youth, the vanishing of their beautiful dreams and a marriage, if they marry, by the savant minister of the worthy Monsieur Villiaume or the edifying stable of the respectable Madame Houdard of the Rue aux Ours.[11]

Sorcerer! Sorcerer! We have left all that far behind; to begin with, we were all fire and flame, tourneys and devices in

---

[10] The military theorist and engineer Charles de Folard (1669-1752) popularized his ideas about strategy in the *Histoire de Polybe* (1729), referring to the Greek historian Polybius, an eye-witness of the destruction of Carthage. Baptiste-Pierre Bisson (1767-1811) was an officer in the Revolutionary Army famous for the ingenuity with which he sustained the siege of the Châtelet in 1793, until it was relieved.

[11] Claude Villiaume was a famous (or notorious) professional matchmaker, who claimed to have invented the first matrimonial agency in 1811. Madame Houdard operated a similar agency, widely advertised circa 1830.

honor of ladies; then balls, dances, fêtes and refreshments at Versailles, in honor of ladies; then again, gallant tales, little verses, fine sighs, elegant lewd talk, in honor of ladies; then, finally, obscene books, obscene engravings, infamous poems, *La Pucelle* and *La Guerre des dieux*,[12] and little houses, and chorus girls, still in honor of ladies, about whom no one any longer talked, and to whom no one any longer paid any heed, and whom, soon, no one will any longer want.

Sorcerer, my friend, before predicting the future of a woman, before luring her with imaginary hopes, this is what you ought to know.

Time flies; the young woman has aged; aged, she is still bored; ennui drives her and brings her back to the sorcerer; now her hand is wrinkled; a thousand pathways divide and fold up on that swollen hand; here and there, time has left profound traces of its passage.

"Sorcerer," says the old woman, in a harsh and shrill tone of voice, "you deceived my youth, would you care to deceive my old age? I'm still bored; what's the remedy for boredom?"

The sorcerer is a good Christian. "Have faith, my daughter; love the Creator in default of his creatures; pray, grow old, fast and whip yourself!"

That remedy against boredom has never failed the sorcerer.

But, O ignorant sorcerer, you're dooming that woman. Nothing is sweeter, in fact, than praying in public, the fast that

---

[12] *La Pucelle [d'Orleans]* was a poem by Voltaire about Jeanne d'Arc, written circa 1730 but unpublished until a pirate edition appeared in 1755, which was condemned as obscene; Voltaire produced a "corrected" edition for publication in 1762, but failed to undo its scabrous reputation; *La Guerre des dieux* (1796) was an anti-clerical poem in the same tradition by Évariste de Forges, Vicomte de Parny, which circulated freely in the Revolutionary Era but was banned after the Restoration

everyone notices, the marks of the whip that they admire; but fasts, prayers and strokes of the whip, the crowd no longer admires, and laughs at; the crowd no longer believes—adieu, faith. It's necessary for many people in the world to believe, or no one. And then, where can one pray? In some church, which has as pastor, a rich, idle and fat abbé in lace and a turned-down collar? Where is the cross that hasn't been shaken? If you have to give advice to an old man, sorcerer, tell him: "Go have yourself burned alive by your grandchildren, my friend, as being no longer good for anything. It's necessary to know one's epoch when one's a sorcerer!"

Once, an artist, anxious when he dreamed, meditated or read, prepared his work, avid for glory, sometimes climbed up to the fifth floor of the pythonist. "Master, will my portrait be beautiful? Will my transfiguration match the subject? Will my song be inspired?" And the artist was anxious, breathless, a poor and honorable serf full of emotion and courage, audacious as a man of the people, trembling like a Carlist.

To such questions, the sorcerer, who had read Winckelmann and Père Buffier, and who had not even head mention of the preface to *Cromwell*,[13] always responded, without any anxiety: "Your portrait will be beautiful if it is large and light, if the sir circulates in its contours, if there is grace in its ornaments, if it's neither too simple nor too crowded. Your transfiguration will be sublime if it resembles, without being a

---

[13] Joann Winckelmann (1717-1768) was the Hellenist archeologist who first applied categories of style on a systematic basis to the history of art, and became an enormous influence on the "Classicism" against which the Romantic Movement rebelled. The Jesuit philosopher Claude Buffier (1661-1737) was a theorist of knowledge much preoccupied with the analysis of "common sense." Victor Hugo's preface to the published version of his play *Cromwell* (1827) was an effective Romantic manifesto, setting out a prospectus for the Movement's esthetic development.

copy, that of Raphael; your music will make people weep for a hundred years if you follow in the footsteps of Mozart."

Thus spoke the sorcerer, and the artist, a spoiled and naïve child, as he went out, said: "What a sorcerer!"

But today, in art, everything has changed, just as everything has changed in the destiny of young women and the future of grandmothers. Art is no longer Michelangelo, Raphael or Mozart. It's Monsieur Jouy, Monsieur Delaville, Monsieur...what do I know?[14] Art is decorated with the Légion d'honneur; art is a chevalier and wears yellow gloves; art has a pince-nez and a false wig; art is red, iron gray, very pale, all colors. So, one laughs in the sorcerer's face today when he talks about all those things: love, religion, poetry—three great words, profaned, forgotten and lost.

From which it follows that there are no more sorcerers.

By way of compensation, we have the masses of Abbé Chatel, the Opéra-Comique and the burlesque poems of Monsieur Viennet.[15]

---

[14] Étiene de Jouy (1764-1846) was a dramatist and librettist popular in the 1820s. Louis Delaville (1763-1841) was a sculptor specializing in terracotta figures of ordinary individuals.

[15] Ferdinand-François Châtel (1795-1875) founded a French Church independent of Rome in 1830, after playing a significant role in the July Revolution, which—among other reforms—introduced a vernacular mass. The soldier-turned-politician Jean Viennet (1777-1868) also played a significant role in the July Revolution; the reference to "burlesque poems" takes in *Le Siège de Damas* (1825), whose preface is an early examination of the contest between Classicism and Romanticism, and *Sédim, ou les Nègres* (1826).

Preface to Contes Fantastiques

I ask the reader's pardon for an ambitious title: *Fantastic Tales*. A slightly more accurate title for these overly hasty compositions would be *Storiettes*, or even simply *Tales*. But in the nebulous literary realm one does not always say what one means, and circumstances carry you away. Most of all, fashion, the sovereign mistress of the masterpieces of an era, imposes exceedingly harsh conditions on her followers, in exchange for a smile that she does not often bestow.

Fantastic tales! My title is a lure. There is very little fantasy in all these pages, and you will not find there any of the precious qualities of Master Hoffman, who has revealed to us an unknown poetry: a poetry of both the domestic hearth and the bachelor apartment; a poetry of the fortunate man who has nothing to do, of the passionate man without passions; a poetry of the drinker who does not get drunk, of the man who sleeps while wide awake; a poetry of the lover of all sorts of tobacco, who smokes in all postures; capricious and crazy, supple, elegant, casually lively, more often unkempt than carefully-ornamented, showing it bosom and its leg to whomever might want to see them, and yet almost chaste and modest. Fantastic poetry is a beautiful and amiable girl, who likes the joys and liberties of the tavern, who delights in the shade of a joyful inn, who seeks out for preference all cheap thrills. Oh, when we saw her, in her negligence, coming to us from the depths of Germany, how surprised and charmed we were! What a difference there is between fantastic poetry and all the other kinds!

Great poetry was beautiful, and like Chérubin's godmother,[16] very imposing. But alongside great poetry, petty

---

[16] Chérubin is an amorous page in Pierre Beaumarchais' play *Le Mariage de Figaro* (1778), the godson of the Countess

poetry is not without its charms; by comparison with the epic poem, the pleasure of the gods, a tale is an indulgence within the range of simple mortals. Chérubin, the amiable child, is afraid of his godmother; he embraces Suzanne, and when Suzanne is reluctant, he courts Fanchette, with whom he is able to dare anything. Hoffmann is the Fanchette of the poetic world; Hoffmann is the tale compared to the poem, or the drama; Hoffmann is the light-footed petty poetry that comes after the great, following in its luminous wake.

With this difference, however: that the tale is manifest within a more modest rainbow. Great poetry descends from Parnassus to reach us; petty poetry, by contrast, rises toward us from the nearby hostelry, where it lodges for preference. Homeric poetry is manifest amid thunder and lightning, on Mount Sinai, or Helicon; the songs of common folk arrive to the sound of popping corks, and if they are often surrounded by a cloud, it is a cloud of tobacco-smoke: innocent smoke fecund in dreams, in fantasy, in tales, in charming dreams.

Are not the *Thousand-and-One Nights* the fantastic tales of the Orient? In the *Thousand-and-One Nights*, and in the *Tales of Hoffmann*, although you encounter kings and princes, the leading roles are played by humble people; already, the merchant, the slave, the mute, the beggar, blind or not, all the people of the Orient, in their most modest functions, are displayed to us, smiling. Come to me, says the enchantress to the poor in spirit—but while the Orient gives us the example of a tale that is both bourgeois and poetic, the nations of the North do not have tales for anyone; they have poems and stories for some, the great and the strongest; and when finally, we have descended from the great poems—or, if you prefer, we have elevated to stories the petty events of bourgeois society—well, there was once a king, Louis XI, and a queen, the Queen of

---

Rosine—a relationship made famous by a song he sings in Mozart's opera based on the play. Suzanne (Figaro's fiancée) and the flirtatious Fanchette also feature in the play as objects of Chérubin's lust.

Navarre,[17] who composed tales to divert themselves, they seemed to be saying to the readers: Whether you like them or not, what does it matter? *My pleasure!*

I do not want to offer a history of the tale in France here; it would be a long and laborious story, which would cost me far more work than it would give you profit. Besides, this is no longer a time for dissertations, and I doubt that even Thomas' *Essai sur les éloges* would have a great success today.[18] My goal is to define sufficiently well the fantastic tale, in order to prove, in spite of the title of my book, that I have never had the right or the desire to aim for the fantastic. In my tales, I only have the fantastic put into them at hazard as they were written, without planning, without choice and without purpose—and I do not think that the phrase "at hazard" is sufficient excuse for you to permit the ambitious title: *Fantastic Tales*.

---

[17] This conscientiously oblique reference is to the first two major compendia of French tales, the *Cent Nouvelles nouvelles* and the *Heptameron*—the French analogues of Boccaccio's *Decameron*. The former was long miscredited to Louis XI, although it was probably assembled by Antoine de la Sale circa 1462. The latter was credited to Marguerite de Navarre—who is supposed to have set out to include a hundred stories but died while the project was incomplete—and published posthumously, initially in bowdlerized form, in 1558. The coarseness of many of the stories might have prompted the true compilers to hide their identities; most of them were probably in circulation as oral anecdotes long before their assembly.

[18] The poet and critic Antoine Léonard Thomas (1732-1785) was famous in his day for his eloquence; his *Essai sur les éloges, ou Histoire de la literature et de l'éloquence appliqués à ce genre d'ouvrage* [Essay on Eulogies; or, A History of the Literature and the Eloquence Applicable to that Kind of Work] was published posthumously in 1812 in two volumes.

But, I repeat, the fault is not mine; it's the fault of circumstances, the fault of fashion, and your own fault, you who want the fantastic at any price and from all hands, as if it were given to just anyone to be a poet in the middle of a cabaret; to draw masterpieces in charcoal on the wall; to love beer and reverie in a great oak armchair; to know the secrets of the violin and the bow—as if it were given to the petty monsieur to whom I am introducing you here to call himself Hoffmann.

On that subject, I've had many arguments with you, my dear Roland. I recall a certain winter night that we spent in the bicolor light of candles and punch. That evening, Roland said everything to me he could say to prevent me from falling into the error of a maladroit mind that wanders at pleasure, without knowing where it is going.

That evening by chance, we were two, he and I—who were ordinarily only one—and we were arguing recklessly. He was glad to see me in dispute and to get the upper hand; there is nothing more redoubtable than placid horses when they get the bit between their teeth and run away.

Our subject of discussion was of great interest. It was a fine night, the fire was good, and we were thinking, for once, like an open book.

Just think how much ground we covered in a few hours! In traveling the imagination, the charger flat out, we had come from Homer to Hoffman, from the poem in verse to the tale in prose; from Athenian Olympus to a German tavern. We had arrived, without knowing how, on the banks of the river Lethe that is known as *the fantastic*. And there we were, listening, open-mouthed, to see whether any light would come from that dark hole, any natural explanation for the unnatural pleasure that Hoffmann gave us.

We had so much time to waste—at that fortunate age, one has nothing to do!—that we began by asking ourselves, like rhetoricians: is there *a fantastic?* And what is *the fantastic?* That lasted a long time; once one gets into Aristotelian divisions and subdivisions one never stops. Then there were other questions: Has our century discovered a new species of poetry, an unknown genre of drama, an Atlantis in the remoter domains of poetry, a lost island rediscovered by Hoffmann: a dangerous island on which the clay of creation still exists?

"Answer my question," Roland said. "Since there is a fantastic, in your sense, where is it, what does it do and where does it come from?" As he spoke, Roland was pacing back and forth, as proud and as happy as if he had written the chorus of the original *Faust*.

I, who know him well and know full well that he takes no more notice of his questions than to my answers, picked up the tongs and started building up the fire while humming the tune *La Grande Pinte*, composed in my home town and composed by you, my ever faithful Jean Paul, whom God protects and rests in the starry sky of the *Thousand-and-One Nights*.[19]

When a log caches fire and gives off joyful sparks one might imagine that young souls were flying out of purgatory, cleansed of all sin.

"Do you see those souls, Roland, flying up and uttering little cries? Do you think that Homer saw them, the great blind man who saw everything? No. Homer did not see sparks flying from the domestic hearth. He saw the heavens; he saw the great stars; he saw the Athenian sun. He plunged into immense light; he was placed higher than Tasso when he discovered Jerusalem from the top of the mountain. Volcanoes, forests, streams, springs, the vast sea and man ten cubits tall! He contemplated Apollo, who ended up resembling Louis XIV. Eve-

---

[19] La Grande Pinte was one of the most famous cabarets in Paris under the Regency, once the haunt of the legendary bandit Cartouche. By the time Janin wrote this it had been demolished and replaced by the Église de la Sainte-Trinité. The name was to be resurrected by several later establishments, including one in Montmartre that became a notable literary café in the 1870s. The reference to a song remains obscure; "Jean Paul" might or might not be the German Romantic writer who used that signature, Jean Paul Richter (1763-1825), who wrote the introduction to one of Hoffmann's collections.

rything was great and sublime; Homer had thrown into poetry a profusion of visible gods, who changed mountains into elegant boudoirs and made clouds a veil for their amorous transports.

"Fortunate were the poets who came first, Roland! The world belonged to those violent souls. They lived in Greece; they filled the house of Atreus. Comedy attacked Socrates. Today, that world is exhausted; Socrates is dead; everything is known. The mysteries of Eleusis are child's play; Egyptian mummies can be bought at a knock-down price. The sphinx and the zodiac of Denderah are celebrated in vaudeville couplets; there isn't a star in the sky that doesn't have its name and its history. And as for men, as numerous as the stars, they go back and forth from their clubs on fixed days; they no longer know what migrations are. Fables, furious combats, funereal games, wars undertaken for the smile of a beautiful woman, old men getting up as Helen passes by, all that appears ridiculous, outré. They laugh pityingly if one talks to them about a siege lasting ten years."

Roland, who was playing with my greyhound, turned to me with an expression of imposing gravity.

"That's true," he said. "The man who lived in primitive times was lucky. I'm sure that Darius' greyhound, adopting Alexander on the eve of the battle of Arbelles, was more beautiful and more intelligent than yours. The beautiful women! The great poets! Yes, but to hear you, one would think that it's the world that lacks poetry, not the poet that lacks a world, and it's not right to chastise the world of the present on the back of the past."

"No," I said, "it's not poets that the world lacks. As long as there's a blade of grass down here, a star on high or a woman before our eyes, there'll be poetry; as long as we have prayer in the depths of our hearts, there'll be poets—but in poetry today, as in politics, it's everyone at home, everyone for himself. And the poet has hidden his poetry, retained his voice, because he's afraid of not finding an echo."

"That's a pity," said Roland. "If we're about to run out of poetry, with what shall we replace it, we who are young? It's a shame; if human respect spreads among poets, that will be the end of poets. Human respect has withered everything among us; it has withered marriage, it has withered love, faith and power; human respect has slipped in everywhere in all its forms; it's called comedy and satire, tragedy, encylopedy, literary lectures; it's ended up being a newspaper. But if poetry becomes a ridiculous thing, you and I are doomed, along with all the others who haven't given themselves, body and soul, possessions and future, present and past, to avarice and ambition."

"You can see," I said to Roland, "that in this respect, too, you're wrong to ask what the fantastic is. It is the only poetry that poets dare to make, and can make, today. It's necessary to respect it, to welcome it with open arms, and not to demand insolently where it's been, friend Roland, as you would of some mistress at your disposal. That strange poetry is as proud as great poetry; she has her caprices, her sulks, her fits of anger, her moments of fatigue. She's an imperious and difficult mistress; she'll throw your cap to the wind, which will carry it away; it's sufficient to displease her, and she'll pass you by— as well as me and the *others*, as you call them."

At the same time, I filled his glass and mine; our glasses kissed, and we sat there, arms folded, thoughts in suspension, hearts tranquil, as happy as two friends, both savoring the sensation of the peace and silence of the night.

After a pause, Roland went on, saying: "And why, damn it, can poets only traffic with the fantastic today?"

When he asked me that question I was in the midst of bidding farewell to Hector and Andromache; I wiped away a tear and said, with the utmost calm: "Poets can do no more; the great deeds are lacking; the great misfortunes are exhausted; the great men are dead to poetry, or, to put it another way, modern misfortunes are such great misfortunes, the great deeds of our day are such great deeds, and contemporary great men are so very great, that poetry, even by summoning all its strength, can never rise up to the level of such grandeurs. Look around you, Roland; what do you expect the ode to do with the battle of Waterloo? What do you expect tragedy to do with Bonaparte? What more touching elegy is there than a king of France abandoning his country, *nos dulcia linquimus arva?*[20] Go back further, to '93, and put yourself in the tumbrel in which the queen of France is sitting, into which the entire aristocracy has climbed. Imagine, invent a novel to tell that story!

"You can understand that one could be three times a poet, and one couldn't add pity or fear to that already-constructed, already-played, already-told drama, stained with its own blood. What need does it have of the words, the passions and the blood of poets? On that count, the ode, the tragedy, the drama, the novel and the epic poem, as they exist, are equally forbidden to the poets of today."

He sat down at the piano and played a tune by Dalayrac,[21] replete with the amorous melody of the eighteenth century. At times he was singing with gusto; then he murmured in a whisper, laughing; he changed, slowed down, hastened the measure at whim. Then he stopped.

"If poets aren't worthy of the ode, why don't the compose eclogues like Dalayrac?" he said. "It seems to me that the times are quite apt; Virgil made use of political allusions under Augustus. Anyone who wrote eclogues today would have no lack of political allusions, it seems to me, with the anger that the shepherds here don't understand very much. Virgil wrote his ten eclogues after the civil wars. If it only requires blood, ruins and exiles for shepherds to be able to devote themselves to contests with the pipes in the shadow of the beech, it seems to me that we have nothing to desire in our day. As for the ode, if the Pindaric ode is forbidden for want o

---

[20] The quotation is from Virgil, usually translated as "our delightful plains," with reference to going into exile.

[21] Nicolas Dalayrac (1753-1809), well-known for his many comic operas, which maintained a certain defiant consistency throughout the period of the Revolution.

warriors and conquerors in the Olympic games, why don't we make petty odes in the manner of Horace: *O nais referent in mare*, etc.[22] And what a beautiful ode to a vessel at Cherbourg!"

At the same time, he began to whistle the tune of "*O ma tendre musette*,"[23] and I waited patiently for him to finish.

When he had finished, I said: "Don't you see that the idyll has never been greatly appreciated here, and now that Monsieur de Segrais[24] and the others have scraped the bottom of the barrel of burlesque compositions, they've run out of jokes. Can one sing about shepherds and woods, and the power of mighty oxen, under the reign of steam engines and railways, of pressure-cookers and wicker armchairs? Since antiquity, physical nature has been no less disrupted than moral nature. The shepherds of Theocritus have been degraded at the Opéra, which has rendered them impossible henceforth. The shepherds of Theocritus were at least plausible, but the shepherds of the Opéra, in pink ribbons, are the despair of all poetry. Alas, machinery has replaced everything. There's no more fear of storms with the lightning-conductor, no more inundations and no more droughts with canals, no more bad wine with the *Manuel de Vigneron*; all dangers have ceased for the shepherd; Virgil's wolves and snakes are as many fables, along with Menalchus and Tityrus.[25] Which revolutions that are carried out in a week—in a week!—where is the poet, I ask you, who will not be forced to erase yesterday's ode before commencing tomorrow's?"

Roland, who sensed that he was defeated, adopted an expression of irony and victory.

---

[22] The full line is *O navis, referent in nave te novi fluctus* [Approximately, O ship, new waves will bring you back].

[23] A very popular song in its day, still regularly performed, composed by Pierre-Alexandre Monsigny (1729-1817), a pioneer of comic operas in the vein taken up by Dalayrac.

[24] The poet and novelist Jean-Renaud de Segrais (1624-1701).

[25] The two *alter egos* that Virgil employs in his *Eclogues*.

"In that case," he said, "if the impossibility of composition is demonstrated, why did you tell me that poets not only can't, but don't even want to write great poetry? At least one would like to know, if by chance a great poet were to be encountered today, why he wouldn't dare try."

"It's because," I told him, "a true poet wouldn't be insane enough to deliver himself to all that impetuosity in the sight of cool-headed men. He wouldn't walk alone on difficult paths while others follow beaten tracks. Believe me, poets never complain honestly of their poverty; their poverty is a fiction they've invented to obtain forgiveness for their superiority over other men; poets have never—no, never, whatever they say and what ever other people say—been devoid of authority and fortune. It's impossible—and, you see, I believe this as I believe in God—that Homer could have been the mendicant that is shown to us, with his staff and begging-bowl; I call as witnesses the seven cities that disputed the glory of being his birthplace.

"Aristophanes was, in his day, the king of opinion; he was the first to commence the great crusade against the new religions that passed from Socrates to Jesus Christ, from Jesus Christ to Luther and from Luther to Saint-Simon, and has ended up now with law courts, correctional police and twenty franc fines, because everything ends up in a ridiculous fashion nowadays. Search history! You will always see the great poet alongside the great Statesman, as his inevitable corollary, Corneille beside Richelieu, Milton beside Cromwell, Racine placed between Louis XIV and his amours. Bossuet dominates the seventeenth century, Mirabeau the eighteenth—and Voltaire, placed between those two centuries link a necessary link, is the absolute master of both at the same time. And you ask me why a poet dare not be a poet today? Where is the means of daring, when no one around us dares to be a great man? To sing a free and pure song, it's necessary to know that one is sustained by an attentive crowd, but the crowd has seen too many things to listen; it has composed too many marvelous poems to listen to any poems but its own. It is the crowd now that says to the Muse, let us sing!"

Piqued, Roland said: "You're damnably eloquent today; could you moderate your expression? To tell the truth, I'd understand much better if you were less of a great orator."

"Roland," I said, "you have to forgive me my great eloquence, at least with regard to great poetry; in fact, all sorts of pomposity hold hands; they're sisters cut from the same cloth, who move at the same pace, in prose and in verse."

"In that case," said Roland, "let's go back to our point of departure, and take small steps. Tell me, very simply, since you're convinced that one can no longer write dramas, odes, poems, idylls—any kind of great poetry—what the poets of the future will do, and what it's still permissible to hope they might do?"

"I will simply say, Roland, my friend, that poets, taking refuge from grand passions in petty ones, will put their art at the level of their vocation, and will make very petty things, as they once, while acting them out, made very great poems. In brief, that's what I was trying to get to, and where I've arrived after taking the long way round: we've fallen from the poem to the tale, and from the tale to *realism*, which is the tale without poetry, and that's why we're raising ourselves to the fantastic, which is to say, the tale with poetry.

"You'll deny those differences in vain; you'll never be able to demonstrate to yourself that a gritty tale by Boccaccio or the *Cent Nouvelles nouvelles* belongs to the same family as a tale by Hoffmann. No, certainly not: those tales of duped and ridiculous husbands, adulterous and rapacious women, dishonest maidservants, imbecilic valets and great seducers; all that vice for the usage of Maître Gonin and Madame Pampinée,[26] to which was added the enchanting genius of La Fontaine, is not of the same family as the tales of Hoffman.

---

[26] The former character is the trickster featured in Laurent Bordelon's farce *Les Tours de Maître Gonin* (1713). The latter name is given to a character in Boccaccio in some French

67

"Hoffmann's tales don't accommodate frivolous and indecent amours or the gallant mockery of gaudily-clad heroes of the bedchamber. Hoffmann's tales are too sage and sensible; they would blush at lewd details. He restricts himself, and even takes pleasure in his naïve tales, to studying and reproducing the most vulgar details; he stops at the bedroom door and goes no further. It's strange but true: our tales of the boudoir and Florentine palaces would make Hoffman's muse—a muse of the tavern!—blush. It's strange to see those ideal figures, those ideal passions, that fresh countryside and that fine society in the gallant undress of the moonlight and the morning, around Hoffmann the drinker:

While being no longer night, it is not yet day![27]

"Oh, the sublime drunkard! He was never drunk enough to cast an indiscreet glance at the phantoms of his creation; in the tavern, when the pretty girls born of his imagination come to sit at his table, and he sees them bare-armed, their hair loose, in the joy and the smiles of their sixteen years, he respects those spring flowers as you would respect your two sisters. Provided that they permit him to go on drinking and smoke perpetually, he will speak to them so respectfully and so tenderly! He will tell them about the amours of the heavens and stories of the third heaven, where St. Paul was.[28] He will

---

translations, derived from a Latin word referring to vine-leaves, and hence implying drunkenness.

[27] The line is from Jean de La Fontaine's "Les Lapins."

[28] *Le troisième ciel* [the third heaven] is a phrase derived from translations of an apocryphal account of the death of Adam, which records that he was buried there (i.e., in Paradise) and from 2 *Corinthians* 2:12, in which St. Paul is generally assumed to be talking about himself when he refers to a man who was taken there, but the more imminent reference that Janin has in mind is a skeptical commentary on Paul's alleged writings by Voltaire, who cites the verse in question in a satir-

be charming with them, simple and rustic Hoffmann! Stay with him, then, chaste thoughts of his soul, adorable daughters of his ever-youthful imagination! Stay with him; he's a poet who scarcely thinks about the external world; he dreams; he only takes account of himself in his delightful stories of terror, pity, misfortune and love."

"I'm beginning to understand," said Roland. "The fantastic poet is an egotist; he plunges at his pleasure into the most beautiful dreams, equally scornful of the criticism and the praise of the world. In that case, God preserve me from these men without heart, who think of nothing but soothing their own ennui, without thinking about soothing the ennui of people who have seen everything and exhausted everything!"

"The fantastic poet, Roland, is a sage. He speaks in a low voice, and doesn't want to disturb anyone! Whoever loves me, follow me..."

"Add to your definition," Roland said, "that the fantastic poet is necessarily a drunkard."

"And I say: the fantastic poet is a great artist, and that is his strength and his inspiration. He's a mage; he's an enchanter; he has no need to put the Sultan to sleep every evening, for which purpose Scheherazade stayed awake and said 'Another story, my sister!' He's naïve; he's credulous; he's chaste.

"Once, the Queen of Navarre exposed her imagination stark naked to the gazes of passer-by. Hoffmann dresses his stories with the innocence of a father who wants to marry off his child, but not to prostitute her. Art has wrought that great change in the tale, it has brought about that important revolution, putting the tale in the hands of the mother and her children, without the mother or the children having to blush. There are positive benefits in that, an incontestable superiority.

---

ical "*Epitre aux Romains*" and asks, rhetorically, whether we are really supposed to infer therefrom that there really is a third heaven.

"Listen to Hoffmann: in the middle of his story he stops, he plays a prelude, he sings, he acts like Kreisler,[29] abandoning himself completely to harmony. He goes from one phantom to another, believing in this one, adoring that one. And that is the man you reproach for a few moments of relaxation in an amicable hostelry? And you think that it's with the aid of an innocent vice that Hoffmann has become such a teller of tales? Would you have more confidence in a tankard of beer than in Hoffmann's bow?

"Oof! Wake up the big words!" said Roland. "Is it mistreating a man so badly to accuse him man of drunkenness and credit him with such a petty vice, in the midst of so many purely human vices? In recognizing the weaknesses of your merry teller of tales, I've recognized one of the causes of his power, the hazard that is fundamental to his tales. Artist! That's a very big word, for the explanation of a futile tale—and how can we be persuaded that the man has become a great musician, a great designer, by recounting a few old tales or old stories without ceremony, without finish, without study, and even without art itself? Have you ever heard the story of the love of a young Italian for the naiad of the Château de Versailles? Yes, indeed, it's a good story! And I'll tell it to you when opportunity arises…Bonjour!"

"Roland," I said to him, "it's a long time since you told me anything. Tell me the story of the naiad of Versailles, please."

---

[29] Johannes Kreisler—which Janin renders "Kreyssler," that being the spelling used in the French translation with which he was familiar— is an *alter ego* featured in three novels by Hoffmann, including the unfinished masterpiece known in abbreviation as *Kater Murr*, and is mentioned in various other works: a choirmaster who is a musical genius, frustrated in his vocation and his personal life alike by his excessive sensibility; an archetype of the Romantic artist, misunderstood (even by himself) and unappreciated. George Sand also adapted the character for her own use.

"I'll do that," said Roland, "but on one condition...I'll tell you what it is when I've finished the story, but in the meantime, swear to me that you'll execute the contract faithfully."

"Whatever your condition is, Roland, I accept it. Tell me your story."

Then Roland commenced:

"In the old Palais de Versailles, in the rotunda, beneath one of those thousand jets of water, a daily amusement for the great king, there was a beautiful and elegant statue of a naiad, so delicate in form, with so much innocence in the smile on her lips, that the satrap known as Louis XV wanted to expel her from his gardens.

"That statue, surrounded by formless blocks, lions with gaping maws, sirens with fishy tales, amours with extended wings, Venuses of every dimension, was alone and sad in the midst of her companions. La Vallière had sat down there one day without seeing her; Montespan had bumped into her in passing; Madame de Maintenon and Madame du Barry had not even touched her. O marble! O mystery! An excellent work of some twenty-year-old artist in his first amorous chagrin.

"In the gardens of King Louis XVI—for the date of my story is recent, scarcely a dozen revolutions ago—a young painter, the child of masterpieces, was going back and forth, gazing at the heavy façades, the trees sculpted into pyramids, the green-tinted waters, the exhausted luxury of a monarchy in ruins. He was triumphant in feeling so superior to all the taste of the seventeenth century and all the barbarity of the eighteenth. He was in one of those admirable instants of irony in which irony arrives at the height of passion. He trampled those obsolete garlands and trinkets with disdainful feet; he was proud of being Italian, in spite of the liberty that was beginning to roar in France with all its might and at the top of its voice.

"Suddenly, by chance—the chance that shows you, dazzlingly, the woman you will love for the rest of your days—the young man discovered, in that chorus-line of grotesque women, the admirable naiad, an entirely Italian creation, a poor, sad woman trembling on the edge of those weary and silent waters. She was cold in that mud. She was beautiful, alas; her gaze was moist; she was pressing her beautiful feet together; her hair was hanging over her shoulders; she was cold, she was so ill-at-ease there, the innocent child!

"Undoubtedly, she had been lost on the road, orphaned of her father and her mother in these desolate gardens, and there, without support, without sustenance, without veils, she was suffering humiliation at the cold hands of fate. Our artist saw her thus made; then he leaned toward her, knelt down, and bowed his head before her gaze. He animated all that marble; he warmed up that ingenuous marble with his hot breath; he made that heart beat beneath his hands, and enveloped the entirety of that woman with such much respect and love that she seemed to be saying to him: 'Until tomorrow!'

"The following day, he talked to her about his love. He told her that he loved her, because she was more beautiful than anything he had ever seen or dreamed. He told her his secrets, with all sorts of mysteries' he told her his entire life story, everything that he had suffered, everything that he had loved.

"She listened to him with a gentle smile; she looked at him with the tender compassion that precedes love. She lent herself entirely to those stories of a stormy and virtuous youth; she loved the young man; she hid her passion, as one hides a beginning passion; she yielded to it without abandoning herself to it; her love was as chaste as her soul.

"And he, seeing her so reserved and so modest, lost himself in his delights of the third heaven. He spent his life looking at her, loving her, talking to her, listening to her...he thought he could hear her, and this is what she said to him:

"'You, my friend, who have divined my presence in the midst of these obscene nymphs, who have come to seek me out in these gardens dishonored by so much royal vice and vulgar amours, how is it that the corrupt air of this place does not make itself felt in your soul?'

"To that plaintive question from the young woman, he responded with a gaze that said so many things.

"She continued in these terms: 'You who are young, with an honest heart, while all the young and the strong are agitating outside to reform the world and relieve humankind of the crushing yoke that oppresses it, how is it that you alone are insensible to the ambition to regenerate France? So, child, I love you; thus, you are happy. Come on, love me as I love you! We must make haste; the clouds are gathering, the tempest is coming, the thunder is rumbling, these thin streams of water are drying up in their leaden grooves. Look at Louis XIV's palace over there, how it is spinning; it has vertigo; one might think it were a yellow autumn leaf. Let us love one another, let us love one another!'

"And he, recklessly, hugged her as if to choke her!

"No, no, it wasn't a marble statue that he was embracing!

"Thus the two lovers spent their beautiful hours, the fresh morning of their love, their summer night: they loved one another in silence, with gazes, with sighs, with endless ecstasies, as one loves oneself. That went on for some time— but the things that the naiad had predicted arrived: the accumulated clouds became a storm and a tempest; the thunder rumbled; there was a racket to frighten the bravest of men.

"The great voice of the populace, a thunder for the usage of revolutions, made itself heard, and everything went away from France: the old laws, the old gods, the old amour, the old poetry, and the old slavery, all gone! Altar and throne, youth and beauty, centuries-old aristocracy, dead in a quarter of an hour! The past expiated the follies and prodigalities of its pride, all in one day! There was a chaos more frightful than primordial chaos, the chaos of created things, the chaos of laws fully made and powers fully constructed. In sum, human passions were reduced to one alone, to the passion that includes all others: revolution!

"To be sure, if the howling mob of the tenth of August had had the time, it would have pointed a finger at the young man pressed by amorous chagrin. My young artist, uniquely

73

occupied with his passion, beheld all these disasters with a serene eye. What did the popular mob matter to him, who encountered such a sweet smile every day? What were the cries of the mob to him, who surrendered himself to an eloquent silence? He belonged to the queen of his dreams. She was his mistress and his sovereign, his glory and his joy; she was everything to him, what did the rest matter?

"For as long as the road from Paris to Versailles was free, and as long as he could devote himself to his cherished amours, he asked for nothing more. One day, however, the people, who also had their passions to satisfy at Versailles, seated on cannons and crying murder and rapine, blocked the road from Paris to Versailles.

"Imagine the young man's distress; it was the day when he was going to see his beloved; she had granted him a rendezvous the day before, sooner than usual. Doubtless she was adorned, she was ready, she as waiting for him...O surprise! O dolor! A living wall has risen up between him and his fiancée; it is a heap of howling men and women, a sea of unkempt heads, an army in disorder that a cannonball could not pierce!

"He was forced to fall into step with the impatient, breathless, desperate people. The people were going to the queen, full of rage; he was going to his mistress, full of love. It was quite a sight, that hatred and that love forced to go at the same pace. It was quite a sight, the innocent passion of that young man and the atrocious passion of that crowd, hitched together, linking arms in the streets, marching through the mud together, all arm-in-arm and body-to-body, the road so long for both of them!

"Finally, the young man arrived, with the crowd. The crowd stopped under the windows of the palace, shouting: 'The queen! The queen! The queen!'

"He left the crowd to its rage and, turning into an obscure pathway, he reached his marble mistress and reassured her regarding his absence; he told her about the shouts, the fury and the dementia of those cut-throat companions.

"She listened tremulously, without understanding any of that fatal story. And the cries redoubled: 'The queen! The queen!' And the abominable people spread out into the gardens.

"Finally, an armed troop, horrible to behold, arrived in front of the young man, who was trembling for his fiancée. 'What are you doing here?' they asked him. Frantic, he threw himself in front of his beloved; he protected her with his body, covering her chaste nudity with his cloak, and he got ready to die with her and for her...

"Oh, misery! His fiancée's refuge was profaned forever, the iron grilles were broken, the guards murdered, all that royal pomp destroyed. She remained without shelter, without servants, without guards, without friends, without protection, like a mere queen! She remained exposed to the gazes of men, the insults of women, the insults of everyone, like a mere queen!

"She darted a melancholy glance at him, which said: 'Friend, don't abandon me to these furious people; take pity on your sister, my brother!' He understood those words, heard her prayer, and resolved to make a wedding day of the day of his fiancée's death. How young, handsome and superb he was! The crowd awaited his orders in silence, so much majesty and grandeur did passion give him.

"'Which of you will lend me a saber?' he cried. Someone handed him a saber—the same blade that had already cut off many heads. He took the saber and turning toward the beautiful marble statue, he said: 'Adieu. Forgive me. Return to the Heaven whence you came. Adieu, my angel; you shall not be delivered to these madmen, these barbarians, these blind men. Adieu! Adieu! Adieu!'

"He broke the head of the woman he had loved so much, and who had loved him so much. That frail neck was detached from its white shoulders. He knelt down over the inanimate body, and began to weep.

"Then the crowd took him for a lunatic and treated him with respect; they resumed their route through the garden, shouting 'The queen! The queen! The queen!' It was all over, for that evening.

"And the next day, the crowd and the lover set out *en route*; they both had what they had come to seek, one the queen and the other his mistress; the queen, it's true, was still alive; he carried away the head of his mistress, snatched from the profaners."

Here, Roland finished his story, weeping.

"Your story has made me feel ill, Roland! Tell me, however, what connection it has with our literary discussion?"

At that question, Roland got up abruptly. "How did that story come to me, and how does it pertain to our discussion? Don't you see, Monsieur, that that story is the cruelest satire one could make on your definition of the fantastic? An artist in love with a statue is ashamed to profit from his passion by making a statue. He adores a marble, he breaks it, and all is said. The man is content, the marble broken. When I began my story, it was on one condition, but I didn't tell you what the condition was. This is it: that you let me go now, right away, without wearying me any more with your literary disputes. Good night!"

That futile dispute came to mind when it was a matter of exposing to the light of day these pretended fanatic tales. Roland's bad temper, and my admiration for the *Tales of Hoffmann*, stopped me at first. I was afraid of the general title of the book, finding too much vanity and too much danger therein. To lack a title for one's book! Oh well, the crime is less treacherous than breaking one's promise.

Take, then, in aid and protection, these essays of an uncertain fabrication, filled with hesitations of every sort. Read them as they have been written, free of any opinion and school. Come to the author, as the author comes to you, extending his hand to you, to you who are the first to love him, to you whom he loves, very glad if, in these scattered tales, you recognize some of the fugitive impressions of your youth, a few more recent traces of your desires, your hopes, your studies, your amours and your dolors.

KREISLER

I was still in the *Frederick the Great* tavern; I had spent the night there. Oh, what a night! The brilliant concert in the midst of a thick cloud of smoke! The pitchers pressed against other pitchers, the glasses clinking, the beer foaming and rising to the rim; like a rustic flageolet combined with a bagpipe, the corks popping to mark the measure better; the barrel standing out like a big drum in the corner of the orchestra. Well played, musicians! Bravo, band! We have thus performed an entire drinkers' symphony in *allegro*, in all tones and all measures. My God! When the sparkle of a generous wine shines on the rim of my glass, I seem to be witnessing a magic spell.

Oh, my genius! Alas, I tell you, my genius is sad; it sees lugubrious things everywhere, even in the tavern: the rattling of specters, the soutanes of monks, the crepe of widowhood and a bride's shroud are so many gaieties compared to the funeral frames of my everyday visions. Do you think I'm cheerful because I go to the *Frederick the Great* tavern every day? You're mistaken; I go there because I'm sad. And what is less cheerful, pray, than a pile of empty bottles? Corks strew the floor, the spit is silent, the cuckoo mute, the bench overturned, the spinning-wheel no longer creaking; in that great dark and desolate bed, the old landlady screws up her old skin, stuck to her meager bones, an assemblage of respectable wrinkles covered in white hair!

O debris, specters, shreds, tombs! Bottles without souls, corks without voices, that wheel devoid of life and that great almost-empty bed—what is emptier? Alas, it used to a bed of roses, just as you, my bottle, were a full bottle, as I was a painter, a musician, when I was full of colors and music. Enchantment was around me, everywhere, morning and evening. You've never heard a spinning-wheel hum louder than Master

77

Hoffman's, hurling more spittle from side to side and producing more chains of good thread. I mean a spinning-wheel agitated by a young foot, amorous and sprightly, a little foot in a short skirt, naked to the absent garter. So where is the little foot that weighed upon me? Alas, Theodor, you resemble the spinning-wheel of that old woman you see there.

I start to cry.

Great God, it's dawn, and I'm not drunk yet! Theodor has wasted his night. Mad poetry has freed his head from the sweet vapors of wine. At every glass I felt something like a cold hand on my forehead, which surrounded me with ivy, the enemy of intoxication. So here I am, sober and cool-headed, like a Dutch housewife. Come on, lads, let's start again; take off your cloaks, hang your hats on the rusty nails in the wall! Let's light the punch with the flame of our pipes, evoke the active salamander on the rim of the pewter mug, summon the fire-spirits to our aid, and chase away melancholy images.

Fire is the enemy of darkness; fire cheers up chaos, returns the lost colors and vanished forms to nature. Look, it's going well: the punch is alight and soon, a thousand joyful spirits will be filling our cups. It's true! The invocation has succeeded! In the midst of that blazing ocean, the goddess with the Bacchic smile is pouring us a drink; liquor is pouring from her hair and streaming over her beautiful breast. I'm going to place my glass beneath her teat, the most fecund of the two, and my glass, a son of Bohemia, topaz at the bottom, rubies in the corners, will soon be full.

Here I am, in my element! I'm a master, and I profit, as an artist, from the slightest accidents of sound and color. I see an entire orchestra with its harmonic gradations in a set of kitchen utensils; a bowl of punch is, for me, the dark-room in which everything stirs and displays itself, a joyous summary of the rainbow after a spring shower. When the punch burns, I contemplate in my fashion, with one eye closed and one eye open, the agreeable silhouettes of my drinking companions.

They really are pleasant figures: thin heads, big noses, fleshy lips. It's a great pleasure to see those worthy folk floating on the wall with all sorts of grimaces. Dance on the walls, jovial companions, as Master Punch, the aerial spirit, the crazy god of my tavern mythology, wishes. I believe that Shakespeare, the divine Shakespeare, has a god like mine: Master Punch, or Master Puck, in *A Midsummer Night's Dream*.

Old Will often steals my gods. He stole Falstaff from me.

Give him back, Old Will; give me back my cheerful monster, or let me complete Falstaff's education; I want to teach the fellow to handle a violin, to blow into a flute, cubby-cheeked as he is. What a shame to leave that fine knight uncultivated! What a fine fantastic dreamer he would have made! O great Will, not only have you stolen my Falstaff from me, but you've spoiled him!

You understand, mortals, that dreaming, gamboling, frolicking in this fashion, always having a world in one hand and a microscope in the other with which to see that infinite world, I can easily spend my nights in a tavern without being a drunkard. The tavern and the night please me. The tavern is my home; it's the realm of which I'm the king, the tribune at which I'm the orator, the altar whose god I am. Sunlight is good; the night is better. Dusk softens all contours; distributes perfume and silence with full hands, makes the nightingale sing in summer and the cricket in winter. The night is my friend, the tavern is my friend.

I said all that is one of those contests of consciousness in which I often indulge myself when I remember the good advice of Her Royal Highness Princess Amalia:[30] "You drink too much, Theodor, and you don't get enough sleep. Promise me to stay at home this evening!" *At any rate*, I said to myself, *the princess won't know that I'm disobeying her this evening.*

I was casting my last glance over the silhouettes on the wall; in the midst of so many grotesque figures, I discovered

---

[30] Princess Amalia of Prussia (1723-1787) made a serious study of musical theory and composition, which brought her into contact with many of the leading musicians and writers of her day.

one of pleasant appearance: it had a tilted head, a pensive attitude, unkempt hair, a friendly face. Oh, how delighted I was when I came to discover the figure, the happiest of all—it was mine. Yes indeed, that amiable individual was me!

I would have admired it for longer, but the last flame of the punch had just died away. Then, everything was effaced…and me too; I disappeared, without having the time to bid myself *adieu* and embrace myself.

At that moment, the daylight appeared, deep blue; a divinity in a nightcap that hasn't yet shaken her golden tresses. I was seized by a fit of sobriety and made my exit from the tavern.

It seemed to me that everything around me was spinning. Every house passed in its turn: the palace, the thatched cottage and the royal garden, with its gilded iron trellises, its marble statues and its majestic swans floating on its full ponds; I also saw the garden of the poor man on his fifth floor, and the goldfish circling around an ocean contained in a glass, between a vase of buttercups and a potted violet.

Everything was going by, rotating, becoming decorated, gilded or flamboyant. The hospital passed in front of me, raising its hat and bidding me an affectionate good day; the prison went by, which liberty has populated more abundantly than slavery ever did; the haughty cathedral went by, holding its dome, shaken by philosophers, in its puny hands; the brothel went by, its door ajar, as silent as a tomb.

I let the entire city pass like that, full of joy!

Finally, the sun came out, tearing off his last sheet, and from the Orient, like an apparition in a painting by Michelangelo, Princess Helena[31] appeared to my charmed eyes, scarcely hatched and shiny with morning dew. I blushed on seeing her; I'd just discovered that I was outside the door of my tavern again, directly under the sign of the *Frederick the Great*.

---

[31] A character in the story known in English as "Nutcracker and the King of the Mice," better known, thanks to Tchaikovsky's ballet based on the tale, as "the Sugar-Plum Fairy."

She saw me standing there, and without complaining, even with her little finger, she said: "Good day, my faithful Theodor, oh, sage Theodor, sober Theodor, up with the lark, who has come to greet the sun. I like you, Theodor, for having phrased the speech you've given me so well; you're an accomplished philosopher; as a reward, I'll permit you to accompany me."

With the stride of a hero and lover, I accompanied my princess. I'm not entirely sure that she's a woman. If she has a body, I've never been able to touch it, not even the hem of her dress with my lips. Her mouth has no breath, merely a perfume like that of a flower; I can't describe the color of her hair; there's no blue in the sky comparable to her gaze. Her clothes are gathered around her like a cloud, embracing her, floating, falling and performing, to please her, a thousand incredible coquetries; they're animated, she isn't; it's her dress that stirs, it's her veil that smiles, her glove that points, her headscarf that throbs, her shoes that walk.

It's said that angels burn...

I followed her as one follows a star through the spaces of the heavens.

She arrived...guess where? At the home of my old comrade, the musician Kreisler! We had studied harmony at the same time, Kreisler and I; he's still a young man, and I'm so old. There has been much debate as to which of us is a more sincere artist. To tell the truth, I have a quicker and livelier imagination than Kreisler; I have more folly and glitter, more intoxication and hazard; I belong to the earth...and Kreisler comes from the heavens! He's the singer of the ideal world, the musician of youth and women; he belongs to the third heaven, alongside St. Paul; he casts his soul as high as it can go, without worrying about it; his music is ecstatic; for him, the external world is nothing; he's not of this world.

Alas, I am.

Kreisler is handsome, better looking than me; his face is inspired, his song is slow and methodical; of, I'm only a buffoon compared with Kreisler; I imagine, however, that Kreisler is happy; he's a dreamer.

The princess listened for a long time to that gentle master, rapturously, with tears in her eyes. She stood there for an hour, contemplating him, admiring him, listening to him. Finally, she withdrew, penetrated, as if she were emerging from a sanctuary.

For the first time, I understood that I was jealous. It was a matter of something more valuable than Helena's love; it was a matter of her esteem.

The serious Helena, having quit Master Kreisler, resumed a jovial tone with me, she esteems me so little!

"But that," she told me, "is what you could have been, had you wished, my poor friend! You could have been a sublime dreamer, an elegant poet, a singer inspired by the heavens, by flowers, by amours. You didn't want to, Theodor. Theodor has splashed his face with mud, corrupted his reason, has been nothing but a poet of hazard, a poor fairground clown."

To which I replied, weeping as I did so: "Oh, Madame, you hurt my feelings. Don't accuse the creator, Madame! He made me...the clown that you love. I'm Diogenes in order to serve you. Too much genius has been my ruin. That excess of genius, it was necessary to use up in improvisation. Don't talk to me about polite geniuses, Madame, nor polite beauties. Accept me for what I am: a poor man; an innocent; a teller of tales; a juggler."

As the streets were already getting crowded, the young princess went back into her palace, or, rather, vanished into the sky. She's in the sky now, looking down on our observatory. And I remained alone with my chagrin!

Funnily enough, when night fell, I found myself back in my favorite tavern, beside the stove, plunged in my landlady's large armchair.

Did I dream all that, then?

HONESTUS

Toward the end of the last century, when all morality was being remade in France, there were so many things to remake, it came about that Paris brought back into question good and evil, virtue and vice. It asked itself whether luxury was a necessity. In brief, the questions were never-ending. At the same time, in the schools, in the salons, in the fields, in the city, at court and in the provinces, rhetoricians came running prepared to sustain anything; it was a rage for perfection that doomed the French people. The plough and the economical supper were perfected; matter and the soul were perfected; little boys were taught the art of thinking, and little girls the art of making intelligent children. Poor Nature was turned upside down, shaken from top to bottom, pierced to the chalk; people rose into the air and lived under water; a sixth sense was added to the five we already had. There were makers of perpetual peace, makers of living eels with flour, makers of ducks that ate and digested, makers of universal happiness. In those days, bottles of inexhaustible ink were sold on street-corners, and plans for strong-boxes that would always be full. It was the most absolute monarchy of quibblers, enthusiasts, dupes, imbeciles, men of wit, fanatics and charlatans.

It was at the height of these strange disputes that a young man of dubious intelligence and an honest heart came to France from the depths of Sweden, in order to be initiated into the profound mysteries of French intelligence and genius. The entire world was occupied with France, and took her craziest dreams very seriously. Scarcely had the young stranger made contact with that shifting ground of fantastic dreams and insensate projects, the last occupations of a dying people, than he was seized by a mental vertigo.

In that immense confusion of sophisms and paradoxes, he understood that if he did not summon analysis to his aid, he would lose himself without assistance in that ocean of theories. And, in the same way that one chooses a horse from a livery stable, he had soon made a choice of a theory with a flowing mane, a loud whinny, a straight head and flared nostrils: a gelding among theories. There was no other like it, not excepting the disciples of Saint-Simon. Then, when his theory was bridled and saddled, he mounted up, dug in his spurs, and away he went, on a loose rein, through the nebulous field of the verities and certainties of his era.

He had a strange and charming mania; he was against all vices, much as the Abbé de Saint-Pierre was against war.[32] His own theory was that of perpetual and eternal virtue: virtue pure and unalloyed, austere, brutal and brusque; stoic virtue. Then, for the sake of virtue, he sought out vice; he took the trouble to see it, feel it and touch it, to live, drink and sleep with the vicious. For the sake of virtue, he devoted himself to all disorders. In the middle of an orgy, he declaimed against the excesses of orgies, made his companions blush for having lost their reason at the bottom of a cup. At that eloquent tirade, the frightened guests removed the drinkers' crown from their heads, and everyone went home, vanquished by the eloquence of the young Swedish Count.

One day, the philosopher found himself sitting at a gaming table; gold was glittering on the green baize, streaming through the rake. He abandoned himself to the intoxication, the color, the subtle clink of the gold. Hazard turned blindly in the midst of all the gamblers, distributing its deadly favors or its severe lessons at random. Suddenly, at the very height of

---

[32] Charles de Saint-Pierre (1658-1743) published his *Project pour rendre la paix perpétuelle en Europe* [A Plan for Making Peace in Europe Permanent] in 1713; it proposed establishing a European Union along similar lines to the one that now exists, but more effective. He was kicked out of the Académie for proposing in 1718 that ministers should be elected rather than appointed, sketching out a plan for a constitutional monarchy.

the intoxication, at the very moment when the wheel, as it turns, saves or kills you, our sage declaimed against gambling...

The game stopped; the rakes remained suspended, the roulette-wheel motionless, and the gamblers waited for the declaimer to leave before risking their fortune, and more, once again on a number...

And our man went out into the street, congratulating himself on his "victory."

On another occasion, he was expected at a little house in the suburbs. The house was somber and black outside, but brightly lit and joyful inside. Inside, there was attentive mystery, elegant luxury, a well-laid table with a beautiful cloth, bright old wine, and a boudoir, and in the boudoir a young woman was waiting for Gustave—for he was a philosopher with a nice smile, a soft voice and a noble heart; he was a laughing philosopher, not very severe in appearance.

He came in; he set himself at the feet of the young woman, seeing her smiling at him; he gazed at her as a young man of eighteen gazes at a woman of twenty-two; he took her by the hand, and that hand was abandoned to him; he spoke to her in a low vice, and the lower his voice became, the better his words were understood.

Suddenly, just as his mouth was about to touch that flowery cheek, as his arm was about to go around that elegant waist, and the last candle was about to go out, the idiot remembered that he was a philosopher. A sermon! He delivered a sermon to Célimène and, seeing her smiling, astonished and nonplussed, he fled, believing himself to be a hero of virtue.

She shrugged her shoulders and, calming down, neglected to retain that other Joseph by the hem of his cloak.

As one can imagine, that absurd war fought against human passions, in all their forms and in any place, was strangely fatiguing for our young man. He was out of breath in that impotent struggle, in which his desires were only braked to the amusement of others. In spite of his efforts, vice continued freely in its course, paying no heed to his clamors.

One evening when, wearied by morality, he had stationed himself at the door of the Opéra, where a large crowd of people was waiting for the box-office to open, he had an adventure that cured his mania and enabled him to esteem earthly pleasures at their true value.

In order to pay for his seat in the orchestra stalls he had already taken a louis d'or out of his pocket; a movement in the crowd caused him to drop that louis d'or, and he was searching for it in vain when a beggar sitting on a boundary-marker, holding out his hat to passers-by, having seen the coin roll away, picked it up and returned it to the sage after having wiped it carefully on the sleeve of his jacket. The man's face was mild, his attitude humble; there was so much resignation about his person that Gustave was touched.

"Keep it, worthy fellow," he said.

"But Monsieur, it's too much for such a small service."

By the time he had finished speaking, our philosopher had disappeared, escaping both the gratitude of the beggar and the necessity of buying a ticket at the door of the Opéra. The young man was far from rich, and that money was all that he had to spend on is evening's pleasure.

He walked through the city, taking long strides, pleased with his good deed, scarcely regretting the Opéra and its loud music, darting pitying glances at the errant demoiselles, still the enemy of vice, and closer to vice than ever.

Having arrived at his house, in a rather distant quarter—one of those old streets of carved stone that are all wall—he knocked. The porter was asleep. He knocked several times; he called out; nothing came of it. The door was mute, inexorably. He sat down on a stone bench and waited, with his arms folded.

He had been there for ten minutes, obsessed with a thousand thoughts, when he saw a carriage with two galloping horses come around the street corner. The carriage stopped almost at his feet. A tall, powdered lackey with an insolent expression, wearing an épée, launched himself toward the carriage door. He opened the door, and Gustave was not a little astonished to see the same beggar to whom he had given his louis d'or get out.

The man was dressed in rags, with a rope around his waist, a beggar's wallet on his back, and sabots on his feet. An old felt hat in the Spanish style had great difficulty covering a head charged with thick and vigorous gray hair. As he got down he leaned on the shoulder of his lackey, with the arrogance of a great seigneur; he gestured to his carriage to move on by a few paces, and then casually sat down beside the young man.

"You seem very much alone, and very sad; the evening must seem long and tedious to you, I feel sure; and on this stone bench, beneath that dappled sky, against the sweating walls of this house, which one might mistake for a tomb, you must be regretting the brand new louis that you gave me, the benches of the Opéra and Guimard's lascivious dancing."[33]

"I only regret one thing," said the young man, "and that's having given alms to someone richer than me, and of having come home on foot, although I'm a gentleman, while my brazen mendicant splashes me with his carriage. You must be a skillful man, from what I can see."

"It's true, my dear gentleman," he beggar said, "that I beg skillfully. It's a science as difficult as that of government; compare the difficult of receiving with the difficulty of giving! It requires a long course of study to learn how to hold one's

---

[33] Marie-Madeleine Guimard (1743-1816) was the star of the Opéra for twenty-five years, from 1762 until the eve of the Revolution. She was as famous for her love affairs as for her performances, including those she gave at a private theater adjoined to her house at Pantin, where she put on plays banned from the public stage. It was rumored that she gave three performances a week there; one for privileged members of high society, one for writers and artists and one restricted to beautiful young women, but the latter allegation, reproduced in the posthumously-published *Mémoires secrets* attributed to Louis de Bachaumont, might not be entirely reliable.

hat in such a fashion as not to be seen to demanding some-one's money or his life; whoever extends his hand to wretches devoid of pity, for the money of a debauchee or a gambler, or alms from a venal girl who only throws into your satchel a glance or half a kiss, requires a strong soul. The work is hard! To flatter pride and baseness, to salute adultery, to go bare-headed and crease one's forehead every evening, on putting on one's night-cap, to give thanks even for one's wrinkles; and then, to mash venomous herbs to make an artificial canker, to be vile by way of speculation, to receive anything, take any-thing and eat anything, even to stroke the dog that bites you...do you think, now, that my carriage is too expensive, young man, and dare the gentleman on foot be jealous of the mendicant who has horses?"

"You talk well," Gustave said to the mendicant. "You're a sage. I forgive you for your carriage, and I no longer regret my charity. So climb back into your carriage, Monsieur; the Opéra will soon finish; you might not arrive in time, and per-haps lose twenty-four sous in consequence, vagabond that you are."

The old man got up, and said to Gustave: "Let's do bet-ter; let's forget the louis d'or that separates us like a abyss; look, I won't return it to you, and I won't keep it." As he spoke, he threw the coin with a vigorous arm into a sixth-floor attic. The coin flew straight to its target; it landed on the mea-ger bed of a poet, who woke up, having been dreaming that he was hungry.

When the coin had made its last clink, the mendicant said: "Now we're equal. You have clothes and I wear rags, but you're on foot and I have a carriage, so everything evens out between us. Let's spend the night together like two friends whose door is closed and who want to forget the hours while waiting for daylight. Besides which, I'll tell you in confidence that you can knock on your door all night and call upon the aid of Francoeur and all the violins in the orchestra, but it would be a waste of time—your door won't open."[34]

"My dear friend," Gustave replied, "I'm happy to go with you, but where the devil are you taking me?"

"Oh," said the other, "I'll take you back into the city, far from this accursed house and your fastidious quarter. We'll go to an abode of leisure and luxury, wine and women, boudoirs and well-stocked taverns. Come with me, my boy."

"Father," said Gustave, "I'd be glad to be your friend for another hour, but, by the wan moon that illuminates you, and the blade of King Christina.[35] I'll never consent to put my blazon under a beggar's wallet; so, don't call me your son, my noble father, and let us, if you have no objection, lower the blinds of your carriage, for fear of an accident."

The old man made no reply; they climbed into the carriage, the young man in the place of honor; the carriage, which had arrived at a gallop, departed at a gentle trot.

On the way, they had a philosophical conversation about vice and virtue; Gustave never talked about anything else. The old man listened to Gustave talk, shaking his head from time to time.

"Humm!" he said. "Vice isn't always a bad thing... Hmm! Vice has its good points... Hmm! The most honest people sometimes fall into it, young man; and you, yourself, a

---

[34] François Francoeur (1698-1787) became one of the musical directors of the Opéra in 1744, along with his friend François Rebel, with whom he composed numerous operas; the two assumed complete control of the Opéra's direction in 1757, although they had to resign in 1767 following a disastrous fire in 1763. The reference is therefore retrospective.

[35] Christina of Sweden (1626-1689), who reigned from 1633-54, is generally known as "Queen Christina," although the official title she was given at her coronation was "King" and she was often referred to as such, encouraged by her masculine appearance and the "irresistible distaste for marriage" that she professed.

sage, who gives alms so casually, even you... What would you say if you became, all of a sudden, a drunkard and a murderer, a parricide and thief? I'll leave it at that."

On hearing the old man speak like that, Gustave started singing, in an ironic fashion, the new song "Sad reason, I renounce your empire!"[36]

While they were speaking and singing thus, the carriage went into a sandy and silent courtyard. A stone staircase appeared; the two friends went up it. They went through a vestibule, a large room with walnut paneling, a small room with mosaic tiles, already more elegant. They stopped in a well-decorated drawing-room. Flames were dancing and sparkling in the hearth; the furniture reflected the light with an impression of bonhomie. Eleven o'clock was chiming when they went into the welcoming place.

"My friend," said the old man, "I assure you that your good will toward me makes me very happy; this hour of the night that you have been kind enough to grant me is precious and dear to me; I want you to spend it in a decent fashion, as a man of high virtue; it's true that a little vice seasons life agreeably, but you have eliminated vice from yours, and we shall be obliged to do without it this evening, since that is what you have resolved."

The young man let the old man speak; he accepted all his kindness in a passably disdainful fashion; he extended himself at his ease in a large armchair, drew nearer to the fire, and established himself in the best place. At the same time, he looked from side to side at the grotesque figures on the mantelpiece, the paintings on the ceiling, the gilding of the cor-

---

[36] The popular song in question credits this sentiment to Louis XVI in his prison, although it is possible that the Revolutionary words were adapted from an earlier version.

nices, and, on painted canvases, gallantries in the Fashion of Van Loo and Boucher.[37]

Eighteenth century decoration is bizarre; it affects little moldings, little facets and contortions of every sort; it proceeds in zigzags, it is gilded, false, niggardly, rich and rococo. It is pretty, stupid and lascivious. That chamber had the elegance of 1745; an echo repeated the ticking of the clock and the clock chimed the hours. The young man found all that charming, but, determined not to be amused, he secretly enjoyed his host's embarrassment and his efforts at diversion.

His host had hurriedly changed costume; he had put on a beautiful robe with long pleats; he had replaced his worn-our fur hat with a silk bonnet. He had prepared the table silently, placing flowers thereon, and beside the flowers a burnished silver dish with a lid; the setting was completed by a crystal glass. He beckoned the young man to the table.

"Oho!" said the latter. "It seems to me, Master that there's an abundance of virtue here. I don't like vice, it's true, but—forgive me—I'm even less fond of making a meal of tulips and roses. Have you nothing else to offer me this evening?"

Without replying, the old man went out of the apartment. He came back in carrying in both hands and under both arms four old elongated bottles carefully sealed in their vestment of ancient cobwebs, as if they contained a full-bodied wine conserved for a long time.

"That's good!" said Gustave. "And a welcome inebriation for my head; with that we can wash down your tulips and drink a toast. But what do you expect us to do with these four little bottles?"

"My guest," said the mendicant, in a soft voice, "if these bottles are not sufficient, I have others; this is a generous wine, whose beard is as white as yours is black. So, make the

---

[37] Presumably Carle van Loo (1705-1765) rather than his brother or either of his nephews, and François Boucher (1703-1770).

most of it, and forgive me for this modest meal; I've been caught out unexpectedly, and this is all I have." As he spoke, he indicated the flowers and the mysterious dish.

Gustave held out his glass. He drank.

The old man, a good companion, poured the wine in large doses.

"That's very good," said Gustave. He held out his glass again...

When the third bottle was opened, he said: "Have you nothing to give me but flowers? This wine gives one an appetite."

"Uncover that dish," said the old man, "and if your heart bids you to, eat from it. But I warn you that, in order to cut into it, you'll need a strong wrist, and this Damascus steel blade won't be too much."

Gustave, driven by the wine and the appetite that wine generates when one is unused to it, lifted the lid from the dished and uncovered a cheese.

"Damn!" he said. "Dairy produce and flowers! We're falling into the pastoral. Come on, come on, my trusty blade..."

As he spoke, he struck the cheese with the saber.

It struck a rough diamond covered in an earthen crust, which was only waiting for a workman's artistry to emit a vivid gleam. With his dagger, Gustave freed the precious stone from the matrix surrounding it. At every instant there was a further gleam, a further flash; the diamond, struck by the steel, ended up shiny and resplendent. Gustave, beside himself, struck and drank alternately.

Then, in the soul of the young man, a horrible conflict began. Passion has strange effects! Scarcely had he seen that miraculous stone shine than the eyes of the man who had been so calm a little while before were set ablaze, and his entire being contracted under the pressure of desire.

Insofar as passion is true, it silences the intelligence and forces the will to submission. The diamond was sparkling with a thousand fires; there was a flame, which visibly grew; it was the first gleam that it had ever emitted—and before that treasure, the young man said to himself: *I must have that treasure! Woe betide the old man who has given me with that infallible weapon the regret for that fortune.* He was breathless, desperate and mute in that horrible contemplation.

He still wanted to act intelligently, but his intelligence was lacking. He wanted at least to destroy his idol and liberate himself from that terrible obsession. He struck the diamond with the blade, but this time, the stone repelled the blade. The diamond had arrived at its purest state. Nothing could prevail against it.

Seeing his blade rebound, and seeing it blunted, the young man was frightened by what he was about to do. He stood up. "Old man," he said, "give me your diamond."

"My diamond," said the old man, "is my blood. I showed it to you in order to honor you. Just as one might say to one's young wife or eldest daughter, a child of sixteen: 'Go place yourself beside our guest, and serve him!' and as one says to one's valets: 'Prepare the best of my rooms, and obey my guest!' I have shown you my most beautiful and dearest possession, my diamond. I have neither a lovely wife to show you, nor a pretty child to sit down beside you, nor numerous domestics, nor musicians with sonorous voices, nor exquisite perfumes. I have my wine and my diamond: wines that are drunk in long draughts, a diamond whose reflections reach into the depths of the soul, and a sharp dagger.

"Well, I have poured you my wine in large doses, I have taken my dagger out of its sheath for you, and I have shown you my entire fortune; thus I have done the honors of my house. Be the judge of that, Monsieur—and now that I have shown you my wife and my daughter, imprudent as I am, you want to steal my wife and daughter from me at a stroke! Now that you have drunk my wine, you want to cut my throat with my dagger! No, young man, and I appeal to your eighteen years of philosophy and virtue; you would not rob the old man; you would not abuse the sharp blade."

Lamenting, the old man was on his knees before the young man. He wept.

"Let's drink!" said Gustave. He held out his glass; he emptied it in a single draught. The fourth bottle was emptied—and the diamond as still there, as brilliant as a star in a nebulous sky. It was still there, launching its flame into the young man's heart. The brimming intoxication overflowed; the diamond sparkled soulfully.

Gustave said to the old man: "You definitely don't want to give it to me?"

"You'll only have it with my life."

"One more time, beggar—your diamond!"

"Beggar, you say! Oh, it's then that I'd be a miserable mendicant, if I gave you my fortune, my name, the escutcheon than shines beneath my tattered garments, the list of my ancestors that is visible through my rags, my universe, my voyage to Italy, my Neapolitan sky, my prince, my love. Let's not say any more; take my blood; strike, and then you can rob the mendicant at your leisure."

With these words he uncovered his breast, where the heart was beating rapidly.

Gustave raised his dagger with the utmost self-composure, for he was drunk. He was about to strike!

The old man's face suddenly changed. He took on the costume, the voice, the gesture, the gaze and the smile that Gustave had always known in his father. It was the same face, the same white hair, the same majesty.

"Gustave, my son!" he said. "Strike, then, Gustave, my son!"

Gustave, beside himself, struck.

The old man collapsed, moaning; his blood flowed; the dagger remained nailed to the ground; the ground shook!

The diamond was covered with a veil, like one of those precious stones that go pale at the approach of poison.

From that blood, that plaintive cry, those tears, that voice, those features, Gustave recoiled in horror. He had just recognized that he was murderer, a parricide. At the same instant, the wine vanished from his head, the desire from his head. He tried to wash his blood-stained hand, but he blood stayed on his hand. He wept; he sobbed; he cursed himself; he cursed Heaven and earth; he tore out his hair; he wanted to die.

The old man resumed his original form. He got up. His wound closed; the blood vanished.

The mendicant said, in a soft voice: "Don't curse men, my son, and when the voice of an old man strikes your ears, don't start singing a frivolous love-song. Oh, my son, depose your pride! Be humble and meek. Don't declaim against vice and the vicious! As I told you, you who are so honest and so good, you have become, at a stroke, a murderer, a parricide and a thief."

Gustave, bewildered, threw himself at the magician's knees—for I assume that he was one.

"O my father," he said, "what a scare you gave me: murderer, parricide and thief! Me, a gentleman! It's the fault of the wine, my father!" And with a furious foot, he kicked the empty bottles.

The old man began to console him.

"Console yourself, Gustave; you're honest and good. You soothed my misery this evening, by sacrificing an innocent pleasure for me; I remained obliged to you. Look—I'm healed! My heart is beating more calmly than yours. Midnight is about to chime. Take advantage of that hour and the new moon to ask me for a favor that I can't refuse you..."

"But Gustave hesitated...

"Do you want my diamond?" asked the old man.

"Your diamond!" said Gustave, recoiling in horror. "No, no! I don't want anything for myself."

"And you don't want anything for others?" said Honestus.

Gustave reflected profoundly. "There's one thing I want for others and for me," he said.

"What?" asked Honestus, already anxious.

"Listen to this," said Gustave. "Listen, this is what I want: that vice should disappear from the world, that crime should abandon the earth—that the reign of virtue should finally arrive. You said that you can't refuse me."

The old man uttered a sigh. "Repeat your wish in a loud voice," he said.

Gustave repeated his wish, in a loud voice.

At the same time, an atrocious and mocking snigger was heard emerging from underground. One might have thought it the laughter of an old upstart apothecary or an enriched bailiff; it was stupid and malevolent.

"Who's that laughing?" asked Gustave.

"The spirit of darkness," replied the old man. "He laughs at the absurd wishes of mortals. His laughter has never been as brutal as today, on hearing your wish. Retract your deadly wish, my son! You haven't yet pronounced it for a third time."

"Didn't you hear me, Old Man?" said Gustave. "It's the abolition of vice that I'm demanding; the complete disappearance of sin; the absolute reign of virtue and wisdom!"

And he repeated his third abjuration in a loud voice.

The coarse snigger was heard again, and the old man raised his tearful eyes to the heavens. Then, with a sigh of regret, he exclaimed: "Let it be done as you wish, my son!"

He took Gustave by the hand. They went out into the street on foot. The sky was clear, the air embalmed, the stars scintillating in the sky; nature was sleeping softly in the shadows and the flowers.

"Alas," said the old man, "bid farewell to this beautiful night; night is the sun's vice, the repose of the day star. No more sin on the earth, no more night for the earth, no more repose for the sun, no more evening shade. Let radiance be extended without release above our heads, Sun! Let dusk no longer close your crystal palace!"

At these words, the young man, thinking that his companion was yielding to a poetic jest, let him speak and went on his way.

At a street corner they encountered a ladder attached to a window; men were climbing the ladder.

"What's happening?" asked Gustave.

"Those are some unfortunate thieves," the beggar replied, "whom your law against vice took by surprise after their theft. Submissive to virtue, which is now the mistress of the world, they've come to return what they stole tonight, hoping that the master of the house won't catch them red-handed in their act of restitution, lest their god deed cost them dear."

Gustave thought, happily, about the joy of the master of the house when he woke up found the objects that had been stolen from his house.

"I know what you're thinking," said the mendicant, "but that man is the commandant of the constabulary; he has a wife and children to feed; the household owes its living to thievery, and the poor wretch will be disagreeably surprised when he finds that there are no more thieves to arrest."

What does it matter? Gustave thought. *Is the virtue of an entire people bought too dear at the price of a policeman's happiness?*

They continued on their way. From a disreputable house they saw several scantily-dressed young women fleeing; their equivocal lovers were also fleeing, alarmed by their disorder.

"Hola!" said Gustave. "Another effect of virtue!"

"Alas," said the other, "I fear that a few women devoid of virtue are necessary, to serve as a foil for honest women. The misery and misfortune of these sluts was an encouragement to other women to do well. Imprudent fellow, I fear that, all these women being forcibly honest, men will not accord much importance to grace and humor."

But this profound reasoning passed Gustave by; he did not understand it.

They paused at a window. A strange spectacle struck their eyes. A woman, beautiful and young, was kneeling beside her child's cradle. The bed was unmade and broken. In a corner of the apartment stood a young man, pale and handsome. During the night, the man and the woman, in the presence of a child and the broken bed, had been taken by surprise, without transition, by the virtue that had suddenly fallen into the world: a sudden scourge that removed its mercy to tears, its tenderness to remorse; a virtue that dried up the soul and ambushed it rather than gripping it.

"What are that man and that woman doing?" Gustave asked the old man.

"That man and that woman were lovers a little while ago," the old man replied. "They loved one another with the most tender passion. The young man had great difficulty seducing his friend's wife; they have been surprised tonight by the virtue hat we have cast into the world. Immediately, their repentance has overtaken their crime. Now the mother is begging the forgiveness of her child for the wrongs she has done to his father. The seducer is going away, cursing the beautiful sinner; everything is disturbed in two lives that were all set for an hour's happiness and twenty years' repentance. The latter have been brought forward by that avalanche of virtue; the woman is mad, the husband very annoyed to have her back, and the lover will marry a novelist within a week. It was well worth the trouble of deranging them with your virtue!"

They continued to walk through the city. They arrived in a large square planted with tall trees; men were running out of all the houses in thousands, a terrifying outflow. Pale faces, stout bodies, rough hands: one might have thought them as many wolves driven from their lairs, arriving in the city in winter. To oppose that howling crowd, the city's soldiers came running, infantry and cavalry, cannons and drums, standards deployed and tapers lighted. The rifles and cannons were loaded, to keep the crowd at bay.

"Where are all those hideous people coming from?" Gustave exclaimed. "What have they come to do in broad daylight?"

"What you see," said the old man, "is the nation of gamblers, pickpockets, debauches, spies and biographers, whom virtue has chased from their occupations and their darkness. Our virtue had fallen on the heads of these people like a bucketful of icy water on a madman's head. Look at them, Gustave, and tell me whether those bandits are made for virtue? Souls of mud and bodies bent toward the earth like those of brutes. Gluttonous appetites, insatiable bellies. The virtue that you have thrown them, as one gives a slap in the face to a liar, is making them ashamed in daylight, far more than their habitual tasks would do.

"Believe me, it's a great misfortune to have extracted from their sewers the insects that hide in that filth. Believe me, Gustave, it's necessary to leave the woodlouse in its mire and the thief in his cave. It's necessary to leave the spider in its web and the prostitute in her den. We should never stir up the mud of cities. See what has become of that entire population of honest thieves! The city is afraid of them, seeing the all united; it doesn't have enough philosophers to maintain them in virtue."

Meanwhile, the daylight was spreading—and yet the silence of the night, frightening by day, was still prolonged. There were no carriages in the street; one could not hear either the cries of the early-rising peasant or the blacksmith's hammer; the markets were deserted.

"Why all this silence?" the young man asked the old.

"Now that they're all virtuous, that there are no more false desires, people are sleeping in peace and resting; they no longer have any need to busy themselves."

At the doors of the bakeries and all the food-merchants, the rich were agitating, holding out hands charged with gold, asking for loaves of bread. All the day's bread, however had been distributed gratuitously to poor people by the virtue of the bakers. Thus, the rich were dying of hunger, because the butchers and the meat-roasters had suddenly embarked on the path of virtue.

At one road-junction, on the bank of the river, unfortunates were rendering their souls. They were spies, professional defamers, forgers, fraudsters, scoundrels and other followers of equivocal trades, who, out of virtue, no longer wanted to continue in their professions.

There were no more guards at the royal palace; the monarch no longer had anything to fear from anyone and to one had anything to fear from him. The courtiers were fleeing as one flees the plague; everyone in the palace was denouncing himself.

"I've stolen from the people," said one.

"I've shed blood," said another.

"I've robbed an orphan," said a third.

"I've filled dungeons and bastilles," said a minister.

All the men of the court were accusing themselves of having sold themselves, and all the women too. It was horrible to see, horrible to hear. The frightened king wanted to abdicate his crown, but out of virtue, no one wanted to accept it; he was forced to remain king.

In sum, that unmasked population, that faceless host, those vagabond virtues, as commonplace as cobblestones, was all vegetating, monotonous, hideous, unhealthy, and bored, no longer thinking about the earth, awaiting death and heaven.

At the sight of that flock of sheep, all obedient to the same impulsion, the young man was gripped by a profound horror. "Oh my God!" he said. "What evil I have inflicted upon the world by removing vice and crime therefrom!"

"By removing vice and crime," the old man added, "you have killed society; you have deprived it of its principal conditions of existence; you have taken away universal morality; in sum, you have deprived virtue of its own esteem by rendering it as common as the gravel of the river-bed. Change all those pebbles into gold, and gold will no longer have any value. Remember this, my son! This sad experience was necessary to teach you that there is nothing more dangerous to human beings than universal virtue. Virtue is like truth. It's necessary to throw verities into the world one at a time; to open the hand too spread them abruptly is a crime. Excessive truth burns and does not shine."

Without replying, the young man went to kneel down at the door of a deserted temple—for since men had become virtuous, they had forgotten to pray.

"Oh, dear God," said Gustave, putting his hands together, "withdraw all this virtue from the earth; return the vice to human beings that units them with one another; return the crime that renders them vigilant and causes them to love laws. Dear God, determine that men are still and always will be thieves, scoundrels, murderers, spies, blasphemers, infidels, that women are and always will be coquettish, treacherous and venal!"

The prayer rose up to the feet of the Eternal.

Everything in the world resumed its accustomed order. Vice returned to human society the movement and charm that virtue had taken away.

As for the old man, he gazed at the young man in satisfaction. "That's good, my son," he said. "You've returned now to the time of fatal paradox; you've convinced yourself that all is for the best in the world, and that to remove the least of its deadly sins—even the slightest of them all, gluttony—would be to derange its savant harmony.

"Adieu, my son. Now that you're indulgent toward the less sage, nothing is lacking in your sagacity. It's necessary, however, that you retain a memory of your friend the beggar. You've refused my diamond, so take these three flowers: this lily, this violet and this iridescent tulip. The lily is innocence, the violet advises humility and modesty; the tulip represents health. As long as the tulip flourishes, the other two flowers will remain in bloom; health is a vessel that contains all the other virtues."

Thus spoke the old man. He embraced Gustave, and they went their separate ways, never to see one another again.

After that, the young sage became such a great philosopher that he died an associate member of the Academies of Dijon, Lyon and Nancy.

HOFFMANN AND PAGANINI

This evening, I felt the need to see you, Theodor, my dear artist, avid pursuer of nothing in all its faces, bold champion of color, sound, form and all the fashions of being a poet, simultaneously as brave as Don Quixote and as wise as Sancho, surrounding for his use invisible paintings and ineffable harmonies, always plunged into a heaven lost up there beneath the stars.

I absolutely had to meet my friend Theodor, and I asked for him in all the corners of the heavens.

Once, when evening came, there were two places where I was sure of encountering Theodor—to wit, the church and the tavern. He loved the uncertain light of the cathedral, its prolonged echoes, its vague perfume, its great extinct candles, its domes, and its organ with the solemn tones, filled with paintings and light. Often, Theodor amused himself by weeping in the old church before surrendering himself to the hectic joys of the tavern.

At present, however, the temple is profaned: no more holy banners, no more virgins with beautiful hands, no more suave perfumes, no more organ with a sumptuous case, no more music and no more anything! Everything is ruination, and silence, and solitude, in the very place where the cathedral stood, and Theodor is reduced by that circumstance, every evening, to go to the tavern an hour earlier.

Let's make haste; it's the hour when our friend encloses himself in his large armchair, disposing his orchestra and distributing the parts to all his musicians, the words to all the singers! Take them, ladies and gentlemen, duets, quartets, trios—choose! Dispose yourselves, instrumentalists! Watch out for the signal, the thrust of the bow, stay in step...and when they've gone away, unsteadily, we're off, for an entire night of harmony and ecstasy.

At this moment, he has a host of musicians at his orders, an entire orchestra, and the most beautiful, fresh and clear voices, which would suffice to delight all the theaters in the world. Let Theodor collect himself, let him surround himself with a few old bottles of Rhenish wine, and you'd never suspect the spectacle and the fine music and the soul of the singers, the ingenious enthusiasm of that orchestra. Theodor is the true creator of the invisible symphony.

He's the artist; he's the god! That inn-table, laden with tankards, Theodor can change at will into a vast theater where all genres are played, the comic and the serious, the grave and the amusing. For the conductor of that orchestra in full flow, the bottles surmounted by their tarred corks represent forests and woods; the pitcher with the broad flanks becomes, by turns, a palace or a cottage, according to the genre, pastoral or martial. Is there need for a volcano, or thunder? Immediately, the bottled gas, let loose, will take you to Vesuvius.

And now that everything is ready: cities, palaces, cottages, vast forests, rumbling volcanoes, lighted chandeliers; now that the orchestra is in position, let's go! Raise the curtain; let the leading lady appear and sing! And behold! Theodor's demon is finally unleashed.

Take heed—he's singing. And lend an ear, listen to that opera, worthy of Mozart. The melody is alternately grave and majestic; sometimes a military march, sometimes the gay and lively movement of a grotesque dance; sometimes the bass and sometimes the tenor; recitation and song—everything is in there. The drama begins; it becomes complicated; it's knotted; it's unraveled; it concludes as soon as Theodor's demon has departed. The demon is obedient to Theodor; it only goes away when Theodor can no longer command it.

Only then does everything disappear: demons, theater and musicians, the music; and the chandelier is extinct. One looks for Theodor; he's fallen, until tomorrow, under his theater; he's dreaming…he's asleep.

So, let's make haste to arrive before Theodor has set up his theater, before he has established his forest, prepared his volcano, lit his chandelier and distributed his parts to the actors.

I arrived at the tavern out of breath. I saw Theodor...he was sad...one might have taken him for a burger of Nuremburg! Lips slack and gaze bleak...his hair was falling over his brow; one might more easily have taken him for a vulgar candle-snuffer than the god of an Olympus raised by his own hands.

When he saw me, strangely enough, he seemed glad to see me, which scarcely ever happens nowadays.

"Oh, my dear Theodor," I said to him, rather anxious on finding him sober and clear-sighted, "Whence this cloud? Do you have a fever? Are you dead?"

"So it's you, Henri," he said. "Henri, I've lost my genius, my head is empty. Would you believe that in this horrible rain and this dismal place, I can't find a single singer at my orders, not one tune in my genius. I've run out of ideas, Henri! I can't find three notes worthy of Mozart. Mozart, Beethoven, Gluck...smoke and visions! I'm no longer a drunkard...inebriate us!"

"That's good," I replied. "Let's drink. For want of art, you've taught me what a fine thing intoxication is. However, my great Theodor, is it necessarily forever that your genius has ceased, and will you never again play masterpieces beyond the reach of your mind? My God! Since your musicians have taken leave of the master, let's go together to hear a great violinist—he'll be glad, and it will relax you."

"You're talking about violins?" he said. "I've heard plenty of violins in my life, and famous ones. Three days ago, with an old French wine, here at this table, I heard a violin concerto such as no human ear has ever heard. Besides which, am I not a true musician myself, able to draw from a magic bow an eloquent suite of the liveliest sensations?"

With an inspired hand he reached for his violin...

The noble instrument as hanging on the wall, between a long chaplet of herrings and a smoked ox-tongue that were waiting for Easter Day. Alas, Theodor's violin was in a pitiful state: two strings missing, the other two loose; the cobwebs had penetrated the interior. At the sight of it, Theodor bowed his head in shame. He wept.

"Weep," I said, "and be ashamed of yourself. Once, it's true, you were a great artist, bold musician. Song was born beneath your inspired fingers; your bow lacked none of the inspiration of our soul and you cast out the elegies that filled your heart. Those were your good times; you didn't devote yourself, egotistically, to these solitary pleasures; the world head your genius, enjoyed it; you played that instrument as a skillful master. Now, the instrument is mute; no more voice, no more expression, no more love; you look at it less often than those kippered herrings and that smoked tongue. Oh, you have every right to weep. It's shameful!"

At these words, Theodor followed me, troubled by my just reproaches, to the Opéra.

"By Castor and Pollux!" he said, at first glance. "What a stupid theater and what a miserable orchestra! What have I done to you, Henri, that you should drag me into this odious cavern? Have so many people with long ears ever been gathered together before? Ears incapable of hearing...and eyes incapable of seeing!"

He laughed; he mocked; he was triumphant.

Suddenly, through the trees of the somber forest, he sees a man...a phantom...a phenomenon!...appear, with a violin under his arm and a bow in his hand, one arm there, one arm there, the body stiff and straight, tall of stature, the face thin and wrinkled, the forehead vast, with floating hair: smile, thought, assurance and scorn, solitude and genius, inspiration...it's all there!

"Do you see how he's made?" Theodor said to me. "At home I have an old tapestry representing Saint Teresa; when she moves, folding herself, refolding herself, coming and going, sometime high, sometimes low, always present, she resembles that man: a phantasmagoria. Oh my, what authority over souls!"

"Silence! Listen! That man...is a violin and a bow!"

At the same instant, like a flail over a wheat-mill, the bow was raised, the violin rested on one shoulder, bow and violin, shoulder and arm, the soul and body of the violinist...they called one another: Legion!

My God! What would Theodor make of that vision? He was listening, in the fashion of Raphael's St. Cecilia, lending an ear to her own canticles. This time, the song surrounded him from all directions; it flowed over him; he was drowned; he plunged into the harmony; the song attacked him, pressed him and oppressed him, swift, slow, mocking and plaintive. There were strange and charming harmonies; there were laughter and tears: a divine song in which everything was singing, in which everything was weeping, an infernal *De profundis*, a *Hosannah* from Heaven! Poor Theodor! He was vanquished; he was no longer the master who could stop the orchestra; he could say "Enough! Enough!" as much as he wished, but the bow would go on, like the sorcerer's broom sweeping water in the German ballad. More and more, and on and on!

When the violin and the bow had accomplished their masterpiece, the violin-player bowed to the audience. He bowed like a chamberlain to his prince, almost to the ground. Oh, the craven! He's bowing, he scraping; he's bowing to the right, to the left.

"There's a sad salute," said Theodor.

"A pedantic salute," I added.

"A musician ought to salute in German," said Theodor. "Oh, when I had my violin—I thought I could play the violin back then—when I had my violin and the crowd said to me: 'Play!' I put my cap on my head, and when the whim took me, I played some fantasy, at hazard; then, at the moment when the audience was attentive, expecting a conclusion, I picked up my glass and I left abruptly. A prostration? Who, me? Salute those contemptible wretches? Thank them for the pleasure I'd given them? Not so stupid! To those idiots, a bow, a genuflection? Silence, though—he's coming back. Shut up and listen!"

The man with the violin reappeared; he played an adagio. It was simple and touching, full of expression and grace.

"Now," said Theodor, "I take you as my witness that I can play an adagio as well as any violinist. I'm not afraid of a human adagio written for humans. I don't recoil before any difficulty, as you know; but I'm afraid of the music that can't be reached; I don't want to run, breathlessly, after impossible notes. Do you remember that mysterious composition that was brought to me one day by some infernal musician, which he defied me to decipher. That was a painful task for me. I sensed, confusedly, that there was a powerful harmony in those notes, but I couldn't find it. Imagine a scholar of your Institut confronted by hieroglyphs from the time of Isis—that's how I was in the presence of those mysterious sonatas.

"What efforts I made to read those scraps! What tortures I endured! My hand remained defeated by them; I put all my muscles to the torture in vain; I was scarcely able to extract a few sounds from my rebellious violin. My bow didn't want to go, at the same time, here and there; my violin bridled; the chanterelle broke. Alas, wretch that I am, in vain I interrogated the sharp, the flat and the mid-register. My violin was mute.

"Now...would you believe it? That other-worldly music...there's that Italian playing it, hurling it at my soul! How is he doing it? How is he doing it? Can you see his hands? Is his hand divided into two, to reach both ends of that violent scale at once? Are his fingers longer than mine, are his tendons more muscular, is his soul greater? I, however, am a great artist; I've dreamed instruments that can embrace the earth and the heavens, which adapt themselves to all known modes—but I haven't invented that violin, that great violin of the earth and the heavens...

"I've seen many musicians...but I've never seen his like. He's deformed...and superb. A child-giant! Utterly crippled, all-powerful! You can see how angry he is, and how he could kill the accompanist, who has missed his note by a ten-thousandth of an interval! His eyes are ablaze, and his violin is demanding a tearful vengeance! Oh, the terrible artist! But now he's finished, and bowing. Oh, the wretch—so he doesn't know his worth, to bow like that, before this dreary audience?

"Damn it! Get up, genius! And don't worry! The people who are listening to you aren't worth a hair of your magic bow. Yes, indeed, they're great lords, sons of kings, representatives of nations—what does it matter? There's only me, in this crowd, worthy to judge you. We're brothers! If you play better than I do, it's by divine right, by virtue of your mother's prayer. Mine simply threw me into the world with the help of a vulgar midwife; I was raised in innocence, amid feasting; I've been happy all my life, loving, drinking, singing, a joyful storyteller, a meek guest, an intrepid drinker—and yet I'm a great artist, like you!"

Thus spoke Theodor, agitated just this once by the only passion that he had ever experienced: envy!

He went on: "Which proves, Henri, that there's something supernatural in this, which surpasses our intelligence; because that violin...can't, has never been able, and never will be able to play a false note. No human mind every conceived a calculation more complicated, no human finger ever executed it in such a precise and clear fashion. Do you understand that, Henri? Not one false note, not one hesitant note, not one mistaken calculation. How can that be explained? Don't you see that none of this is real and that we're both dreaming?

"Oh, accursed violin, you've made Theodor a vile slave! To your slightest whim, I'm obedient. I only go where you want to take me, and no further. Wretch and insensate that I am! I've been deceived by my violin; it has thrown me to the ground. Instead of turning the head of my horse away from the sun, as Alexander did, I've tried to tame my steed like a vulgar squire, and here I am, on the ground. Alexander is mounted. Wretch that I am!"

"Wretch that I am, I wasn't able to say to the ill-tamed instrument: 'There you are; march! Obey! Sing my joy and weep my tears! You're going to repeat all the mysteries of my soul, and all the transports of my heart...' And here's this miserable Italian, who, to mock me, is breaking three strings of his violin. Harsher to himself than the Areopagus of Sparta, he's only keeping one…one single string for so much passion! One alone, for all that soul! One string for that song thrown to profusion!"

And Theodor, breathless, unquiet, mouth agape, listened, laughing lightly with a smile of naïve credulity. Worthy Theodor! He went out at a run.

"Did you find that beautiful?" I asked him.

He stated running. He went slowly; he went quickly; he sang; he wept; he found admirable tunes; he became frantic; he played his most beautiful dramas, and then became discouraged. In the end, he turned round, and, after an hour, answered my question:

"Was it beautiful? Was it beautiful? My God!"

He became even more animated; his voice rose even higher; he was all music, body and soul. He sang for me alone.

And that's my inspired genius, alternately furious and tender, imposing and burlesque. He's the tyrant, the young woman and the great lady; friend, he growls, he weeps, he laughs, he mourns; he's all drama, an orchestra, a god. How many times he has caused me to expand, and how many emotions he has roused in my soul!

I understood, on the evening I'm talking about, how much passion there was in that worthy man; and at the same time, I understood why I loved him. I loved him for his genius and his generosity.

Don't be so malcontent, dear Theodor, to have found your equal or your master. I know full well that you don't understand the strange alliance of the two words *art* and *theater*, art and daylight; fortunately, there are exceptions to the general rule of poetry and drama. Fortunate is the artist who overcomes that great difficulty! He reigns. He arrives in the midst of human beings like a revelation of their power; he brings them unknown pleasures; he informs them of the strength of the beautiful, when it is simple; he excites them by the emulation of genius; he forces the young woman not to blush at her passion or her talent. Give thanks, therefore, for what forces you no longer to be a great artist for yourself alone.

Now, how did we find ourselves back at the tavern door? I don't know. The landlady was in bed, and the vast curtains surrounded the bed with an impenetrable wall; the lamp was still burning. Scarcely had we gone in than Theodor picked up his violin. He turned the remaining string; he searched for his bow…in vain.

"Bring me a bow tomorrow," he said to me.

"Do you also want three strings, my friend?"

He repeated: "Bring me a bow."

Then, seeing that I was looking at him anxiously, trying to divine what he might be missing, he said: "My friends have doomed me with their pampering. Thanks to you, scoundrels, I haven't had anything one might call an instant of unhappiness; I've never once been poor, nor ill; health is killing me! What do you expect me to invent, with these chubby cheeks and this rubicund nose, this thick hair, that heavy slumber, this vast chest and bulging stomach? One is nothing but a contemptible wretch with so much hair. Oh, my dear fellow, I haven't had enough misfortune to be a genius.

"By contrast, the man with the violin…everything has served him: no father, no mother, abandonment in infancy! Adventurous youth! That man has begged for his bread to live…he's done worse than beg, he's given lessons in his art; he's had pupils! Can you imagine that martyrdom, Henri? To come at a fixed hour, to obey some idiot, and say to him: 'Do this, do that!' and then hold out your hand. And that imbecile, after ten years, brags about his master! He says: 'I was Theodor's pupil!'

"The man with the violin has suffered all those tortures, and many others. He's known all miseries preliminary to his glory. He's been envied, slandered, persecuted! How pale and thin he is! He looks like a ghost. And now he's the foremost in his art, he greatest, the only one; musician and singer, thinking and rendering his thought, a man who could be killed by a breath…and who has killed me with a stroke of a bow.

"It's only through suffering that one becomes a genius, Henri. Fire burns, and consecrates.

"Beneath that lightning is the masterpiece of great passion, great dolor!

"As for us—the petty, the living, the odd—let's drink, laugh and sing, and make girls dance, sitting on a barrel, between a howling clarion and a screeching clarinet."

He picked up a glass. "Honor to Paganini, the miracle! Health to Hoffmann, the fiddler!"

BEETHOVEN'S DINNER

In 1849 I was in Vienna. Whatever people might say, Vienna is a French and German city, even more French than German: an intelligent city, which gives as much time to the fine arts and pleasures as Paris gives to politics. Vienna, as you know, is the musical city *par excellence*; one can feel the music there; the air is charged with chords. All the great musicians and all the great singers have passed through Vienna.

Hence the feeling of wellbeing that one experiences, without knowing why.

On the day I'm talking about, however, there was a great silence in Herr von Metternich's city. That day, I was wandering the streets at random, waiting for the hour of my departure; I was due to leave the city that evening.

At the moment of my greatest boredom, I saw a man go by in the street—one of those men that one sees right away, even in a crowd. The crowd itself sees them and notices them; by some mysterious admirable instinct, it flattens itself against the wall to let them pass, salutes them with its gaze and its soul, respects them without knowing their names, recognizes them instantly without ever having seen them before.

At any rate, on seeing him, it was difficult not to divine that he was a man above others. I can still see him: he had a big, bushy head, long hair, half-gray and half-black, loading his head and falling in waves to either side; his head was entirely covered by it; one might have thought, seeing it bristling pell-mell, in disorder, that it was the mane of a lion; and beneath that mane shone little wild eyes, whose gaze combined marvelously with a sardonic and singularly witty smile.

The man was walking at an uneven pace, sometimes rapidly, sometimes slowly; he looked from side to side, smiling, but his gaze was distracted and his smile was bitter; one could see that he was already a man outside the real world, as far as anyone ever had been. As soon as I saw the man I felt intrigued, almost emotional. In spite of myself, I wanted to know who he was, and I followed him.

After many comings and goings, many turns and detours, he went into the music shop on the Kohlmarktstrasse. The shopkeeper greeted him very politely; he offered him a seat with the utmost haste, but the unknown man remained standing. I couldn't hear what he was saying, but I could see him through the transparent window of the shop. His manner of conversation was strange; he spoke, his interlocutor wrote. I deduced that my unknown was deaf.

Suddenly, he adopted a more preoccupied expression than usual, and, turning toward the door of the shop, rapped rhythmically with his fingers on the glass to which I was glued. Could he see me, or not? I don't know. The fact is that he reached for me with his large hand, and I felt as if the man's powerful fingers were crushing me.

As he had not paid any heed to me, I paid none to him. He started beating out some unknown symphony on the glazed door; it was slow, it was fast. Sometimes he paused to search for an idea, and then his fingers stopped; sometimes the idea came to him swiftly and abundantly, and then his fingers fluttered here and there on the resonant glass, as if he were playing a keyboard. Evidently, the man was composing something great and beautiful. Then, while composing, his gaze became animated; his hair flew up from his brow, his smile became melancholy again, his face satisfied; the poor great man was happy.

He remained thus for a full quarter of an hour, after which he turned round and gestured to the owner of the shop. Immediately, a pretty girl, entirely German, with a chaste German gaze, an honest German smile and a German freshness, came to the man and placed a pen and a sheet of music paper in front of him. Then I saw him write rapidly. Undoubtedly he was writing down what he had just composed on the shop window. He wrote without pausing for breath, and when he was finished he held the piece of paper out to the shopkeeper without reading it. The shopkeeper gave him a gold coin in return.

Then my man came out of the shop. Scarcely was he outside that he resumed his grim and mocking expression, but his step was lighter. That morning, I was on good form in matters of divination; I divined that our man was going to the tavern, just as I had divined a little while before that he was a musician. There are people who think that the tavern is the consequence of music, but there are also people who are never content.

So, he went at a sprightly pace to the smoky hostelry that has for a sign *The Spinning Cat*. It's said that the cat in question was designed by Hoffmann, after his own cat Murr, to which Hoffmann has given, as to the inn, such a great celebrity.

That day, which was a Friday, the inn was deserted. Even the main room was silent; the stoves were extinct and the mistress of the establishment, a fine German landlady, was busy polishing her copper vessels and giving all the pewter tray as much polish and gleam as one gives silver trays,

You might well think that it was a bad moment to come to ask the good lady for one of those excellent culinary fabrications that had made her the queen of all the eaters and drinkers of her time. Even so, our man was in funds; he advanced boldly and asked without overmuch ceremony for a *kälbern*—a slice of hot veal.

"I don't have any hot veal," said the landlady of the *Spinning Cat*. She was still polishing her pewter trays.

"In that case," said the unknown, "give me a slice of cold veal."

"I don't have any cold veal," said the landlady of the *Spinning Cat*.

"Damn!" exclaimed the man—and he withdrew, sad and disappointed. His disappointment distressed me, and I saw him go away with a profound sentiment of chagrin. When I had lost sight of him I went into the inn. I took off my hat very humbly and, speaking with the most profound respect, I said to the landlady "Can you tell me who that man is, Madame, and where he lives, if you please?"

Hearing me speak in such a polite tone, she left her pewter pot alone momentarily, and, gratifying me with the most amiable smile that she could contrive with her toothless mouth, she said: "You're very honest, Monsieur. The man is some kind of musician, an eater and drunkard, a friend of Hoffmann—another drunkard, who's dead. I know his maidservant, Marthe, quite well. She lives over here, in the little house on the left next to the cloth-merchant's. I believe his name is Beethoven."

At that great name I felt my heart break in my breast. It was Beethoven!"

The landlady of the *Spinning Cat*, seeing me go pale, thought I must be feeling ill. "My God, Monsieur, what's wrong?" she said.

I pulled myself together. "Madame," I said to her, "in the name of German hospitality, I'll ask you for a great favor, if you please." Then, as she looked at me in astonishment, I went on: "Madame, yes, Madame, if you're good and charitable, you'll immediately put a piece of veal on the spit— immediately, Madame. I won't leave until I have my piece of roast meat in my hands."

"Shh, Monsieur!" she said, pointing at the kitchen range, which was lit. "What you want is in there, and you'll have it in an instant." At the same time, she summoned her maidservant, who was feeding the ducks in the poultry-yard.

The maidservant came in and opened the oven door; a delicious odor of roast meat was exhaled into the vast kitchen. How agreeably the poor deaf man's sense of smell would have been excited! Meanwhile, the landlady prepared the sliced veal herself on a large tray.

"Why," I said, "didn't you want to give that poor devil Beethoven the slice of veal that he asked for just now?"

"Monsieur," said the landlady, "that man is a wastrel who eats everything, a glutton who wants meat every day. He hardly ever has any money to bring me. I take as little of it as I can, out of pity for him, poor man—and besides, Monsieur, I've promised his housekeeper."

Poor Beethoven! Poor great man! Unfortunate noble artist! Ambitious fellow, who wants to eat roast meat, hot or cold, every day!

"Madame," I said, "which is Beethoven's preferred wine?"

"Damn, Monsieur," said the landlady, "I don't know. These people drink all wines, and as long as there's wine, it doesn't matter much to them what they drink. I think, however, that if he had a bottle of my old Rhenish wine, he wouldn't be disappointed, you know."

"Give me two bottles of your best Rhenish wine," I said to the landlady. "It wouldn't be too good for what I want to do, if it were Herr von Metternich's own wine."

At that redoubtable name, the landlady, as if she hadn't heard me, opened a door to one side of the entrance door, which led to a cellar, and went down. A few moments later she came back with two old bottles, black with dust, clad in coats of cobweb spun by some ancient spider.

"Good," I said. "That should cheer Beethoven up!"

"Would Monsieur like all that to be delivered?" the landlady asked me.

I paid her without answering. I put the two bottles in my side-pocket and picked up the plate of veal in both hands, and went out into the street as proudly as if I'd received the great sash of the Order of Prussia.

On the way, I said to myself: *No, I won't cede the honor of serving Beethoven to anyone else! O, I won't blush at an action that does me such honor! No, I won't renounce the honor of loading his table and going to say to him, with my napkin over my arm: Monseigneur the King of Harmony, Your Majesty's dinner is served!*

Ordinarily, I don't remember places very well; I'm a distracted man, and my vagabond imagination can never recognize the abodes of others as easily as its own, but this time, the name of Beethoven had struck me as forcefully as if it had been inscribed on the door of the house in letters of fire. It was, if you recall, a little house with the square door and narrow windows hidden even in daylight, solitary in the midst of others: an honest and poor house both decent and miserable in appearance—which is as rare for a house as it is for a woman, of course. I had soon arrived at Beethoven's house.

Beethoven lives on the first floor; that is the only luxury he permits himself. His door is garnished with broad-headed nails, which gives it at first glance a rather formidable appearance, but the nails in question are useless for the defense of the house; the lock is badly attached, and in any case, the door is more often unlocked than locked, and one can open it by pushing it with one's foot.

I went in. There was nothing in the antechamber but a table covered in a coarse cloth, a canary that was singing joyfully in its cage, and a large sitting on a footstool, which was gazing at the empty table and uttering the occasional mewls of a cat more idle than hungry. They were Beethoven's table, canary and cat!

I put my covered plate and my two old bottles on the table; I stroked the cat, which arched its back for me, and saluted the canary, which continued the song it had begun without paying any more attention to me than had been paid to its master in the publisher's shop.

In the meantime, Beethoven's housekeeper came in.

She did not seem any more astonished to see me than the cat or the canary, but she said: "You can't see him today; he's in his room; he's so sad that he doesn't want dinner."

At the same time, she opened the door of Beethoven's room for me; I went in.

He was sitting by his window, looking attentively at a lovely carnation he had planted; a host of little green insects was devouring his beautiful carnation. He was picking them off with the utmost precaution. The carnation wasn't alone on his window, either; long nasturtiums had climbed up to top, and their mat green leaves formed the most admirable blind against the ardors of the sun.

As you know, he's deaf; he didn't hear me come in. There were writing materials on his table. I wrote: *I've bought you hot veal and Rhenish wine. Let's eat.*

I held the piece of paper out to him.

He finished saving his carnation from the little green insects; then he read my piece of paper. Then, all of a sudden, you would have seen his eyes light up and his smile reappear.

"Be welcome," said, "be welcome!" You're a Frenchman—that's good. Do me the honor of dining with me." At the same time he shouted: "Marthe! Set a place for the gentleman." Then he turned back to me. "You've done well to come," he said. "I was very sad. It's only the countryside that makes me happy; the city is killing me. I'm stifling here. I hear all sorts of strange noises, but I can't hear myself sing. That's a great shame, isn't it?"

As he saw that I was amazed, he went on, with tears in his eyes: "Oh yes, it's because I'm quite alone, all alone; no one talks to me, no one asks what has become of poor old Beethoven; I don't know myself any more what my name is and who I am. Once I was the master of a world; I commanded the most powerful invisible orchestra that has ever filled the air; I lent my ear night and day to ravishing symphonies of which I was simultaneously the author, the orchestra, the singer, the judge, the king and the god; my life was a perpetual concert, an unending symphony. What delightful ecstasies there were, in those days! What lyrical transports! What mysterious and holy voices! What an immense bow, which departed from the earth to touch the heavens!

"All that had an echo in my soul; my soul then received the slightest sounds from the air or the earth: birdsong, the sound of the wind; the murmur of water, the sights of the nocturnal breeze, the swaying of poplars in the sky, the familiar gaiety of the sparrow, the active buzz of bees, the plaintive murmur of the cricket on the domestic hearth, were as many harmonies for me; I received them all in my heart, in my soul, for me, who lived on sounds, dreams, silence, sighs, ecstasies, amity, amours, poetry!

"But alas, one morning, all that fled! One morning, adieu to my visions! Adieu my admirable singers! Adieu my omnipotent organ, my holy harps played by the angels' hands! Adieu sounds of the earth and the heavens! Adieu also to silence! Adieu to everything! I've lost more than Milton, who only lost his sight and kept his poetry; I've lost my poetry, I've lost my universe; I'm a poor exile now from the domain of harmony. Poor man, poor man that I am! Here I am on the edge of my tomb singing my funeral mass! But you say that you have brought me two bottles of Rhenish wine and a slice of roast veal, Monsieur?"

His housekeeper signaled to us that dinner was served.

He took me gallantly by the hand, invited me to precede him into the little dining-room. Only two places were set at the table; his housekeeper, doubtless jealous of her master's consideration, had yielded her place at the table to me, and she served us.

They meal was cheerful on Beethoven's part; he put so much verve and wit into it, and spoke so well, with so much pleasure, that I had soon forgotten the infirmity about which he had been so sad a short while before.

Beethoven was one of those old men who have lived their entire lives with a single idea. One great idea suffices for existence of those exceptional men; it absorbs them, it's all of their joy, it's all of their chagrin, it's all of their past and all of their present; it grows with them and grows weaker with them, and, when the idea is exhausted, the man is dead.

The old Rhenish wine had reanimated Beethoven so forcefully that at the end of the meal he got up abruptly and went into his room.

"I want to show you," he said to me, "that old Beethoven is not as deaf as people claim. There are people who no longer hear me, but I can still hear myself. Judge for yourself."

As he spoke, he sat down at his piano.

The piano in question is an admirable instrument made by Broadwood in London. It was a present that Messieurs Cramer, Kalkbrenner, Clementi, Ries, etc. had sent from England to the musical Homer. Neglected as he was, misunderstood and almost forgotten as he believed himself to be, Beethoven had been very touched by that excellent gesture by those great artists, an almost-posthumous gratitude that did equal honor to their talent and their heart.

So, he placed himself at his piano, and there, suddenly, he began to play a symphony of his own composition.

Merciful Heaven! The piano was out of tune and screeched like an old chat!

Beethoven struck his piano like a deaf man. No, never had more piercing sounds, never had more disastrous chords, never had a more discordant symphony rent my ears. For him, entirely given over to his momentary enthusiasm, happy and proud finally to have a listener—him, Beethoven, one listener!—he continued the symphony he had begun; he lost himself in its sweetest ecstasies; he shivered; he wept; he smiled; he was beside himself.

I kept my gaze lowered; I would have liked to stop up my ears; I would have liked to flee. Oh well—we were both right. I was on earth, listening to the most abominable charivari that one could ever hear; he was in Heaven, listening to the music of Beethoven!

Finally, my torture came to an end; his joy concluded. He stood up, harassed but very happy.

"Isn't it true," he said to me, "that that's still beautiful? Isn't it true that old Beethoven still has good blood in his veins? Isn't it true that that's music, and that I've been myself for one more hour? Oh, they can say 'Poor Beethoven! Unfortunate Beethoven!' Poor unfortunate Beethoven is still the only musician in Germany! Am I not right, my dear friend?"

At the same time, he pressed me with his large hands; his broad torso drew closer to me, and he moistened me with a large tear. I responded as best I could to his caresses. Good and worthy Beethoven!

Then he said: "I have to give you something. You can take away something of me, an entirely new song, something for yourself, for you alone."

As he spoke he left the piano and went to the window. He set about tapping the window with his right hand as he had in the music-seller's shop. He was listening internally, composing.

And he gave me that piece, which I still have, which he touched with his hands, which he composed with his genius, and of which I will give you a copy, in order to give this story all the authenticity it needs.

I left the worthy old man filled with admiration and pity, penetrated with respect, ashamed on behalf of Germany and Europe of the poverty and abandonment that I had seen.

For him, he had spent a good day; he had eaten roast veal, he had drunk Rhenish wine, and he had played his music on his piano.

He accompanied me as far as his door and watched me go downstairs; and when I was at the bottom of the staircase he shouted to me, loudly: "Adieu! Adieu! *Bon voyage!* Love me! Think of me! Your Rhenish wine was excellent, and your roast was cooked to perfection, my friend!"

THE GREEN MAN

This is an adventure taken from the memoirs of a musician. The details of the story are so simple and so touching that I have gathered them all together in order to render them, exactly as I learned and received them, to all the musicians, young and old, who are reading this, united as they are in the love of the art, that beautiful and innocent passion!

I was still a child, but a child of sixteen (it's the German musician who is speaking), when I already thought myself a master. I was so young! And because my violin resonated beneath the bow, in a thousand chords, I thought I had nothing more to do. A happy presumption of the age!

My father, who was a musician of the old school, was proud of me, not as a master is proud of his pupil, but as a father is proud of his son. Furthermore, I worked night and day. My violin was my life, and I abandoned myself all the more to that musical ardor because I already believed—me, the poor beginner—that I was about to obtain perfection.

I was not the only one obsessed with that same passion, however, in our little German village. Several young masters like me abandoned themselves to the same musical frenzy. We had soon formed a quartet—the quartet, that first dream of all musical beginners!

The entire street came to my father's house three or four times a week to listen to our quartets. We gave all our neighbors as much harmony as they could take in one evening, and more. They listened to us, they praised us, they admired us, they applauded us; they played their part marvelously in the concerts of our musical education. For myself, I don't believe that I've ever played the violin with more enthusiasm and pride at any time in my life.

One autumn evening, the air was sweet and clear, the sky was calm, the earth seemed to be rotating on its axis more slowly than usual, and our violins were sensing all that calm sweetness in my father's large drawing-room, where we gave our concerts, when, all of a sudden, we saw a man of the strangest appearance come in.

He was wearing short, narrow trousers of a very ancient style, violet in color, in a poor, threadbare velvet that had lost its sheen; his stockings were blue and checkered; his stoutly-soled shoes were ornamented by silver buckles. That costume, already so bizarre, was completed by a parrot-green coat heightened by large and flamboyant steel buttons. Above that coat one saw an immense black cravat, and above that cravat a melancholy face. His head was ornamented by long, curly hair.

The man was unsmiling, but his eyes were keen and ardent. He came into my father's house without introduction; then, seeing an empty seat in the corner next to my pretty cousin Nanrel, he went to sit down there, after which, adopting an attentive expression, he lent his ears to the quartet.

The presence of that stranger, however, had struck us all with an immense and inexplicable fear. Scarcely had he sat down next to the pretty Nanrel than our four violins lost the measure. My father came to our aid—and my father was a skillful musician—but in vain; nothing could be done. The entire quartet was in disarray.

Then the stranger came up to me and said, in a severe tone: "Young man, your ardor carries you away; you've adopted a bow too impetuous for you. That's an instrument which shouldn't be touched unwisely, for fear of burning one's fingers."

Then, turning to my three colleagues, he addressed reproachful words to each of them, expressing doubt as to their artistic future, which made his words very cruel. For myself, I confess that I felt a mortal chill circulating in my veins when I saw the stranger's scornful expression; I thought I was such an excellent violinist! Meanwhile, the green man picked up my bow, which I had dropped, took my violin from me, and began to play. Then I felt more humiliated than ever.

But also, what verve! How admirably he played! What heavenly chords! Whet harmonious plaints the stranger drew from my violin! One might have thought that an invisible soul, concealed in that sonorous wood, had suddenly been woken up by a ray from on high. Never, no, never, even in my summer dreams, had I dreamed of that ideal! Yes, for sure, it was an invisible and charming spirit that sang in my violin, obedient to the fingers of the green man.

When the stranger had put his instrument down, everyone was still listening. At the first notes that his bow had brought forth, the entire assembly had risen unanimously to its feet; now it was no longer listening, it was applauding with that silent murmur that is worth more than all the bravos in the world. My father was the first to take the stranger's hand, and addressed respectful words of welcome to him. The green man, however, all his natural modesty having returned, blushed at so much praise.

Finally, the members of the crowd took their leave, and my father, myself and the green man remained alone.

We knew that there was, that same September, in our pleasant little town, a meeting of the great German masters, who would hold a scholarly and practical musical conference. Naturally, we were convinced that the green man was a master newly arrived for the assembly, and my father hastened to offer him the hospitality of his house. The green man accepted and offered us his hand.

He thus became our guest, sat down at our table, sat down at our domestic hearth as if he were my father's brother. Simple, good and knowledgeable—God knows!—his special and inexhaustible subject of conversation was the manufacture of instruments, and the best schemes to employ in order to arrive at incredible and entirely new results. Once started on that subject, the green man never shut up.

That was the life we led for a fortnight, surrounding our guest with all the concerns he merited, listening to his lessons, and blessing him in our hearts for all his advice, when he said to us: "Love music, young folk; it's the bread of souls. Music helps us to understand the goal of life; it's the earthly immortality." That was the way he talked. But if, by chance, a stranger came, our knowledgeable friend fled into the garden. He liked to be alone, or at least to be alone with us.

One day, however, a friend of my father's named Kurz came to his house—a wealthy local timber-merchant. To tell the truth, Herr Kurz was not a man I liked. He was rich, he was generous; the only thing he knew was selling dear and buying cheap. He was a man like any other—less than nothing to me, the son of an artist who only liked artists.

At the sight of the timber-merchant, the green man went out in haste, but Kurz had already glimpsed and recognized him, and followed him with his eyes.

"What kind of man have you taken into your home?" he said to my father. "My word, you have a singular guest there—and in truth, I'd rather he were at the bottom of the sea than in your house." That was the way Herr Kurz talked.

"Do you know him, then?" asked my father, with ill-disguised curiosity.

"Do I know him!" said Herr Kurz. "He lived in my village for a long time. His name is Beze and he's a carpenter by trade, but he's an odd fellow who doesn't pay much heed to things of this world. There was once an organ in our little church that had lost its harmony, so our congregation decided to have a new one. Immediately, your guest, Beze, offered us his services. He took responsibility for building the organ all on his own, at his expense; he only asked us for the materials. He seemed so convincing, and his offer was so tempting, that it was accepted.

"He sets to work; he makes preparations, puts things together and takes them apart; he throws himself into his task body and soul, spending all night and all day on it, forgetting to eat and drink. Finally, his work is concluded. The organ resounds in the church and nothing so beautiful has ever been heard. People come from miles around to admire the masterpiece. We all come running, the notables of the locale. The entire village is on tenterhooks.

"Meanwhile, Beze explains the mechanism of his instrument; he goes into the most minute detail; he follows up each of his demonstrations. At the same time, for a final demonstration, he sits down at the organ and starts to play.

"We're all ears and all silent, but we can only hear a thousand confused sounds that make no sense. Immediately, the old parish organist comes forward, impatient to show us what he can do with such a noble and beautiful instrument— but the instrument is rebellious to any melody. Then a thousand gibes rain down on the unfortunate workman; with a common voice his organ is declared to be detestable.

"Finally, there's a great tumult in the church. Beze, however, isn't intimidated; he goes out, casting an ironic glance at us, as if he'd created an unknown masterpiece. That, my dear friend, is the illustrious guest you've received in your home."

Thus spoke Herr Kurz, with the starchy facility of an ignoramus who thinks he has enough money to rise above fatuity. I don't know what the merchant said after that; it would have been impossible for me to hear him talk about my friend like that any longer. I went into the garden to join him.

He was, in fact, in the garden, in his usual place, on the grass at the foot of the big apple tree, his face turned to the setting sun. When he saw me he beckoned me to come nearer.

"Look," he said to me, in an emotional voice, "how the sun's setting over there in all its splendor. Well, the slightest cloud might impede that fiery glare. Such is the story of the man of genius; the words of an ignoramus can tarnish him in an instant—but also, the slightest breath of wind can blow away the temporary cloud."

I was profoundly moved by those melancholy words; I wanted to reassure my friend.

"Oh," he said to me, "I have no fear; my soul can't be troubled by the vulgar; I'm well aware that progress isn't so easy to make, and patience is everything in that game. The example of our forefathers has been useful to us; any perfection is bound to be rejected by people; take them out of their routine and they'll make the sign of the cross, as if they'd seen the Antichrist. But before God, time is the master. That beautiful organ I've constructed, that great work of my hands, possesses a soul, but it requires a man who can awaken that dormant soul. It's the story of Alexander's horse, which could only be mounted by Alexander."

At the same time, the sun bade one last adieu to the entire landscape; the light, fading by degrees, climbed into the sky as it glided lightly over the mountains.

"Anyway, my friend," said the green man, "what does the insensible soul of an instrument of wood or lead matter, when one thinks about the immortal soul? Oh, how many errant souls are out there in that envelope of dew, embalmed by the perfume of flowers!"

And when darkness had fallen, he said: "Come on, my son, let's go play the violin."

Gradually, meanwhile, our village was animated by a new crowd. The time for the musical competition having arrived, the masters were coming from all directions. There were people throughout the village ready to give them hospitality worthy of their great names. Music is the pride and joy of our dear Germany! Every newly-arrived great musician was received like a king; his entry was a veritable triumph; we went to see all the masters as they passed by, to applaud them. One by one, we saw all the famous masters arrive: Graun, the inexhaustible genius who drew all his inspiration from his heart; Fux and Hasse, his two faithful companions; the great Telemann, who had been entrusted to us by his great city of Hamburg; then your Gassmann, whose future glory Germany anticipated; finally, we saw a letter arrive from Gluck himself, unable to attend the festival of the arts.[38] Gluck told his pupils

---

[38] The references are to Carl Heinrich Graun (1704-1759), Johann Fux (1660-1741), Johann Adolphe Hasse (1699-1783), Georg Philipp Telemann (1681-1767), Florian Gassmann (1729-1774) and Christophe Gluck (1714-1787)

how he regretted his absence. His letter concluded with the sincerest wishes for the progress of German art. In sum, a circle formed in our little village of the most interesting and the most curious grandmasters of our era.

Those great men were, at the same time, the simplest and best of men. Their lectures were more than public; they were held in the largest hall of the best inn in the town, at the sign of Saint Cecilia, where one could see and hear as much as one wished. Although timid, I was not about to miss that great festival. I slipped between the tables and hid in a corner, and from there, for entire hours, I listened to those marvelous speeches and contemplated those noble faces. From time to time, the masters interrupted their conversations to offer one another a few large glasses of an old German wine that rejoiced their hearts.

One evening, when they were all assembled and I was at my post listening to them, the conversation turned to the subject of the green man. Each of them repeated that he had heard mention of a mysterious musician who hid from all eyes. "By Heaven," said Graun, "it shall not be said that we did not make the acquaintance of a man of genius; let's have him come, children, that he might be one of us, that he might speak with us and drink with us, sharing our conversation and our pleasures."

Then, very humbly, I advanced into the middle of the group. "My masters," I said humbly, "the man of whom you speak is indeed a great musician, a genius who hides away; but you'll invite him in vain—he wouldn't want to come."

Astonished, they repeated: "He wouldn't want to come!" And a thousand questions followed, urgently.

Seeing that they were attentive, I told them the story of the neighboring village's organ, and how no one could play it, and how it had been a great subject of reproach and chagrin for my friend.

When the masters had heard that story they were gripped by a great ardor. "My friends," said Graun, "early in the morning tomorrow, Sunday, we'll go see this organ that doesn't want to sing. By King David, it'll be strange if any instrument can resist so many masters brought together."

At these words, Hasse and Fux applauded. Telemann added that he would think of a means to bring to the foot of the organ the mysterious workman who had made it—but young Gassmann uttered a sigh and exclaimed: "My friends, there's one man in the world who can extract sounds from stone. But where are you, our divine master, Emmanuel Bach?"[39]

A rendezvous was arranged at the organ for the following morning.

The next day, the most beautiful dawn was rising over the little church that enclosed the master carpenter's organ when two pedestrians entered the church through the cemetery door. One of the two men was in his prime; the profundity of his thoughts was visible on his broad forehead and his large blue eyes shone with a soft, calm gleam. The man who accompanied him was young, sprightly and benevolent, with a face blossoming with youth.

"Master," the latter said, "why have you stopped on the way like this? The masters' meeting will be finished when you arrive."

"My son," said the other, "a voice in my head urged me to enter this church. Did you not hear yesterday what a travel-

---

[39] Emmanuel Bach (1714-1788) was the fifth son of Johann Sebastian Bach. He became prominent during a period of transition between the baroque style exemplified by his father and the cited composers and the more romantic style that followed it; his own distinctive expressive approach to composition and performance as known as *empfidsamer stil* [sensitive style]. He was, in consequence, a significant forerunner of Romanticism, the French version of which paid considerable homage to Jean-Jacques Rousseau's "cult of sensibility." Many readers of the *Gazette Musicale*, where this story first appeared, would have known that, and would therefore have found the story's symbolism relatively transparent.

er told us about a mysterious organ that no one has yet been able to played? The traveler called the organ the work of madness; Heaven has sent me to discover whether it might instead be the product of genius. Let's go in, then, my boy; pray to Heaven in a whisper: I'll accompany your morning prayer on that organ."

They went in. The master meditated, seated in front of the organ, while the pupil guarded the door to the loft. Soon the church was filled with the faithful who had come to hear the Sunday mass; then the masters, faithful to the rendezvous they had agreed the previous evening, arrived at the church, and as the priest was at the altar, they knelt down to pray.

Suddenly, a sound descended from Heaven made the little church reverberate: the best-nurtured sounds, divine sounds, emerged from the organ that had so far been mute. The faithful were dazed, as if they could hear an angel; the masters raised their heads, each one trying to determine who among them was playing the organ, and became frightened on finding that they were all present, kneeling in the same place. Even the priest was seized by a secret terror.

Meanwhile, the organ, played by an inspired genius, was alternately grave, sublime, melancholy, passionate and plaintive, sometimes fluty, sometimes thunderous, sometimes praises of God, sometimes the terror of men. Everyone listened, admired, and remained prostrate.

In that crowd, one man alone raised his head: the green man! He was near the altar, leaning against a pillar, and he gazed at his organ, his work brought to life—or rather, he gazed at Heaven. Finally, then, his thought was manifest to human beings! Finally, then, his revelation was complete! He did not weep; he did not pray; he scarcely listened; he thought he was dreaming. He was the happiest of all the members of that happy, emotional, impassioned gathering. When he saw that all gazes were fixed on him, with pride, he went out of the church at a rapid pace, and the mass continued.

When the mass was concluded, the masters gathered at the door of the organ-loft in order to discover who the angel was who had played like that.

The door opened, and they all exclaimed: "Emmanuel Bach! Emmanuel Bach!"

It was him, Emmanuel Bach. "Good day, my friends," he said. "Your brother has arrived—but where is the man of genius who has made this organ? Where is he, that I might embrace him—or, rather, that I might throw myself at his feet!"

They replied to Emmanuel that the man in question was invisible, and the masters added: "Come and have breakfast with us, Master, at the sign of St. Cecilia."

That evening, Emmanuel Bach and Graun were strolling in my father's garden. They were searching for and calling out to my friend, the green man.

Finally, they found him under his favorite tree—but in what a state! O Heaven! My poor friend's head was leaning against the tree-trunk; his eyes, still open, were vaguely seeking the last rays of sunset; His hands were extended on his knees, and no movement of his heart announced that he was breathing.

I ran forward; Emmanuel Bach ran forward; Graun took hold of my friend's head; we called to him.

Then he opened his eyes; his hands spread out as if he were about to play the organ; then, perceiving the foreign masters, he said: "Ah! You're here, my Masters! Ah! You're here, Emmanuel Bach, my god of this morning—oh, forgive me if I'm not receiving you with all respect; I can't do any more; the emotion has killed me; I've succumbed to the happiness, crushed by the sound of my beautiful organ. I'm dying."

The two masters sat down next to the poor carpenter.

"Yes," he said, I can die. "Graun to my left; Emmanuel Bach to my right!" Then he turned to me, and offered me his hand. "Adieu, my son," he said to me. "You, my Masters, bless me!"

The last ray of the beautiful sunlight bore away my friend's soul in the roseate cloud; the gentle dusk fell over that noble face like a silvered net, and in the distance, everything fell silent to listen to a simple and pious melody that escaped from Graun's enchanted flute.

THE GOOD SISTER AND THE BAD SISTER[40]
An Unpublished Chapter of the Devil's Memoirs

It was about a week ago. A rainy, cold and somber autumn had cast its mantle of cloud over the earth; the night was black and dreary; one might have thought that winter had suddenly arrived, without any warning, and had no intention of leaving again. The wind was whistling, the trees roaring; the leaves were being shed only half-yellowed.

On that bleak night I was walking alone in the beautiful Parc de Saint-Cloud, whose superimposed pathways are somewhat reminiscent of an immense ladder of verdure. Under those trees, thrown into a corner, the château is usually hidden; it's rather difficult to discover even in broad daylight; but that night, the château was sparkling with a thousand lights; one understood that life, thought, celebration, joy, grave concerns and powerful inspirations were behind those walls

And that was exactly why I had the courage, at that hour, alone on that fatal night, to take a stroll in the Parc de Saint-Cloud.

You know that there are several ways to reach the Lantern if Demosthenes (by what caprice has Diogenes' lantern

---

[40] There is no way to reproduce in English the complex set of double meanings contained in the adjectives in the French title "La Sœur rose et la sœur grise." It is worth pointing out, however, that just as *grise* could imply either "gray," in the sense of "dreary" or "drunk," so *rose* could imply either rosy-cheeked innocence or (as in such phrases as "la vie en rose") a life of pleasure. It is not entirely clear, therefore, which of the sisters is which in the metaphorical scheme of the titular description.

been stolen?), which is the culminating point of the park; the simplest is to follow the lower pathway and to go up the water-slope to the upper pathway, and, at the end of that path, to take another even higher, and so on, as one does to climb the great stairway at Versailles. That's the vulgar way; but to arrive at the famous lantern, from which the view embraces the whole of Paris, without encountering a human being, there's another way, admirable and difficult, which you've all taken in your youth, uttering squeals of joy. That beautiful route of youth consists of going straight ahead, via uncleared paths.

At the very bottom of the mountain, you raise your head, and, while gazing at a certain point in the sky, a fugitive star—your eighteen-year-old star—you say to yourself: "That's where I'm going!" As you do as you say; you go through the brambles, over the ravines, the grass and the sand; you keep on climbing; sometimes you come to a rock; you climb the rock; sometimes there's a fallen tree; you climb over the tree-trunk; it's an authentic steeple-chase, for which one never has enough arms, enough legs or enough breath.

As you climb, the shade thickens around you; at our feet, however, you discover something like a nebulous ocean whose waves rise up behind you, so effectively that, thanks to that fantastic mirage, any retreat becomes impossible, and it's necessary for you to climb, to climb further, to keep on climbing.

And that was exactly the route I took that night, for my stroll in the Parc de Saint-Cloud.

But on that difficult path, you see, I had a beautiful escort! I saw rising before me, as Jacob saw his ladder, a white myriad of beautiful angels, al the profane angels who, in our heyday, had scaled the mountain with us, nostrils flared, hair scattered, lips parted...

We were young then, we and they: they were uttering joyful little squeals in the air; they were going forth to conquer, and their scarves served as oriflammes; they made many false steps on that route, but they got up prouder and more animated than before.

That night, it seemed to me that I heard and saw them all again, those vanished beauties.

Thus escorted, I marched in their wake as before; as before, I held out my hand to them; I encouraged them with gestures: I called on them to follow me; and such was the power of memory that I arrived thus at the summit of the mountain without perceiving that I was alone.

Directly facing the Lantern of Demosthenes is a terrace; from that terrace, when it's dark, one overlooks an abyss; you can see in the distance something like an immense mass of paper laden with wit and blasphemies that one has just reduced to ashes; in those black ashes, little sparks glow momentarily and are extinguished, faint dying gleams that are disappearing forever. That black mass, however, is Paris; those sparks that are shining and disappearing are the soul and the thought of the eternal city, which is going to sleep, perhaps to wake up again tomorrow.

I was standing there, in my contemplation, when I felt two little hands—but so cold!—over my eyes.

Although I say cold, one of those hands was burning; it was an incredible sensation that no one could define. The icy hand was rough to the touch, as if it were covered with a recently-sheared fleece; the burning hand was slender and soft, like the hand of a forty-year-old woman.

At the same time, I felt that the invisible creature had sat down behind me, and I heard it say to me, in a mordant voice: "Guess who!"

"It's the Devil!" I exclaimed, immediately.

And he, returning the use of my eyes, said: "Well guessed, my secretary Theodor!"

Undisconcerted, I replied: "And that, my dear Master, is where you're mistaken. I'm not your secretary Theodor, and I'm very sorry; I'm a poor man, to whom you've never dictated anything at all, to whom you've never recounted the slightest story, while you have indeed heaped your beloved friend Theodore Hoffmann with all your favors. What the hell! Monseigneur, I'm not as fussy as you are! Limp or no limp, you've penetrated into all houses and all souls; not one roof, not one conscience, has any secret from you; you know the history of humanity entire; you've studied it in its saddest aspect, but also the most fecund; you are, incontrovertibly, the greatest observer in the world; and when you want to write your commentaries, you only summon, every fifty years, a single secretary! You leave your other servants to mope at your door and divine, as best they can, some of the marvelous mysteries that you lavish upon your favorite. Has no one ever told you that Caesar wore out four secretaries?

> *As Caesar once, at the same time,*
> *Dictated in four different styles.*

"All well and good! Leave me in peace to tell myself the beautiful stories that I know, in whispers, in my heart, and if you have time to kill, go wake up your secretary Theodor, who's sleeping soundly under some tavern table at present."

"La la!" said the Devil, with the mocking expression with which you're familiar. "Let's not get so upset! It's true that I love my friend Hoffmann; he's a powerful intelligence who contests with me in finesse and naivety, and who has never trembled. I don't know any man who takes the most frightful stories as seriously. He loves the odor of sulfur as others love the odor of roses. At any rate, I love him; but as for you, my son, I don't hate you either. You've rendered me some good services, without knowing me, which I haven't forgotten; to begin with, you took up the cause of King Louis XV, who was my friend, and his mistresses, and I said in talking about you: 'There's a good companion!' You like rouge and beauty-spots, and the odor of musk doesn't displease you; now, in moral terms, from a woman's rouge to the Devil's tail, from beauty-spots to his horns, and from musk to sulfur, it's only a short step. What you haven't enough of, for my taste, and which prevents you from every being worthy to write to my dictation, is belief. You don't believe in anything; that's all right, it's in your blood. You don't believe in the Devil, so how do you expect the Devil to believe in you? Even now, when you're looking at me, you're sniffing me, opening your eyes wide, as if I were a Phalansterian, a humanitarian, a so-called Muse of the Fatherland. Reassure yourself, my son, I'm only the Devil. And since it's dark, and cold, I'll tell you a story if you want."

As he spoke those words, I remembered that Frédéric Soulié, in *Les Mémoires du Diable*, which the Devil had surely inspired in one of his finest moments of verve,[41] with insolence and cruelty, informs us of one of his hero's favorite habits, and I searched in my pocket for a cigar. The Devil divined my politeness.

"Here," he said, offering me a piece of dead wood. "Smoke this for me..."

At the same time, he rolled some willow-branches in his fingers; he rubbed one of those improvised cigar-stubs in the palm of his hand, and there we were, smoking like two brothers. Except that I noticed that the Devil, who doesn't do anything like other people, but the lighted end of the cigar in his mouth—a remarkable particularity that Frédéric Soulié forgot to mention in their memoirs.

"Now," said the Devil, "What do you want me to tell you?" Then, reading my thoughts, he said: "Oh! Anything you like, except that. No, it's not me who'll tell you what happened, five years ago, in this palace that's so calm today; no, that's not a story of the kind that the Devil can tell a man, or a man the Devil. There are too many dangers in such a story for me to want to confront them. A throne lost, and that throne the throne of France! An old man going to die far away, in such sad exile! Marie-Thérèse d'Angoulême, a saint on earth who

---

[41] The feuilleton version of Frédéric Soulié's novel *Les Mémoires du diable* ran in *Le Journal des Débats* between June 1837 and Mars 1938; Janin's story appeared in the September 1837 issue of the *Revue de Paris* in 1937. Soulié had, however, published the first of two brief "Extraits des mémoires du diable" in the *Revue de Paris* in 1836.

drives even me to pity! And finally, a child, a poor child expelled from these groves like a leaf yellowed by autumn! No, I won't recount all those dolors, but we can talk about something else if you want."[42]

Thus speaking, the Devil turned his head away from the heights of Saint-Cloud, to which my thoughts had gone in spite of him—there are thoughts so strange, desires so violent, that they're more powerful than the Devil. In my turn, involuntarily obedient to the being sitting beside me, I darted a glance at the narrow and rude path that I'd followed in order to arrive at the place where I was sitting. The path, so dark a little while ago, was illuminated by a dubious glow. In that wan light, several people were moving, men and women occupied with all the cares of everyday life. The men had become fat and heavy; the women had lost the charming bosom and soft pallor of their sixteenth year a decade ago; they were all occupied with a thousand cruel worries, a thousand paltry ambitions and a thousand puerile desires.

"What's that villainous troop, then?" I exclaimed.

"Oh," said the Devil, "that's the singing and gilded company that accompanied you just now through the bushes, singing crazy songs of love." The Devil took me by the arm, and added: "Which proves to you that whenever one does as much as cast a backward glance, it's a great imprudence not to go further than ten years or so. Less than ten years is something so paltry and so sad, it's a past so miserable that it makes one horrified by oneself. You might as well say to the clock that

---

[42] This passage explains why the location of the story had a particular symbolism for Janin, in connection with the July Revolution of 1830, apart from being that of a famous panoramic view over Paris. He had no way of knowing that the Prussians would set up a battery there in 1870 in order to shell the city, and that the shells with which the French retaliated would set fire to the royal and imperial residence, necessitating its subsequent demolition, but he might have appreciated the extra dimension of irony that it would add to his story.

has just chimed midnight, 'Chime again!' The clock can only tell you what you already know, that it's midnight. So, when you want to evoke the past, do so in such a way that the past in question is so far away that you won't be compromised by the solemn evocation. Come on, it's all right—and since you wish it, those old men of thirty and those old women of twenty-five will disappear. I'm not here to cause you chagrin."

At the same time, he blew on the path, and all the sad faces disappeared, and I could no longer see anything but a few scraps of blue and white scarves, hanging from the flexible branches, and light footprints in the grass, and little squeals of joy in the air, and I understood that, in order to evoke vanished youth, there is something in us more powerful than the Devil, which is the heart!

The Devil overheard my thought.

"Now," he said, "it's necessary for me to begin my story; I've been preparing you long enough. In that mass of black houses, not far from the dome of the Invalides, which looks from here rather like a cooking-pot inverted over some pasha with three tails, in those streets that intersect in a thousand different fashions, between two gardens, there's an ancient Carmelite convent…do you see it?"

"I can only see a black, formless hidden mass," I told him, "feebly lit by a few fire-follets that flutter as they fade away."

"Well then, look," he said.

At the same time, he placed in front of my right eye, by way of a monocle, the icy hand that I mentioned just now. That hand produced an incredible effect on my optic nerve. Monsieur Arago, at the top of the tower where he watches for stray comets, ready to show them their way, has no optical instruments as clear and as infallible.[43]

---

[43] François Arago, appointed director of the Paris Observatoire in 1834, modernized its equipment extensively, but this story was written before the installation of the Coupole Arago to install a new equatorial telescope.

"Yes!" I exclaimed. "Now I can see the dome of the Invalides! It's glistening like Mambrin's golden helmet over Don Quixote's skull. I can see, at the end of a street, to the right of the hostel, a house in ruins, and that house is still filled with cells, dormitories, refectories, and—what a horrible sight!—there's a terrible dungeon, devoid of air, devoid of light, devoid of hope!"

"Keep looking," said the Devil. "What do you see?"

"Now I can see that a thick wall separates that monastery from a calm, somber and tranquil house. The walls of that house still retain the unequivocal vestiges of considerable luxury; the ceilings are decorated with amours; figures and emblems, half-effaced, are still shining on the walls. There's a striking contrast with those other walls, cold, inanimate, terrible and bloody. But what are you trying to get at, Monseigneur?"

Here the Devil rubbed his hand on his breast, as a young dandy at the Opéra does with his monocle when that great and powerful beauty Taglioni,[44] our regret of every winter evening, slowly descended from the third heaven where she was hidden among the flowers. It appeared to me that the magnifying glass had become even more terrible.

"Look closely," the Devil continued. "Can you see, in the wall separating the convent from that elegant little house, once consecrated to all the vices, a door, cleverly-hidden on the side of the convent by iron nails, and on the side of the little house by lascivious paintings?

"I can indeed see a wall, and in that wall an almost-invisible door; to the right, a nun's cell; to the left, the boudoir of an Opéra girl. But as far as I can judge from the stage that you're setting so carefully, Monseigneur, you're going to tell me a vulgar story, half sacred and half profane, which unfolds simultaneously beneath the veil of serge and the veil of

---

[44] The ballet dancer Marie Taglioni (1804-1884), famous for dancing *La Sylphide* (1832); in which her skirts were shortened in order to show off her *pointe* work to full advantage.

gauze—some stupid intrigue between a marquis of the *ancien régime* and a nun retained in that cloister by eternal vows. If that's the case, Seigneur Devil, you can keep your story; we've known it for a long time."

"Impatient young men!" exclaimed the Devil, spitting out the fire of his cigar. "With their rage to guess everything, it will soon no longer be possible to tell an honest little story!" He added: "But I'm going to tell you my story anyway, and you'll listen whether you like it or not. You've fallen into my claws, and it won't be said that you got out of them so cheaply. So take your medicine patiently. Once, to punish you for your impoliteness, I'd have taken and carried away your soul, but what's the point nowadays? I have more than enough souls. So listen to me, and permit me, before having my drama acted, to dispose my theater as I wish.

"As the Devil, I'm at least entitled to the same rights as any writer of melodramas explaining to the stalls that the palace into which his characters are about to enter was built expressly for the dramatic fable at hand; that there's a false door there, and a subterranean passage further on; that this window overlooks the Alps and that other one the Apennines; that there's a balcony to the left and a precipice to the right. At the same time, our man hands you a bunch of keys, as in the tale of Bluebeard. If, unfortunately, you forget a single one of the indications of the dramatic architect, if you lose a single key from the bunch...pop! No more melodrama! It's the story of the goats passing the goatherd in *Don Quixote*.

"So, I'll continue with my story.

"That convent that you see over there, beside that pretty house, which is occupied today by a timber-merchant, was still filled with Carmelite nuns in 1788, who lived in all the severity of their Order. The house beside it, which bears a sign saying *House to Let*, and which no one wants to rent, because it's too far away from Parisian vice and nor is it fashioned to bourgeois habits, was at that time one of the remote little houses in which the great seigneurs of old came to relax from the excesses committed in broad daylight, by means of other nocturnal and hidden excesses, thus doing their best to recall beautiful nights in the petty apartments of Versailles.

"Don't worry, I'm not going to make any speeches on that subject or offer you any moral. I've never understood how people can have so many emotions of every sort with regard to a historical fact. The historian who becomes impassioned for or against the history he's recording seems to me to be insane; a fact has no need of commentary, simply because it is a fact. But let's not replace one speech with another.

"So, nearly fifty years ago..."

At these words, I interrupted him. "Stop there, Master!" I exclaimed. "It seems to me that you're scarcely in accord with yourself. Didn't you say just now that it's not worth the trouble of evoking memories so recent, and that there's surely nothing for us to collect from such evocations but humiliations?"

"I said," the Devil went on, "that I'm a fool and a lunatic to speak thus, in the simplicity of my intelligence, with such incomplete and petulant beings, who know nothing and don't want to know anything. I must, in fact, be at a really loose end to pause with a listener of your sort, who interrupts me disrespectfully every time I start a sentence. Do you take me for a writer of third-rate vaudevilles? Do I look like a street poet? Know, then, that what makes the Devil the Devil—which is to say that power is power and that will is will—is, on the contrary, the inexorable logic of the Devil's thoughts and actions; for a being like me, everything holds together: the beginning, the middle and the end.

"Just now, when you turned your head away in fright from the grisettes, soubrettes, actresses, young wives and the other young people who used to be the friends and companions of your foolish youth, I explained to you that you were wrong to evoke those ten years of life, and how, if it's permissible for a man to go backwards, it's never by passing from one day to the day before—but now that I'm talking about fifty years, you stop me and say: 'That's too little.' Fool! As if those fifty years didn't include a revolution, and as if that revolution couldn't count for at least three centuries! As if, in the fifty years I'm talking about, humankind—which is to say, humans and the Devil, body and soul, thought and action—hasn't lived more than it has since the beginning of the world!

"But I'll take no notice of you, and take up my story were I left it...

"So, fifty years ago, more or less, the old French society, undermined from within, still believed itself to be eternal; it toyed with the principles that were to overturn it from top to bottom; it called that *playing with paradox*. Meanwhile, everything was standing and had maintained an appearance of strength and incredible life: the army, the Church, the city, the court, parliament, the aristocracy, the nobility and all the common people, who still trembled before the Lieutenant of Police and were afraid of the Bastille that could no longer stand up to a gust of wind. That was how things were—or, rather, how they appeared to be.

"In the midst of that organized chaos, seemingly immobile but already anticipating the hour off triumph, was an army of minds in revolt, a thousand times more formidable than the army of rebel angels about which Milton sang. Oh, Satan, Satan, if you had only had such a phalanx under your command—Voltaire, Diderot, d'Alembert, Rousseau, Montesquieu—what a hole you would have made in the celestial phalanx! But, poor devils that we were, we only had for weaponry the great cannon of which Milton speaks. In order for it to have any range, that hollow and empty cannon, it would have needed to be loaded with the pages of *Le Contrat social*."

The Devil paused. "Forgive me—I think I'm getting lost in vain dissertations. What do you expect? I have a head so full of modern novels, modern dramas, memoirs and revelations, not to mention that someone's just invented another kind of mental torture called *Histoire des salons de Paris*—it's enough to make one lose one's head—but fortunately, one has a strong head.[45]

"So, fifty years ago, more or less. Far from Paris and far from Versailles, lived an honest gentleman full of common sense and courage. He had so much sense that he had divined that, in order not to perish so quickly, the French aristocracy ought to have be defending itself and not abandon itself to pleasure. He had so much courage that he dared not resist the double invasion of philosophy and the people. In the incredible delirium that had taken possession of all the people of his class, the old Comte de Fayl-Billot—that was his name—lived alone with his sad presentiments.

"He had lost his only son at the battle of Fontenoy, and he thanked Heaven for it, for at least he knew that his name was extinct, and he had no anxieties on that score. Although his son was dead, he still had two daughters, Louise and Léonore, who were completely different in character. Louise was the angel, Léonore the demon; the one was so pure that no evil thought had ever been able to get near her head, even in a dream; the other was already perverted at fifteen. Both of them were beautiful, with a similar beauty...but I'm not going to tire myself out giving you descriptions as if I were some common-or-garden storyteller. Instead, look..."

I did, in fact, see, still with the aid of the Devil's transparent hand, in a beautiful garden of olden times, two young women of almost the same age—scarcely sixteen. I recognized Louise by the calmness of her beautiful face, by the pale transparency of her complexion, by the gleam in her eyes, as blue as the sky; I recognized Léonore by the vivacity of her

---

[45] *Histoire des Salons de Paris* was one of several long works with which Laure Junot, Duchesse d'Abrantès, the widow of one of Napoléon's generals, followed up the breezily spiteful memoirs she had published in eighteen volumes in 1831-34. When Janin wrote this passage, the history in question was still in the process of publication; the last of its six volumes did not appear until 1838.

expressions, the petulance of her stride and the impatient agitation of her entire person.

The revolution that was brooding dully in the French nation had penetrated the most hidden corners of the population; it had not stopped at the doors of temples or the thresholds of convent; it was fermenting in the youngest hearts and the most candid souls. In those days, more than one young woman stayed up late at night to read, by the light of an infernal lamp, Voltaire's *Pucelle* or Diderot's *Religieuse*; there was in every consciousness, young or old, a muffled murmur, frenetic and implacable in its opposition to received institutions. I had never understood how general that revolution of action against idea, the present against the past, and philosophy against the law, was until that moment, when I saw Léonore's face; I had never understood human beauty in all its perfection, grace in all its innocence and virtue in all its serenity until I saw Louise's sweet face.

"Now do you understand what I mean?" the Devil said.

"Yes," I told him. "Simply by seeing the two sisters, I understand that Louise is a young woman tenderly blossoming in the breath of her sixteenth spring, while Léonore is a flower violently opened to the agitation of all the interior passions."

"That's a very ambitious metaphor," the Devil told me, "of no great worth. I didn't want to demonstrate a metaphor; I wanted to prove that my story is true, although very strange. The truth of my story is proven by the faces of the two sisters—and how glad your novelists would be if they could see the faces of their heroines like that in their mind's eye! They wouldn't be reduced to giving us such long, detailed and obscure descriptions; they'd be able to see more clearly in their imagination and their intelligence.

"Unwittingly, the father of those two daughters you see there, the old Comte de Fayl-Bilot, was a philosopher, but a philosopher in his own fashion. When his two daughters were sixteen, he divined, as you've just divined, the inclinations of each of them. Obviously, Louise would be the consolation of his old age; Léonore would be its dishonor. He saw that clearly, without hesitation. He blessed Louise and was afraid of Léonore—and, just as he'd already renounced his dead son, he resolved to renounce that living daughter. In consequence, he declared to Léonore that she would no longer set foot in society and would remain in a convent, as dead as one can be without dying.

"You probably think that Léonore was frightened by this news and that she tried to change her father's mind, but hers was too firm and too energetic an intelligence to lower herself to pleading for anything whatsoever, down here or up above, especially from her father. In that general relaxation of all power, Léonore had understood very well that paternal authority was only hanging by a thread, just like royal authority. She sensed in her own consciousness that the social edifice was undermined and that it was about to fall into ruins, and she felt sure that in the midst of those ruins she would be able to find a crack wide enough for her to be able to escape and be free. She therefore told her father that she would take the veil; and, indeed, she took the veil on the very day that her sister Louise was married.

"All her life, Louise had been afraid of her sister. Léonore's sarcasm afflicted everything around her, and Louise had never understood how anyone could laugh like that at all propositions, beliefs, affections and duties. Louise was like a poor girl escaped from Saint-Cyr, from the chaste tutelage of Madame de Maintenon, suddenly finding herself catapulted into the orgies of the Regency.

"Her father, who loved her and who had invested in her all the affections of his life, married that beloved daughter to a handsome young man, the Marquis de Cintrey, who was renowned at that time for his good morals. But alas, my son, if you knew what good morals were in those days, how scornful you would be of the gilded youth of that century!

"When by chance I see your fashionable young gentleman, those you proudly cal your rakes, your debauchees, your libertines; when I compare your Lauzuns, your Richelieus of the present century, even with the valets of Monsieur le

Maréchal Duc de Richelieu, I put on a pitying smile: all those petty gentlemen, whom your era regards with admiration as the *nec plus ultra* of human roguishness, could not hold a candle to the sagest abbé of Saint-Sulpice in 1764. Those messieurs were dead drunk from the moment the eighteenth century started drinking; a single day's gabling ruined them to the third generation; they ran, from the age of ten, in a filthy circle, after half a dozen girls who were always the same, without there being any means to avoid them, even if they found a god marriage and a good position somewhere. You absolutely cannot, therefore, with the aid of today's petty messieurs, form the slightest notion of the virtue and sagacity of the Marquis de Cintrey.

"Even so, the old Comte took him for a son-in-law for want of anything better. Cintrey was proud; he didn't talk much, he was discontented with the court; he had received a large scar in the middle of his face in a duel; he was an avid reader of Letourneur's translations of Young's *Night Thoughts* and Shakespeare; he was insolent with everyone, especially his vassals; he had not subscribed to the *Encyclopédie*; he hated Voltaire and despised Rousseau; he raised his hat when he mentioned Louis XIV. Old Fayl-Billot was therefore able to believe that his dear Louise would, in fact, be very happy with a man of such noble character.

"Indeed, in the early days of their marriage, Louise considered herself to be happy and worthy of envy. At that time, good girls obeyed their father meekly; they were little disposed to fits of nerves and the vapors; they loved, without disgrace, the husbands they were ordered to love. When I see in the women in your novels, young and old, weeping and moaning and wringing their hands over a *yes* or *no* that goes against their wishes, I don't know what to think. The honest women of those licentious times were much superior to the honest women of these virtuous times.

"Louise loved her husband; she had a beautiful child by him, and her love for her husband increased. At twenty, the young woman was cited everywhere as a model of filial piety, conjugal virtue and maternal love; she had the respect of all men and the respect of all women. Unfortunate creature! She suffered a great deal!"

That exclamation of pity, in the mouth of the Devil, astonished me to the highest degree. "What's the matter with you?" I said. "It seems to me that you're weeping over virtue. Please don't be ridiculous to that extent."

"Eh? Why not?" the Devil replied. "Can't I have a good impulse from time to time? Where is the man—and I mean the most wicked—who, after having killed his enemy, doesn't feel some emotion in looking at the cadaver at his feet? Personally, I'm not so made that I suffer from both the misfortunes of honest folk and the success of the vicious; everything that's in the order of things revolts me, and also everything that's outside that order, and that's exactly what proves that I'm utterly accursed. The woman about whom I'm talking was very unfortunate; that's one of the masterpieces of my wickedness of which I'm proudest, and which saddens me the most.

"In those days, though, I only had to commit a few isolated petty crimes in order not to go rusty in idleness. In the epoch of the Revolution, events were stronger than me; I was obliged to set myself aside in order not to get carried away by that horrible whirlwind myself, along with the throne and the altar, and in order that after the tempest, something superhuman would still remain in the France of François I and Louis XIV, which I've always loved. As it wasn't given to me—I am, after all, only the Devil—to finish the French Revolution, any more than it had been given to me to start it, for it was a masterpiece beyond the reach of a power as mediocre as mine. I spotted that woman in that little corner of Paris—that Louise, beautiful, honest, esteemed, beloved and happy—and I said to myself: 'Let's leave it to more powerful intelligences to turn France upside down; that woman will suffice for me.'"

Then the Devil added: "Look—can't you see our little house suddenly sparkling with a thousand lights?"

"Yes, indeed!" At the same time, I looked, with all the strength of my soul, and saw that everything was ready in that house for a splendid party: the sculpted silver, bronze and gold; the crystals as light as air; the rarest flowers; the velvet extended over the carved wood; the lace and ivory competing in lightness and transparency.

"What cheerful forms! What sparkling masterpieces! What universal intoxication! One might think that everything in that beautiful place were smiling at you, with an eternal smile; the sofas holding out their arms to you like so many delirious prostitutes; the armchairs cradling you gently while singing drinking songs; the beautiful carpets carrying you without your touching them; satyrs dancing while carrying lighted candles; the fire-dogs trailing at your feet, charged with odorant flames; the pendulum-clock prancing gracefully and sounding the hours you love most; the gods and goddesses of fable emerging lightly from the floor, the ceiling, the walls; heads crowned with roses, belts loosened, bosoms beginning to heave gently.

"What wit! What murmurs! What sighs! What audacity! In truth, those women entering like that, holding hands, burn you merely by the sight of them. Their feet are flames that illuminate their legs to the knee; sparks spurt from their hands, and pearls fall from their hair; their necks are as slender as serpents; their throats are in delirium and their hearts are as cold as marble; the gauze hardly touches them and parts, quivering.

"Have you noticed"—by now I was addressing the Devil as *tu*—"the one who's hiding a little black mark in the crease of her smile? And the one whose mat white arm is crushing the gold that surrounds it? And the other one, smiling like a madwoman? And the other one, admiring herself in the shiny mirror, turning her head languidly to look at her shoulder, devouring her own beauty with a lewd eye, as far as a gaze can go! Oh, let's end it, let's end it! I'm succumbing! I'm dying..."

Saying those words, I cast that intoxicating spectacle far away; the Devil was enjoying my astonishment and my emotion.

"Isn't it the case, young man," he said, in a mocking tone, "that in those days we understood a little better than you do today all the paraphernalia of pleasure and amour? We were past masters in all the fine details of celebration and joy. By our luxury alone we were recognizable as people born amid gold, grandeur and silk; we were natural gentlefolk—and since then, you've only seen miserable counterfeits of our princes and vices of old.

"Pour petty bourgeois that you are! I've often laughed on seeing you go to great pains to arrange an eighteenth century for your use in a few separate rooms in a five-floor house. My petty messieurs, you can gild and regild your old furniture as much as you like, you can order brand new sofas, but neither your paintings nor your velvets resemble our paintings and velvets. And even when you succeed in imitating a little of all that luxury you see there, it's a joke! You introduce into your homes dressmakers, the wives of bailiffs or notaries' clerks: a paltry, ridiculous and far from amorous parody of human dignity!"

Thus spoke the Devil. I, however, was no longer listening, and, entirely given over to the spectacle that I had before my eyes, I watched. When the fête had been fully prepared, pretty omen, indecently clad, entered pell-mell along with handsome young men, witty and stylish in their finesse. All the fine manners of high society were deployed at ease in the rich salons; invisible and hurried servants set the table; the wine, the flowers, the ice-cream, the game-birds enveloped in brilliant plumage, all the things that smile naturally in glass, in porcelain, around the chandeliers, around the women, were smiling on the table with an abandonment that was the ultimate in artistry; never had all those splendors appeared to me so vividly, even in my dreams of summer.

"My God!" I said to the Devil. "I understand now why all those people died without complaint; they knew what life was worth; they had picked all its flowers, emptied all its cups, studied and squandered one by one, or all at the same time, all graces, all voluptuousnesses, all nudities My God! It isn't so difficult to die when one has arrived thus at the highest point, where one can display wit, revolt, pride, power, egotism and scorn for everything but oneself!"

"I will point out to you," the Devil relied, "that your interjection 'My God!' isn't polite, in addressing my person. It wasn't so long ago that I would have been obliged to disappear brutally at the mere pronunciation of that word, leaving behind me a strong odor of roast flesh. The progress of the century and the annihilation of every species of prejudice had fortunately dispensed me from that ceremony. More than that—if you were to make the sign of the cross with holy water, my duty as a well-brought-up devil would be to take no notice. However, I warn you that the thing isn't very agreeable to me, for the simple reason that one doesn't like to talk about people with whom one has fallen out.

"You poor fool, though! As for what you say about that life of feasting and opulence, I find it, in truth, utterly insane. If you knew what miseries those smiles hide, what vanities those velvets conceal, what plaintive moans those sofas have heard! It's not me who'll draw you a moral, but if I cared to lift a corner of that silky and nonchalant drapery, what tortures you'd see! All the young people you see there, I loved them dearly; they were my companions and my brothers; I fought with their épées, I ran around town under their cloaks, I borrowed their white hands, their armories and their faces to tame, to seduce, to doom forever more than one blushing innocence that was lost as eyes were closed. More than once, behind the masks of those petty marquises, whose grandparents had been scythed down by Cardinal Richelieu, and who were awaiting the scaffold themselves, I lost myself at the Opéra ball, quite simply seeking the Queen of France...

"And yet, while sharing in all their disorders, I cried out within myself: 'The imbeciles! How they're losing themselves in pleasure! They have neither pity not respect for themselves! All the privileges that their forefathers heaped up at the cost of so many perils and so many eternal damnations, they're throwing to the wind, as if, tomorrow, they were going to be masters of that dust and say to it: *Obey us!* The insensate fools! They don't even think of defending themselves against the roaring beast they have unleashed, and which they call *the people!* They play with the lion as if the lion had no claws and teeth! To amuse themselves without danger in such orgies, which doom the past and present of a people simultaneously, it would be necessary to be, like me, almost eternal.'

"That's why, even in those mad nights of debauchery, if you cared to look into their depths, you'd find something sad and fearful..."

Here the Devil started laughing at his own moral.

I, however, was still gazing into that house filled with light, with passionate silence, with gluttony, wit and amour. All the young people invited to the feast had arrived; only one was still missing, and it already appeared that no one wanted to wait for him any longer, when we suddenly saw him arrive.

He was a man still young, of a severe aspect. He had adopted a serious attitude early in life, and he conserved that grave appearance even in an orgy. He was dressed in black; his épée was not tied down; his wig was almost devoid of powder. He took incredible care to moderate the vivacity of his gaze and the gaiety of his smile; he was one of the Tartuffes of the era—for, alas, all eras have their Tartuffes—except that in those days, virtue was no longer a devoted virtue, it was an austere virtue. He had renounced the hair shirt along with the disciplinary whip, in order to cover himself with the mantle of Brutus and the hat of William Penn.

The man was very curious to study. His friends and his mistresses accepted all that humor very well. In general, there is in hypocrisy an almost supernatural omnipotence that makes one accept it, almost in spite of oneself, and no one—not even a drunken whore—can or dare tackle it head on. It's an idea that might have come from the genius of Molière to put Alceste, his misanthrope, at odds not with Philinte but with Tartuffe. It's a meager glory for Alceste, that of crushing Philinte—especially a Philinte defenseless against his competitor's brutality—but what an admirable spectacle it would have been to see Alceste unmasking Tartuffe! There are two rude jousters who would have been able to fight with equal weapons! But I don't know whether the misanthropy of the one was worthy to fight a duel against the hypocrisy of the other.

Anyway, since Molière didn't do it, it must be the case that it's impossible. In fact, hypocrisy will always be bolder and more powerful than virtue. The hypocrite is as clever as the virtuous man, but he has his rascality as well. He has studied virtue so carefully, if only in order to adopt its attitude, its language and all its external appearances, that he knows its strengths and weaknesses, and most often attacks it with its own weapons. Add that virtue disquiets vice, while hypocrisy reassures it. A vicious person is never more at ease than when in company with a hypocrite; they understand one another marvelously, protect one another and defend one another; the hypocrite lends the vicious individual his mask, and the vicious individual lends him his mistresses; when the vicious individual totters, the hypocrite supports him, and when he falls, he covers him with his cloak. Thus, even in a society lost to vice, there are hypocrites.

One of the most skillful hypocrites of those times was the austere and gallant seigneur who had just come in, the Marquis de Cintrey.

"Now," the Devil said to me, when his[46] literary dissertation was complete, "do you understand what is about to happen?"

"In truth, no," I replied, "for you've promised me a story that won't be a vulgar story, and thus far I've seen nothing but a petty house, a set table, a splendid supper, Opéra girls, young men with bulging eyes, powder, beauty-spots, pretty

---

[46] Janin was occasionally wont to lose track in the course of his philosophical dialogues of exactly who was saying what, partly because he was writing in haste and partly because he was, in essence, always debating with himself, even—perhaps especially—when using the Devil as a mouthpiece.

feet, fatigued faces, shining eyes, pearls stirring over heaving bosoms—in a word something splendid and magnificent in its form, but fundamentally, something as trivial as one of Monsieur Ancelot's vaudevilles."[47]

"Do you see now," the Devil went on, "there, to the left, a poor woman who is slipping, tremulously, into that dimly-lit boudoir? See how pale she is! It's impossible to have a whiter skin, a sleeker neck, a better-formed arm, a smaller hand; it's impossible, too, to have more sadness in the soul, more despair in the heart. Yes, certainly, that woman is beautiful; you recognize her, of course: it's Louise, the Marquise de Cintrey!"

"I believe," I exclaimed, "that I'm beginning to understand. Madame de Cintrey, a young woman in love with her husband and unworthily deceived, a poor woman driven by jealousy, has come alone, at his hour, to this soiled house, in order finally to learn the full extent of her misfortune."

"You'll never understand anything," said the Devil, "if you always want to get ahead of me. Come on, declare a truce on wit and intelligence; don't be like those idiots who whisper eloquent words to Monsieur Thiers from their places when Monsieur Thiers is at the Tribune. Monsieur Thiers knows better than they do, doesn't he? And I know almost as much as Monsieur Thiers.[48]

---

[47] Jacques-François Ancelot (1794-1854) was a clerk in the Admiralty who wrote tragedies, including Louis IX (1819), which earned him a generous pension from Louis XVIII, but he lost his pension and his status in the July Revolution and had to write vaudevilles thereafter to get by.

[48] Adolphe Thiers (1797-1877), one of the prime movers of the July Revolution, served the first of his three terms as prime minister in 1836. Janin was not to know that he would be relegated to the political wilderness after 1840, until his return as President of the Republic in 1871, after the fall of the Second Empire and the Commune.

"Look, now, on the other side of the wall, at the obscure and terrible side of the house, at that nun who is abandoned, all alone, to the most violent fit of the most frightful despair: she is crying out, blaspheming, wringing her hands in rage, foaming at the mouth!

"Yes, yes!" I exclaimed, alarmed. "Through those thick walls and in that dense shadow, dimly lit by a sepulchral lamp...oh, it's frightful to see and hear! How beautiful the woman is, too—but she's fighting like a lioness. At her feet, a pitcher has tipped water over some black bread. A death's-head, smiling hideously, is placed beside the lamp, the somber light of which fades away in those hollow eyes and strays insensibly over those gleaming teeth. One might think it were a soul in torment playing the *De profundis* on those enamel keys. In a corner of the wall, above that disordered straw pallet, a frightful bloody crucifix looms up, and even into that holy image the inquisitor who sculpted it has found the means of putting more wrath than indulgence. It's all quite horrible. The unfortunate woman is wearing a cilice that is bruising her beautiful flesh, and yet it seems to me that the marble throat is on the point of breaking that terrible mesh. The woman's hair is full of straw; her gaze is full of fever; her heat is full of rage...who is that woman, then?

"Who do you think she is?" said the Devil, shifting his weight from one leg to the other. "It's Léonore."

I was moved to the highest degree; the drama whose heart I was thus approaching took possession of me passionately; I told myself that I was, indeed, about to witness something strange and bold.

Suddenly, however, the Devil took his hand away and disappeared like a puff of smoke carried away by the wind, and I no longer had anything before my eyes but the confused shadows of the palace and lairs plunged into an impenetrable darkness.

The Devil had abandoned me thus at the critical pint of his story. Even the cigar that he had given me, which I had been smoking voluptuously, had reverted to an insipid piece of wood.

Left alone, I went back down from the disenchanted heights as best I could, opening my eyes without seeing anything, pricking up my ears without hearing anything, pursued by a thousand bizarre visions and a thousand confused noises, searching in vain for a denouement for the story that had been poised between virtue and vice, between austerity and debauchery, between the straw of the dungeon and the sofa of the boudoir.

Several days went by before I saw my fantastic historian again. I regretted, albeit with an indescribable thrill of fear, the mordant irony and the brisk and mocking tone of the damned individual who could see so profoundly into all the twists and turns of the human soul. To chase after him, to summon and invoke him by a magical incantation was very old and hackneyed. Besides, which, what would be the point? The Devil is like poetic inspiration; he's not at anyone's beck and call. He goes, he comes, he pauses, he goes away and comes back when he wishes. Where is the great poet who can say to himself, when he gets up in the morning happy and refreshed by the night's dreams: *Today I shall be a poet*? Where, again, is the man who can say to himself with certainty: *This evening I shall see the Devil*? But I saw the Devil again one evening, when I was not expecting it.

The evening was calm and serene. I was standing on the terrace at Belle-Vue, a noble dismantled château that has been divided between several bourgeois housewives who do their best to play the role of princesses of the blood.[49] Suddenly, I saw a slim and vigorous young woman by my side, who seemed to be sharing my mute contemplation. Her pale face

---

[49] The Château de Bellevue at Meudon, built in 1750 for Madame de Pompadour, and subsequently occupied by three daughters of the late Louis XV, was demolished in 1823 and new residential buildings were erected on the site.

was magnificently illuminated by two large dark flashing eyes; that burning gaze plunged down on Paris with a feverish ardor. In that new disguise, I recognized the Devil.

"That's very fortunate!" I said. "I've finally found you again, Monseigneur. Why, then, did you leave like that the other day, when I was listening to you with the greatest attention? It's a miserably petty oratorical artifice unworthy of an intelligence like yours."

"You're taking a very familiar tone!" Satan replied. "But who are you to have a storyteller like me at your orders? A fine job, to have to amuse Monsieur! Do you take me, then, for your Basile or your Grippe-Soleil?[50] Anyway, why are you so unintelligent? If you haven't seen me sooner"—as he spoke those words he flashed me a half-smile so full of intelligence as to be terrifying—"it certainly isn't my fault. Since the night you mention I haven't left you, but you've never wanted to recognize me. Do you remember, the other day, the old bookseller who sold you Apicius' treatise *De re culinaria* for its weight in gold? That was me! And the old woman who brought you that anonymous letter full of insults and bad grammar? That was me! I was close to you the other evening when that young woman of twenty came into the theater whom passion had paled and curbed, who bore without succumbing to it all the genius of Meyerbeer—but you scarcely paid attention to her.

"I was close to you yesterday morning when you were reading that elegy by Tibullus in which he speaks of the beautiful Neaera, but at the most touching point of the elegy the book fell from your hands. In the bushy wood where the Parisian beauties come to dance you saw me carrying away, in the rapid whirl of the waltz, that frail Spanish girl whose shoulders shone like lightning; you scarcely deigned to dart a distracted glance at us. So, it's entirely your own fault is you ha-

---

[50] The music-master Basile and the shepherd Grippe-Soleil are gossip-supplying characters in Beaumarchais' *Mariage de Figaro*.

ven't encountered me in your path. At least, however, you divine my presence when you have need of me; it would be too embarrassing if I were obliged to tap you on the shoulder and say: *I'm the Devil*."

As the Devil was speaking, the night descended more somberly over the great city of Paris, and gradually, I saw the two-part stage light up in that transparent shadow on which the strange drama of which I had been the witness was being enacted. This time, however, I no longer saw anything but the remains of the feast; the door that separated the boudoir from the cell was hermetically sealed; the nun had disappeared; among the guests, who were drunk, a newcomer was sitting, a woman who seemed to dominate that delirium while taking part in it.

"Ha ha!" said the Devil. "Now you're embarrassed, because in what you see there you no longer understand very much of my work. Poor petty intelligence, who can't divine anything! Provincial spectator for whom it's necessary to light the Argand lamps and the chandelier, who needs decorations and costumes! It's always the same with those who are obliged to read the comedy that's been acted for them! That's the way you're made, my worthy fellow! Fortunately, I'm here to explain the scene to you, half of which is already in the shadows. So listen...

"Louise, the young and beautiful Marquise de Cintrey, wife and mother, had soon understood that all the conjugal felicities had come to an end. In vain, her husband, the Marquis de Cintrey, was cited in society as a ridiculous and sublime model of fidelity and constancy; Louise soon realized what she ought to think of that virtue. It was a frightful blow for the poor woman: she believed in her husband's love as she believed in God. In that universal shipwreck of all the domestic sentiments, Louise regarded her household as a place of refuge that was still afloat. Around her and alongside her, Louise saw nothing but corruption, disorder, broken and reconnected unions, adulteries, lies, perfidies and all sorts of vices, pell-mell, eating, laughing and drinking together, taking one another, leaving one another and retaking one another alternately, without choice, without taste and without measure—but she, poor woman, had believed, had hoped, that she might be saved from that disorder.

"As I've said, however, her husband was a hypocrite. He soon wearied of his feigned virtue and quite his wife for other women. I knew about those adventures from the start; I warned Louise, and I made her jealous; I led her by the hand to that den of debauchery; I placed her in that discreet little apartment, from which she could see and hear everything—and, indeed, she saw those men and women, she heard their tender words, she understood all that unrestrained audacity of the mind and the heart. She was afraid for her husband, when she saw how similar he was to all those men. She stayed there, however, mute, desolate, insensible; and I confess that I no longer knew what to make of that woman with her mute despair, when an admirable idea suddenly occurred to me—one of those ideas that you call *infernal ideas* without being fully aware of what you're saying."

Then, as if he were talking to himself, he said: "Yes indeed, that was well done, Satan! And if you wish, you can make it into a fine melodrama for the Théâtre-Français!"

He went on: "Yes, it was quite a *coup de théâtre*. You'll recall that alongside the little redoubt where Louise was hiding, lending an ear to that conversation of skeptical libertines, mingling lust with blasphemy, was the cell where Léonore was waiting in vain every day for the liberating revolution that she had promised herself but which hadn't arrived. I'll make Léonore's story as short as Louise's...

"Scarcely had she entered the convent than Léonore became frightened and began to doubt her imminent liberation. So long as she hadn't pronounced her eternal vows, she'd been sure of the total ruination of all established institutions, and she'd looked forward secretly to finding herself free again amid that universal upheaval of which she had no doubt.

"Once captive, however, veiled and cloistered, she was no longer her own mistress; she no longer had the patience to wait for the times predicted in the *Encyclopédie*; that mind, in secret rebellion, rebelled openly. She had the terrible fever of a robust young woman devoured by passion and seared by doubt, subject to the simultaneous revolt of the mind and the flesh. Thus, she soon became an object of fear in the convent, which had conserved all the rigidity of the order, a subject of terror among those saintly women, all the more inexorable because they could foresee the collapse of the celestial Jerusalem.

"Soon, therefore, all the rigors of the cloister weighed upon Léonore: fasting, vigils, prayers, the cilice, the whips. Nothing worked; she was indomitable. Frenzy gripped her several times a day, and then she tore off her habit, her veil, her shroud, and in that complete nudity she defied Heaven, and invoked men. Often, in the middle of the choir, by night, when the Mother Abbess was intoning matins, Léonore, raising her voice, recited the most violent passages of her beloved philosophers.

"Several times, the chapter was assembled to pronounce on the fate of the unfortunate; she was condemned to the oubliette. By dint of starvation and blows she was reduced to silence; she was covered with a mortuary veil, the *De profundis* was pronounced over her; she was lowered to the sepulcher that you have seen, and they gave her no further thought except to send her a pitcher of water and some back bread every day.

"That was the moment at which I opened the hidden door that separated the dungeon from the boudoir, and the two sisters found themselves together."

At this point the Devil started crumpling, in a very dainty fashion, a little embroidered handkerchief that he was holding in his left hand; then, suddenly, as if he were tired of playing the role of a woman—which he was playing rather badly—he resumed his original form: the form of a tall young man, indolent, bold and rather badly-built. Then, abruptly placing himself in front of me, he continued.

"I shall describe with regret, for my personal amusement and not for pity's sake, that terrible scene between the two sisters; I'll never see its like again. That door, contrived long ago by a mysterious amour, had been locked for a long time; it suddenly opened under the efforts of the recluse, aided by me. Then, Léonore, beaten, famished, bewildered, bloodied and whipped, finding herself in the presence of Louise, so free, so happy and so richly adorned a short while before, could scarcely retain herself from devouring her sister.

"'Oh!' she cried. "You're here! You've just been listening, sitting here on silk, to my cries of agony on the straw! Oh, dressed up are you are, you've come to see, through the cracks in my cell, how pale I am, and thin, and feverish! A curse, a curse, a curse upon you! There's no God in Heaven; there's no father on earth!'

"Saying these words, Léonore stood in front of Louise, and Louise closed her eyes.

"At that moment, the guests next door were singing a drinking song, and those horrible cries did not reach them.

"Meanwhile Louise, bewildered but calm, had gradually opened her eyes, and made sure that it really was her sister. Yes, it was her sister, as truly as that was her husband in the grip of wine and indecent amour—for, while contemplating Léonore, Louise, cocking an ear, could hear her husband celebrating wine and the love of whores. Thus placed between two miseries, the unfortunate woman did not hesitate any longer.

"'Since you envy me so much,' she said to her sister, 'and since I envy you so much, would you care to exchange roles with me, Léonore? My boudoir for your cell; my lace for your cilice; my husband, who is in there'—she pointed to the dining-room 'for your crucifix and that death's-head; my rich clothes for your coarse robe; my liberty for your slavery? Would you like that?'"

The Devil stopped, as if he were seeking to recall Louise's voice, gestures and imploring inflections.

Impatiently, however, I said: "Well? What happened?"

"What happened is that Léonore agreed to the exchange. She took off her cilice in order to put on Louise's clothes; she threw Louise into the cell and on to that disordered straw; she closed the iron door again, and over the closed door she pulled a thick silk curtain.

"It was done: Louise was the recluse; Léonore was free! After which she cast a glance over the shiny pier-glasses, and smiled delightedly at her own beauty, of which she had been long deprived. She plunged her hands and face into limpid water prepared for the guests; she decorated her sister's chaste clothes as best she could, striving to render them immodest. Then, when she was thus fully-armed, she heard the Marquis de Cintrey drinking an ironic toast to the health of his wife— and, abruptly opening the door to the dining-room, she cried: 'Here I am!'

"You can imagine the astonishment of those men and women, plunged into drunkenness, at the sudden appearance of the chaste and honest Louise, who came into their midst half-naked, demanding something to drink. Indeed, Léonore resembled Louise as the Devil resembles an angel; she had the same slim and supple figure, the same fire in her gaze, the same face. Louise had not often gone into society; society had seen her at a distance, without daring to get too close to that inaccessible virtue; so all the guests imagined that it was indeed the Marquise, who was finally throwing away the imposing mask of virtue. Even the Marquis thought so, but it must be admitted that his head was reeling.

"A drink! A drink!" cried Léonore. "At the same time she threw herself, famished and delirious, upon the wine and the meats. She looked at the men; she embraced the women; she was already drunk, with the double intoxication of wine and the flesh. Never, in the muddy hollow of her cell, in her iron cilice, on her putrid straw, in the presence of her death's-head, in the most violent moments of her dementia and indefatigable blasphemy, had the wretch dreamed of so much indecent porcelain, so many naked breasts, so many avid gazes, so many wines and so many flowers. In the midst of that disorder she felt that she was finally born; she was like a fury, but beautiful and powerful.

"And, indeed, I shall let you be the judge of whether that was an incredible transition: to pass thus from a Christian dungeon to a Voltairean orgy! She did such things and said such things in that initial delirium of enthusiasm and passion that she even frightened the guests, as if lightning were about to strike them; more than one of them, who voluntarily abandoned the orgy, hid their eyes and wanted to flee the damned soul; the bravest among them gazed at her in bewilderment, not daring to speak.

When Léonore had drunk and eaten, she said: 'Who's going to sing us a drinking song, then?' To a young pupil of Mademoiselle Duthé,[51] already worthy of her mistress, she said: 'Is it you, my darling?'

"Then she sang a song of revolt that she had composed to the rhythm of an ode by Piron,[52] the music of which she had composed with the aid of the *De profundis*, which she parodied as best she could. At the same time, she emptied all the cups polluted by all those licentious lips, ripped away all the flowers that were still veiling a few dubious nudities; then,

---

[51] Rosalie Duthé (1748-1830) was one of the most celebrated courtesans of her era, who danced at the Opéra and was much in demand among artists as a nude model, with the result that she is still on display in several of the world's great museums. She was acquainted with the future Charles X, and Louis-Philippe was said to have introduced her to his fifteen-year-old son in order that she might teach him "the facts of life"—but as her "memoirs" were forged after her death by Étienne Lamothe-Langon, the latter anecdote might not be entirely reliable

[52] The dramatist Alexis Piron (1689-1773) was kicked out of the Academy in 1753 when his enemies called Louis XV's attention to an obscene "Ode à Priape" [Ode to Priapus] that he had composed in his youth.

when she had exhausted all those terrible excesses, Léonore started singing and dancing at the same time.

"She had invented in her dungeon a certain Oriental dance, all of whose poses she had designed with the lustful exactitude of a bayadere and the vindictive perseverance of a nun who feels her flesh tremble under the double impact of the disciplinary whip and ill-contained passions. When she had danced, she asked where her husband was. He was pointed out to her, lying on the floor, prostrated by admiration, astonishment and drunkenness, not knowing whether he was dreaming or awake. She went straight to him, looked down at him lying at her feet, and found that he was young and handsome.

"'So, Marquis,' she said to him, 'I'm yours, the harvest of virtue and good morals. There's no God in Heaven, and nothing on earth but dupes and rogues. I've been your dupe and my own for long enough. I thought you were a philosopher, you took me for a virtuous woman; we were both mistaken; we're quits. So, throw away that tedious mask and, as you sang a little while ago, let's enjoy life! Can you hear the earth quaking beneath our feet? It's the signal for a fête that is going to swallow us all...'

"After saying these words, she called the prostitutes 'my friends,' invited the men to a feast at her house the following day, and arranged to meet them all at the Opéra; she escorted both parties to their carriages. And finally, left alone with her husband, she said: 'Monsieur Monsieur, why hide ourselves now? We'll indulge our vice in the open, if you please. I demand, therefore, that you give me the keys to the little house, in order that it can remain closed, being henceforth unnecessary to our hypocrisy.'

"And thus it was that she took possession of the keys of the little house, in order that no one could go into it except for her. The Marquis took her back to his town house, in broad daylight."

Having concluded this tirade, the Devil looked at me in order to see what I was thinking. In truth, I was more emotional than I could say. I understood, confusedly, all poor

Louise's misery, buried alive and innocent in the oubliettes of a Carmelite convent; I understood, confusedly, all the rascality of Léonore, suddenly emerging from her tomb to take the place, the name, the face and the honor of an honest woman—and yet, I had a great need for the Devil to explain all those horrors to me.

"Yes," he went on, "it happened the way you think. Frightened Parisian society was informed the following day of the sudden excesses of the Marquise de Cintrey. People recounted, but still in whispers, how the woman in question, surrounded by all the respect of men and women, had abruptly cast off the mask of virtue that covered her face; how, to commence her new career, she had done the honors of a horrible feast of debauchees in her husband's little house, and shocked the vilest whores with her disorders.

"People lost themselves in a thousand conjectures on the subject; bets were laid for and against; there was a duel. Soon, however, all doubts fell away before the scandalous conduct of the woman in question. She was an unchained lioness; she shocked the city and the court with her excesses; she threw her husband's fortune to the wind; she was devoid of pity and respect for anyone.

"Her father, the old Comte de Fayl-Billot, was on his death-bed. The old nobleman, before quitting a life full of anxieties, was counting, at least, on the support, the prayers and the last and pious smile of his beloved daughter; he called for Louise, his Louise!

"His Louise was in the dungeon, but instead of the saint he saw Léonore come in. O terror! She retained her vengeance, however. She asked to be left alone with her father. No one knows what passed between the old man and that woman, but after that fatal and final conversation, the old man was found dead in his bed, his hands raised toward Heaven, as if he were demanding justice.

"What can I tell you? Never had insolence, vanity, pride and scorn for divine laws gone so far. I'm talking to you with self-satisfaction, you see, for that woman was my masterpiece, the equal of the Marquise de Merteuil. Thanks to her. I contested with the work of that Laclos, of who I was jealous.[53] More than that: I hoped to compete with Danton, and later with Robespierre, saying to them: 'Behold my masterpiece!' Insensate that I was!"

Here the Devil suffered a shudder of horror, evidently excited by the horrible names of Danton and Robespierre. I felt sorry for the poor loser, who was no longer good for anything but telling stories. In order to distract him from his sad reflections, I said: "But in the end," I said, "where are you going with this?"

"Oh," he said, "there's nothing simpler. You know what happened when the Bastille was taken, and how '89 raced toward '93, and how all the orgies of power and beauty were interrupted at a stroke, and how proscription extended over the entirety of France, like the plague, but more rapidly and more ferociously. You've read all that in books, but you didn't see it, and even those who have recalled those bloody events didn't see them, for, before such horrible spectacles, all courage remains in suspense, all thought stops and every voice becomes mute. Well, in that general proscription, the people, who had their moments of justice came one day to stand beneath the windows of the Marquise de Cintry and demand the head of that soiled and stained woman, as if the head were innocent and pure. The Marquise was not at home that day, and no one, not even the domestics, who she beat, or the maidservants, whom she insulted, or her creditors, whom she ruined, could say where she'd gone.

"Do you know where that woman was hiding?"

Here the Devil placed himself astride the iron bar that serves the admirable terrace of Belle-Vue, where I was listen-

---

[53] The Marquise de Merteuil is the vicious anti-heroine of *Les Liaisons dangereuses* (1782; tr. as Dangerous Liaisons) by Pierre Chodelos de Laclos, the definitive portrait of the decadence of the pre-Revolutionary aristocracy.

ing to him, as a balustrade. I thought he was about to cast himself down, into the cloud that rose up gently to our height.

"In fact," he went on, "I might as well finish my story now. You'll recall that the woman in question, that Léonore, had taken the keys to the little house and kept them, as the jailer does of the doors of a prison Well, to escape the popular fury, the woman had gone back to that house; she'd gone back to the hidden door that led to the dungeon. She'd opened that door and had seen her sister Louise kneeling in the straw, praying to God."

After a pause, the Devil went on: "I'm only a demon, but I wept. Yes, I wept on hearing Louise speak to her sister.

"'My good sister,' Louise said. 'I knew that you'd come back to me and that you hadn't condemned me to an eternal prison. I've suffered a great deal; I've done a great deal of penance in your place; I've prayed for you a great deal, my sister! How many years have passed in that suffering? I don't know, alas, but it seems to me that it's been a century. When I was plunged alive into this tomb, I had a husband, and I had a child. Where are they?

"'Oh, my sister, my sister! Oh, Léonore! What crimes had you committed, then, to be condemned to this penitence? But finally, here you are; I forgive you. You've come to return the open air and my child to me; I'll forget that I have suffered. Adieu, then…but know, however, my sister, that your prison will soon be open. I've been instructed by my jailer every day; she has begged me, in the name of Heaven, to be patient, saying that the hour of forgiveness is about to sound. Oh, thank you, thank you, Léonore!'

"And, indeed, Léonore put on Louise's rags. Louise covered herself with Léonore's clothes; she fled that house, where she had suffered so much. Léonore threw herself down on the straw of her dungeon and breathed more easily, feeling far away from the people...

"But what do you expect me to say? Is it really necessary to go on?"

"Yes, certainly!" I cried. "What a sad mania, to cut your story short at the very moment when it becomes gripping! You've stolen that singular fashion of narration from that charming devil known as Ariosto, but he wouldn't have dared to undertake stories like yours. You, however, who dare to begin them, ought not to be afraid to finish them."

"Then I will," said the Devil. "So, Louise, having been freed, scarcely escaped from that fatal house, was returning to her town-house at a run. Already, she could see her husband, and she was saying to him: 'I forgive you...' Already, she was embracing her son, the child she had left so small; she was falling into her father's arms, and pressing her lips to his venerable white hair.

"Thus agitated by a thousand thoughts that were dividing her heart, the poor woman did not notice any of what was happening around her, nor the unchained people who were parading their insolent victory everywhere in the newly-conquered capital, nor the cries of agony that were resounding in the streets, nor the images of a funereal liberty drenched in blood, nor the horrible scaffolds erected in the public squares, awaiting their daily prey. She was running, breathlessly, and already the Brutus of the crossroads had marked out with his finger as a victim.

"She finally arrived at her husband's house. At the sight of her, the entire indignant street rose up, a thousand cries of death were heard. At the moment when she set foot on her beloved threshold, frightful men armed with pikes and coifed in red bonnets took hold of her; the mob cried: 'That's her! That's the Marquise de Cintrey! Down with the vicious slut! Down with the pitiless tyrant! Death to the parricide!'

"In the midst of all that noise and fury, what could she do, poor woman? She looked, she listened, she drove that horrible dream far away from her eyes, her ears and her mind. She was carried away unconscious, and when she woke up, and found herself on the straw of a dungeon, she was reassured, and she said to herself: 'What a horrible dream!'

"While Louise woke up, only to return to the sleep of death, Léonore, already impatient, ran out of the house in her nun's habit, shouting: 'Help! Help!' At those screams, the people arrived; they were everywhere, the people. Léonore told them who she was; that she belonged to the convent that is now in ruins; that she had been forgotten ten years ago in a dungeon, where implacable fanaticism had kept her imprisoned; and that she had fled just now, and here she was demanding justice. The people replied to her with the word *Vengeance*.

"The convent, half, destroyed, was searched again from top to bottom. A few miserable women who were hiding in the ruins were discovered, and their severed heads soon served as trophies for Léonore's triumph. The people cried: 'Long live Léonore!' and she was carried in triumph to the house that she had quit the day before as a fugitive.

"Do you know my story now?"

"Yes," I replied, "yes. Now I know it in its entirety, that catastrophic story, and I can finish it without you. Thus, twice over, the horrible Léonore cast down the gentle Louise. While Louise was wearing Léonore's cilice, Léonore wore Louise's party dresses; while Louise prayed and fasted in Léonore's stead, Léonore heaped up on Louise all manner of maledictions and opprobrium; on the day when the people wanted to render justice to Léonore, Léonore expelled Louise from her cell and delivered her to the people in her stead. Oh, that's a frightful story!"

"All the more frightful," said the Devil, "because in those days, human justice was violent, and did not stop once it was unleashed. Oh, it's a dismal sovereign, Terror; it degrades the noblest, causes the bravest to go pale, throws the most intelligent into panic. It made the entire French nation into the most stupid butcher's meat that was ever driven to the abattoir.

"So, no sooner had Louise de Cintrey replied to the Revolutionary Tribunal that she was indeed the Marquise de Cintrey than she immediately heard herself condemned to death, and that was that."

169

The Devil added: "The most beautiful aspect of the crime is that, on the day when Louise climbed into the fatal tumbrel that was to carry her to the Place de la Grève, cursed by her husband, cursed by her son, her sister Léonore was carried in triumph as a saint; she was proclaimed a martyr, and she blessed the people. I think she even had the courage to bless her sister, who was going to the scaffold.

"That's the whole of my story. Are you content?"

When I saw that the Devil had nothing more to say to me, and that my curiosity had to be satisfied, I felt much more at ease with the Devil.

"To tell you the truth, Seigneur Devil," I replied, "you've gone to a great deal of trouble to make your story something full of interest and pity, but you've missed your goal. If anyone is to be pitied in all this, it's you. What! The most terrible revolution ever to change the face of the world falls upon France, and you can find nothing better to amuse yourself than to doom a poor virtuous woman, to the profit of a horrible criminal. You must be very idle. So, with heads being cut off by the hundred, you say to yourself, like Pilate: 'I wash my hands of it.' That frightful phrase, an egotistical comment, with which all crimes are accomplished! And you, meanwhile, are only occupied with a trick worthy, at the most, of a fairground conjuror! I can assure you that you are, at present, a far from dangerous individual."

"And you're right, Master," retorted the Devil, "all the more so because, even in the subaltern mischief that I permitted myself, I was beaten by the red-bonnets. They too, on hearing the story of the Marquise de Cintrey, would have been jealous of me. To put an end to my diabolical pretensions once and for all, can you imagine that they cut off the head of the king's sister, Madame Élisabeth?

"That day, I confessed myself utterly defeated; I recognized that I was no longer the Devil, and that all my malevolent power had been permanently overtaken; I felt sorry for myself when I compared myself to the least of those executioners. I repented of having doomed, without gaining anything in my own esteem, that saintly woman Madame de Cintrey; and if anything consoled me, it was the thought that in those horrible times, even if I had had spared her, that virtuous woman would have had no chance of escaping the guillotine.

"Furthermore, you'll see that I'm not as weak as you say; never have I regretted more not being human, in order to have had the honor of sending Louis XVI. Marie-Antoinette, Charlotte Corday and Monsieur de Malesherbes to the same scaffold. Since that time, I've led the saddest life that any demon has ever led on earth. Incapable of evil, incapable of good, agitated by remorse, poor and alone, weary of heaping up the souls that throw themselves at my head, being no longer loved or hated, I've ended up making myself a historian, an author, a novelist...what do I know?

"Perhaps I'll end up running a reading-room. In my idleness, having no more evil deeds to commit, I imagine them; I search in the crowd for the men the crowd listens to, and I tell them strange stories. At present, I'm like all poets, sometimes in the heavens, sometimes below ground; I have my moments of prophetic inspiration, and my hours of mortal discouragement.

"While all Europe was in arms with the emperor—what means was there of plying the Devil's trade with such a man as that?—I lifted up on to my knee, with a more-than-paternal solicitude, a beautiful English child that I made into a poet; it was me who dictated to him, from end to end, his poem *Don Juan*. Well, scarcely was my poet cherished than he threw into the souls of his contemporaries more desolation and dread than even Voltaire had thrown into them. Then my poet let himself die because he discovered one day that that he was slightly lame in the left foot and weighed ten pounds more than he had the year before!

"When I lost him, I lost all my poetic verve; I've been living from day to day like a freelance writer: I turn out dramas at which people laugh and vaudevilles at which they shed tears. I've tried my hand at all sorts of frivolous things, as best

I could; I've often got drunk with my friend Theodor, who's dead and in Heaven now. Now, here I am, more alone than ever, telling my stories like a man talking nonsense, stories adapted to the dreariness of the present day. Where, alas, are the times of my wandering expeditions over the rooftops of Spanish cities, when I was the devil on two sticks?"

As he spoke these words, the Devil stood up straight on the light iron bar on which he had been sitting astride.

"What became of that frightful Léonore?" I asked him.

"She died before 1830," he replied, "in an odor of sancti- ty, loudly imploring Heaven to be merciful to her sister Louise. Louise's ashes have been cast to the winds; Léonore rests beneath a marble slab covered with golden tears. She's been canonized since the July Revolution."

So saying, the Devil plunged into the thick cloud and disappeared, uttering the plaintive sigh of a mere mortal.

THE MAGNETIZED CORPSE

With regard to good stories, here is one that was told to me by a trustworthy man, who claimed to be the friend of a friend of an eye-witness who played a significant role in the drama that I am about to relate to you briefly, not without making the ardent wish that the story in question might be honored before long by an adaptation for the theater—which is, as everyone knows, the greatest honor that can be desired nowadays.

Not six weeks ago, a young Englishman named Belfort was dying, quite simply from a bad chest and a few crazy years recklessly spent. The young man, although he was nearing the end, did not regret losing his life too much, for he had had his fair share of amours, duels, bad debts, picnics, and even fine sermons—in short, his fair share of all the Parisian joys.

One of his friends, a man of science but a good enough fellow regardless, seeing that Charles Belfort would soon render his last breath, came to say to him, in his softest voice: "If it wouldn't displease you too much, my dear invalid, I'll use my abilities to magnetize you, and I'll choose the moment when you render up your soul; it seems to me that it will be a fine experiment, and that there's nothing about it likely to displease you. What do you say?"

"Not only doesn't your experiment displease me," the other replied, "but it seems to me to be very amusing and interesting, and I thank you for having thought of me for the proof, which will be decisive. Count on me, my dear doctor; you'll be content with my patience, I hope, and I'll be sure to let you know when the moment comes."

With those words, the two friends shook hands and separated, saying that they would see one another again soon. They were both full of hope, and it would have been difficult to decide which of the two was the more content, the moribund or the magnetizer.

Two days went by—two centuries—while the magnetizer waited impatiently for the final agony, which did not seem to want to arrive for good and all. The dying man, for his part, lost patience, and he said to his friend: "Damn it, my dear chap, it's not my fault if death is treating me with such ill-will, but what consoles me is that you won't lose anything by waiting, and I'll be a magnificent subject."

On the night following this conversation, the sick man had a final crisis and fell into a comatose ecstasy; he started sketching fantastic spider-webs with his finger, and yet, in the midst of the most abominable grimaces, he still had the presence of mind to say to his comrade: "You have to lift my head, to hide the light that is hurting my eyes."

The other obeyed. He propped his moribund up in a sitting position, took away every importunate light and set about the operation; which is to say that never, absolutely never, had such beautiful passes and counter-passes—the whole customary apparatus, in short—been performed. The magnetizer was in the swim; but in the end, when he had enveloped the moribund—who lent himself to it with exemplary willingness—with his all-powerful fluid, and saw that his subject had arrived at magnetic perfection, the magnetizer started to interrogate him.

"How are you doing, Belfort? Where are you?"

"My dear friend," the other said, "I'm just dying; you've caught me just at the moment when the breath was leaving my body, and now it depends entirely on you to let me finish the job or to keep me here, suspended between being and non-being, which doesn't seem to me to be a disagreeable state, so far."

"Let's wait," said the magnetizer. "There's no hurry, Belfort, my friend." And with that, the magnetizer went to dinner, without taking the trouble to demagnetize his friend.

The next day the maker of magnetism reappeared in the mortuary chamber; everything was in its place, including the cadaver.

"Belfort," said the scientist, after a few preliminary passes, "what have you been doing since you died?"

"In truth, my dear chap," the dead man replied, "I've been obliged to follow you everywhere you went."

And with that, the dead man told the living one everything that the latter had done the day before: he had dined in a cheap eatery, and from there he had gone to stand on the steps of the Café de Paris; he had been given a ticket to the Vaudeville and he had seen some young women who were pretty enough, but some of whom sang out of tune; finally he had gone back home, and read a little of a novel that he had picked up on the way.

"And if you'll permit me to make an observation," the dead man said, "so long as I'm attached to you by a thread that only you can break, eat better, I beg you, remembering that I'm sharing the experience. You know that I like music, so don't expose me to hearing quavering voices that would spoil the most beautiful faces. All alone here, I'm getting bored, and I wouldn't be sorry if you were to read a good novel from time to time, but at least, for pity's sake, read it all the way through. Finally, if you please, don't go to bed so late; I become irritated not sleeping, because for twenty-four hours, I ought to have been sleeping eternally."

With these words, the man slumped back, and the magnetizer left the room, slightly discomfited by the strange spy that was dogging his heels.

The next day, the living man came back, and found his dead man a trifle numb. He warmed him up with a further dose of magnetic fluid, rendering him, if not life, at least a little color and the ability to speak.

"Ah!" said the dead man, raising himself up. "You're not showing me any charity. What! You go to see such hideous sick people, and I have to hear them coughing, spitting, howling, moaning and all the rest! In the street you follow a horrible woman reeking of musk, a woman in old shoes and a dirty skirt, and I have to keep you company counting the holes and the stains of the filthy creature! Then you go to meet up with some young people, and you tell them about your good luck! You make the streetwalker into a duchess, and a cotton apron into a silk skirt! When you're dead, you know, lying makes you feel ill. And what makes you feel even worse, when you're dead, is stupidity—some quip that would have made me laugh when I was of this world appears to me to be utter nonsense now that I can hear your mind with the ears of my own. So try to talk better my dear chap, and, if it's all the same to you, I'd be obliged if you didn't get drunk on adulterated wine; my throat's been torn apart by the alcohol you've swallowed."

Who do you think pulled a face? It was the living man, who was beginning to think that his dead man was damnable hard to please—because, after all, the previous evening's indulgence hadn't been deserving of such scorn. As for the lady with the worn-out shoes, the living man hadn't noticed the shoe, but only the foot and a little bit of the leg. However, he was fond to his dead man, and he resolved to keep a better eye on himself, in order not to give poor Belfort further reason for discontentment.

When he came back two days later, he found the deceased in a state of incredible excitement. The dead man was sweating copiously, with indignation legible on his distressed face.

First of all, the magnetizer set about trying to calm that anger; he blew his most soothing breath upon those irritated nerves, and appeased that motionless and frozen heart as best he could, which beat in memory.

"What is it, Master Belfort? Who's upset you? And for God's sake, what's the matter with you?"

"What's the matter with me?" replied the cadaver, after a long pause. "What's the matter with me, imbecile that you are? A curse upon the brazen threads that attack me to a fool like you! What's the matter with me! But my dear chap, for two days you've been going from one stupidity to another. The day before yesterday, it's true, you were well-groomed and well-dressed, but you'd fastened your belt too tight and I nearly choked. Your boots—or, rather, our boots—were well-polished, but they were too small, and if I could still walk, I'm sure that I'd be limping with my right foot.

"I've nothing to say about the lovely salon to which you took me; it was pleasant and it was calm; the clothes weren't at all garish; the mature ladies kept to their place, leaving the foreground to the young women; no one played the slightest sonata or read the slightest sonnet; people only spoke in even voices, neither too loud not too quiet, and said the nicest things—trivial but light, benevolent and sonorous. In brief, had it not been for your belt and our footwear, I would have blessed you for having taken me to such a beautiful place. But good heavens! Could you have been any more gauche, maladroit and absurd?

"In a corner of the little room to the left, a more beautiful woman than I ever saw with my mortal eyes was sitting; by dint of attention and will-power, via your terrestrial intermediation. I had attracted the benevolent interest of that amiable lady; already she was looking at me with a certain tenderness, and she was about to smile at me; our two souls were no longer any but one, and we were about to fall in love, when you turned your head like an idiot to greet I don't know what starchy spirit. Then the image of my beautiful lady fled, and if you live for a hundred years you won't find either another face as beautiful or another heart as noble.

"Idiot that you are, having done that, what do you do next? You know that I've left some glaring debts, and that I don't even have a tomb. You haven't a sou yourself; you live from hand to mouth; your rent hasn't been paid and never will be; in brief, you're as poor as a poet and an actor rolled into one—which is to say, abominably poor! Well, you sit down at a card-table, tremulously risk a wretched pistole, and, having won the hand, you pocket the money and run away like a thief!

"Now, do you know what you did there, Monsieur Idiot? You renounced getting your hands on a round sum of four lovely thousand louis d'or, for you'd have won the next thirteen hands, my son! With your four thousand louis you'd have had a carriage and I'd have had a first-class funeral. You'd have had a new suit and I'd have had an embroidered shroud. You'd have gone to seek your supper in the chorus of the Opéra, and I'd have gone to look for Monsieur Gannal.[54]

"Damn your feeble intelligence—you can't make use of what little sense you have, but you amuse yourself dragging another man's intelligence around with you. Go away—you make me sick, wretched living individual that you are!"

When our magnetizer finally understood that whatever he did would surely attract criticism or sarcasm, he fell silent. Now that he felt that he was being followed and observed at close range by some invisible entity that he had retained on the boundary between the two worlds, the scientist dare not take a step in the street; he scarcely dared answer yes or no to the simplest questions that were addressed to him; if was as if he were deaf and dumb. At times he wondered whether he might be the magnetized man and the magnetizer that great motionless—but not speechless—cadaver, the mere sight of which had ended up making him shiver.

An idea, a thought, is such a powerful thing, even independent of life! An idea pursues you, obsesses you, more tenacious than a shadow, as eloquent as remorse or hope, full of starts, excitations and perils!

However, our man went back to his friend Belfort three days later. This time, once again, a great change was evident

---

[54] Jean-Nicolas Gannal (1791-1852) was the pharmacist and inventor who founded and developed the modern techniques of embalming in the early 1830s, winning the Prix Montyon three times by virtue of the benefits thus provided to human society. In 1837 he obtained a patent for his embalming fluid and set up a commercial laboratory in the Rue Saint-Hippolyte.

in his inanimate face; pure and simple scorn had replaced indignation and anger. The half-closed eyes seemed to be saying: "Away with you!" The tight lips were expressing an indescribable disdain. Every muscle, taut from top to bottom, held a contempt suspended from every thread connecting it to the soul.

"What's the matter now, my friend?" cried the living man, "You seem dazed. You can't say this time that I've done or said anything stupid, because I've stayed at home, alone, entirely given over to my thoughts."

"Oh, my dear fellow," the dead man said, "it's the contemplation of your thoughts that's giving me nausea. Motionless as you were, I was forced to look into the depths of that chaos you call your soul. But what kind of animal are you to occupy yourself with so many ignoble, frivolous and shameful things? When I was alive and I called you my friend, everyone said that you were a gallant fellow; you had a reputation for keen, even eloquent wit; you were credited with philosophy, probity and tact.

"For three days, unable to help it, I've been watching you very attentively—but my dear fellow, you're a complete mess! What you know, you know poorly; what you don't know, you replace with words as empty as your head. Your generosity is a certain organic weakness that ends up making your eyes red, and that's all. Your intelligence is represented by a few mechanical cog-wheels that rotate of their own accord like the wheel of a water-mill incessantly repeating the same tick-tock. Your courage—I've seen all the way its depths, your courage!—is a cardboard mask that frightens children. Your probity—let's talk about your probity!—is written in the margins of the commercial Code and the penal Code.

"Shame upon your vices, those of a badly brought-up child! I wouldn't give four sous for your vices; they make me sick, your wicked shameful vices: they're like a kind of boasting! As for your virtues, they're so worthless I wouldn't even give them to my lackeys; there's something limp and vain about your virtue, which bears some resemblance to a badly-cooked broth. Oh, I advise you not to lay bare the inside of your brain and your heart—it's not a pretty sight, although, on the other hand, it's very sad.

"And what ideas you have about other men! What thwarted ambitions! And I don't envy your work at all, my poor sir! What! You aren't ashamed, even of your castles in Spain, when you amuse yourself rambling on for entire hours in petty daydreams?

"Anyway, Monsieur, let's leave it at that—but I'm damnably sorry that I ever called you my friend!"

It would not have taken much on this occasion for the magnetizer to destroy his work and liberate himself from the unwelcome thought that was obsessing him. He left the mortuary chamber in a very bad mood, and on the way home he said to himself that it was, after all, quite an accomplishment to have stopped Belfort's discontented soul half-way.

Then again, the living man said to himself, sadly, *what good has it done me to have retained that dead man in the edge of his grave? To have myself told such rude home-truths, to hear the story of my everyday life told in such a cruel and grotesque fashion, no longer to be alone with my conscience, my thoughts, my ambitions, my self? If the clairvoyant that sees everything were, at least, to indicate some unknown science to me—a remedy for the gout or some hidden treasure easy to extract—I'd be rewarded for my troubles, but no! For having carried out the most difficult task, the most excellent miracle that magnetism has ever accomplished, here I am dragging behind me a bilious inquisitor who isn't content with anything, and who'll end up making me disgusted with myself.*

Thus the clever man reasoned; he was very annoyed, and firmly resolved to put an end to his dealings with such a miscreant, no matter what it cost.

As he was unable to sleep, the magnetizer went back to Belfort's house that same evening, at midnight.

Belfort watched him come in, and without waiting to be interrogated—for the magnetic fluid becomes, it seems, a habit, and replaces life as a well-lit candle replaces with winter sun—the dead man cried: "I'll tell you what you've just done, amiable doctor! You've quite simply decided to murder me! Yes, you're jealous of this artificial life, you're furious at my revelations, and you've decided to extract me abruptly from magnetic sleep in order to return me to dust and silence!

"That's handsome of you, Monsieur, it's glorious, what you're doing, coming to murder...a dead man! Coming to trouble a cadaver in his coffin! Attacking the thought of a man because the man, having become, thanks to you, a part of eternal life, is no longer able and no longer wants to flatter you!

"Well, get on with it, then, and turn me to dust—but that dust, when you've cast it to the wind, will summon to its aid another, bolder thought, to follow in your tracks, another gaze, even more clairvoyant, to read the depths of your soul, another avenger, even more implacable: remorse!"

At these threats the magnetizer fled, but, in his distress, he left the door ajar.

The neighbors of both sexes, who had initially kept their distance, took the chance, one after another, and finally all together, of coming to greet and interrogate the dead man, and picked up, here and there, some of those fine verities—I mean a few of those eternal, ever-living truths—that only the dead know how to voice appropriately. Husbands, wives, children, tenants, owners, masters and servants, the rich and the poor, all the way to the porter, each obtained a parcel of justice addressed to them.

The dead man spoke true words and expressed true notions, and what he said was, admittedly, cruel. If you asked him where fortune lay, he would point out a wart on the end of your nose; if you mentioned ambition to him, he would talk to you about modesty, economy and bonhomie. The female neighbors found him so ungallant that they slammed the door violently.

That was all that the late Monsieur Belfort wanted.

A week went by without the magnetized and the magnetizer seeing one another again; they were sulking, but it was obviously not up to the dead man to make the first move. The scientist finally understood that, and came back to his subject's bedside.

"I've thought about everything that has happened," Belfort said to him, "and I'd be glad if you were to carry through the plan you made the other day. You're right: wake me up, so that I can finish dying quietly. It had made such a good beginning, when you came along to disrupt it, that I'd already be devoured by worms and returned via the thousand pores of universal decomposition into the ocean of life and light. Wake me up, then, and I'll die entirely—and joyfully, for, this time, I'll amuse myself by gazing, not at your soul, which isn't beautiful, but at your body, which is very ugly.

"Only the other day—I caught you in that agreeable occupation—you were telling yourself how fortunate you were before, but please, where are these women who can look lovingly at an ape like you? You're badly-formed; you always have one shoulder higher than the other, this one over that one or that one over this one. Your hair started falling out a long time ago, and what's left is hanging on to rotten roots, like last year's thatch after the winter. Your eyes can still see, but I can see some sort of pellicle extending over your line of sight that doesn't augur anything good.

"Oh, if you could see those layers of yellow chalk encrusted in the joints of your fingers, which are corrupting your bones and are going to break them bit by bit, like the boot of torture, but more slowly, more insidiously and with a more obstinate verve!

"Your heart is swollen, my dear chap, and the point is being torn by some viscera or other that is wounded in its turn. Your left lung isn't much better than my right lung. Gradually infiltrating between your skin and your softened tendons I can see layers of thick fat which makes you resemble some sort of sea-cow. Your teeth are already turning yellow; they're loose in their bloody cavities. In your brain I can see veins swollen with apoplectic blood, ready to burst. You're doomed, you see, and—give me your hand—you're dead!"

On hearing those lugubrious words, the magnetizer begs the magnetized for mercy, pity and forgiveness. And, in order to free himself from the vision that is obsessing him, to expel from his mind that voice, which is pursuing him with such bruising stubbornness, in order not to remain exposed to that mockery and those prophecies of misfortune, the magnetizer sets about countermanding the magnetic fluid and destroying that artificial life.

The dead man resists, but in vain; it is necessary that a corpse, which is dead, should yield to a man who is still alive.

Gradually, the voice fades away. It utters one last gasp, and then Belfort, so eloquent a little while before, is no longer more than I don't know what, that which I don't know how to name in any language...

It was, in fact, for three weeks already that death had had possession of the cadaver, and now the magnetic breath had ceased, corruption and the worm took hold of their prey again and did not let go.

One shivers at the mere idea that the magnetizer might have died before having demagnetized his friend Belfort. How long eternity would have seemed to the latter then—unless his thought, obedient all the way to the abyss, or to Heaven, had followed the soul of magnetizer.

That would be another trial to attempt!

THE REVENANT

Once upon a time, on the heights of Montmartre, there was a little enclosure of about eight or ten thousand square meters all told, which the sun illuminated with its first rays, and which overlooked the entire city. The location was charming, to such an extent that it only suited artists, poets, dreamers and good people retired from the world and content with the present moment.

It was necessary to climb for some time to reach the Clos Champenois. That was the name of the oasis, filled with vines comparable to be best in Suresnes and Argenteuil. Whether it was a good year or a bad year, one could easily have pressed a little wine in the Clos Champenois, which would have liked nothing better than to sparkle in a glass; but the local girls and art students—a hungry and disreputable race—cleared it out regularly, disputing the fine vintage with the local sparrows. Oh, it was a good place for work, for pleasure, for celebrating and singing.

When our story begins, it belonged to one of the most fortunate young men of his century. He was twenty-five years old at the most; he had dark eyes, dark hair and a mat complexion; he was handsome, with that somber, almost romantic beauty that does not displease a grisette or a marquise. Finally, to cap it all, he was a veritable artist, and better still, in the esteem and to the astonishment of bourgeois Paris, he was the owner, with no mortgage, of the Clos Champenois, which he had bought very cheap. At his own expense, he had built a large studio there with a double exposure to the north and south. The previous year, he had won a gold medal; six months ago he had been appointed a Chevalier de la Légion d'honneur. At every exhibition his paintings were acquired by a mysterious buyer, who paid the asking price without haggling.

His latest work, in the turbulent style of a Casanova of battles, represented a genuine massacre, a frightful pell-mell of Poles slaughtered by Russians, children killed with axes, young women treated to fire and blood, while younger ones extended pleading hands in vain as they died. The crowd, avid and curious to see the spectacle gratis, had flocked to that abominable melodrama, which sobbed all day long in the grand salon of the Louvre, but people of taste, while recognizing the fever and the hand of a master in the canvas abundant with lamentations, said to one another: "In truth, perhaps it's a fine work, but it wouldn't do in the house. We don't need to be depressed."

They were right. Some paintings that suit an immense gallery would be out of place in a bourgeois home, the attentive friend of gentle and calm emotions; they belong in museums. A great battle is all very well, but a rural scene, a nice landscape; an idyll in short skirts in which one can see nothing but shepherds; a picnic on the grass, in which the sprightly Aglaia offers her cousin Myrtile a lovely fruit that one might think had been picked in the gardens of Alcinous…as long as the painter has a skillful hand, those are the true pleasures of an honest domestic roof.

Well, strangely enough, for that painting, very well-treated by the critics and abused by connoisseurs, which the government had not wanted—because governments, like people, have their days of sensibility—the intrepid yearly art-lover had offered two thousand écus. Imagine how gratefully that handsome and very unexpected sum was accepted.

To obey the most violent instincts, to give the most terrible lessons to the despots of the North, to depend on the vengeance of peoples, to defend yourself and love yourself in the open—O outraged Pole!—and to march without any hindrance along paths full of vengeance, to represent a grand fête, and when the thing is accomplished to the whim of our passions, to sell the book or the painting, which we think unsalable, at a good price—that's what one calls a fortunate outcome, a great joy!

What could be more just? One has not retreated before public taste; one has not ceded anything to the little mistress, to the handsome petty gentlemen, to the bourgeois, the bête noire! And yet, success arrives, and popularity cradles you. Then, content with yourself and content with others, you touch the stars.

The lesson had been profitable, however. The more the young man had feared the annoyance of having to take the work back to a corner of his studio, the better he understood that it was imprudent to exhibit such miseries too often, and he reverted to his natural good humor. Besides which, that is the grace and gladness of serious talents: to pass from one idea to its opposite, today in the full-blooded history, tomorrow in rural romance. And nothing can impede or sadden them. The go freely into free space as soon as they sense that they are followed, heeded, granted approval.

Our happy painter combined that rare talent with a beautiful soul and a tender heart; he willingly obeyed all the inspirations of youth. He already had, while still so young, to love him, to surround him and, in sum, to please him, two adoptive children who lived his life and knew no other: his pupil and godson Zacharie, otherwise known as the art-student Toiras,[55] whom he had found playing in the garden when he was very small; and his adoptive daughter Edith, who had been brought to him one day by one of his colleagues at school in Rome, a certain Malvoisin, a misunderstood talent who had had no success at all.

"I'm giving her to you," his comrade had said, "because she's an orphan, because she's charming, and because I'm incapable of raising her. She's a true Roman, a Transteverine, one of those heads before which Monsieur Ingrès, our illustrious master, paused, and studied thoughtfully. She's a budding

---

[55] "Toiras" was the name by which the 17th century Maréchal de France Jean Caylar d'Anduze de Saint-Bonnet, Marquis de Toiras had generally been known. As governor of the Ile de Ré he withstood a long siege by an English army in 1627.

artist. More than once I've caught her holding a pencil in her light hand; oh, how I regretted then being an impotent painter, a Bohemian abandoned to all hazards! Do you think, however, that I would have chosen to confide this precious deposit to you if I thought you unworthy of it? It's not in vain that we in Paul Delaroche's studio call you Nicolas the Sage, after Poussin, your true master.[56] Younger than us, you give us an assiduous example of the good morals. A joke makes you blush. You scarcely dare look a model representing Flora or Venus in the face. How much fun we've poked at your innocence! And now, the cruelest of the persecutors of your virtue inclines humbly before it, and deposits at its feet this pale and meek burden. The poor child has lost her mother, or at least she's an errant vagabond, far from a vagabond like me. If the father isn't worth much, the mother's worth even less, and the greatest good fortune that could befall this amiable child is that she be preserved from her father and mother alike. Farewell, then! I'm going back to Rome, where talentless Raphaels live so easily, with so much leisure."

With which he left, his eyes full of tears, easily dried up. He had not reached the foot of the hill when he had already forgotten his good resolutions, his sadness and his repentance.

Such were the three inhabitants of the Clos Champenois. It is necessary to add, for the sake of completeness, an excellent housekeeper, who did her best to fulfill the double function of doorkeeper and grandmother; she watched over the two children, not sparing the art-student clips round the ear or the little girl caresses. She also took great care to water the garden, art-student Toiras remaining in charge of pruning the trees and young Edith of tending the flowers.

---

[56] Hippolyte Delaroche (1797-1856), familiarly known as Paul Delaroche, had a famous studio in the Rue Mazarine, through which many prestigious students passed, but he was in Italy between 1838 and 1843, when his father-in-law was director of the French Academy in Rome.

The great generosity that he had, no less than his talent, had attracted to the master of the house all sorts of pupils, from whom he very rarely demanded any fees, in memory as well as following the example of his own first master. Not only did he help them with his advice, but also his purse. More than one Corot of either sex could already be cited whose bankruptcy he had prevented with sums of between four and five louis. If, therefore, there were people outside his enclosure who were jealous of him, he saw no one in his studio or his garden but happy faces, good workers in beautiful paint, who did not spare their praise and admiration. He heard nothing but songs, gaiety and the joy of living in the fortunate shade of the pleasant vineyard. One would have had to go a long way to encounter such great contentment in such a small space.

We have not yet revealed the name of the fortunate young man in question, and he did not pronounce it willingly himself. He was called, not Nicolas Poussin, which was his fine-weather nickname, but quite stupidly Nicaise de Kinseton.[57] Hazard, more than the fortune of his birth, had made him a Baron: Baron Nicaise de Kinseton. A Nicaise and a Baron as well: too good reasons to see him exposed to all the jokes of his brother art-students, when he had still been a mere aspirant to the honors of painting. How they had laughed in his face at his barony! How they had poked fun at Monsieur de Kinseton and his châteaux!

It's true: a college and a studio, a notary's *étude* and the stage all represent full equality. I don't believe that a lieutenant has ever been called Monsieur le Baron such-and such; no one has ever seen a Comte or a Marquis on a theater poster. Wait, young man, for the hour to come; then, if it pleases you, you can call yourself at your ease Baron Dupuytren, Baron Gros, Baron Gérard, Baron Cuvier, Baron de Sacy, and you

---

[57] The French forename Nicaise was often used to refer to a simpleton, presumably because of its similarity to the adjective *niaise* [stupid].

will be neither greater nor diminished in consequence. Talent, that is the true title, and well-brought-up people take care not to call Madame Spontini the Comtesse de San Andrea.[58]

In the meantime, our artist, after the initial ragging, gradually felt those petty chagrins lessening. To begin with, he rectified matters. In the catalogue of the Salon every year, and in society, he simply called himself "Monsieur Kinseton." The name was agreeable to artists; it sounded suitably bourgeois, especially when one added: "You know, Monsieur Kinseton, who has built such a fine studio in the Clos Champenois."

At the moment when the story we are about to recount begins, joyous April was swaying the flowering almond-trees, and the newly-hatched paintings were shining in the halls of the exhibition, so the moment was full of hope, and each of the exhibitors—an alert race devoid of doubt—was secretly buying his own works at fabulous prices and pinning the gold medal on himself. All of those great unknown artists were coming and going through the vast galleries, keeping watch on the most indifferent gazes, listening to the slightest comments.

Monsieur Kinseton was perhaps alone at that moment in belonging entirely to the inspiration of such a beautiful morning. Forgetting the exhibited work, he was only thinking about the work to come, and seeking to recognize himself in the first preparatory sketches. A sketch has so much charm and authority! In the eyes of connoisseurs, it is already the work entire, and when it is beautiful and big, in bright light, the master is so content with his enterprise!

In the vast studio all was spectacular, interesting and curious. An even and soft light fell from the ceiling over so many things shining for the pleasure of the eyes! Here and there, beautiful works of ancients and moderns—German, Dutch, Flemish, French most of all—were hung without order, but not without taste, in the midst of that elegant confusion. Oriental fabrics, Spanish armor, fragments borrowed random-

---

[58] The Italian composer Gaspare Spontini (1774-1851) was given the title Comte de San Andrea in 1844.

ly from all centuries, were placed on all the items of furniture of all epochs.

The various inhabitants of the house, so calm outside, so laborious inside, were united in that common joy, and, truly, they each had their fair share of it. On a Persian rug that covered half the parquet, the cat and the dog, two friends, were waiting to be fed; they were playing together, competing in trying to seize passing sunbeams. A blackbird with a gilded beak was whistling in his cage, the door of which was open.

A girl with blonde hair—her father's hair—and her mother's dark eyes, was sitting, or, to put it better, sprawling, in a vast armchair embroidered on a frame by some duchesse at Versailles. She was engraving in the wood, in a nonchalant manner, a slight design that she had copied from the surrounding rosebushes. Leaning on the armchair, a joyful student, slim and nimble, still frail and more ugly than handsome was alternately watching the girl draw and the master work. He was seeking both to divine the dream of those beautiful eyes and comprehend some of the mysteries of the painter's great art, for which he had more passion than talent.

Posed, beneath the most beautiful daylight, before his easel, charged with a canvas of mediocre dimension, the young painter was completely absorbed in his well-commenced work. He saw nothing but his painting; everything else was, for him, darkness and confusion. His soul and his mind belonged to the idea; he was not longer a man, he was a great artist. Thus, the work was going well, bright and neat, and profound—and anyone who looked at that vast conflict of light and shadow, would have seen beauty, youth and love surging forth: all the graces of the nascent spring, and the ingenious drama that those fifteen-year-old gazes contained.

In the excellent sketch, the idyll appeared in its flower; the smile burst forth in its grace; forms, beauties and the dream were confusedly visible. Something trivial made the gaze gleam; an inner light illuminated the charming brow. The painter proceeded thus, in the ideal, realizing the visions glimpsed in the obscure chamber of his brain. If he was sometimes indecisive, like a traveler who loses is way in the midst of intersecting paths, he took his point of reference, and with a rapid glance at the girl with the blonde hair he came back immediately to his model. He looked at her without seeing her.

She, however, moved and charmed, divining that she had entered unwittingly into the enchanted program, remained motionless for as long as he felt that she was the object of attention. Then, in her turn, she glanced at the young master.

He would, in any case, have attracted the attention of someone less clear-sighted. He was wearing the most beautiful costume, clad in a full-length garment in black velvet edged with red. He was shod in a pair of slippers embroidered with gold thread. His beautiful hands held his palette and brush. A light down blurred his eloquent upper lip. Shadow and radiance disputed his superb forehead; forgetful of everything else, he was only thinking about the ideal perfection that is forever fleeing.

Certainly, the moment was solemn; everyone was maintaining silence around that labor, which a savage, or even an idler at the Maison-d'Or, would have respected, without understanding whence all his respect came. Even the cat and the dog were no longer playing; they were watching the young man in contemplation before his canvas—and the blackbird had stopped singing. Thus, all those gazes, all those human and animal souls, were fixed upon that luminous point: the artist and his work. O ineffable and holy power of inspiration!

The imposing charm of the work even made itself felt outside the studio. One might have thought that the passers-by fell silent, that the schoolchildren were moving alongside the wall in silence. Sitting on the doorstep, cursing the lateness of her breakfast, Madame Robert, the doorkeeper, was awaiting the master's pleasure.

"I would like to speak," a newcomer said to her, "to Monsieur Kinseton the landscapist."

"He's at home, Monsieur," said the concierge, "but he's still working, and the entire mountain is accustomed to respect Monsieur's work. But you can wait, if you wish; I don't think you'll have to wait for very long. The blackbird's in the middle of the lawn, there's the cat on the window-sill, and I can hear Zémire barking. Look, there's the student calling me."

"Breakfast! Breakfast!"

"Off we go! Off we go! You can go in now, Monsieur. I'm going to serve breakfast."

While she put a white cloth on the slate table, a bowl of warm milk for Mademoiselle Edith, and I don't know how many cutlets and potatoes for the master and his student, the visitor introduced himself to Monsieur Kinseton.

The newcomer was still young, and well-dressed. On a rural jacket in iron-gray cloth he wore the ribbon of the Légion d'honneur. His whole appearance was imprinted with rustic elegance; an intelligent generosity was legible in all his features. Merely by the way in which he looked at the paintings in the studio, the painter understood that the man was a connoisseur, and that discovery added to his favorable disposition toward the stranger.

"You've arrived at a good time, Monsieur," Kinseton said to him. "We've done some good work this morning and now we're going to have breakfast. If your heart commands, be our guest; we'll give you eggs from our chickens, and, if you wish, milk from our cow."

"With potatoes from our garden," added art-student Toiras.

"Better still, Monsieur," the artist went on, "you can offer your hand to Mademoiselle Edith...here she is...and now, to the garden!"

The man in the gray coat did not stand on ceremony; he seemed utterly charmed by this amiable invitation. Walking and good humor had given him an appetite; he ate almost as much a young Toiras; he praised the cow's milk and the hen's eggs. He applauded everything, like a happy man. Except that, warned by the color of the petty wine, he lifted the glass to his lips with a certain hesitation.

"It's the same for all of us," he said, cheerfully, with an intention devoid of flattery, "we vineyard owners! We find nothing better than the wine of our own vintage." And he laughed.

"It's obvious that Monsieur has never drunk ours," replied young Toiras. "this little Beaugency is Clos Vouegot compared to Clos Champenois."

"It's my fault," said the visitor. "I admit it, and henceforth, Monsieur Art-Student Toiras, I'll send you, every year, for beautiful Mâconnaises the same age as Mademoiselle, or very nearly. Yes, it's my fault!" And as he saw the astonishment on the three faces, he extended his hand to Kinseton and said: "My friend, you're seeing me for the first time, but we're old acquaintances. I've loved you for a long time already. For one thing, we have the same name. I too am N. Kinseton."

"But N. isn't a name," said the student. "Are you Nicaise Kinseton? Are you, like us, Baron Nicaise de Kinseton?"

"Alas, no," replied the new Kinseton. "I'm N. Kinseton, as you're N. Kinseton in the catalogue. And yet, a little thing like that made such an impression on my heart and mind that I've followed you in your career like a brother following a brother. Each of your successes I applauded with all my might; I have to have the N. Kinseton painting every year, at any price. You're my family, and my pride."

"So, Monsieur," the young painter exclaimed, "you're the constant, devoted, paternal buyer that I've encountered for what will soon be ten years, indulgent and generous! Welcome to my home...to your home! A thousand thanks. But you've had some sad dealings with me, and I'm ashamed when I think that you bought me *Oedipus*.

"Yes, Master, and ten years later, I willingly bought your charming *Daphnis and Chloe*, in which young Chloe dances, laughing, the cyclops dance."

"Oh, so it's you who owns the *Oedipus* and the *Chloe*, and the *Templar Brian de Bois-Guilbert*?" exclaimed young Toiras. "It's you who own all our works! How glad I'd be to see them again! Yours too, O Maecenas, are our *Amaryllis*, a daughter of Virgil, and our *Galatea*, a nymph of Theocritus? Oh, you really are a true friend, a veritable Kinseton."

"So the acquaintance is finally made," said the visitor. "I'm just coming back from the Salon, where I've seen..."

"Our Béranger *Bohemians*?"

"I've also seen, by a certain student Toiras, pupil of Kinseton, *La Tortue et la Bergère*, and I've come to ask Monsieur Toiras whether he would care to let me have the tortoise and the shepherdess for fifty louis d'or? I'll place his painting not far from the Bohemians and Brian de Bois-Guilbert."

"Fifty louis d'or for me?" exclaimed student Toiras. "Do you mean it, Monsieur le Chevalier? Fifty louis d'or! It's true that the shepherdess is quite similar to someone I know. That's why I want to buy that someone a brand new dress, a lace skirt and shoes the color of the sun."

With these words, the painter smiled at the girl, who returned the smile. And the three friends, having concluded their meal, went on to the Terrasse de Montmartre. It's said that the Devil, having taken Our Lord up to that terrace, showed him the great city of Paris, traversed by its beautiful river, and said to him: "If you bow down to me, Paris is yours!" Our Lord resisted the temptation. It's true that the tempter could only show him the Paris of 1867 years ago; the temptation would be almost irresistible today.

When they had lit their pipes and recognized one another, by certain signs, as honest men, Kinseton the painter told Kinseton the vineyard-owner that he was originally from the Midi, from an ancient family, and the last of his line. He had lost his mother when he was still a child; his father, an old soldier of the Empire, had had a profound scorn for all painters, musicians, poets and writers. He knew nothing but the saber; he loved nothing but battles; after a battle, he liked nothing better than good wine, his compatriot; and when his son left him to go study painting, the indignant father had cursed him. After his death, however, he had left his son some petty property, which he had exchanged for this promising terrain on the summit of Montmartre.

"And that, my dear Kinseton, is all that I know about my family. In your turn, tell me what you know about yours, and let's at least try, as bearers of the same name, to remain cousins."

In his turn, Monsieur Kinseton the vine-grower recounted, not without a certain emotion, that he was orphaned of both parents, that he had been picked up, half-dead, on the Breton coast. He had a confused memory of the shipwreck and the tempest, of a woman who wept as she embraced him. A smuggler from Roscoff had picked him up and taken him home. Fifty louis d'or had been found on him, in an ivory jewel-case, and with that money he had been raised. He had been taught French, mathematics and Bas-Breton, but above all, he had been taught courage and perseverance, to believe in God, and never to despair of Providence.

When he was of an age to see the world, he had studied mineralogy and the best ways of employing coal to manufacture gas, and later to animate machinery for the railways. That was how he had made, fairly quickly, a fairly tidy fortune, and had retired early to the exceedingly busy repose of agriculture. He had been one of the députés who saw the throne of Charles X fall, and the remorse of his unjust opposition to the best of all princes had brought him back forever to his vineyards.

As for the name of N. Kinseton, he had found it engraved on the ivory jewel-case, which had doubtless served the parents he had lost as a seal. But the arms were, as the saying has it, speaking arms: a spade in saltire with two oars. That was all he knew about himself. And now, he was asking the young painter for indulgence, amity and fraternal generosity.

From that day forward, he was a friend and guest of the Clos Champenois. They both liked calling one another by their own name. The painter had a great talent, but the art-lover had a clear and correct appreciation of beautiful painting. He had visited all the great museums, and from that beautiful voyage through various schools he had come back very smitten with the French school. Thus, very rapidly, he was adopted by the amiable inhabitants of that cheerful little corner of the Earth, incessantly open to honest impressions.

That festival of amity lasted a full six months. The master of the house, the girl and the student—especially the student—were infatuated with the vine-grower who picked such beautiful peaches, the lover of paintings who brought forth such good grapes.

"I'll paint your portrait," the student Toiras sometimes said to him, "and you'll possess a veritable Velasquez."

In the meantime, he fulfilled his obligations, and as they succeeded by virtue of irony and good humor, one found them on all the surrounding walls.

Kinseton the painter made good on his student's promise. "My dear friend," he said to his friend the vine-grower, "you'll pose for me; it's a good means of seeing oneself. I'll only keep you for a week; it will be as much gained."

Indeed, the painter had soon represented the vine-grower. For his part, the vine-grower wanted to have the painter's portrait; thus they made the most amiable exchange, and almost simultaneously, the Baron N. de Kinseton decorated the château of N. Kinseton, his friend. The adieux were painful on both sides, however.

"Alas," said the latter to the former, "your life is hopeful. You almost have a son in young Toiras, and you will, I expect, have an amiable wife on the day when the girl with blue eyes gives you her beautiful hand as full of glints as her gaze. Be greatly thanked, however, my host and my friend. Count on me as one day I shall count on you, for you will never forget, I imagine, that you and I bear exactly similar names, and just as I claim a fraction of your glory, you shall have, inevitably, a share of my shame."

As he spoke thus, large tears formed in the worthy man's eyes; his heart was full of foreboding. And when he had taken his leave, definitively, of the Clos Champenois, the studio, young Toiras, his friend and young Edith, it was evident that he had great difficulty quitting that beautiful place and those good people. He gave student Toiras an important commission; he gave young Edith a bracelet for the days of her pink dress, and two diamante buckles for her shoes the color of the sun.

"As for you, my dear Nicaise, my younger brother, whom I've lost and found, I leave you my pipe and my cane, and this puppy of my dear Zerbine. He was born in Paris, he knows no other domain than the Clos Champenois. Farewell to you all! I'm going back to my vineyards, one single grape of which is worth ten times your entire vintage, and yet see how I'm weeping. Adieu! I'm reserving all your works; I want them all; and the man who wants to usurp our bargain will have to be very rich. Once more, adieu! And don't forget, on your somber days, that out there, on the peaceful banks of an enchanted river, on the slopes of hills full of intoxication and joy, to the sound of the god Pan's pipes and the tambourines of errant nymphs, you'll find a house, cool in summer and arm in winter, the house of Chevalier N. Kinseton."

As soon as he arrived at his vineyard, the Chevalier Kinseton wrote an amiable letter to his three friends at the Clos Champenois, in which he claimed the painting in the imminent exhibition, and a small painting by student Toiras representing *L'Aigle et l'Escargot*, while awaiting *La Tortue*. At the same time, he sent his friend Toiras, as he had promised, two beautiful burgundiennes of a good age and condition, in brand new clothes, with an invitation to make use of them.

"May they be blessed!" cried the student. "We're finally liberated from Bordeaux from Argenteuil and Clos-Vougeot from Suresnes!"

And when he saw that he was the proprietor of six hundred red-sealed bottles, he took out of their niche half a dozen beautiful glasses engraved by Louis XV's glassmakers with the Bourbon arms. The old wine, which all the friends of the studio were generously invited to share, added, one might have said, an unexpected gaiety to all the prosperities that that garden of the Hesperides contained.

"Oh, away with you, drunkard!" cried the indolent Edith. Then, half laughing and half irritated, she touched the young man's glass with her blooming lip, and the latter emptied it, to the last drop, to the health of the earth and the sky.

Returned to themselves, they went back to all their old habits, except that the beautiful Edith was wide awake and very attentive to everything that was happening around her. She was, in the nonchalant hours, reminiscent of some dormant passion; anyone who had seen her beautiful eyes lowered, in those long silences, shading her face, would surely have said "There's a child!" but as soon as she woke up, one divined the young woman.

She said herself, with a certain pride: "My baptism lied about it; I must be older than fifteen."

She did, in fact, have the stature and the bearing, the shoulders and all the rest of a beauty gently blossoming to the breath of eighteen springs. She had more than that: she had intelligence and talent, with all the gifts of an exquisite nature; and when she deigned to speak, to smile, to listen, to interrogate or to reply, the finest and most intelligent minds remained, so to speak, frightened by the eloquence and merits of that fifteen-year-old child. But she did not listen much and only responded rarely. She lived an intimate and discreet life. She knew that she was loved, honored and surrounded; she was content with that, but did not express it.

Student Toiras, a great lover of bric-à-brac, had bought the day before, while going along the Quai Voltaire, an elegant mandolin with a long shaft, which bore in relief the arms of the Princesse des Ursins.[59] It was a beautiful instrument,

---

[59] Marie-Anne de La Trémoille, Princesse des Ursins (1642-1722) was married young to Adrien de Talleyrand, Prince of Chalais, who was forced to flee France after a fatal duel; when he died she settled in Italy and married Flavio Orsini, Duke of Bracciano (her assumed title being a corruption of Orsini). She was recruited by Louis XIV to help place members of his family on the Spanish throne, and spent many years in the Spanish court, where it was alleged that she plotted to become queen herself before being expelled and returning to Rome.

made of ivory and ebony, with a beautiful sounding-board on which light fingers had left faint traces. Student Toiras, who knew everything, had replaced the neglected lute's four brass strings, and tuned them rather slowly to the high-pitched notes for which the beautiful Transteverine was evidently awaiting impatiently.

Finally, no longer able to contain herself, she snatched the instrument from the young man's hand. The strings were tuned in the blink of an eye, and two charming hands rendered life and song to the rejuvenated instrument.

How long had that sonorous lute been buried in the second-hand dealer's attic? What route had it followed in coming from Madrid to Versailles? What pedantic songs had it accompanied in the hands of his first mistress, better made to bear a scepter than to hold an amorous lute? That was certainly a problem to which Monsieur de Kinseton gave no thought, nor student Toiras. Sometimes, they were both amazed and submerged by the deluge, simultaneously energetic and tender, of the liveliest and most alert notes.

At such moments, the valiant Edith had forgotten that her two friends were listening, and, utterly charmed herself by the long-forgotten but suddenly rediscovered cantilenas, abandoned herself to the joy and good fortune of hearing them. In its turn, the docile instrument obeyed that sovereign inspiration, and when it had finally yielded all the sounds it could contain, and it was absolutely impossible to go any further, the young woman's beautiful voice added its powerful vibrations to the sonorities of the vanquished instrument. She sang, and the lute obediently accompanied, marvelous songs of another age and a distant country, until the moment when, vanquished in hr turn, out of breath and inspiration, she returned the instrument to the frightened student.

"Mazetto," she said to him, "that's how to make an old instrument that has fallen into your hands obey you. You'll never be a musician, Mazetto. And now, put the old guitar on its hook."[60]

He obeyed without replying. He was ashamed, humiliated and charmed. He looked at the master, who, knowing that the demoiselle did not want to be admired, had already picked up his brush and palette—but it was evident that he was scarcely working.

Often, I'm listening still, when the song has ceased...

Edith profited from that long silence to make a tour of the studio and the garden. In her capacity as a mystery, she experienced some embarrassment at the revelation that passed her off as a great musician, when she had scarcely been granted a petty talent for designing and engraving woodcuts for illustrated books. It was true that admiration annoyed her. An overly persistent gaze at her incontestable beauty put her ill at ease. She liked silence and shadow, and now that she has sung, how could she resist those who said to her: "Sing to us? Sing again"?

Oh, silly fool that I am! she said to herself.

Thus discontented, she went back into the studio, where the master and the student had finally pulled themselves together. Monsieur de Kinseton seemed fully occupied in giving a lesson to the frightened student Toiras on a beautiful, slightly grainy sheet specifically made for a three-pencil drawing. It was certainly not the first time that the disciple had drawn under the master's eyes: a Diomedes, a Niobe, a Perseus or a Venus, even a Laocoon. This time, however, either because he was conscious of his scant talent or because he was troubled by the unexpected discovery of a short while ago, or because he could still hear the instrument resounding under the pressure of those feverish fingers, it must be admitted that student Toiras was hesitant.

---

[60] It seems probable that Edith has borrowed the name Mazetto from the peasant in Mozart's opera Don Juan.

He had already begun twice, erased some image or other uncertain in his mental vision, when the Roman girl, who was watching him, said: "O *maledetto!* He'll no more be a draughtsman than a musician. Give!"

And, taking the charcoal from that trembling hand, she set about—O miracle!—drawing with broad strokes the non-plussed young master's own image. In four or five strokes of the pencil, it was already him. It really was that innocent face, with the alert gaze and the thin smile with the malice of a woodland faun. That image, with the pointed ears, has often been encountered, and the poet Horace sang it.

There were the lips with the two corners raised provocatively, and the cheeks, where the dimples were ironic, and those round eyes sparkling with innocent mischief. At certain moments, she forgot the model and remembered some divinity from the *Metamorphoses*. You have remained in these Roman souls, charming god of the amorous idyll, whom Virgil borrowed from good Theocritus, and nothing can efface your cheerful memory. That was how the Italian girl, now, returned without knowing it to the banks of the Arno, and was intoxicated by the charming sound of the little waterfalls of Tivoli. She simply copied the gentle profile of Melibea or Tytirus,[61] mingling in the most original fashion the human and the demigod, the student and the shepherd, grace and intoxication.

So absorbed was she in her work that she heard the sound of pipes, and breathed the sickly odor of beautiful cups carved in beech and traces of odorous wax. It was charming, alive, shining. It was rustic and splendid at the same time. A beautiful blue sky, a sky of the month of June, completed that image borrowed from the shores of Gallese, the mordant waters of Liris, the vines of Formia.

Oh, the masterpiece! Our friend Kinseton had already been contemplating it for a long time, holding back his enthusiasm breathlessly. He trembled lest the vision dissipate, in

---

[61] Melibea and Tytirus are featured in one of Dante's *Eclogues*.

that air as transparent as crystal. Then, when the young woman had finished that improvisation of genius, he knelt before her, and with his hands joined, he raised that marvelous drawing to his lips.

Bewildered, understanding as little of the work as of its executrix, student Toiras dared not recognize himself, and sought confusedly in the picture what he had scarcely glimpsed in the excellent work of Italian masters.

Exhausted, and almost ashamed, the young woman had fallen back into her seat. Panting, she closed her eyes.

A loud knocking on the door to the street announced visitors who had the right to enter. Indeed, it was two art-dealers, great adventurers trawling the studios of painters whose renown was secure, and artists whose renown was yet to be made.

One of those dealers, strangely enough, was an expert on beautiful paintings, and when he put the name of a master a picture, ancient or modern, he was rarely mistaken, so it was affirmed. He loved painting, he honored it, and often bought paintings for his own pleasure. That is doubtless why he had already spent two fortunes to satisfy his passion.

The other was much younger, and, fortunately for him, perfectly ignorant in the matters of his trade. He was deceived a hundred times over, but always to his advantage. He had declared a host of run-of-the-mill paintings masterpieces, and declared detestable beautiful works that he had ended up buying for far less than their value.

Rivals as they were, they remained good friends, and as they had the same tastes, that is easily understandable. If they ran into one another in Monsieur de Kinseton's house this time, it was not hazard that had led them there; it was a commission given to them by one of the great noblemen of England, loaded down with pictures and no longer liking, at the present moment, anything but drawings by masters. He said that drawing was more sincere and truer than painting; that one could see the excellent imprint of the artist more fully therein, and that the naked work had an ineffable charm. It was, therefore, precisely to obtain from the famous artist some of his primitive compositions that the gentlemen in question had come to his studio.

"We're here," said Monsieur de Kinseton to the student Toiras, "and they're very welcome. We haven't had any money for a fortnight."

The student had hardly had the time to deploy the folding screen behind which the Transteverine was accustomed to hide. There, she was absent; her body was present, but her soul was elsewhere.

Scarcely had they come in, and without telling the painter what they wanted, when the two men stopped dead, so to speak, before the drawing that the young Kinseton was in the process of adoring. Such is the authority of a beautiful work; it bursts forth and shines at the same time. One glance is sufficient to grasp the ensemble and the detail. The person most ignorant of the mysteries of form and color soon yields to that divine magic. He looks; he admires; he contemplates.

Thus the four men, before a word as pronounced, found themselves halted before that work, still palpitating with the shudders of creation.

In the end, the connoisseur dealer broke the silence. "Ah!" he said. "That's what's called a thing of beauty—and until today, Monsieur, you'll willingly agree that nothing so perfect has emerged from your hands."

"Hmm!" said the other dealer, the inept connoisseur. "At first glance, one can't deny the effect of the image, and I'm as struck by it as you are—but what trouble and effort! How taut it all is, too virile, and much too contrived. But all in all, such as it is, I'd take it for a hundred écus."

"You think so?" said the other. "At twenty-five louis, that puny faun wouldn't be paid in full, and I'll offer a thousand-franc bill."

"You're spoiling the trade," the skeptic replied. "With a thousand francs, well-employed, you could have a little painting..."

"That's true," replied the enthusiast, "but I wouldn't have what I want: a drawing."

They were there, in their contemplation, when the great nobleman we mentioned arrived in person. He was one of those connoisseurs as blasé about the fine arts as everything else; they need some exceptional work, such as they have never seen, and which strikes them. Such people, fatigued by possessing everything, sleep on their paintings without seeing them, and on their money, without dipping into it. As soon as something is theirs, its charm and attraction suddenly vanishes. Their eyes, veiled with ennui, scarcely light up in the fire of an auction sale.

The nobleman felt awakened by the appetite for something unknown, and immediately offered a thousand écus for it, for the pleasure of burying it in his album. Three thousand francs! That was a lot for three hours' work, but Kinseton did not think that it was enough. He would not have given it away for anything in the world.

A furtive glance that he darted behind the screen put him entirely at his ease.

"Alas, Milord," he said, "I'm sorry for Your Lordship, but that image isn't for sale, and it wasn't me who made it. It came to me from another hand, and I couldn't console myself if I were unfortunate enough to lose such a perfect composition."

There was such great conviction in his tone as he spoke that the three men withdrew without persisting any further. That same day, there was a great celebration in the Clos Champenois between the painter and his student.

"Oh, Master," said the latter to the former, "how well you did, and what a precious ornament for our fortunate house."

Hidden in the depths of her abode, the proud Edith made herself very small, and regretted being thus delivered to the admiration of her two comrades. *To be loved and humbly take lessons from the Master was all of my glory*, she said to herself. *What will I become, now that they admire me in their turn?*

In the meantime, Monsieur de Kinseton was commissioned to paint a chapel in honor of the Black Virgin in one of the old churches of Paris.[62] He was only asked to bring his sketches and have them approved by the ecclesiastical authorities. He was, therefore, gripped by the fever of great compositions. He dreamed about it by night and thought about it all day.

He knew the legend and the history of the Black Virgin, and immediately started searching for a model.

In the end, he found one in the vicinity of the Théâtre Montmartre, among idle actors warming themselves in the September sun: a daughter of Abyssinia, strange to behold, but of whom a skillful painter could make good use. It was not very difficult to make his request to the woman in question, exposed to all the hazards of the theater and the studio. She had no other ambition than to live and ornament herself. At

---

[62] A *Vierge Noire* [Black Virgin, or Black Madonna] is a kind of icon or statue, Medieval in origin and often Byzantine in style, of which nearly two hundred samples were known to exist in France when this story was written. The original significance of the dark-skinned images of Jesus' mother is enigmatic, and it is highly probable that most of them are the result of deteriorated pigmentation or blackening by votive candles, but French legend-mongers were not to be caught at a loss, and manufactured various stories to account for the images; although Janin does not specify which one springs to Kinseton's mind, we shall subsequently discover that his family hails from Aigues-Mortes, and he would therefore have been familiar with the story associating such images with St. Sara, the patron saint of gypsies: the black servant who allegedly accompanied Mary Magdalene, Mary Salome, Mary Jacobe and Joseph of Arimathea to the Camargue after the crucifixion. The town of Saintes-Maries-de-la-Mer is not far from Aigues-Mortes.

present, she was due to dance in a ballet composed with her in mind, to the music of a pupil at the Conservatoire—in brief, the utmost depths of dramatic art. And yet, he had found nothing better in spite of all his research.

There he was, then, attracted by that olive-skinned dancer, searching her face, ravaged by hunger and thirst, for the radiant features of a daughter of Heaven. And so hard did he search in those abysms of vanity and rags that he ended up, imprudently, being caught by those miserable traps.

No explanation, no excuses; by virtue of studying that inert body, he began to find it likeable; by raising all that abasement to the dignity of a work of art, the ornament of a altar, the unfortunate fellow became the dupe of his own work. He treated that filthy model as Pygmalion did his statue; he called an Abyssinian woman brought from the slave-market the Black Virgin!

He did not hide from himself in order to obey his sad inclination. It seemed to him that his passion was the consequence of the task undertaken. On that account, he did not see the profound horror of young Edith for those amours of the street, and when the student wanted to close the door on the woman he called "the Negress" that unfortunate painter became so angry that the whole studio trembled. It was necessary to obey, and whether the Negress arrived through the main courtyard or the corridor leading to the street, she found the door open. Like her painter, she had no suspicion that anyone could find her conduct reprehensible.

In those somber hours, the painter was at his canvas, and the student went out with his friends into Paris, the great city. Alone in that abode, where she had spent such beautiful hours of innocence and pride, of which her voice had once filled the joyful echoes, in which her slightest desire was a command, Edith proudly bore that ordeal. In fact, she lived, in a corner of the Clos Champenois, in an old Montmartre windmill, which the young painter had repaired for his ward's use.

As soon as she had crossed the abrupt threshold of that place of refuge, she was truly at home, under the benevolent protection of Madame Robert. Sometimes she read the beautiful books of her Italian homeland, Ariosto or Tasso, and most often old Dante; or else she sang in a low voice. She drew, she dreamed; she heard the voice and agitation of the great city surging from the distant vapors, similar to those lakes of somber fire in which a conflagration is dormant.

That disquieting year, however, whose commencements had been so peaceful, its middle so tender, and whose recent days had hidden so many storms, dissipated for the sad Edith in mortal discouragement. In such a short time, hope had given way to despair, shadow to darkness, work to exhaustion. Simply because that happy house had welcomed that Egyptian woman, that daughter of the Dead Sea, and because she came, every day, to represent graces and virtues of which she did not know the first thing, nothing lived any longer, nothing sang. The blackbird forgot to chatter, the linnet and the chaffinch had nothing more to say. There was nothing joyful but the osprey and its ally the hawk, which filled the air with their furious and murderous screeches.

In the meantime, winter, baying its furies, heaped up the snow and the fog on the miserable heights. Everything froze; everything was confused. The studio creaked and lamented in a grim fashion. Unending rain fell from the inexhaustible urn.

Oh, Montmartre is beautiful when a radiant sun rises, in the vast aspect of a flamboyant noon! And in the evening, what is more charming than light in decline, fluid and pale, through light clouds filled with caprice and fantasy? One feels alive, and the heart palpitates at those charming impressions; the mountain wakes up, reawakening the sleeping plain, or the plain, in the first zephyrs of the morning, pushing back its veil through the softened air. A charming concert of all noises and all silences; a radiant echo of all the delights of earth and sky! But as soon as the hour is somber and the air severe; in the midst of obstacles that surge from below, and in fear of the abysms on high; when disorder is king, and the tumult arrives, accumulating north winds in tempests; when there is no longer anything but solitude and noise, menace and frisson, nothing can compare, for sadness and ennui, to those dwellings of lamentations. The idle man, looking at them from below, asks himself whether they are really inhabited by rational creatures.

To get back to our story, for nearly an entire fortnight the earth had been inundated. An incessant infiltration was heard beneath that seemingly solid wall of chalk. Sometimes there were terrible gusts of wind, with pitiless roars, which made the stone-carved windmills tremble. Everything was groaning, weeping and lamenting in that cloud and that desert, and God knows how cold the young Roman girl was in her retreat neighboring the hurricane.

It was in one of the last days of the month of December, and Christmas Eve, that after many futile rehearsals, the Abyssinian was finally advertised in her ballet. She was playing the principal role on one of those operatic-balletic-poems that are neither dance, nor drama, nor song. The audience, however, was considerable, attracted as much by midnight mass as the black dancer.

Scarcely had the hall opened that Monsieur de Kinseton, driven by the double interest of the painter and the lover, was at his post. Sometimes he hid, ashamed of himself, and sometimes, outside his box, he contemplated as only a painter can that strange model, full of horror and beauty.

One might have thought that the public shared the charm and repulsion of the painter. They applauded wildly; they whistled furiously. The woman was an inexplicable mystery for the people; they would willingly have said, as Nero did of his mistress: "I want her put to the torture, in order that she can at least tell me why I love her."

She talked as if she were yapping; she danced...it was not dancing, but bounding. In that bounding there was a certain intoxication akin to ecstasy. The savage truly had a plastic beauty, and the painter was well within his rights to gaze at her deliriously. Monotonous music and other-worldly songs were a worthy accompaniment to that lugubrious ballet, in which one might have thought that the dancer had discolored her entourage.

Outside, the rain was falling in torrents, the wind was whistling and the trees were lamenting.

Suddenly, the entire theater trembled on its foundations, and the spectators, woken up with a painful start, remained frightened by that *coup de théâtre*. A formidable noise charged the echoes with the most terrible threats, but silence soon resumed its authority over the shaken mountain.

At that moment, by a profound intuition of his misfortune, the young painter, bewildered and frightened, ran out, abandoning his goddess, appealing to all the vagabonds in the vicinity, the beggars lying in the ruins and the thieves asleep under lime-ovens—a Parisian society devoid of bread, shelter and fear.

"Help! Help!" he cried. And in his hectic course he saw those specters emerging from the shadows, those old men without morals, those women without laws, without children, without God.

They had understood, at the first sound, that they were being summoned to an immense ruin, that they would have their part to play; and, pale and silent, creeping through the shadows, they obeyed the misery that was summoning them. Imagine the astonishment of those ghosts, on seeing themselves invoked as if they had had light and hope!

Thus, without any other word of instruction, they gathered at the bottom of the hill, down which the fortune and the studio of the unfortunate painter had slid. *Hic jacent!*

And let us do justice to the artist; he did not give any thought to his buried work; he did not weep for his devastated house; he had no concern for so many beautiful things heaped up at such great expense. No, no! His pain and disorder, at that moment, came from his young pupil, buried under those ruins.

"My dear child! My friend! My student, my little student, where are you? Answer me?"

He searched by the light of torches, and it was with great difficulty that the bandits that had run in answer to his appeal pulled him out of the densest part of the ruin, where he had been thrown. Finally, God be praised, he found the poor child, half-broken on his bed. He was still alive; he was still breathing.

"Oh, my friends," said Kinseton, "I have my wealth—you can have the rest..."

And the invading troop carried everything away: the pillars, the debris; all the broken, soiled things that had previously represented so much joy and happiness.

At daybreak, the place was clear; one would not have thought that beauty, genius and youth had passed that way.

That great noise, those sinister plaints, that reckless storm on the mountain, had snatched the valiant Edith from a sleep full of torpor. We have said that she lived alone, with her maidservant, in the lodge of which old Madame Robert was the concierge, but that evening, the watcher, inadequately watched, had left her post and, tranquilized by the locked door, had gone to midnight mass, That is why the young woman, mute witness of the great cataclysm, remained motionless at her window, calling, but in vain, for help.

She had divined, rather than having seen, the great disaster. She could not understand it at all. She thought she was having a bad dream. She asked herself what the meaning was of that dark mass and that noise.

Oh, when she heard the loud cries of Monsieur de Kinseton calling to the young man and asking the rain. the storm and the ruin for him, and when she saw, running from all their caverns, all those savages, who would have sufficed to demolish the palace of Versailles within twenty-four hours, she understood all that misery. In her turn, she cried: "Help! Help!"

For more than an hour, she listened to his moans and his tears, until the moment when, the door having been opened, she raced out in her night-dress to the side of the young man who had been pulled out, in the midst of so many perils, from that crumbled roof.

While the night-prowlers, at the sound of the summon beaten by the guardians of the city, went back into their holes, as one sees the ashes of a burning piece of paper gradually devoured by invisible flames, the poor child, an innocent victim of his fidelity to the lodgings where the young woman lived and the studio where his young master worked, was carried into the old windmill.

The old windmill had remained standing; it had stood up to all tempests for two hundred years!

There was a kind of convoy full of sobs and tears, which each of them was trying to hold back.

The student, transported to that place of safety, recognized at his bedside, leaning over his agony, everyone that he loved in this base world: Edith and Monsieur de Kinseton. He recognized them with a smile.

In the end, summoning up all his strength, he took their two hands in his dying hand, and, touching them to his lips, expired.

The young woman and the young master remained silent and mute, searching for a residue of life...

He was dead.

"I loved him!" said Edith, looking at Monsieur de Kinseton.

And the latter felt himself pierced to the depths of his heart.

When daylight came, the disaster appeared in all its formidable magnificence. A part of the Clos Champenois had collapsed and been precipitated in an avalanche through the rain-drenched terrains. There was no longer any vestige of the studio, which, the day before, had been full of hope and endeavor. In a matter of seconds, the unfortunate possessor of so much wealth, which was his joy and his pride, had lost everything: his adoptive son; his brushes; his palette; and all his canvases, every one of which, unfinished, was a subject of study, a force, a memory. He had lost those precious studies that the artist only makes once in his travels through the museums. The storm had reduced to nothing those albums, those sketches, those dreams, those puffs of smoke, those memories that the pencil confides to the album of a traveler. The ruin had created a tabula rasa.

He could scarcely remember so many works commenced or imagined in that frail space now completely covered in mud and slime. But the veritable object of his pain and the subject of his tears, his inconsolable affliction, was young Edith's three words: "I loved him!"

Then, he saw again, very clearly, the gaieties of those two natures, so dissimilar to one another at first glance. He heard the young man's sparkling laughter; he rediscovered the slightest tone of the young woman's mockeries when she was in a good mood. He would have given anything in the world to have saved the image of the little faun, a masterpiece that she had made with a deft hand.

In that formless despair, he saw everything in its place once again, with the tone, the gaze and all the enchantment of before. He understood his fault fully now, and how Edith, whom he had neglected, and treated as a soul that he did not doubt, had ended up being secretly smitten with the innocent Student-Toiras. And still he could hear those words in his lacerated ears: "I loved him!"

Edith, however, that semi-dormant child, the languishing Edith, seeing the peril of the situation and her young master's infinite dejection, had suddenly woken up. A single incident had made the girl into an absolute lady, a force of will presiding over everything.

She had followed student Toiras' coffin to the nearby cemetery, carried by six young friends of the studio. She had designed the tombstone herself, and when she received a hundred louis from her friend the vine-grower for that good work, she felt so much gratitude that nothing, henceforth, could have made her forget such a reward.

The funeral was scarcely over when Monsieur de Kinseton received an absolute order from the city. Within twenty-four hours he had to quit his final shelter, that tottering house, and seek his fortune elsewhere. It was another hard blow; he had planned to establish himself within those walls and remake a garden in the chaos. Nevertheless, he obeyed without saying a word, and, descending from the heights where they had been so peaceful, Edith and he found lodgings at the bottom of the mount, in a new and poorly-constructed house in the shade.

The ruination of artists and kings proceeds rapidly. The greater you seem in prosperity, the more misfortune overwhelms you. Gradually, without yet admitting it, Edith and Kinseton, sensed necessity weighing upon their innocent heads. Edith had a fever; she had been exposed to the storm for too long, and she simply did not have the strength to go any further.

Another difficulty: the young artist had incurred debts. How can one not incur debts at an age replete with temptations, when money is so easy to make and enthusiasts snatch your works from your hand as soon as they are begun? One says to oneself: "I'm the king of the world." One finds an excuse for every whim. With that great word, *artist*, one goes from passion to passion; one buys on a whim, everything that pleases the eye; curiosity becomes second nature, and one congratulates oneself, out loud, for loving such beautiful things. Add that the credit is so generous for the painter adopted by the public.

It's true that, at the slightest accident, the credit disappears, often never to return. The merchants and second-hand dealers of Paris are unworried as long as they can seen the paintings, marbles and porcelain heaped up in the rich studio and answering for their owner, but when they learn of the entire ruin and the irreparable loss of so many riches, which they regarded as their guarantee, they hasten to present their bills.

"This time, my dear master" said young Edith, "you have a good motive for going back to work. Courage! Forget, for a moment, the pain and the chagrin for the present necessity, and, when the public have rediscovered their familiar artist, as soon as you've exhibited a beautiful canvas, and the merchants come back, as eager as before, you'll calm all these anxieties with a word. Then, the men who are pressing you will be at your feet. Meanwhile, take this money, which I've earned engraving these little woodcuts that aren't too unworthy of publicity. The young shade of our friend student Toiras will be pleased to see us profiting from the fruits of that work, which is his as much as mine. How many times he abridged my task, and how happy he was when I woke up to find that I had no more to do than the fine and delicate lines, the rest having been removed by the poor friend I so often discouraged."

"You're right, my dear and courageous Edith," replied Monsieur de Kinseton. "It's no longer the time when I could intoxicate myself with dreams and lend an ear to the early morning song of the skylark. We're entering into a life of austerity, and work alone can save us. Let's be patient! Let's allow inspiration to return. At the moment, an insurmountable force is stopping me and holding me back. In sum, you see, I don't even have a canvas, a palette and colors. The one who made my palette is up above!"

"If you please," Edith replied, "I'll make it myself. Everything has been foreseen, Monsieur Artist. Now, here's the canvas and the brush, and pencils. I've saved, thank God, the first sketch of the painting that was lost. Here it is. Copy it. That will be the least trouble, and you'll soon have recovered the shadows, the light, the grace, the landscape and the charming background, and the radiance on the waters wrinkled by the morning breeze."

Speaking thus, she was exceedingly engaging; she was irresistible. She sat down on a wretched armchair, without thinking too much about the Trianon armchair.

Vanquished by so many pleas, and above all by the tearful gaze that encouraged him, the young artist finally picked up the pencil offered to him by the beautiful hand.

He could already see again, in that errant shadow, the idyll commenced so well. He told himself that he would go to find his beautiful model, and that the model, understanding the necessity of success, would resume the calm assurance and glad attitude of last April.

There he is, trembling with an ineffable emotion, wanting to cast on to the canvas a first impression of the painting destined to recover his fortune and his courage...

O misery! O woe! His hand was trembling; it is trembling still. In vain he leans it, effortfully, upon the painter's staff...

Oh! This is the final blow, the final torment! He has lost the sureness of his hand; it no longer obeys his glance; it goes further than his thought or lags behind. Imagine the stupor of the unfortunate young man; can you understand his fear, at that irresistible quaking of his fibers?

Was it true, then? Since his great misfortune, he had had a premonition of that further disaster.

Then, bowing his head beneath implacable necessity, he covered his eyes with his afflicted hands, and he felt them quivering over his eyes, which were weeping.

At this point, a profound silence entered into Edith and the young man. She sought in vain for a consolation. He sought, without finding, a glimmer of hope. He really was definitively doomed. Henceforth, what could he do and what would become of him? Never had distress been simultaneously so great and so complete.

"Oh, my dear Edith," he said to her, seeing her prey to the fever that had not let her go, "I've been very afraid of losing you, and I want you to survive. Where would you have found a tenderness equal to mine, and a more honest adoption? And if I've sometimes neglected the cares of my guardianship, alas, that forgetfulness came precisely from the great happiness that surrounded us. Now, you're ill, and that's fortunate for my glory. I know you; you would have worked in my stead. Alas, hardship and work are made for those as well as you and I were six weeks ago. God be praised, your youth will soon get the upper hand. The great artist that you leave in the shadow, who woke up once with so much brilliance, will reappear in all her force. Oh, what a beautiful image you made, of which I would have been jealous, had I not preferred you to everything!"

He hoped for a long time that the crisis was temporary. Impatient to work, he expected every morning that his hand, so long valiant, would have recovered its energy and accuracy.

Vain hope, alas! Although the glance was just and clear, the hand still trembled; the indecisive image went here and there, full of caprice and hazard. What misfortune, when the pencil fails the design, the instrument the will, the form the color!

In that energetic struggle, all of whose dolors he alone knew, the unfortunate artist felt the last days of his youth being consumed. As much as he could, he hid his misery, but the clients, incessantly and endlessly refused under various pretexts, renounced their requests.

Some said: "He's a hypochondriac."

Others said: "He's mad."

The most malevolent claimed that he had lost the better part of his talent in losing student Toiras. One morning, as he was walking in the sun, he was able to read on a wall, in capital letters: KINSETON, CRETIN.

Woe to the vanquished! Thrice woe to the vanquished! Always the pitiless word of our ancestor Brennus, which he applies to the painter, the poet, the lover, the captain and the Statesman.[63]

In those days, all painting was occupied in saluting the two newcomers, the two masters of color: Marilhat, the Orientalist, and Decamps, who came back fully laden with the booty of our conquest of Algeria.[64] There was also, to keep the world attentive to his exploits, a kind of hero named Eugène Dela-

---

[63] Brennus was a Gaulish tribal leader who led the Senones in a attack on Rome in 387 B.C. He is credited by the Roman historian Livy, improbably, with uttering the famous cry: "Vae victis!" [Woe to the Vanquished], which became ironic when the Gauls were subsequently beaten by Camillus, subsequently hailed as the "second founder" (after Romulus) of Rome.

[64] Prosper Marilhat (1811-1847) first exhibited in the Paris salons from 1837-41. His fellow Orientalist Alexander-Gabriel Decamps (1803-1860) began exhibiting slightly earlier but would still have been reckoned a newcomer at that time.

croix, full of the nascent pride of the *Massacre at Chios*.[65] Then, in the distance, a fine spirit, who had become in twenty-four hours, and just that once, a very great painter. His name was Charlet. That Charlet, of battles, soldiers and children, showed the attentive people, in one moving canvas, the battle and heroes the Béranger sang.[66]

Behold, therefore, the somber oblivion, the supreme oblivion, that has fallen like a crepe over your renown, unfortunate Kinseton!

Full of strength and life, and a powerful imagination, he witnessed, disarmed, the greatest and most generous struggle of new talents of French painting. And the more he contemplated those marvels, the more he rendered the justice to himself that perhaps he was not unworthy to enter that illustrious arena. Finally, driven to the extreme of delirium, he could not console himself for having been stopped by that nameless accident: a nerve disturbed, a finger that no longer worked. His talent was at its apogee, and his impotence too!

Certainly, the courageous Edith played her part in these indescribable miseries. She sensed that she was indispensable to that unfortunate man, whom she had seen in such fine fortune; she sensed that he was living dependent on her life, and by virtue of a kind of filial piety she resolved to save the young man to whom her father had confided her.

She said, later, that she had never lost hope. She did well.

First, she acquired the certainty that she and he would be able to live, just about, on their work. He learned fairly rapidly to draw and engrave with his left hand. He succeeded in pro-

---

[65] Eugène Delacroix's Massacre at Chois was exhibited in the Salon of 1824, which implies an earlier date than the previous citations, although it could still have been plausibly reckoned to be "recent" in the early 1830s.

[66] Nicolas Toussaint Charlet exhibited three oil paintings of military subjects in 1836, 1837 and 1843, but the subsidiary reference must be to his lithographs of peasant life, of which he produced a renowned set of fifty between 1838 and 1842.

ducing etchings that were immediately acceptable. He signed them with Edith's name; she smiled at that unexpected glory. Edith, for her part, with her mastery of charcoal, composed great designs, full of genius and imperfection, which she proudly signed: E. de Kinseton. There never was a more innocent deception. Thus, he had his second string—but the connoisseurs regretted the original painter. They bought the drawings, but demanded paintings.

Gradually, their affairs were put in order and, thanks to numerous commissions, the humble household glimpsed better days. As good fortune does not come alone, help arrived, on which they were no longer counting. They were of the proud and laborious race that does not know how to put out a hand, but they were not very astonished when they received a second letter from Kinseton the vine-grower.

Friend, he said to his homonym, *is it true that you're no longer doing anything? Some say that you've gone mad; others say, which is worse, that you no longer have talent, that you lost it in losing student Toiras, the true author of your most beautiful works.*

In vain, for nearly eighteen months, I've been asking for Monsieur de Kinseton's new painting. All that anyone has been able to send me is a sequence of beautiful etchings by your pupil Edith, and truly they represent, with no possibility of error, one of the characteristics of your old talent: poetry and the ideal. In that confusion, in which one finds both a virile hand and the talent of a young Muse, one senses life and movement, errant plants and distant songs, the murmur of fresh waters, the hum of tall grass, the rustle of woods. Everything and nothing! But the vulgar do not appreciate these unfinished beauties. You and Edith will have difficulty living, once the first fervor of these metamorphoses is over.

Finally, I'm afraid, even on seeing certain drawings signed by you, that you might soon be weary. I have, therefore, collected, on your behalf, all my ready money. It's not very much. Accept it with as much heart as I offer it to you, and, henceforth, no longer count on me. I have lost my liberty, mis-

erably. Since the day when I left you, my heart full of all your affection, an evil passion has taken over my entire life, and I have lost the right henceforth to open my house to courage, innocence and virtue.

From now on, my dear Kinseton, I am no longer your cousin. I shall no longer have the honor and happiness of calling the beautiful and proud Edith my relative. She shall not come under my dishonored roof. I'm lost to her and to you. Don't thank me; you would bring down a great storm on my head. Don't write to me again, I no longer read any but letters that have been torn up and soiled.

Pray for me. Weep for me.

The unfortunate N. de Kinseton

When they had opened that horrible letter, Edith and her friend looked at one another in silence; they tried to understand, and the very effort redoubled the cloud. The letter enclosed a sum of money at least equal to all the debts they still had.

"Let's obey the wishes of this dying man," said Edith. "Let's pay our debts; let's be free, and then we'll think about going to the aid of that friend who hasn't forgotten the honor of the poor and the repose of the dead. As true as there's a God in Heaven, if you'll let me do it, my young master, I'll save Monsieur de Kinseton."

Speaking thus, her gaze was full of hope; an aureole was upon her brow. Anyone who did not believe in the inspiration of that good genius would have been a criminal or a madman.

"And me," exclaimed the artist, drunk on hope, "and me, my dear Edith, are you forgetting me in your miracles?"

"No, no!" she cried, "you'll be saved, you too!"

The next day, as he was finishing off a patch of sky with his left hand, she said to him: "You didn't notice, although it would have been worth the trouble, the seal on that letter from our friend the wine-grower?"

"That's true," the artist replied. "But what does it matter?"

"What does it matter, you say? But the seal is a revelation. The arms are the same as yours, and come, I'm sure of it, from the armoried jewel-case found on the child after his shipwreck. There's no need to compare them any longer to be sure of the resemblance, and, the identity being clear and striking, given that you're a gallant man, a friend of justice and grateful for a favor, we're going to leave immediately for Aigues-Mortes, your birthplace, in order to seek information regarding that lost child, who must belong to our family."

"Well," replied Monsieur de Kinseton, "let's suppose that I do, in fact, rediscover a Kinseton forgotten in those sands, which gives me sufficient explanation to establish my kinship with the benefactor that fell from Heaven for us, what difference would it make?"

"What difference would it make?" exclaimed Edith, indignantly. "As soon as we have proof of a common origin and those rights that relatives have in respect of one another by natural law and human law, you'll be able to that abandoned individual who is as avid for a family as a deer for the water of a spring: 'Here I am; I belong to you, you to me; we have the same name, we have the same origin, and it's my duty, as it's yours, to protect our common honor.'

"What difference does it make? The difference we'll have the right to knock on the door that is closed to us and chase away therefrom the tyrant who's oppressing us. Thus, sick or healthy, rich or poor, fortunate or unfortunate, as soon as this friend is recognized as a Kinseton of our family, he'll become for us an object of solicitude. That's why, if you please, we're leaving immediately!"

And she immediately set about making arrangements for the departure. She wanted to pack the palette and the paint-box herself.

"Is it true, then, my dear Edith," said the artist, "that you'll bring me back cured?"

"Yes, cured," she said, "with a family, and more talent than before."

The painter was about to abandon himself entirely to his joy, but he stopped when he saw the young woman mingling with her most beautiful dresses the costume of the young student Toiras, his Sunday clothes, so clearly marked that the buttonhole still bore a sprig of the wild thyme that perfumed the obliterated garden.

Three days later, the young painter, Edith, the old maid-servant and even the faithful dog, climbed gravely into the Midi diligence. Things did not proceed very rapidly as yet in those days. The railways were still extending their branches with difficulty, and diligences did the rest.

Scarcely was she installed beside her traveling companion when Edith uttered a deep sigh of delight.

"Ah!" she said. "Finally, I can rest. Agree, my dear friend, that for what will soon be an entire year, Edith has done nothing but work. Don't commend me; allow me to praise myself: Edith has maintained courage and hope. Oh, these men! They'd get lost in the pathways of Meudon, they'd drown in the Swiss fountain! For a few paintings lost in a studio foundered in sand and clay, I know one of them who'd have died of despair. For a tremor in his right hand, he no longer slept, and lamented in whispers. So, believe me, all those dolors are trivial. It's only our unfortunate companion who merits our regret. But what joy! Now we're off! Bon voyage! And let me sleep at my ease, or gaze at the landscape while dreaming. Look, it's so beautiful! It's so charming, to close one's eyes and bring back the vanished landscape! Nothing to do, being transported through space, going to one's destination, painlessly and effortlessly. Already I can breathe, and I feel well!"

Throughout the first day they were almost alone in the diligence. There were travelers from one town to another, and that very succession of different faces was another pleasure. Sometimes an old lady and her granddaughter chatted with open hearts; sometimes a fat merchant calculated his future profits in his notebook. A commercial traveler, of a race now extinct, took possession of the table in the inn and deployed all his grace before the beautiful Edith's eyes. Every village, at the relays, came out to see the people passing through. Madame Robert and her dog experienced the delights of the cabriolet.

There was even a moment when the seat opposite Edith and Monsieur de Kinseton was occupied by a girl and a young cousin who were slowly following the long-armed telegraph with their eyes. That old telegraph was a good friend to runaway lovers; if, by chance, they were close to being caught, he turned his kindly face away, and terminated his betrayal with the benevolent sentence: *interrupted by fog.*[67] The fog was his accomplice. Oh, how many innocent heads the old telegraph and the fog have saved! Today, poor lovers, no more hope! A pitiless machine that nothing stops; an incessant tattletale with little strident screeches that warn every gendarme and travel like the wind to surprise, on arrival, young Chevalier des Grieux and the beautiful Manon Lescaut.[68]

When they had passed Lyon, on the ridge, at the moment when the Midi appeared, a traveler who was still young but full of gravity, wearing a white cravat, climbed into the heavy carriage and sat down, without saying a word, beside Monsieur de Kinseton. The newcomer was obviously in a great hurry to get home, and was already gazing into the distance as if he ought to be able to see it.

Near Ampuy, at the relay of the *Croix d'or*, the curé of some neighboring village was standing, who had just dined in the presbytery, to judge by his eyes, brighter than usual, and the last words spoken to him by to his host, the local curé:

---

[67] The "telegraph" in question was the semaphore system invented by Claude Chappe in 1792 which was installed throughout France in the Napoleonic era and remained in use for some time after the invention of the electric telegraph, which gradually displaced it.

[68] In the 1731 novel by the Abbé Prevost, usually known as *Manon Lescaut.*

"Adieu, my dear colleague; a pleasure to see you again. Expect me in a fortnight."

"I'm counting on it," said the traveler. "Adieu, my dear Curé; thank you, Brigitte."

He took his little valise from Brigitte's hands, and, as the coachman plied his whip, off they went again.

Not one of these little details escaped the curious gaze of young Edith, but as soon as the errant drama of the highways fell silent, the young woman, fatigued by two days of travel, retreated into her corner and went back to sleep. Then, the artist covered her with his cloak and, with the blinds lowered, he listened to her sleeping, watching over her with an entirely paternal care.

Most of the time, the travelers began by respecting that slumber for four or five minutes, the time it takes a girl to fall asleep. This time, however, the curé had scarcely sat down when he exclaimed: "Is that you, my dear notary? I'm glad to see you again! Where are you coming from? What have you been doing? I left town this morning, and I can give you good news. All's going well. Madame your wife was at the window, and Messieurs your clerks seemed very busy with their writing when I went past your house."

To these words from his curé, the notary paid great attention. He was utterly charmed by the good news of his wife and staff, and as he had not talked since the morning, he took advantage of the opportunity.

"I'm coming from Paris, Monsieur le Curé, where I took a sum of money on behalf of a client who instructed me to bring back a painting that I haven't found. I'm annoyed, for the worthy fellow is extremely sad, and we no longer know how to cheer him up."

"I know who you're talking about," the curé replied. "Your client is one of my flock, and I think he's very ill. Terrible tales are being told about him, but you know them better than I do, and since we're almost alone, the road is level and the horses are moving at a steady pace, tell me, if you please, about the great changes that have made that peaceful house into a Hell, and that Christian a skeptic, and that benevolent man, a friend of joy and good works, into a veritable were-wolf. You know, my dear friend, that if I'm interrogating you, there's far less curiosity in my question than sympathy and charity."

Here, the notary's gaze went to the side of the carriage where young Edith was asleep under the eyes of her guardian. The artist seemed fully occupied with the sleeping girl. Thus reassured, the ministerial officer commenced his story in a prudent voice, although it's true that the voice rose in volume as the interest of the story increased. A squeeze of the hand told Monsieur de Kinseton that he was not alone in listening.

"You know, Monsieur le Curé, that it will soon be ten years since a stranger, who was not from these parts, took possession, at the price of half a million, of the beautiful vines and manor of Saint-Gilles. He paid for his acquisition with cash. He renovated the dilapidated house, replaced all the dead wood in the vineyard. He was good to the poor, easy on the vine-growers, and everyone soon took to him because he sold his harvest at a modest price, without any finesse or secrecy. He stated his price to everyone, and everyone could believe it. He would have blushed at the vulgar skill that consists of quoting one's neighbors a fictitious price. If he kept his harvest, he did not hide it. In the meantime, one could see immediately that he was a good vine-grower, that he knew his vintages, and knew how to treat them, as a father and as a worthy and honest merchant."

"All that's true," the curé replied, "and I can add that the brave man accomplished his Christian duties in a worthy manner. He never failed to celebrate the major festivals with us; he rendered the blessed bread a little more often than in his turn. If he saw me passing by on my gray mare, coming and going between the rich and the poor, he came to his doorstep and gave me a good greeting. 'Monsieur le Curé,' he said, 'won't the manor of Saint-Gilles have the honor of your visit today?' I went in without being asked twice. Whoever disdains benevolent hospitality discourages the person who offers it. Many a time, under the thick trellis and in the heat of June, I tasted the humble white wine of the Côte Saint-Gilles, which doesn't have the celebrity that it merits. And there were the beautiful fruits, the beautiful peaches, the Muscat grapes that he made me carry away at the petty trot of my well-rested gray, who was very familiar with the taste of the oats of the fields of Saint-Gilles!

"Now it's all somber and closed. There's not a hole in the hedge through which a child can slip to eat his fill. The carriage entrance is reinforced with iron. The vine-growers have stopped singing. The poor are neglected on the estate where they used to be welcome. To cap it all, we hardly ever, even at Easter, glimpse the faithful soul that I once called, secretly, the churchwarden of Saint-Dizier, our parish.

"Thus far, the evil is without remedy, and the danger seems to be increasing every day. That's where we are! That joyful spirit, that gentleman, surrounded by all the graces of life, seemed unreachable by any misfortune. He was rich, loved, honored; everyone knew that his fortune was well-earned, and earned with difficulty in the bowels of the earth, and that the longer he had lived in darkness, the more he loved life in the open air, in the sun. The coal he had exploited doubled the price of the vintage; at the sight of an espalier laden with autumn fruits, he always talked about his brothers the miners. He blessed coal, because it had made his fortune; he cursed it when he thought of the unfortunate creatures who lived in those abysms, by the pale light of fetid lamps, under the threat of firedamp.

"All was benevolence in that noble heart. He would gladly salute his cousins the skylarks and his friends the nightingales. His unique chagrin was to have no other family…and yet, he ended up discovering a celebrated artist who bore his name, and even his forename; and, by virtue of an infinite hope, he attached himself to that excellent painter. He bought his works every year; he made them the ornament of his manor. He talked to us about his adoptive daughter, as beautiful as an angel and as proud as a queen. He even bought paintings by the student, a scamp, and made me a present of them. You've been able to see them in my drawing-room, with the portrait of my wife in their midst."

"An unfortunate journey he made to Paris lost all that. He stayed there for six months, and came back very content with the time he had spent in that sympathetic milieu; he re-called so much good laughter and so many fine tales, the joy-ful gazes of the young girl, and the mischief of the student. He had collected several clues that might lead him to recover his family...

"Alas, his misfortune dictated that he set foot on the boat that goes from Lyon to Mâcon...within an hour, he was lost. A woman was there, half lady and half servant. An unbleached apron covered a fur-trimmed dress; she had the mittens and shoes of a duchesse, the skirt of a seaman's wife and an Italian straw hat. She was insolent and seductive. She attracted some by her courtesy, and drove others away with her rudeness. The Prefect is certainly not a man to be put off by a refusal; every-one knows that he has tamed the most rebellious, and that his plea is a command, but she treated him like a good-for-nothing. Scarcely had she caught sight of the lord and master of the manor of Saint-Gilles, however, than she divined that she had just found a slave, and, as she was in search of a place to sit down, she placed herself at his side.

"She was genuinely young and beautiful, with the gaze of her feline race: an insolent gesture, a humble attitude. She told that man, intoxicated by her presence, whatever she wished. He did not struggle for a single instant; he obeyed the charm; he followed her with open eyes.

"Imagine the universal amazement when the town—which readily comes out to watch the arrival and departure of the ferry—saw that man, honored by everyone, take his hat off and offer his arm to that stranger, whose overnight bag he was carrying! All the ladies flocking on to the jetty, and others more serious, who were leaning on the parapet of the quay, stood there, mute witnesses to the scandal, and the marriagea-ble demoiselles and young widows shut their eyes, weeping over their collapsed châteaux. The two of them disappeared, in the midst of the astonishment—let us say more, of the universal scorn.

"Our story ends there. We have nothing else but conjectures. We only know that the manor's faithful maidservant, the worthy Alison, was pitilessly dismissed after a week. All the older servants found themselves replaced by unemployed lackeys from the suburbs of Vèze. The Megaera has invaded everything with her unmitigated domination. She commands; it's necessary to obey. It's said that she has struck her slave more than once, and if, by chance, the poor fellow rebels, he comes back a moment later on his knees to beg for forgiveness.

"Believe me, Monsieur le Curé; he's very unhappy! He has renounced all joys; he has chased away all his friends. The ladies whom he liked and visited, the good-humored Burgundiennes whose houses were open to him, he avoids. The paintings that he bought out of glory, the sight of which rejoiced his charmed gaze, the Megaera has locked away. In the dark hours when the captive might perhaps escape his jailer, she weeps in her turn, she laments, she invokes his devotion with loud cries, and, as she is very beautiful, she is heeded and victorious.

"Thus, the torture goes on every day, the pain every hour. Isolation and abandonment have placed their tabernacles upon that dwelling, formerly so content.

"What can and ought to be done? How can the poor man be saved and rescued from himself? He's reached the limit of his strength, and the limit of his credit. His cellars are empty, his casks exhausted. He's already sold two fine fields, the honor of his domain. If he still had one relative, one friend, to defend him, someone to protect him...but there's no one. For a moment, I thought that he still had a family in Paris...vain hope. He loves, it's true, the poor devil of an artist whose works he once bought, but it appears that the poor young man has lost his talent, and is no longer good for anything much. So, from that direction too, there's no hope."

As he finished his speech, the notary glimpsed, by the roadside, a young woman and two lovely children who were waiting for him, bouquet in hand, smiles on their lips, with joyful cries. He got down first, and when the curé took his leave he said: "You're right, Maître Honoré, let's pray to God for that unfortunate, for God alone can save him."

Naturally, these words, whose meaning could not escape them, caused our two travelers to reflect. They illuminated an unexplained mystery with a sudden light. So that was why, when they had expected to see their friend the vine-grower come to their aid in their misery, he had scarcely given any sign of life. They understood everything now, and God knows that they felt the most profound pity for the unfortunate fellow.

"Alas," said the young painter, blushing deeply, "he too has encountered the Black Virgin, and, to make things worse, he hasn't found the angel that could drive the demon away."

The rest of the journey was nothing but silence and meditation. The following day, in the mot modest fashion, they came into the town of Nîmes, where Roman civilization has left so many half-crumbling masterpieces.

Scarcely were they in Nîmes when one might have thought that Edith the Roman had rediscovered her homeland. Content and superb, she traversed the Pont du Gard built to carry, in turn, armies and birds, strong and light is its workmanship. She visited the great circus, where so many generations had spent, in glory and in pleasure, hours filled with license, eating their masters' bread and lending their ears to the roars of lions and tigers. She admired the Roman ladies' baths, the crystal encased in the marble, and, pricking up her ears, it seemed to her that Delia, Lesbia and Lalage,[69] plunged into those fresh waters, were applauding the elegies of Propertius

---

[69] These are three of the names in a slightly longer list cited in René de Chateaubriand's *Mémoires d'Outre-Tombe* as a company of shades perched on broken cornices and babbling mysterious words to visitors to some Roman ruins near Elbogen.

or the songs of Horace. Edith truly was a daughter of antiquity, and would have remained in that ecstasy for a long time, but for the memory of their friend the vine-grower.

Between Nîmes and Montpellier, a side-road took them over a fertile plain to a crenellated line of ramparts surmounted by a gigantic tower. It was necessary to cross the Vidourie, a little river that serves as a boundary between the départements of Hérault and the Gard.

The further one advances, the more arid and sandy the soil becomes. One step further, and you encounter vast marshes covered with reeds; only a few sea-birds sometimes traverse those solitudes. You finally discover, in those marshes, a long causeway that seems to be defended by a square tower open in arches. That is the tower, the causeway and the ancient ramparts of Aigues-Mortes.

Everything in that place of desolation is, in fact, dead. The waters are silent, the marshes inert, the terrain scorched; the battlements have collapsed. You might take it for a desert in Africa or the New World. There are only a few scattered clumps of wild fir-trees, intercut with sandy edges and damp strips. Brambles and brushwood, reeds and rushes, saltwort and tamarisk make up the entire vegetation of those dolorous regions. The ground is infested with reptiles; clouds of bloodthirsty insects swirl in the air. Wild bulls run furiously through the scrub, seemingly threatening any traveler bold enough to wait for them. Masterless horses seek their livelihood in the salty grass of the marshes. Tropical sunlight makes the desert sands sparkle at a distance like expanses of water in Egyptian mirages. Only long salt-traps testify to the passage and work of humans in this intimidating region.

The region does, however, have a history. It is mentioned in the life of Marsius and the life of Caesar. The Saracens, beaten by Charles Martel, traversed these marshes in their flight. An abbey had replaced all these transient forces. A day came that saw King Louis IX digging out the port of Aigues-Mortes and embarking for the crusades, after having razed the feudal tower of Roger du Clorège. He went forth preceded by

the oriflamme, dominating by his tall stature the knights form-
ing his cortege: Hugues de Saint-Pol; Geoffroy de Sargines;
Gaston de Goutant-Dervic; Roland de Cossé; Gaucher de
Châtillon, poet and soldier; Roger, Comte de Foix; Gaston de
Béarn; Guyet-Philippe de Montfort; Pons de Villeneuve; Oliv-
ier de Termes; Trencavel, Vicomte de Béziers; the Sires de
Turnon, de Crussol, de Mailly; the Vicomte de Polignac; the
Chevalier de Montlaur; the Chevalier de Kinseton.[70]

At that name Kinseton, gloriously mingled with the
greatest names of the crusades, Edith and her traveling companion experienced a moment of joy and hope. Evidently, the
young painter belonged to a warrior race; he belonged to the
feudal land that had contained so many thousands of soldiers
whose weapons and bucklers glistened in the sun, so many
vessels come from Genoa and Venice. Here, the oriflamme
had deployed all its splendors, mingled with the standards of
barons and knights, while the sound of fanfares raised the *Veni
creator Spiritus* to the heavens: the spectacle of a day; an immortal memory.

Edith and the young painter spent the first two days after
their arrival getting their bearings, and establishing themselves
comfortably in the ruins. They ended up encountering, in the
shelter of the Grau-Louis, which is a formidable crag, a humble house made up, on the ground floor, of a room and an ancient barber's shop, while the first floor as divided into two
separate bedrooms, which seemed designed to lodge a mistress
and her servant. There they took up residence, glad to be in the

---

[70] The inclusion of the final name in the august list is, of
course fictitious. Kineston does survive as an English sur-
name, as do what are presumably the alternate renderings
Kyneston and Kynaston, but it does not seem to exist in
France. Although there are references in the English national
archives to minor noblemen whose name is rendered as de
Kyneston, that probably does not signify a Norman origin, let
alone one traceable to the Midi—but who knows?

shade and shelter, and anticipating that their journey would not be futile.

Kinseton already knew that his name belonged to the town's nobility; he soon found out that one of his relatives, the Reverend Abbess Marie de Kinseton, lived in seclusion, plunged into the most extreme devotion, in the convent of the Dames de la Visitation d'Aigues-Mortes. They were told, however, that it would be very difficult to gain entry to the convent.

The young man was prudent; he did not want to rush things; he knew how to wait for a favorable opportunity. In any case, he was reluctant to show himself to his relative, not as he had previously been—a great artist surrounded by all the honors of painting and the absolute master of his talent—but as an unskillful and vanquished master whose name as already almost forgotten.

In the end—what can I say?—he had faith in the advice of his valiant pupil, and as soon as they were settled in he said: "This is the time, my dear Edith, finally to render me the strength and security that I have lost, or, at least, for me to know that there really is no more hope."

To this supreme appeal, Edith replied with a smile. She had clay suitable for sculpting brought to the ground-floor apartment. "Now, dear Master, have confidence! Firm up your still-tremulous hand in that clay, and you'll soon have found energy and force enough to command those nerves that render you anxious, or, at least, no longer able to be a great painter, you'll have the honor of becoming a great sculptor."

Kinseton was initially convinced that the remedy for his trouble had been found. It was not the first time that he had entered the sculptor's domain; he had produced, while playing with potter's clay, more than one image that Pradier[71] would have gladly signed. It is a painter's recreation to play the sculptor, and the most dangerous game of sculptors to attempt

---

[71] The Swiss-born French sculptor James Pardier (1790-1852).

the hazards of great painting; truly, very few have excelled in both arts.

The young painter was not in a position to be choosy, however. Full of fury, he threw himself into a plan that might save him. At the sight of the obedient earth, he felt inspiration come to him, and not for an instant did he doubt the success of his enterprise.

At that degree of power and inspiration, painting and sculpture are the same. The same genius is necessary, and the same model can serve. After the first endeavor, the painter was scarcely trembling. He held his pencil in a firmer hand, and, in order that his work might be complete, he set on his easel the canvas that he had tried in vain to cover with a life.

"Oh, God be praised," he said, "here I am, a painter and a sculptor." But as ever, in gratitude, he came back to earth.

"Edith," he said, "stand here, before me, that I might begin by realizing my most beautiful dream."

And the young woman, wearing an elegant crown of acanthus and green vine-branches, represented the beautiful goddess of Youth at the banquet of the immortals.

The artist was truly delighted, at first, by the apparition that emerged, smiling and pensive, from the inanimate block.

Meanwhile, the Visitandines' door remained closed to the headstrong Edith. The lady she sought was none other than the abbess herself, and her order was absolute. Nevertheless, as the festival of the Virgin was celebrated, in the midst of flowers and canticles, Edith, having confided herself to the aged organist, sang in so touching a voice, and in the veritable accent of the pupils of Porpora, the canticle of Stradella[72]—the fugitive musician slain by the daggers of assassins who had followed him to church—the Abbess of the Visitandines, moved by that tearful voice, summoned the unknown singer,

---

[72] The references are to the famous teacher and composer Nicola Porpora (1686-1768) and Alessandro Stradela (1639-1682). The Stradella piece the Edith sings is probably *Ave Regina Coelorum*.

and, when she saw her at her feet, looking up at her with such a tender, she finally said: "What's the matter, dear child. What's troubling you? What do you want?"

Then Edith explained, in all frankness, saying that her father was a vagabond who had confided her to one of his friends, an artist. Although she was sure of being a legitimate daughter, she had never known her mother. She had had no other shelter in her early years but the Villa Medicis, a palace in Rome to which France sent every year, at her expense, master painters, musicians and sculptors. Her father had been one of them; his talent, she said, was full of promise, but, carried away by his passions, he had broken his palette and brushes and set off adventuring, forgetful of his wife and child. The French in Rome, especially the guests of the Villa Medicis, still talked about that story—and that was how, adopted by one of her father's friends, she had found an entirely paternal adoption in the home of a young man, in the midst of the most devoted respect.

At that point, the girl stopped, fearful of saying too much, and the old woman, attentive to the moving story, said: "Why stop on such a beautiful road, my daughter?"

"Alas, Madame," Edith replied, "it's because the hour of our destiny, as yet uncertain, has now come, to be designed and decided in the depths of your mind. That's why I'm hesitant. In sum, my last hope will be dead if you remain indifferent to the name that I am about to tell you: the name of my adoptive father, the young painter Nicaise de Kinseton."

At the name, the lady remained silent. A slight blush invaded the faced paled by prayer. "And why," she said, in a clipped voice, "would I refuse to recognize a child of my family? The man you call your adoptive father was the son of a man whose great-aunt I was, and I'm very happy and proud to know that he is an intelligent, honest man respectful of his adoptive daughter. That's not what's worrying you. Go on! Courage, and no half-truths!"

"The fact is, you see, Madame, that it's not just a matter of Kinseton the painter; his life is set; he has been subject to the most dolorous ordeal for an artist like him; he has been stripped of his glory. It's a matter of another Nicaise de Kinseton, our friend, if not our relative, a very worthy and very unfortunate man, perhaps unfortunate without remission, unless he finds a family that he has lost, and of which he has no other indication than the name and forename that served to refer him to us. So we—my adoptive father and—beg you to help us to find the proofs of an affiliation that have escaped us. He's from the north, this Kinseton with no family, and the true Kinsetons belong to the Midi. He's the son of a shipwreck and a tempest, and we were born here, in the halls of Saint Louis. He's alone, and, unfortunately, devoid of dependence. It's necessary to save him by giving him a family."

Edith stopped talking.

After a pause the old lady said: "Now that the austere age and severe aspect of human things have cured me of all pride, there will be no further cost to me in recognizing in this Nicaise de Kinseton the lost son of Monsieur de Kinseton and a Breton maidservant, whose misalliance cast as much shame as chagrin among us. In those days, my child, we were an implacable family, and God, who does well all that he has to do, has justly imposed the most formidable trials upon us. All those nobles, so proud of their fortune and their nobility, have been subjected to necessity. Their lands have been sold, their châteaux razed, their heads cut off, and their names destroyed, or, at the very least, the Baron has become a painter, or the Marquis a musician: that is our history, and our injustice is not to have learned those severe lessons. It's true that, the eldest son of the Kinsetons having disappeared in a shipwreck on the Breton coast, we thought that his child had died with him; but it will be necessary to rely on the evidence that you have collected, my declaration, and the papers I have kept. The Terror destroyed all the rest.

"And now that we have spoken seriously, go fetch me my grandson, whom God has brought back to me, that I might hold in my arms before dying."

In all haste, young Edith opened the door that led into the sanctuary, and, taking the hand of her companion, who was waiting there, gazing at a flamboyant Gothic statue, she led him into the visitors' room, where the saintly woman was waiting impatiently to bless them. They remained there until the evening, and they left with both the archives of the house of Kinseton and the old lady's benediction.

They came back from that accomplished adventure utterly charmed and pensive. The last rumblings of the Rhône were audible in the distance, and the waves of the Mediterranean were brilliant with all the fires of a radiant sun. The evening was full of prayer and perfume. It was the hour when Lamartine, an unknown poet, sang a mystical canticle to the sun.

Suddenly, as they were approaching their lodgings, Edith and her guardian heard a charming sound of young and friendly voices, mingled with the strident accompaniment of lutes and guitars. They were singing as one sings in Venice at the hour when the Adriatic is free or, in Verona, at the hour when Juliet is waiting for her lover, who will come.

Edith and Monsieur de Kinseton stopped, uncomprehendingly. Finally, they discovered that the nocturnal serenade and the enchantment of those beautiful voices were addressing themselves, through the open widow to the head scarcely born beneath the firm and light hand of the artist N. de Kinseton. She was so charming and so lifelike! A daughter with lowered eyes, a face akin to a star, a newly-born bosom, with the broken rays of the calm and gentle moonlight shining through her crown of vine-branches.

What benevolent gaze had discovered that masterpiece, and what devoted hands had placed it on that pedestal, covered with the new season's flowers? The great mystery was soon explained. A dozen artists and their companions, worthy children of Italy, were undertaking a tour of France, and had just disembarked on the shore of Aigues-Mortes, at the very spot where Alphonse, Comte de Poitiers, the brother of the king, Jeanne de Toulouse, his wife, and Mathilde de Brabant, Comtesse d'Artois had disembarked in August 1250.

This time, the company was less brilliant but it made at least as much noise. Those crusaders of poetry and the fine arts, bearers of the most vulgar names, although several of them were famous, had been going along, poor but inspired, singing, looking around, and admiring. For those twenty-year-old enthusiasts, the road was easy; at the sight of them, all doors opened; there was no museum intimate enough to escape their research and their admiration. As they were traversing the square where our young folk were lodging, they had discovered, through the partly-open door, the marvelous recently-finished bust, and, having admired it all day long, they had resolved to sing to it all evening—hence the concert.

Edith and her sculptor were completely charmed. "Friends and companions," they said, "the house is too small to contain you, but our neighbors will set up tables or you in the street, and you can drink until tomorrow to the health of Nicaise de Kinseton."

The name alone awoke all sympathies and caused the guitars to be strummed again. The leader of the ambulant orchestra was a jovial individual with a handsome face illuminated by large dark eyes, older by half than all the others. Beneath his graying hair, inspiration still lived. At the name of Kinseton, it was evident that the cheerful Bohemian was gripped by an inexplicable tenderness.

"Oh, it's really you!" he cried, hugging him in his muscular arms. "You, Kinseton, the great painter, the great sculptor—a double miracle! And you haven't recognized me!" The vagabond turned to address the angelic head: "O grace and beauty! And me, whose heart has beaten so forcefully on finding you in this corner of the world, beneath the crown of Virgil's shepherds, O my daughter! O my abandoned and rediscovered child! It's necessary for you to forgive your father, by virtue of his repentance!"

The man, half-poet, half-musician, a painter and a sculptor as well, was indeed young Edith's father.

He laughed, he wept. "My child! My child!" he said. "I departed precisely to rejoin you, and to see you again.

What a joyful scene, and what pleasant confusion!

The following day was Sunday, and our Italian singers, invading the altar, brought to the lady abbess, by way of an offering and an *ex-voto*, the bust of young Edith, ornamented with the inscription: *Sancta Maria, ora pro nobis*.

On receiving that masterpiece in the name of Nicaise de Kinseton, at the sight of that admirable head, imprinted with both innocence and youth, the aged and saintly abbess experienced more contentment than she had felt in her entire life. She understood all the grandeur—I almost said majesty—of great art, and that an artist is at least the equal of the sons of Saint Louis. Thus was dissipated the final cloud in that superb spirit. She was glorified by her glorified name.

"My children," she said, to the bearded painters tanned by the sun, "permit me to thank you." And as she had remained, in her humility, beneath her veils, a noblewoman, she gave those bandits a hundred louis to drink the health of the Mother Superior of the Visitandines, Marie, Baronne de Kinseton.

The joyful band would soon have to break up, each returning to his work, in Rome, in Bologna or in Florence. In all haste, as soon as they have breathed their natal air, Parisian artists head for Paris, to which the immense and radiant Louvre attracts them, by its invincible and omnipotent charm. The Louvre! After the sun, there is nothing greater for souls in love with the ideal; an immense series of revelations fills its sublime vaults; every step brings forth a masterpiece. What is astonishing, then, about the miracle, momentarily forgotten for other miracles, suddenly resuming all its force and reconquering all those vagabond souls?

That is how, the farewells having been made, our travelers found themselves alone, reinforced by the charming Bohemian who recognized young Edith as his daughter.

He had arrived just in time; they needed his help. All three of them took their places in one of those large barges drawn by vigorous horses that went up the Rhône in those days, until the moment when the Saône, in its turn, took the travelers in lighter vessels.

That as the final phase of a long journey full of confidences and leisure. They had time to recognize one another and tell their stories.

The worthy Cervantes did well when he gave his heroes Rosinante and Grison for their mounts. They went at a moderate pace, necessarily, through the lands of fiction, seeking and fining adventure. Invent a railway through Spain, or even enter the pathways of the Sierra Morena at the gallop of two English horses, and the enchantment of the journey abruptly disappears. There is no longer a hostelry, and no longer a noble hotelier on the joyful threshold. The revenants have disappeared from those cleared paths. Dorothea with the white feet, which she is bathing in the water of a stream, is no longer waiting for young Stenio, driven mad by love. Even Ginés de Pasamont falls into the hands of the Alguacil within twenty-four hours.

The old world went slowly; the ancient fable loved to amble, and even better, to travel on foot. Those gentle rivers, those beautiful roads which marched alone, bore from one world to the other a series of stories that will never be replaced. Even the most beautiful rivers, shining with a thousand gleams, flowing through hills covered with vines, serve today to carry coal and quarried stone. They have forgotten the song of the traveler, the gay smiles of errant girls and the joyful oaths of soldiers coming back from the war, or going in search of it in the midst of thunder and lightning.

So, our travelers, going up the profound river, recounted to one another at their leisure all the things they needed to know: how young Edith was the legitimate daughter of the painter Malvoisin and a young Transteverine; how, scarcely married and their daughter scarcely in the world, the newly-weds had separated, amid ill humor and ill will, never to meet again; how she had even abandoned her daughter, and had fled to some unknown abyss.

"I was very young in those days, my daughter, scarcely eighteen years older than you; I was only good at useless things. If I had loved you immediately, and immediately had you adopted, well, that was by chance. But now, I'm entirely disposed, if you wish, to love you seriously. I'm a good man, and, may it please God, I'll finally make up for my eternal youth."

He took two days to make this confidence, and in those first two days they did not ask any more of him. They were all plunged in an ineffable contemplation: the young woman thinking about the happiness she was about to make; Monsieur de Kinseton full of glory at the sight of his right hand as obedient and light as before; Malvoisin looking alternately at his daughter and the landscape.

Oh, how beautiful she is! he said to himself. *And look at those rich hills, filly laden with the vintage purpled by the fires of day!*

At the same time, he followed his colleague's drawings with a delighted eye, or, taking up is guitar, he sang cantilenas of his composition to the echoes. He had forged the words, he had made the music, and truly, in those little things that the wind carries away and does not bring back, he was a man of talent.

Once, when he seemed lost in his ecstasy and his memories, Edith stopped him in the middle of his speech.

"That's all very well," the young woman said, "but that whole story doesn't explain, my dear father, why you abandoned your daughter and why you've gone such a long time without seeing her."

"I wanted to every day," said Malvoisin. "I thought about my daughter and I thought about my friend Kinseton. I continually ran into Gallo-Romans who gave me news of you. I painted pictures from which I expected fame and fortune, and I saw myself depositing a golden crown on my beloved daughter's head. Unfinished paintings and dreams! At other times, I wanted to come to see you and to leave right away, and live at our expense making the skies at which I excel, with furniture and clothes entirely accessory.

"Yes, indeed, I'm not unskillful—but these inconstant and sick heads, one might thing that their wings flutter in every wind. Anyway, Italy has so many charms, and Rome is so naturally the august shelter of mediocre talents and musicians of my ability! Rome is full of connoisseurs who know nothing. There one meets Russians, Englishmen, Germans, who aren't embarrassed to buy second-rate Raphael's and Titians.

"In spite of all their pretensions, the Italians themselves aren't such great connoisseurs, and people who are afraid of them honor them beyond their merits. In twenty-four hours one can arrange a libretto to suit them, and compose the music in six weeks; once the opera is skimped, one puts it on in four or five principal towns during the carnival, after which the boards take possession of it and one starts again in the first days of April. Nothing is simpler.

"Out there, one can be a great man on the cheap. One runs into a host of petty princes there who give you, in abundance, knights' crosses, chamberlains' keys, sometimes even a hundred-écu diamond or some snuff-box bearing their arms. Would you like to be a baron? You are—but the rights of the seal will be an obstacle. In sum, what am I telling you? Out there, there's the unexpected, while here, everything is arranged, coordinated and settled in advance.

"In the final analysis, my dear Edith, why are you grumbling? Here I am. I looked for you, and I've found you, and God knows that I recognized you by your smile."

Thus, the father and the daughter, by dint of explaining it to one another, ended up discovering that Malvoisin's conduct was the most natural thing in the world. Not once was the name of the mother and wife pronounced during that double outpouring. The cloud and the mystery were there; nowhere else. It was like an insurmountable abyss. Edith sighted; her father sighed.

Meanwhile, our travelers made haste. Edith and Kinseton felt drawn by their friend the vine-grower; it sometime seemed to them that they could hear his plaint: "Oh, my friends, help me! Come quickly, I'm dying! Bring with you the calm and peace of my best days!"

And that is why, having arrived in Lyon, they departed in a hurry the following day for Châlons, borne by a more placid stream.

At such moments, the traveler, lulled, after so much noise, by those silent waters, passing from the torrent to the gentle river, experiences a great relaxation. He feels at ease; he converses with himself. One might think that the calm and freshness of the new river was invading the soul and transporting it beyond the clouds.

Nevertheless, the sky, radiant until then, was somewhat veiled; the wind was blowing from the mountains of the Dauphiné. The silence had gradually invaded our travelers. Sitting in a corner of the boat, the young woman was thinking about past events, and contemplating, without overmuch far, the future opening before her. Astonished by that great calm, to which he was not accustomed, Malvoisin quickly returned to his everyday contentment.

"My God!" he said to his friend Kinseton. "If one let oneself go, one could fall back very rapidly into seriousness. That sky is sad and those mountains appear to me to be utterly solemn. What madness led you to go up this monotonous river? Have you sworn never to arrive?"

"My dear friend," said Kinseton, "you don't know how right you are. We are indeed falling into seriousness. Our task, at this moment is to come to the aid of my first protector, my best friend, my worthy relative, Kinseton the vine-grower. The long road that I've traveled with your daughter Edith had no other goal that retrieving the titles of that brave man, and my right to come to his aid.

"He has fallen, I'm told, into the most dangerous of traps. An unworthy woman has cast her net over my unfortunate cousin; she has imprisoned him in his own house; she has separated him from his friends and neighbors; she has devoured his rich heritage with avid teeth. In vain my unfortunate relative has struggled against the toils of that horrible enchantress…he has succumbed; in vain he has called for help…he is at the limit of his strength, so powerful is an evil woman to torture an unhappy heart!"

"To whom are you talking!" Malvoisin replied. "There's nothing worse than an evil woman; she is shame and disorder; she is ruination. One curses oneself on seeing the abjection into which one has fallen. But try for an instant to break the bonds that are crushing you, unfortunate man, and they tighten, the chain becoming heavier. Oh, I know that terrible yoke. It weighed upon me for too long, and whatever the tyrant of our friend Kinseton might be, I can't believe that she can ever compare to the late Madame Malvoisin.

"There's one who was skillful in the art of torturing an honest man! She had all the secrets that make an unhappy household into a veritable Hell. Given certain features that you've described to me, I wouldn't be at all surprised if your friend had fallen prey to some pupil and disciple of Madame Malvoisin. Look at me! Merely by virtue of talking about that woman, it seems to me that I've gone pale. So, my dear fellow, don't count on me to confront the Minotaur. I've fought too much on my own account, and so much the worse for anyone imprudent enough to let himself be caught in those sad toils."

When they had spoken thus, our two travelers returned, each on his own account, to his mute contemplation. An ineffable fear seemed to overtake those two friends who were returning from joyful lands. The closer they came to the shore, the more solemn the moment seemed to them.

Finally, at eight o'clock in the evening, they docked safely. A carriage harnessed to two gray horses was doubtless waiting for a traveler who was about to arrive.

Strangely enough, the coachman of the caleche in question, bearing the initials N.K., on seeing the young painter, who was in the lead, arriving, said: "Good—here comes my master."

Astonished, the artist was about to reply when he perceived, by the curious expressions of the passers-by, that he had indeed been mistaken for his cousin the vine-grower, and, without saying a word, he had Edith and her father climb up into the carriage, and climbed up on to front seat himself. The coachman was wearing mourning, but the young painter had not had time to notice that, and, taking the reins, he allowed himself to be led where the horses took him.

That took less time than it requires to tell, and yet, there was a kind of ominous shudder in the excited crowd. A little dog that had come from some distance away, to judge by its gait, had soon climbed on to Kinseton's lap, with cries of joy.

"Oh!" said Edith. "There's our little Brack." And that name, pronounced by the soft voice, seemed to increase the fear of the curious observers.[73]

Nevertheless, the horses, proceeding at a fast trot, went through the village, and Kinseton recognized his traveling companion the notary looking out of his window. His wife was by his side, and they were both open-mouthed, frightened by the unexpected encounter.

A quarter of an hour later, they turned into a dark and profound road between two hedges, and the team stopped at the front steps of a house of beautiful appearance, but sad and silent. A groom emerging from the stables experienced such a shock on seeing the man holding the horses' reins that he fell on to a grassy bank.

_____

[73] This incident is enigmatic, given that no prior or subsequent reference is made to a dog named Brack. Is this the dog that was with the travelers when they left Paris, and which disappeared mysteriously *en route*, along with Madame Robert? Was that the puppy that Kinseton the win-grower gave Kinseton the painter when he bid him farewell in Paris, or the dog that the family already owned? Either way, what is it doing here?

Edith and her father, preceded by Kinseton, went up the unlit steps. A maidservant opened the door, and started weeping at the sight of the newcomers.

"Master! Oh, Master!" And sobs burst forth.

Then, all three of them looked at one another, frightened in their turn.

"We must be the victims of some unfortunate misinterpretation," said Kinseton. "Let's go in, though. We'll know soon enough what we're dealing with."

As they went in, preceded by the young maidservant, who was holding in her trembling hand one of those antique lamps of Roman design, like those miners have retained for digging coal, they perceived a woman in full mourning, who came toward them with a smile.

Evidently, the woman was expecting someone other than Monsieur de Kinseton. The feeble light scarcely illuminated the newcomer; Edith and her father remained in the shadows, and the woman in mourning had to look twice to take an exact account of the phantom that she had before her eyes.

She too went pale, and began trembling.

Monsieur de Kinseton recognized her right away by her beauty, and especially be certain signs of malevolence that could not escape a disciple of Titian and Velasquez. He took the lamp and raised it toward that face, where all the terrors were painted.

"Would you care," he said, "to tell me who this house belongs to, what is happening here, and who you were expecting?"

She was certainly very bold; she had been playing a abominable role for a long time; she had exercised all her furies against an innocent and defenseless man; but, addressed in such a lofty and solemn voice by the phantom, and finding such a complete resemblance between the phantom and the unfortunate she had tortured, the woman at bay was breathless, and her eyes were haggard.

By what fascination did she, too, find in the features of the living Kinseton the features of the Kinseton who had been dead for a fortnight? Conscience alone can explain these fatal visions. The woman was prey to remorse. She was expecting a businessman; suddenly, she was confronted by the exact image of a portrait with which her dwelling was crowded, and, by virtue of a perfectly natural confusion, she mistook the living man for the dead one.[74]

Imagine, then, how her terror was augmented when suddenly, in the shadows, she perceived—but this time it was not an illusion—her legitimate husband.

He was gazing at her with the sad and disdainful expression that she had so often glimpsed in her dreams. He was there, in front of her, saddened and scornful. A great pity was legible in that handsome face, and an immense dolor.

On suddenly rediscovering that bewildered woman, stammering a humble excuse to the dead man she had tortured for such a long time, Malvoisin saw again, in the blink of an eye, all the evils that he had suffered himself. He had loved that wretch with all his heart; he had thrown his most beautiful years at her feet, and now he understood that she was about to expiate all her crimes. It was, therefore, for her that he was afraid.

As all four of them were contemplating one another, fathoming the abyss, a door opened and a neighbor, Guillaume, a true Burgundian, said: "Is it true, my friend, that you're not dead? Let's embrace, and let's empty, if you please, one of the twenty-five bottles that you were keeping to celebrate the welcome and the sojourn among us of your favorite painter."

The worthy Guillaume, at that moment, could not contain his joy, and when he saw that his dream was…a dream, he said: "Oh, forgive me, Mademoiselle et Messieurs, for that brief moment of cruel illusion. Oh, I loved the worthy

---

[74] This incident, too, is profoundly enigmatic, even though the painter did give his namesake a self-portrait as well as the one he made of him. In this instance, apparently, two did constitute a crowd, and a confusing one.

Kinseton like a brother! He was so free and content, and if you only knew what a friendly house: how we enjoyed ourselves in these rooms full of beautiful things, in these gardens where the roses and the carnations struggled advantageously with the Muscat grapes! How many beautiful hours we spent drinking little sips of the white wine that has no equal in all of Maçon! But that woman"—he pointed at her with an irritated finger—"has doomed him. She's sold his crops, chased away his friends, and forced the poor man to kill himself."

And as he heard poor Edith sob, he added: "Yes, Mademoiselle, one single woman has filled these beautiful places with mourning. Death, devoid of pity and devoid of respect, now occupies this haven of joy, and we shall give thanks to the phantom of my poor friend if he can aid us in purifying this roof, so peaceful for so long, and so sad today."

Meanwhile the young maidservant had lit the candles in the drawing-room. The woman in mourning had disappeared, and the sound of a carriage indicated a flight over the mountain.

The neighbor Guillaume, interrogated by degrees, recounted what he knew of the long martyrdom. He had been the confidant of all the troubles the poor man had suffered, perpetually harassed by his fury and brought back by passion.

The poor man had broken his chain, but had come to take it back again; overwhelmed by the woman's scorn, he was intoxicated by her gaze. He allowed to become the absolute mistress of his home; she disposed of everything; she dismissed the servants; she insulted his friends. The unfortunate Kinseton had deteriorated by the day; his weak reason became impotent to console him. "I'm dying of it," he had said, "I'm dying of it." Among his curiosities he had a beautiful weapon, an ancient pistol damascened in gold. One evening, while playing with it, he had blown out his brains, and although it was difficult with such a weapon, he had counted on his voluntary death being recorded as an accident.

The neighbor Guillaume loved to talk, and talked a great deal. Had there been any need, he would have invented the right of interpellation. He went as far as anyone could wish along the road of the most deplorable revelations.

"But now," said the young painter, "the woman has disappeared. Are we sure of finding her again?"

"Certainly," said the neighbor Guillaume. "She'll be found on the mountain, in the home of the vine-grower Bernard. Madame Bernard, his wife, is a good nurse, and for a week she's been feeding a little boy with no father or mother, who'll come into a large inheritance one day."

When there was nothing more to be got out of friend Guillaume, our three travelers retired to their rooms. Edith and Kinseton each recognized their apartment from the description that their friend the wine-grower had given them.

The day after that formidable night was a renaissance.

At the first crow of the cockerels replying to one another, the phantom disappeared and his reality became evident in his coat the color of the sun. Edith alone had slept the divine slumber of youth. Monsieur de Kinseton had had beautiful dreams; his friend, Malvoisin, had uttered deep sighs.

They came together again, all three, in the house from which their mere presence had expelled mourning. Through the open window, adieu to death! Life entered in abundance beneath the vaults, to which calm had been restored. All the noises reappeared in all their joy, whinnying to the stables and clucking to the poultry-yard. On the roofs, the pigeons cooed, forgetful of the hand that nourished them.

Reunited in the drawing-room, where that late Monsieur de Kinseton had accumulated the most beautiful items of his intimate museum, the three friends contemplated all those works. The painter and young Edith, especially, were charmed by all the paintings, the first products of the artist's genius and his studio. It seemed to Kinseton that he was seeing the errant image of his youth again. He recognized the peaceful landscapes, the joyful faces, the dreams borrowed from Hugo's *Feuilles d'automne*, Lamartine's *Méditations poétiques* and Balzac's *Comédie humaine*. He was tempted to invoke them as so many young gods that had crossed his first paths.

One of the heads, above all, attracted the gaze of the beautiful and sincere Edith. Her beautiful eyes moistened with an involuntary tear at the sight of that cheerful face smiling at them from the depths of the tomb. "Oh, my poor friend, my dear student Toiras!" the lovely girl murmured.

Monsieur Kinseton, in a sad and penetrating voice, replied: "I loved him too. But he's done me too much harm for me to weep for him still."

"What harm did he do you?" Edith retorted. "He loved you like an elder brother; he lived in your shadow, and the most beautiful deed you ever did was to risk yourself in the ruins to save that sweet companion of our finest days."

"I'll tell you what he did," the painter replied. "He loved you too much, and you loved him too much, my dear Edith. You're inconsolable. His image will remain between you and me forever."

"Ingrate!" the young woman replied, holding out her hand to him. "So you can't distinguish simple amity from love? I only ever had amity for that poor child, who was younger than me."

As she spoke those words, her gaze shone with a discreet flame. She offered the young artist her forehead to kiss. Her father, who was looking in another direction, turned round at the exact moment when, in a silence inspired by all the passions of tender hearts, those two young people, without saying a word, swore eternal love to one another.

After a pause, Malvoisin said to his daughter: "Come on! At a time like this you can't refuse anything to the imprudent father who put you into the world. He's given you, my dear daughter, too beautiful a present for you not to come to the aid of his remorse. Happy lovers, egotists, as one is at your age, you've already forgotten the friend who killed himself invoking your name, and you're not thinking about the destiny of the unfortunate woman who mistook you for phantoms yesterday. Well, that woman is mine, and better still, she's your mother, Edith. She didn't recognize you, and that's her first punishment. I committed the grave sin of giving her the first example of a life of abandon and an infidel marriage. Others can curse her; we only have the right to weep for her."

At these words, Edith threw herself into her father's arms. "Come on, Father, let's both erase, if possible, so many cruel memories."

And the two of them took the road to the mountain.

For his part, the young artist went to the house of the notary—the same one who had told him, unwittingly, the principal events of the story. He found him to be every inch the honest mind and intelligent man that he had appeared to be in the diligence, and they were soon in accord with regard to the facts.

The late Monsieur de Kinseton had written for his "cousin"—for he did not doubt their relationship—a letter *in extremis*. In that letter, he testified to the double intention to institute his cousin as his sole heir, on the sole condition that his child, if he had one, would be recognized as having a right to that fortune, to the name, and even the title of the Seigneurs de Kinseton. That was said in a few words; it was written in a sure and firm hand. It was evident that the unfortunate man had decided to die. There was not a word about his mistress and his tragic amours.

After the attentive reading of that testamentary will, the artist and the man of law each sought, in the depths of his conscience, the means by which they could obey that instruction of a dying man without outraging the honor of the living.

"It's difficult," said the notary.

"Only one person can get us out of this predicament. That person is, for me, the law and the prophets; she has the genius and the talent of truth in everything. What she says is well said; and what she does is well done."

The artist was speaking like a man of common sense. Only women have the thread to the labyrinth, if the labyrinth is the human heart.

No one ever knew what passed between Edith and her mother, and how the two women met and recognized one another. The mother was insolent to the highest degree, and her crimes served her as a bodyguard, but the daughter was irresistible; she had the sacred gift of tears; she knew how to invoke divine providence; she was eloquent and touching; and she ended up softening that heart of stone. Her visit lasted all day.

The father and the daughter came back silently, but much calmer than on departure. Evidently, the daughter had a plan firmly settled in her head and her heart, but the father did not know what it was.

The night passed, and another day. And when the artist finally explained for the third time a situation full of doubt and confusion, the young woman suddenly said: "Listen to me, and, if you do as I say, everything will be saved. Our cousin Kinseton's child will not be deprived of his fortune and his mother will not be dishonored; he will bear his father's name; he will be the Baron de Kinseton."

Having said that, she retreated into her mystery. "Make a start," she said to the artist, "unless you've changed your mind, on the preparations for our happy marriage: a large poster at the Mairie and public banns at the church that will bless us."

In the meantime, the town was abuzz with rumors; it too had believed in the revenant; it had mistaken the newcomer for Kinseton the wine-grower—whom he did not much resemble, it must be said. Both they both bore the same insignia, the same names, and they were dressed in the same way. A dead man is so quickly forgotten! The living man who replaces him is so easily welcomed.

The notary acted in Kinseton's interest. The woman in black had disappeared, and no one had any news of her.

On the first Sunday when the curé announced to his congregation the marriage of the Baron de Kinseton to Mademoiselle Edith Malvoisin, there was another indescribable shiver. People ended up, however, by getting accustomed to the appearance of the same names and forenames, and when the great day of the marriage came, at the exit from the civil contract, to which few people had been invited, the doors of the church were opened wide.

The church was full, a crowd of curiosity-seekers having arrived in the hope of finding the key to the enigma.

Imagine how the curiosity increased when they say—O surprise!—the beautiful and proud Edith, blushing beneath her virginal crown, carrying a baby in swaddling-clothes, embroidered by the fairies.

The child was laughing and playing with the orange-blossom that decorated the waist of the young bride. She marched at a firm pace to the altar; one might have thought that she was proud of her burden. Then, the voice of the priest who was to marry them welcomed her with so much tenderness and respect that not one member of the audience dared to smile. He began by baptizing the child; after the baptism, he married the father and the mother, invoking with his solemn voice all the blessings of Heaven upon the young man and, especially, the young bride.

A woman was there, a mat-complexioned Burgundienne in rustic costume, and as soon as she was married to Monsieur de Kinseton, the beautiful Edith gave the child back to her nurse, and the nurse, happy with the offspring that had been returned to her, went down the parvis of the temple to the sound of the organ playing "Victory is ours!"

The day after that happy adventure, the good Malvoisin took his leave of his daughter and his son-in-law.

"Adieu," he said to them. "Be happy. I'm going back to Rome, to Florence, to the land where one forgets—and yet, I shall never forget my children!"

251

Afterword to "The Revenant"

Jules Janin's preliminary note to "Le Revenant" in *Petits romans d'hier et d'aujourd'hui* dates the composition of the story as January 1868. It might be a pure coincidence that Dentu had published a novel by Paul Féval in 1867 titled *Les Revenants*—a novel originally serialized in 1852 as *Le Livre des mystères* and initially reprinted in book form in the same year as *La Soeur des fantômes*—but even if it is a coincidence, the similarities between the two texts are interesting. As pointed out in the Afterword to my translation of Féval's novel, *Revenants* (2006)[75], that novel's plot reflects a deep confusion regarding the propriety of employing fantastic materials, which eventually resulted in a conclusive "rationalization" of the plot that is blatantly false; although the narrative voice implies in the final chapter that there were no "real" *revenants*—i.e., ghosts—in the story, a careful reading of its previous statements strongly suggests that there was at least one, and perhaps more.

If Janin read the book in question, he would undoubtedly have noticed that anomaly, and recognized its kinship with the struggles with propriety that he had undertaken himself, and it would not have been untypical of him to set out to write a story of his own in which the presence of real ghosts was deliberately but falsely denied by the terminal remarks made by the narrative voice. Whatever his intentions might have been when he set out to write "Le Revenant," however—and he might not have had any if, as he claimed, he never planned his stories in advance, but simply let them develop at hazard—they do not seem to have been fulfilled. The existing text seems rudely truncated; had the narrative pace of the first twenty thousand words been sustained, the events of the final

---

[75] Black Coat Press, ISBN 978-1-932983-70-8.

three thousand would have occupied far more narrative space, even if one sets aside the strong probability that further complications might well have been added to the plot.

Perhaps that apparent truncation is itself an artifact, mimicking and mocking the fashion in which *romans feuilletons* such as those that Féval produced in such profusion were ever likely to be cut short on editorial instruction, no matter how much damage was done to the plot in consequence. Perhaps, on the other hand, Janin simply tired of his endeavor and decided to kill off a story of whose direction and purpose he was no longer certain, because it had eluded his narrative grasp. Either way, however, the questions remain of what on earth was supposed to be going on in the story, and why it is called "Le Revenant" when it does not appear, at a first retrospective glance, to feature a *revenant*, except in the feeble sense that Kinseton the living artist is briefly mistaken for Kinseton the dead vine-grower by the latter's neighbors, servants and mistress.

Readers are, of course, perfectly free to make up their own minds about that, and there can be no correct answer. There is, however, no harm in my offering some suggestions for consideration, in my capacity as a translator.

First of all, it is worth raising the question of *how* Kinseton the vine-grower's acquaintances make the mistake of misidentifying Kinseton the artist for the dead man, even in a dim light, given that we are specifically told that the two men bear no particular resemblance to one another. It is suggested that the evil *femme fatale* is the victim of a "fascination" as well as an "illusion," but even the narrative voice begs leave to wonder how that can have come about, and seems to have no idea how the widespread mistake as to the newcomer's identity ought to be interpreted. It is surely possible, going on the evidence that the narrative voice provides, that the error really does have a supernatural component, and that there is some sense in which Kinseton the artist, when he finally arrives, too late to save his benefactor, really is, in some sense, a ghost? Indeed, is any other interpretation possible?

The confusion of the two leading characters' identities is not, of course, restricted to a mere temporary appearance. What Kinseton the artist has discovered in Aigues-Mortes (a significantly-named location if ever there was one) is that it was Kinseton the vine-grower, not him, who was the real Baron de Kinseton, and, that although he seemed to become the heir to the title when his cousin was wrongly assumed to be dead, his entitlement to that inheritance now that the Baron really is dead is confused by the existence of Kinseton the vine-grower's illegitimate son. In terms of feudal symbolism, the "real" identities of the two individuals are deeply confused, further complicating their already-intricate and very peculiar relationship.

If Kinseton the artist does become, at least temporarily, a "ghost" in a deeper sense than a mere error of misrecognition on the part of those who see him, the corollary question arises of whose ghost it is that "takes possession" of Kinseton the artist. Is it the ghost of Kinseton the vine-grower, or, taking into account the fashion in which the esthetic logic of the narrative makes the two Kinsetons into exotic *alter egos*, is it some remoter spirit of the Kinseton family, representative of some kind of supernatural barony, as opposed to the trivial and falsified barony that Kinseton the artist has never been able to take seriously?

This question is further complicated if it is juxtaposed with that of the other possessive ghost featured, a trifle unobtrusively, in the plot: the one that takes possession of Edith during her fit of preternatural inspiration, when she discovers a frankly-impossible ability to play exotic music on the mandolin and a highly-improbable talent for interpretative portraiture. Where does that spirit come from? The overwhelming probability, if one accepts the possible reality of ghostly possession, is that it comes from her mother's side of the family, and that the tangled pattern binding Edith's mother to both her father and to Kinseton the vine-grower involves a supernatural element extending back through the centuries, perhaps all the way to the crusades.

Given that the mandolin bears the arms of the Princesse d'Ursins, there is a temptation to suppose that her ghost might be lurking somewhere in the plot; her equivocal reputation when alive allows plenty of narrative space to make her the ancestor of Madame Malvoisin (whose family name we are never told). The angelic Edith, however, is set up in opposition to her evil mother, so whatever the untold story behind her possession is, the likelihood is that it involves two hungry spirits rather than one—perhaps residual components of an instance of the eternal triangle whose apex was a Baron de Kinseton. Alas, the untold story not only remains untold, but hardly even implied; the revenants playing covert roles in the strange destiny of the story's characters remain frustratingly intangible.

Perhaps that is an appropriate fate for revenants in an era that has put away belief in revenants as a childish thing. Jules Janin was certainly troubled by a matter of conscience whenever he contemplated the possibility of allowing the supernatural to intrude into one of his stories. Perhaps, though, he was being oversensitive. After all, it does not necessarily follow that because an era has no further use for sincere belief in ghosts, they can play no further role in literature. Indeed, it is not inconceivable that the reverse is true: that the obliteration of real belief ought to function as a liberation for the literary imagination, which becomes free to invent, reinvent, symbolize and allegorize to its heart's content, no longer fettered by vestiges of faith.

Is that not in fact, what has actually happened in the literary history of the last 150 years?

At any rate, the underlying logic of the narrative of "Le Revenant" suggests, and blatantly demands, that the eventual confrontation between Kinseton the artist, Edith, Malvoisin and the nameless *femme fatale* should have been far more dramatic and far more extensive than it is in the existing text, and that a far more elaborate explanation ought to have been offered of her uncanny power and her motivation, whether that explanation involved revenants or not. In the event, all of that was omitted, perhaps because Janin could not actually think of a half-way satisfactory explanation when the moment came to provide one—but to say that the omission is conspicuous by its absence is surely a drastic understatement.

In my opinion, it cannot possibly be the case that the plot of "Le Revenant" is devoid of "real" ghosts, even though the narrative voice pusillanimously leaves that interpretation open to readers allergic to such narrative intrusions. The story *is* a *conte fantastique*, in the usual sense of the term, as well as in the highly idiosyncratic sense that Janin attempted to develop. Would it have been a better *conte fantastique* if its fantastic quality had been fully brought-out and appropriately elaborated? Well, perhaps—lovers of fantastic fiction would presumably agree with me in thinking so. On the other hand, it is arguable that what is uniquely interesting and precious about Janin's work, seen *en masse*, is his insistence on not doing the expected thing, or even the logical thing, even at the expense, as in "Une Histoire de revenant," of producing a story that will generally be considered not to make any sense.

"Le Revenant" makes no sense—but that is not necessarily a bad thing, in literary terms, no matter how much we might desire, perhaps hopelessly, to make sense of the real world, and our actual lives within it.

Brian Stableford

SINCERITY

If one exercises the profession of *belles-lettres* with a certain zeal, it is necessary not to neglect anything. Everything is of use, or might be of use. Who would have thought that, in an old collection of Latin sermons, devoid of a date but which reeks of the distance of the sixteenth century, a nameless Dominican would have collected, in the manner of *Sermones discipuli de tempore*,[76] two hundred and twelve dramatic stories for all the Sundays and principal festivals of the year? "I have called these sermons 'The Sermons of a Neophyte' because there is nothing magisterial in these innocent stories, and any schoolboy might have written them, or made them up." With the result that young preachers, when they want to keep their audience attentive, will only have to dip their hands into these tales, whose entire merit is in their naivety.

That said, the Dominican gets down to business, and from among those storiettes, we have chosen the present story of the Devil and the bailiff.

The bailiff in question was the scourge of a dozen unfortunate villages in the Jura, grouped around a wretched fortified château, where devastation, conflagration and war had left their formidable imprint.

People had been breathing sadness in that desolate region for a long time; if one were searching for the worst possible place to reside, the cleverest individual could not have found anything more propitious than that heap of sufferings and

---

[76] *Sermones discipuli et tempore* (1418) is a famous collection made by the Dominican preacher Johann Herolt, also known as Discipulus. Herolt also collected exemplary stories for use in sermons, similarly circulated in manuscript and widely reprinted as *Promptuaria exemplorum*.

ennuis. Nature herself, in her most charming beauties, had been vanquished by tyrannical force.

In that desolate place, the echoes had forgotten the refrains of songs; the somber woods were inhabited by silent guests; the osprey and the vulture were the sole inhabitants of those Northern firs whose savage cries were heard. On the shores of depopulated lakes no frogs croaked. The livestock went hungry; the errant bee had been chased away, poor thing, from its smoked-out hive.

There were no more paths in the fields, no more bridges over the streams, not single barge on the river. There was still a banal mill, but no bread for the oven. It was said, however, that the villagers had once cooked buckwheat galettes in that oven, and that, on days before festivals, a little meat at the bottom of a covered dish—but the dish had been broken.

Fire and plague had been the only distractions of those dolorous houses. The militia had taken away the strong, fever had carried away the young. A few old people still remained to utter curses.

The devouring hyena and the wolf had passed through the cemetery. The church was empty; the bell no longer rang for want of a rope, with which the provost, for the sake of economy, had hanged the most unfortunate. That was the sole charity that the poor could expect.

Thus, of the Lord above and the lord below, there was not a trace. In vain it is written: "No land without a lord, and no Heaven without a god!" It was true, however: God was no longer there! The Marquis de Mondragon, the absolute master of the seigneurie in question, was absent; his wife no longer came to the place, and his children no longer came.

Shame and dishonor had preceded that ruin. Oh, there was nothing but rags to cover that man's vassals, and nothing but wild plants to nourish them. The leeches had scarcely left those poor folk a little flesh stuck to their bones. Woe unto them! For such a long time they had supported the men of war, the men of business, the king's men, princes of the blood, officers of the crown and gentlemen in His Majesty's service—so many birds of prey and plunderers.

In the end, when they had been visibly reduced to nothing, the kings, princes, lords, captains and the marquis seemed to have forgotten that that little corner of earth existed. That was a release, and the race in question, taxed and worked to exhaustion, might perhaps have ended up finding a little hope and a few ears of corn, if Monsieur le Marquis had not left his bailiff behind in his devastated marquisate.

With a little more courage, the bailiff in question might have been a man-at-arms in the service of some provincial ravager. He had not become a man of war because he had not dared to carry a torch or wield a sword. He had given himself the unique task, having the right of low and high justice for ten leagues around, and being the sovereign judge, to leave nothing in the hovels: not a single egg, or wisp of cloth, or loaf of bread, or bundle of straw. He came back from every expedition carrying something, and suspecting his peasants of hiding their money and their livestock. Four times a year that torturer set out on campaign—and every man for himself!

Now, one somber and rainy day in autumn, at a time when the north wind and winter were already advancing, the bailiff of the Sires de Mondragon emerged from the château, warmly wrapped up in the cloak of an unfortunate farmer that he had sent to the galleys. Two serfs followed him, carrying empty sacks. He was mounted on his horse, well-nourished on oats and hay—such good oats that the Christians of the regions would have baked bread for their wedding-feasts with it.

The sight of that man was terrible. He advanced, however, at a careful pace in the solitude and the silence. He understood that hatred was at his heels, and that vengeance went before him—but nothing stopped him in these supreme expeditions.

When he had gone past the cemetery and the church, at a bend in the road, he entered a heath as sterile as all the rest, and went into a stand of old trees that it was absolutely necessary to go through before reaching the villages of the seigneurie. Not encountering anyone, he had gradually begun to feel reassured, when he saw a man—or, at least, a phantom—step out from behind an old oak whose top was lost in the sky, and place his powerful hand on the horse's rump.

A tremor ran through the horse's entire body. Then the rider, turning his head, dared to look his silent companion in the face.

He was not so much a body as an image, a shadow. Two implacable black eyes were shining in his face; even their whites were black. They were shining, menacing and burning.

The bailiff had no difficulty in recognizing that he had just met his grandfather, the Devil, in person.

The other said to him, in an unearthly voice: "I know where you're going, and I'm going the same way. Let's travel together."

They were going on in that fashion when they saw, at a crossroads in the forest—it's incredible, but it's true—a peasant leading a pig, coming back from an acorn-hunt. By that miraculous means, he had saved the pig, and was taking it back home, trembling lest he be spotted by one of the bailiffs assessors.

Certainly, the latter would not have liked anything better than to put the animal in a sack and go back to the château, to set out on campaign again the next day; but the horse was obedient to the tenebrous hand. At the same time, the pig refused to go any further, and started struggling with all its might.

"May the Devil take you!" cried the peasant.

At these words, the bailiff, who was beginning to tremble forcefully, felt entirely reassured, because it is customary among the demons of the other world, and the demons of this one, that as soon as the Devil has found his prey, he must necessarily accept it and go away, in search of another adventure.

Thus, if you encounter Satan himself, you can give him to take away the first creature that is offered to his eyes. "Agreed!" Satan will say. Then he will have to be content with a black hen, or a sheep, or even less—a frog in the middle of the road. These sorts of pacts, however, don't displease him, because hazard and Satan are good friends. More than once he has encountered the old father, or the wife, or the son of the same companion, who has thought that he has got out of it cheaply.

Alas, it's the story of Iphigenia or Jephthah's daughter.[77]

So, the bailiff, his little eyes radiant with cunning, said to the black eyes: "Since it's been given to you, friend phantom, take your prey and go away. Well, what are you waiting for? That's the pact, and I'm saved from your claws."

To which the black man replied with silent laughter, and little blue flames emerged from his mouth. "Yes," he said, "I'll take the prey that I've been given, and I'll leave you, unless, of course, this gentleman hasn't given me his pig sincerely. It's the sincerity that makes the gift, as you know. It's not a matter of saying something; it's necessary that the intention should be wholehearted. Let's wait."

As he spoke, the Devil and the bailiff saw a dozen charcoal-burners coming through the wood, who, on seeing the pig coming in their direction, uttered cries of joy.

"Oh, my God!" they said. "Where did you find so much fodder, friend Jean?" And they surrounded the animal and its guide. They could not contain their joy. They danced around, singing: "Friend pig! What a feast and what joy! We'll eat your blood, we'll eat your flesh! We'll make chops, sausages and black puddings; your head and trotters will give us relief from a long fast!"

And they were all so contented, so joyful, that they did not even see the bailiff. The latter went on his way.

---

[77] The story of Jephthah's unwise promise to sacrifice the first creature he meets after returning home from defeating the Ammonites is told in *Judges* 11. The most familiar versions of the story of Agamemnon's sacrifice of his daughter Iphigenia, as told by Homer and Euripides, do not introduce a similar twist to the story.

"As you see," his comrade said to him, with a malevolent snigger, "those starving peasants hadn't given me the pig sincerely."

The bailiff lowered his head, wondering what the Prince of Darkness was getting at. He knew that, of all the logicians of the Aristotelian school, the Devil was the greatest. There was no argument that he could not twist, no syllogism in which he could not immediately find a fault.

Meanwhile, they arrived at the door of a hut, and on the threshold they found a humble old woman who was spinning with her distaff and agitating a little crib with her weary foot. The baby was crying and moaning, calling for his mother; he was hungry. The mother had gone out to collect dead branches, and the baby was crying incessantly.

"Oh, accursed child," said the old woman, "may the Devil take you!"

At this, the wicked bailiff conceived a glimmer of hope again. The old woman was so poor! One child more in that hovel was one mouth more! The miserable bailiff imagined that toil had reduced those men and women to be nothing more than savage beasts of the woods.

One might have thought that his colleague with the cloven hoofs was of the same opinion. Already, he was reaching out his hand to take possession of the frail jetsam, and when that was done, the Devil would be vanquished...

But as soon as the shadow had touched the crib, the old woman, whose arms were still vigorous, carried the baby away to her mother, who had just arrived, laden with branches, singing: "Mister Wolf, don't listen, get thee gone/A mother can hear her crying son."

"You're here, at last, my daughter!" cried the grandmother. "The child's calling for you—he's thirsty and hungry, and I can't rock him anymore."

The young mother, throwing down her burden, uncovered her breast and showed it to the child, who began to smile.

"Oh, I pity you," said the Demon to his companion. "You can see that I acted in good faith, but you can't maintain that the old woman had given me her little child with a good grace. Come on, courage! Let's look for something else. We still have a way to go before we get down to your business. But it's good to hear the words of that song; it's an old tale from before my time."

And they went on their way.

The further they went, the darker the sky became, and yet noon had not yet sounded. They were going between two hedges, the bailiff thinking about his destiny and searching his arsenal for some ruse, the Devil murmuring an old song derisively. The two sack-bearers were perfectly indifferent to everything to that was happening around them, for their humble condition sheltered them from the anger of the Prince of Darkness.

One might have thought that the solitude had magnified and that the road was growing longer of its own accord. There was no sadder sight than those four monotonous travelers.

There was, however, an unexpected bright spot: a new house of cheerful appearance. It was built in good stone and covered with tiles, and with lattice windows—very rare in those days—that were glittering in the sunlight. One might have thought that the masterpiece in question had been brought to the hillside ready-made during the night, for exhibition to the rising sun. A great ease and excellent order presided over the habitation. A vigilant cockerel could be heard crowing; dogs were yapping; a beautiful cow with full udders was wandering freely in the thick grass. Pigeons could be heard cooing on the roof, and ducks splashing in the pond, and vines were running over a trellis alongside the vegetable garden.

The Demon contemplated such great abundance without envy, and turned to the astounded bailiff. "My opinion, Master Cut-throat, is that here's a dwelling neglected by your procedures. Beware, lest I tell your master—doubtless he'll throw out an accountant as negligent as you."

The bailiff did not know what to say. He was both happy to have discovered this new subject of mortmain and ashamed of not having exploited such fortune before. He was so covetous of it that he forgot his companion momentarily. Finally, and having made sure that he had his ink-pot and parchment bearing the lord's watermark—it as a broken pot, a telling image of feudalism—he looked for an open door in order to institute proceedings against a vassal bold enough to be a little better lodged than his seigneur.

The doors were closed, but the window was open, and from the height of his horse the bailiff was able to contemplate at his ease the crimes contained in that honest house.

The first crime was a beautiful walnut table, covered with a white cloth, and on the cloth—O forfeit!—a loaf of white bread, and white salt in a salt-cellar; a joint of venison on a rick pewter tray, shinier than silver, announced a meal such as had been eaten before the crusade under Saint Louis. Two silver goblets were filled to the brim with vermilion liquid. A tankard carved by a master, and beautiful plates representing the king and queen of France, added their splendor to all those bourgeois riches. The furniture was not unworthy of everything else.

Finally, two young people, a husband and wife, in all the gleam of youth and strength, were sitting there, surrounded by three beautiful children dressed like prince, and doubtless not very hungry, to see them laughing and chattering to one another.

As the bailiff's eyes devoured that meal, which an ancient knight errant would have found cooked to perfection, and as he was already making an inventory of that suspect wealth, a sharp and loud argument suddenly broke out between the husband and the wife. It seemed that the latter had bought, without telling the former, a gold necklace from the neighboring town, and the husband was reproaching her for the expense.

After the first skirmish, they very rapidly came to angry words, to finish up with these, so full of danger:

"To the Devil with you, Wife!"

"To the Devil with you, Husband!"

At that moment, we can agree that the temptation was great even for the Devil, and that the prey was luscious. A wife of twenty, a husband of almost the same age: to carry them away immediately would represent a good diabolical day's work.

"What's stopping you, friend?" said the bailiff to his comrade. "Where will you find two such beautiful souls, and more tears than those in the eyes of the three children? Play your part; I'll play mine; and we'll part as good friends."

All seemed lost, therefore. The bailiff was triumphant; the beautiful house trembled to its foundations. The children were weeping. The mother and father were damned...

But in the depths of their souls, they loved one another too much to be at odds with one another for long.

"What have you've done, my darling?" cried the young man, throwing his arms around his wife. "What have you done? I'm a wretch for having scolded you for so little! A thread of gold! To reproach you for a thread of gold, when I ought to have covered you in diamonds and pearls!"

"No, no!" cried the young wife, with large tears in her eyes. "It's my fault, not yours. Why, indeed, have I had so little heart as to spend our children's dowry on vanities?"

Then, quitting her husband's embrace, she kissed the two little boys and the beautiful little girl ardently, the children no longer knowing whether to laugh or to cry. And when, finally, all five of them wiped away those soft tears and found their smiles again, they placed the little necklace on the Madonna's head, by way of an *ex-voto*, and all five of them knelt down before the divine mother, and recited, with their hands joined: "Hail Mary, full of grace!"

At this point the Devil felt so touched that a tear escaped from his eye and trickled down his cheek. A *pssst!* was heard: the sound of a drop of water falling on a hot stove.

The bailiff was not in the least touched. He felt his fury increase, and not for anything would he have retraced his steps—but with the Devil, it is always necessary to go forward. He is the voice that says: "Forward march! One, two!"

In vain you want to call a halt in some beautiful part of the enchanted land. "Forward march! One, two!" In vain the city offers its singular beauties to your eyes. "Forward march! One, two!" In vain the libertine requests a moment of respite to quit his bad mores and marry some innocent. "Onwards! Forward march! One, two!" There are even moments in which the traitor and the tyrant would gladly call a truce in their criminal maneuvers. "Forward march! You've let repentance pass. Arrive, limping, at the punishment that will claim you!" Thus, too, go the ambitious man, when he renounces ambition, the miser when he renounced money, the soldier when he renounces murder and the debauchee when he renounces his daily pleasures: "Forward march! One, two!"

It is necessary to obey, all the way to the yawning abyss. It is necessity.

So the bailiff marched. Nevertheless, as he was cunning and a past master in devilry himself, he said to his companion: "It's my right to go forward along the road I choose."

"That's your right," the other replied, "incontestably."

With which the bailiff, reassured, took a little path over the mountain.

That path lengthened the journey by a full league, and the Devil—who is quite easily caught out—had a suspicion that the bailiff was playing a trick on him. "Are you setting a trap for me?" he said. "Let us, as they say, put our cards on the table, and let each of us be content."

"Everyone has his turn, Monseigneur," the bailiff replied. "You had me a little while ago, and now I have you. Incompetent! It wasn't worth the trouble of running all over the country and setting all those traps for me, only to fall into my ambush! Where are we, at present, comrade? Don't you see that we've taken the path that leads to the convent of Sainte-Croix? The convent has disappeared—I'm the one who razed it, and I took possession of all its domains—but I respected the calvary, raised on these heights on the very day of the Passion, and that calvary contains the relics of Saint Peter the Martyr, Saint Eutropius, Saint Bartholomew, Saint Catherine, virgin and martyr, and ten thousand crucified martyrs. That's where I'll wait for you, Messire Demon, and we'll see whether you dare pursue me into the shadow of the cross.

Who was irritated by this declaration? It was Satan. He was annoyed with himself for having forgotten the formidable rampart that the saints had erected with their pious hands on the mountain. He was aware, moreover, of the strength and authority of certain relics buried in that calvary. Finally, he was annoyed with himself for having been duped by a bailiff of the worst sort, and for having met someone more cunning than himself. It was his battle of Pavia.[78]

I'll get my revenge another time, he said to himself, sulkily. However, as he did not want to go away empty-handed, he said to the bailiff: "I'll go to seek my fortune elsewhere, if you'll at least give me those two scoundrels marching behind you. Is that agreed?"

"You won't get them from me," said the bailiff, flicking a yellow tooth with a fingernail. "Those two men are necessary to my high and low justice. One is the executioner of our domains. No one knows better than he does how to whip a rebel with bloody rods, to brand a poacher with a hot iron marked with two fleurs-de-lys, or to rivet a chain around the neck of a convict destined to row His Majesty's galleys in perpetuity. The other is the concierge of our prisons and the executor of our sentences; he excels in hanging insolvent debtors, and has put substantial sums into our coffers more than once. It's impossible for me to do without either of them. So go back whence you came with empty hands, and good night, Master Demon."

As he spoke, they were already half way up the mountain. The Devil was about to go when he decided to dig his heels in.

---

[78] At the battle of Pavia in 1525, François I was defeated by the Spaniards and taken prisoner; he subsequently wrote to his mother: "Madame, all is lost, except honor."

"Come on," he said, laughing ominously, "at least let's promise to spare one of those wretches?"

"Not one," aid the bailiff. "They've caused me too much trouble this morning."

"At least spare the residents of that new house!"

"Oh, their account's drawn up. I'll have the gold necklace in my pocket this evening, and if you come back this way a month hence, the entire area will be covered by brambles and stubble."

"But the little baby at the teat!"

"He'll pay for his mother's milk!"

"And the pig?"

"My acolytes and I will eat it this evening."

"In sum, neither pardon nor pity?"

"Neither pity nor..."

At this point, the bailiff's voice catches in his throat. He is looking hard, but he can no longer see the calvary. In vain, his interrogative gaze searches in every direction. The holy cross that ought to protect him is not there.

"Ye, indeed," said Satan. "You're searching in vain for your strength and your support. The unfortunates that you've created have felled the calvary. By dint of poverty, they've ceased to hope and believe. Insensate! There are the ruins that your malice and cowardice ought to have foreseen. Those desperate folk have taken their revenge on the relics of the martyrs, and now it's you who'll be punished for the profanations of all those unfortunates."

At that revelation, whose justice he understood fully, the bailiff fell off his horse, and the horse, relieved of its double burden—the man and the Devil—ran off at a gallop, striking up such a firework display, with so many sunbursts, bombs and rockets, that it would have been enough to celebrate the birthday of the greatest king in the world.

Seeing the man crushed by shame and fear, Satan raised him gently to his feet, as an affectionate father might have done for his only son, and all four of them went down the gentle slope that led to the various villages of that abominable seigneurie.

They went past the first houses, without hearing anything but moans and tears—but no curses, as yet. The people were afraid, trembling in their every limb. The sick held their breath and children put down their toys; frightened women went to hide in some covert, and the dogs forgot to bark. Finally, however, when they had traveled the length of an entire street, they heard murmurs, cries, plaints and maledictions emerging from the debris of the cottages. The unanimous curse was incessant and ever-increasing.

In the second village, the neighbor of the first, anger had replaced complaint, and the unfortunates were crying:

"Down with the brigand who has stolen my son!"

"Death to the blackguard who caused my father to perish under the rod!"

"There's the pitiless monster!"

And the children threw stones at the infernal sinner.

"Give us back our bread!" said the women.

"Give us back our honor!" said the men. "Give us back our beds and our cribs! Look—famine is undermining us, and our feeble hands could no longer hold the implements that you have stolen from us!"

At that immense racket, in which teeth were grinding and eyes blazing, in which those meager and desiccated torsos emitted hoarse cries and feverish whistles, villagers of both sexes came running, and as their vengeful fingers pointed at the impious man, they all shouted: "To the Devil! To the Devil! To the Devil!"

And the echoes repeated: "To the Devil! To the Devil!"

Then Satan, in a voice that filled the plain and the mountain, said: "Comrade, it's agreed that I will only accept a gift made with a good grace, and with one voice, without any of the donors wanting to retract it. Well, how does this seem to you? What do you say to this unanimous malediction? Now you're mine, well and truly mine. Not one of them is claiming you or forgiving you."

And, picking up the bailiff by the shoulders, he suspended him from an oak that was no less than sixty feet high.

The entire country applauded that act of vengeance! Alas, for want of justice, one takes revenge, and that is why it is necessary to be just before all else.

The man in question having disappeared from the domain, order and peace were gradually seen to return to the region.

The church was rebuilt, and the bell once again called the faithful to prayer; they obeyed the sacred summons, precisely because they had ceased to be miserable.

The men returned to the plough, to the harrow and to all the instruments that give life and enjoyment to humankind.

The pig, saved by a miracle, had an abundant progeniture.

The little baby grew up and became a great dispenser of justice, the leader of a parliament whose voice was sovereign.

No one was astonished when, one morning, the old château was disemboweled, its materials used to build an aqueduct, a bridge and a highway.

Finally, you will have guessed that the new lord was the young man from the new house.

They had begun by renouncing their right to the scaffold, their right to the galleys and the gibbet; they had converted the scaffold into a signpost to guide travelers in the forest.

We have one more adventure to relate, and all will be said. On the day when the bailiff disappeared, the elders of the village who had maintained their composure had clearly seen that Satan, his hands full of lightning-bolts, had engraved something unknown on the highest branch of the old oak. The old oak died of old age, and the woodcutters, when they stripped it of its crown, found a memorable word written in streaks of fire:

JUSTICE!

SF & FANTASY

Adolphe Alhaiza. *Cybele*
Alphonse Allais. *The Adventures of Captain Cap*
Henri Allorge. *The Great Cataclysm*
Guy d'Armen. *Doc Ardan: The City of Gold and Lepers*
G.-J. Arnaud. *The Ice Company*
Charles Asselineau. *The Double Life*
Cyprien Bérard. *The Vampire Lord Ruthwen*
S. Henry Berthoud. *Martyrs of Science*
Aloysius Bertrand. *Gaspard de la Nuit*
Richard Bessière. *The Gardens of the Apocalypse*
Albert Bleunard. *Ever Smaller*
Félix Bodin. *The Novel of the Future*
Louis Boussenard. *Monsieur Synthesis*
Alphonse Brown. *City of Glass; The Conquest of the Air*
Emile Calvet. *In a Thousand Years*
André Caroff. *The Terror of Madame Atomos; Miss Atomos; The
Return of Madame Atomos; The Mistake of Madame Atomos; The
Monsters of Madame Atomos; The Revenge of Madame Atomos; The
Resurrection of Madame Atomos; The Mark of Madame Atomos*
Félicien Champsaur. *The Human Arrow; Ouha, King of the Apes;
Pharaoh's Wife*
Didier de Chousy. *Ignis*
Jules Clarétie. *Obsession*
Michel Corday. *The Eternal Flame*
Captain Danrit. *Undersea Odyssey*
C. I. Defontenay. *Star (Psi Cassiopeia)*
Charles Derennes. *The People of the Pole*
Georges Dodds (anthologist). *The Missing Link*
Harry Dickson. *The Heir of Dracula*
Jules Dornay. *Lord Ruthven Begins*
Alfred Driou. *The Adventures of a Parisian Aeronaut*
Sâr Dubnotal *vs. Jack the Ripper*
Alexandre Dumas. *The Return of Lord Ruthven*
Renée Dunan. *Baal*
J.-C. Dunyach. *The Night Orchid; The Thieves of Silence*
Henri Duvernois. *The Man Who Found Himself*
Achille Eyraud. *Voyage to Venus*
Henri Falk. *The Age of Lead*

Paul Féval. *Anne of the Isles; Knightshade; Revenants; Vampire City; The Vampire Countess; The Wandering Jew's Daughter*
Paul Féval, *fils. Felifax, the Tiger-Man*
Charles de Fieux. *Lamékis*
Arnould Galopin. *Doctor Omega*; *Doctor Omega and the Shadowmen* (anthology)
Judith Gautier. *Isoline and the Serpent-Flower*
Léon Gozlan. *The Vampire of the Val-de-Grâce*
G.L. Gick. *Harry Dickson and the Werewolf of Rutherford Grange*
Edmond Haraucourt. *Illusions of Immortality*
Nathalie Henneberg. *The Green Gods*
V. Hugo, P. Foucher & P. Meurice. *The Hunchback of Notre-Dame*
Romain d'Huissier. *Hexagon: Dark Matter*
Jules Janin. *The Magnetized Corpse*
Michel Jeury. *Chronolysis*
Gustave Kahn. *The Tale of Gold and Silence*
Gérard Klein. *The Mote in Time's Eye*
Fernand Kolney. *Love in 5000 Years*
Paul Lacroix. *Danse Macabre*
Louis-Guillaume de La Follie. *The Unpretentious Philosopher*
Jean de La Hire. *Enter the Nyctalope; The Nyctalope on Mars; The Nyctalope vs. Lucifer; The Nyctalope Steps In; Night of the Nyctalope; Return of the Nyctalope; The Fiery Wheel*
Etienne-Léon de Lamothe-Langon. *The Virgin Vampire*
André Laurie. *Spiridon*
Gabriel de Lautrec. *The Vengeance of the Oval Portrait*
Alain le Drimeur. *The Future City*
Georges Le Faure & Henri de Graffigny. *The Extraordinary Adventures of a Russian Scientist Across the Solar System* (2 vols.)
Gustave Le Rouge. *The Vampires of Mars; The Dominion of the World* (w/Gustave Guitton) (4 vols.)
Jules Lermina. *Mysteryville; Panic in Paris; To-Ho and the Gold Destroyers; The Secret of Zippelius*
André Lichtenberger. *The Centaurs; The Children of the Crab*
Jean-Marc & Randy Lofficier. *Edgar Allan Poe on Mars; The Katrina Protocol; Pacifica; Robonocchio; Return of the Nyctalope;* (anthologists) *Tales of the Shadowmen 1-10*
Xavier Mauméjean. *The League of Heroes*
Joseph Méry. *The Tower of Destiny*
Hippolyte Mettais. *The Year 5865*
Louise Michel. *The Human Microbes; The New World*

Tony Moilin. *Paris in the Year 2000*
José Moselli. *Illa's End*
John-Antoine Nau. *Enemy Force*
Marie Nizet. *Captain Vampire*
C. Nodier, A. Beraud & Toussaint-Merle. *Frankenstein*
Henri de Parville. *An Inhabitant of the Planet Mars*
Gaston de Pawlowski. *Journey to the Land of the 4th Dimension*
Georges Pellerin. *The World in 2000 Years*
Ernest Pérochon. *The Frenetic People*
Pierre Pelot. *The Child Who Walked on the Sky*
J. Polidori, C. Nodier, E. Scribe. *Lord Ruthven the Vampire*
P.-A. Ponson du Terrail. *The Vampire and the Devil's Son; The Immortal Woman*
Edgar Quinet. *Ahasuerus*
Henri de Régnier. *A Surfeit of Mirrors*
Maurice Renard. *The Blue Peril; Doctor Lerne; The Doctored Man; A Man Among the Microbes; The Master of Light*
Jean Richepin. *The Wing; The Crazy Corner*
Albert Robida. *The Adventures of Saturnin Farandoul; The Clock of the Centuries; Chalet in the Sky; The Electric Life*
J.-H. Rosny Aîné. *Helgvor of the Blue River; The Givreuse Enigma; The Mysterious Force; The Navigators of Space; Vamireh; The World of the Variants; The Young Vampire*
Marcel Rouff. *Journey to the Inverted World*
Han Ryner. *The Superhumans*
Brian Stableford. *The New Faust at the Tragicomique;The Empire of the Necromancers (The Shadow of Frankenstein; Frankenstein and the Vampire Countess; Frankenstein in London); Sherlock Holmes & The Vampires of Eternity; The Stones of Camelot; The Wayward Muse.* (anthologist) *News from the Moon; The Germans on Venus; The Supreme Progress; The World Above the World; Nemoville; Investigations of the Future; The Conqueror of Death*
Jacques Spitz. *The Eye of Purgatory*
Kurt Steiner. *Ortog*
Eugène Thébault. *Radio-Terror*
C.-F. Tiphaigne de La Roche. *Amilec*
Louis Ulbach. *Prince Bonifacio*
Théo Varlet. *The Golden Rock. The Xenobiotic Invasion; The Castaways of Eros; Timeslip Troopers* (w/André Blandin); *The Martian Epic* (w/Octave Joncquel)
Paul Vibert. *The Mysterious Fluid*

Villiers de l'Isle-Adam. *The Scaffold; The Vampire Soul*
Philippe Ward. *Artahe*
Philippe Ward & Sylvie Miller. *The Song of Montségur*

MYSTERIES & THRILLERS

M. Allain & P. Souvestre. *The Daughter of Fantômas*
A. Anicet-Bourgeois, Lucien Dabril. *Rocambole*
A. Bernède. *Belphegor; Judex* (w/Louis Feuillade); *The Return of Judex* (w/Louis Feuillade); *The Shadow of Judex*
A. Bisson & G. Livet. *Nick Carter vs. Fantômas*
V. Darlay & H. de Gorsse. *Arsène Lupin vs. Sherlock Holmes: The Stage Play*
Séamas Duffy. *Sherlock Holmes in Paris*
Paul Féval. *Gentlemen of the Night; John Devil; The Black Coats ('Salem Street; The Invisible Weapon; The Parisian Jungle; The Companions of the Treasure; Heart of Steel; The Cadet Gang; The Sword-Swallower)*
Emile Gaboriau. *Monsieur Lecoq*
Goron & Emile Gautier. *Spawn of the Penitentiary*
Rick Lai. *Shadows of the Opera: Retribution in Blood; Sisters of the Shadows: The Curse of Cagliostro*
Steve Leadley. *Sherlock Holmes: The Circle of Blood*
Maurice Leblanc. *Arsène Lupin vs. Countess Cagliostro; Arsène Lupin vs. Sherlock Holmes (The Blonde Phantom; The Hollow Needle); The Many Faces of Arsène Lupin*
Gaston Leroux. *Chéri-Bibi; The Phantom of the Opera; Rouletabille & the Mystery of the Yellow Room; Rouletabille at Krupp's*
Richard Marsh. *The Complete Adventures of Judith Lee*
William Patrick Maynard. *The Terror of Fu Manchu; The Destiny of Fu Manchu*
Frank J. Morlock. *Sherlock Holmes: The Grand Horizontals; Sherlock Holmes vs Jack the Ripper*
Jean Petithuguenin. *The Adventures of Ethel King*
Antonin Reschal. *The Adventures of Miss Boston*
P. de Wattyne & Y. Walter. *Sherlock Holmes vs. Fantômas*
David White. *Fantômas in America*
Pierre Yrondy. *The Adventures of Thérèse Arnaud*

SCREENPLAYS

Mike Baron. *The Iron Triangle*
Emma Bull & Will Shetterly. *Nightspeeder; War for the Oaks*
Gerry Conway & Roy Thomas. *Doc Dynamo*
Steve Englehart. *Majorca*
James Hudnall. *The Devastator*
Jean-Marc & Randy Lofficier. *Royal Flush*
J.-M. & R. Lofficier & Marc Agapit. *Despair*
J.-M. & R. Lofficier & Joël Houssin. *City*
Andrew Paquette. *Peripheral Vision*
Robert L. Robinson, Jr. *Judex*
R. Thomas, J. Hendler & L. Sprague de Camp. *Rivers of Time*

NON-FICTION

Stephen R. Bissette. *Blur 1-5. Green Mountain Cinema 1; Teen Angels*
Win Scott Eckert. *Crossovers* (2 vols.)
Jean-Marc & Randy Lofficier. *Shadowmen* (2 vols.)
Randy Lofficier. *Over Here*

ART BOOKS

Jean-Pierre Normand. *Science Fiction Illustrations*
Raven Okeefe. *Raven's L'il Critters; Rave's Faves*
Randy Lofficier & Raven Okeefe. *If Your Possum Go Daylight...*
Daniele Serra. *Illusions*

HEXAGON COMICS

Franco Frescura & Luciano Bernasconi. *Wampus*
Franco Frescura & Giorgio Trevisan. *CLASH*
L. Bernasconi, J.-M. Lofficier & Juan Roncagliolo Berger. *Phenix*
Claude Legrand, J.-M. Lofficier & L. Bernasconi. *Kabur*
Franco Oneta. *Zembla*
L. Buffolente, Lofficier & J.-J. Dzialowski. *Strangers: Homicron*
Danilo Grossi. *Strangers: Jaydee*
Claude Legrand & Luciano Bernasconi. *Strangers: Starlock*
T. Mornet & Juan Roncagliolo Berger: *Guardian of the Republic*